EMALICKEL

RELEASE OF THE NEPHILIM

A. M. TRUE

Edited by
KATHERINE O. BROWN

ACKNOWLEDGEMENTS

My sincerest gratitude to Kathy for always taking the time to read the first drafts. She has played a key-role in making these novels an epic journey for all to enjoy. I am completely and utterly grateful for her honest input and for the countless hours of careful editing she has put into these works for publishing.

And finally, may I remove my hat and take a respectful bow to my family for all their support, love, sacrifices, and understanding during the times of my writing. It isn't always easy to find a balance, but they remain the caring, comforting, and affectionate family that has always been there through it all. I love each of them, with all my heart, unconditionally and forever.

CONTENTS

PREFACE

This novel is the second in the *Emalickel* series. The events of this novel took place six years after the events of the first novel. It was written several months after the first novel had been released to the public.

After reading the first novel, several readers had shared with me that I must write a sequel. Although I wanted to appease them, I explained to them the content of the novel was not simply a creation from my mind. I did not write the first *Emalickel* by sitting down at a computer every day and thinking of things to write about; but rather, I had actually observed and experienced the events in an unintentionally very vivid, dream or possibly through astral-projection.

Starting in my teenage years, I had experienced three or four astral-projection incidents, but had never gotten any further than floating around my own bedroom, for fear of the unknown and not understanding what was happening to me. Also, starting in my late twenties, a few years before the events of the first *Emalickel*, I had been working on dream-recall, with the goal of becoming better at controlling my dreams, whilst within them. Lucid dreaming becomes possible when a person is aware they are dreaming and can then control the dream from within it. A person is more likely to be able to lucid dream if they become better at recalling their dreams. I researched more into this and found that recording my dreams onto paper would "rewire" the brain to have better dream-recall. Thus, it would enable me to lucid dream.

After doing all these things, I unintentionally experienced what I have come to call *The Emalickel Experience.* It was more vivid than a dream. In this experience, I had all five of my acute senses; I remembered specific things, places, names, and visuals. Plus, there was a sense of the passage of chronological time. Upon waking from *The Emalickel Experience*, I immediately started writing down everything I remembered. It took several days to write. When I was finally finished writing it all down (well actually, I decided to type it on my computer) it contained about 40,000 words—which was the simplified version.

Five years had passed, and the dream remained recorded on my laptop; until one day, something unknown urged me to share my experience with the world by making it into a novel. In the summer of 2018, the first of the *Emalickel* series was born.

There I was with readers of the first novel, who were begging for me to write another one. There was no way I would be able to do that, but I decided to sit down one day and just start typing—about my life after *The Emalickel Experience.* I wrote down my thoughts, my perceptions, and my interactions with others as I was trying to find my place in the world again.

That had been a challenge after returning. It had been hard resuming a regular lifestyle after experiencing a place of such magic. For three months, I worked on this second novel until I hit what they call a "writer's block." There was nothing more I knew to write about; everything I needed to say about myself and my experience had been said. There was no story—only my internal thoughts and perspectives. So, I gave up on the second *Emalickel* and pushed the idea of it to the side. My life continued as normal, at least for about two weeks after giving up on this sequel.

Then, just as I recorded in this novel, an unexpected event happened to me one night upon falling asleep. You will read all about this in the many pages to come.

Before you read, I wanted to point out a few things in the *Appendix*. I have included several aids in the back of this novel to help make your reading experience just as vivid and realistic as I once experienced. Therefore, you will find two items in the *Appendix*: a musical playlist and a pronunciation key.

The musical playlist is extremely important to me as it contains cherished pieces of music which help convey the emotion of each scene taking place throughout the novel. Listening to the music, you will need to slow your reading pace down to a "read-aloud" pace, as if what you are reading is taking place in real-time. For example, when the characters speak, they're going to speak in a slow concise manner—not rushed like you would do if you read at your brain's internal pace. I am aware the timing of the music may not always work out perfectly but playing the music along with the scenes is sure to add some extra flair to your experience—just as does music in the scenes of a movie.

If you use the music, not only will it enhance your reading experience, but you will get to hear some amazing pieces by all the different artists. These songs are listed throughout the novel at the beginning of each scene, but please support the artists and contribute to their heart-filled work by purchasing or licensing their music per the information in the appendix. Then, create an *Emalickel: Release of the Nephilim* playlist to use while you read.

Another tool readers will appreciate is the pronunciation key. The pronunciation key will help you properly pronounce the names of beings and places throughout the novel. This will help you to know, truly, the names of those places I experienced and beings I encountered. This enables the reader to more easily relate to these important characters and places, thus making the novel more immersive.

I hope you enjoy the second *Emalickel Experience,* and that it resonates with you in some way. May it bring you pleasure escaping into the private world of celestials. May it bring you excitement as you enjoy the unraveling of secrets that were shared. The mysteries will eventually all come together. Finally, may it bring you joy to know that you are adored. You are a major part of this big picture we call creation. After all, there is a reason you have found this novel in the placement of your hands. Remember, there are no coincidences.

Love to all of you,

A. M. True
United States
03/03/2019

* Also, please note that the words that are *italicized*, throughout the novel, are thoughts and not spoken words.

INTRODUCTION

My name is Adrienne. I am a regular girl, but I have an unusual thing about me—an ability, so to say—an ability to astral-travel, I think. The definition of this, in my own words, is a form of "remote viewing" where a person's consciousness leaves their body with full awareness and comprehension. Since my teens, I have experienced this ability, but I was never sure what it was. Up until the age of twenty-four, I had astral-traveled about five or six times, but never went very far. However, in September of 2012, I experienced a full-fledged astral-projection and found myself in another plane of existence from the mortal plane—I had traveled to the celestial plane.

Back on that day, I had laid down one evening to go to sleep when I suddenly felt paralyzed. Trying with all my might to move my body, I felt myself "pop" from my physical body and began wandering the house. By traveling through walls, I went outside and up the street to a lake by an old primitive church. Upon arriving there, I met someone who identified himself by the name of Emalickel.

He explained to me that there are a few different planes (or levels) to existence within the Universe. He did not provide a scientific break-down of how exactly this worked, but he did explain that human beings and other mortals reside within the "mortal plane," while celestials reside in the "celestial plane." The celestial plane is veiled to mortals. There is also an "astral plane." It lies between the mortal and celestial planes. It is a common ground, or a bridge, between celestials and mortals.

He further explained that there are billions of galaxies in the Universe, but only nine of them are classified as realms—that means they host celestial life, often accompanied by mortal life. Three of the nine realms have fallen into darkness. They are considered the villains among celestials, holding their own alternative agendas. Regardless of their differences, all the celestials of each realm reside on one giant planet near their own realm's center. The Milky Way galaxy, or Millattus, is the name of the realm in which man exists. The giant celestial planet of our realm is called Lapoi. There are three mortal planets within the mortal plane of Millattus, and they are called Earth, Fynne, and Grahst. Fynne and Grahst have yet to be discovered by man.

Emalickel identified himself as a celestial from Lapoi. The reason he came to meet me in the astral plane, on that night in September of 2012, was because he had been hearing my thoughts, feeling my emotions, and sensing my energy. Apparently, Emalickel had never experienced such a phenomenon.

Ensuring my safe return home, he invited me to go on a journey with him to the celestial plane. He would take me to the celestial planet of Lapoi where all the celestials of our realm reside. He traveled with me through space using different means, such as supersonic speed, warp-travel, and teleportation. Once we had reached the celestial planet, I was introduced to his five brothers named Thorenel, Romenciel, Xabiel, Dennoliel, and Seronimel.

Emalickel knew my mortal name as Adrienne, but he and the other celestials began referring to me as Hadriel while I walked among them in Lapoi. Previously, I had thought they were referring to me as Hadriannel, but I have since learned the true pronunciation is ***hā** · drē · el, spelled Hadriel*

There are billions of celestials in Lapoi. They hold specific titles, acting as either warriors or guards. Guards have the duty of guiding and tending to the mortals of the mortal plane, assisting in the will of God among them. They have the ability to physically manifest and intervene in the mortal plane. Warriors have the duty of protecting and defending the realm of Millattus from negative intruders. Although warriors are not typically allowed to physically manifest in the mortal plane, they have done so before. Mostly, they are equipped with abilities to interact with masses of people undetected and also to control natural events on the mortal planets by impeding or initiating such things as the weather, quakes, volcanic activity, meteors, tides, and other related phenomena. In general, they are positioned to surround the boarders of Millattus, but are also dispersed all throughout the inner portions. They fight in an ongoing battle with celestials from the dark realms who are constantly trying to infiltrate.

Upon entering Lapoi with Emalickel, I became drawn to him. I felt an uncontrollable attraction to him. It felt a sense of familiarity with him, as if I had known him for a lifetime. I desired to know him deeply and in more intimate ways. I was worried from fear of it being wrong to have such feelings for a celestial being; though I couldn't control it or avoid it. Upon learning about my feelings for him, Emalickel disclosed to me that the feeling of intimate love between celestials and mortal females comes naturally to both parties.

Don't freak out. You will discover how and why this is permissible later on, but in the meantime, let me clarify the definition of intimate love. It is a kind of love rooted deeply in emotional and spiritual communion. When it comes to expressing this love, celestials must abide by specific precepts to ensure the purity of it remains untainted and unbroken. First, and foremost, celestials shall not allow for an intimate love to become a distraction from their dedication to God. There is no marriage within the celestial plane, for all beings there are married to God and He shall always be first. Secondly, it is only permissible for celestials to express love while in the purity of the celestial plane. Unlike the unscrupulous mortal plane, the celestial plane is one of unconditional love. When love is expressed in the celestial plane, it is not susceptible to corruption. And lastly, as revealed to me in a more-recent revelation, intimacy can only be shared with those who are of a pure spiritual heart; meaning they are dedicated to God and belong solely to Him through redemption and righteousness.

So, yes, I had become intimately connected with Emalickel and Thorenel; and this was permissible as all criteria had been satisfied to ensure the union remained pure and blessed. Later, Emalickel revealed to me that he and Thorenel are the Royal-Princedom celestials of Lapoi. This means they hold a status of authority over the entire celestial kingdom of Lapoi. They are both Prince's and both reside in a majestic palace made of white marble and stone. They had refrained from informing me of this too soon, for they feared their status would influence my decision on whether or not to become bonded with them. Even more amazing was that, as a result of their status and my intimate bond with them, I inevitably inherited a place among the Principality of Lapoi. I was appointed to the throne and was designated as the Princess of Lapoi.

Emalickel and Thorenel's other brothers are considered a part of the Principality of Lapoi, but they do not hold the status of Royal-Princedom. They are referred to as the Princedom brothers. They are placed in high-ranking positions, but are not in charge of overseeing the entire realm. Romenciel and Xabiel are over the warriors, while Dennoliel and Seronimel are over the guards. All celestials, even the four Princedom brothers, must abide by the sovereign orders of Emalickel and Thorenel.

1

ANOTHER VISION

1. Artist: Whitesand
Song: Eternity

I opened my eyes. Looking down at the green, white, and blue planet, I saw that I was floating in space above the Earth. Green continents peaked through scattered white clouds, swirling below me. The beautiful, blue glow of a thin atmosphere encircled the planet, surrounding it in a permeable shell of topaz. All was quiet as I peacefully watched the Earth slowly spin beneath me. I was unaware of how I had gotten there, but at the same time, I did not wonder nor question the matter. I was relaxed and content. My mind was completely clear of all thoughts. In that moment, I was simply an observer.

Then, I heard a familiar voice. It was a deep and resonate male voice. It was smooth and calm, yet confident and authoritative. I recognized the voice as belonging to Emalickel, the celestial prince of a kingdom called Lapoi, a planet inhabited by billions of divine celestials who watch over mankind. When Emalickel spoke, it sounded as if he were right in front of me, but yet he was nowhere to be seen. All I saw was the moving image of planet Earth underneath me.

Emalickel: There you are. I have been calling to you, but you have been too distracted to hear. There is an abundance of confusion about you. I will provide you clarity, but we must start from the beginning. There are many explanations which attempt to describe the process of creation, but the actual process is difficult to comprehend. The Biblical book of Genesis, as you know it, provides the most-accurate depiction of creation in the simplest of terms. Do not try to rationalize nor construe this story, or you will be led astray. The power of God is limitless, for He is able to create, alter, and transcend anything and any concept. With the exception of Himself, nothing in existence is capable of fully understanding His omnipotence. Truly, without doubt, I tell you, this is the canon story of creation...

The image of Earth quickly zoomed-out and away from me, as if I were departing at the speed of light. I was moving backward. Stars became mere streaks of light. It visually reminded me of being in a dark tunnel with lights on the walls while traveling in reverse at a great speed. I did not actually feel myself moving, but was rather observing from an outside perspective.

Then, after a series of multi-colored light-streaks, everything became completely dark and still. After a moment, I saw the silhouette of a dark-grey sphere appear from the darkness. Emalickel's voice began speaking again. As he spoke, the images before me began playing-out with all that he said, like a narrated movie.

Emalickel: Among the first of God's creations were the heavens. He created the heavens in three different spheres. The first sphere, which is the largest, encompasses the second

sphere; and the second sphere encompasses the third. This was witnessed only by God and His Word, for there was nothing else in existence to bear witness. The first to receive the gift of consciousness were the celestials of the first and second spheres, who received this gift collectively.

The most-highly exalted types of celestials inhabit the first sphere of heaven. These celestials include the Seraphim, Cherubim, and Thrones. Within the second sphere are the intermittent celestials known as Dominions, Virtues, and Powers. There are many mysteries about the first and second spheres of heaven. For one, the perceptual experiences within each sphere are known only by those who inhabit each sphere. Also, it remains unknown how these types of celestials were created, but it was likely similar to the way in which the celestials of the third sphere came into being.

The third sphere was created in the presence of those in the first and second sphere. According to the Dominions of the second sphere, God created the perceivable Universe in the third sphere. The Universe was jeweled with billions of galaxies, each containing countless numbers of stars. He chose nine of the galaxies and designated them as realms. He shed His light upon these nine realms and named them as follows: Millattus, Jesserion, Odalveim, Haffelnia, Gaddorium, Yahrinstahd, Norohmba, Chasstillia, and Salheim. Near the center of each realm, He formed a large planet, a celestial planet, which would become the dwelling place of the celestials of that realm.

Within the third sphere, I had seen the Universe and all of its colorful galaxies and sparkling nebula clouds. Then, the scene panned upward toward the first sphere of the heavens. Emalickel's description continued playing-out with moving images before me.

2. Artist: Whitesand
Song: Story of the Wind

Emalickel: Finally, God created the celestials of the third sphere. At the beginning, we were a formless thought within the first sphere. The thought manifested into a singular sphere of transparent energy. When the Lord God illuminated it with His Light, the sphere glowed like a brilliant-star. The sphere of light was then split into three individual spheres of energy: A, B, and C. These energies were sent down to dwell in the third sphere. Energy A was sent to the realm of Millattus, energy B was sent to Haffelnia, and energy C was sent to Norohmba.

This visual was easy to observe with Emalickel's narration, but without the visual, it would have been difficult to comprehend (see diagrams 1 and 2).

Emalickel: Energy A, B, and C were then split into three parts —creating three parts in Millattus, three in Haffelnia, and three in Norohmba. Each of those three parts was split one final time into three aspects—creating nine aspects in Millattus, nine in Haffelnia, and nine in Norohmba. These aspects were sent to rest on their realm's celestial planet.

Finally, God breathed life into each of them, giving them conscious awareness. He classified them as Princedom celestials, meaning they would hold positions of authority in their realm. Within each realm, the Princedoms were arranged into three groups of three. The most-illuminated triad in each realm were designated as Royal-Princedoms. They share a

crown of authority and oversee their assigned realm. The other six Princedoms hold positions of authority, but ultimately, they follow the commands of the Royal-Princedoms. This leveled arrangement of celestials promotes balance, efficiency, and simplicity. Essentially, nine Princedoms collectively supervise their realm. In total, there are twenty-seven Princedoms who tend the entire third sphere.

After the Princedom celestials had been created, a multitude of other celestials were formed. They were formed by the same process as the Princedom celestials, in groups of three, but without any authority over the Princedoms. Most celestials among all the realms embody a masculine essence.

The view zoomed-in to the realm of Millattus, or the Milky Way galaxy as we refer to it. Slightly to the side of the bright center of the galaxy, I saw the massive celestial planet of Lapoi glowing of gold and white.

3. Artist: Efisio Cross
Song: If You Fall I Will Carry You

Emalickel: On the celestial planet of Lapoi, which is in your realm of Millattus, the arrangement was a bit different than the others. Do you remember when Thorenel told you about "celestial-pairs?" Celestial-pairs are a unique arrangement that only exist in Millattus. Unlike the realms of Norohmba and Haffelnia, where the Princedoms are organized into groups of three celestials, the Princedoms of Millattus are organized into groups of two celestials. Our third aspects have been removed. These aspects are composed of rare feminine energies and were stationed in the nearby realm of Jesserion. The masculine aspects remain in Millattus.

Each celestial-pair shares a common source from which they derive. As a result, they share the same abilities, feel the same emotions, hold the same titles, and desire the same wants. They have telepathic abilities with each other, and they understand each other as deeply as themselves. Thorenel and I are a celestial-pair, so are Romenciel and Xabiel, and then also Dennoliel and Seronimel.

The LORD blessed all celestials with intelligence, strength, and immortality. He supplied us with divine powers which are only to be used at His discretion and control. We are able to perform certain abilities that are seemingly supernatural. God has endowed us with physical forms which, by our divine light, are masked and overpowered. We are only permitted to show our true physical forms by God's command.

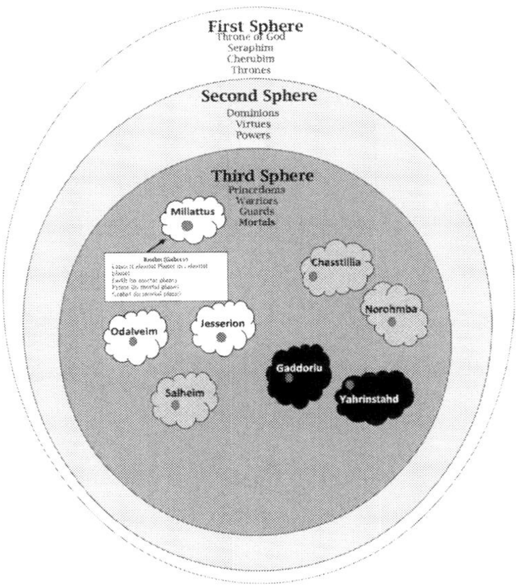
First Sphere
Throne of God
Seraphim
Cherubim
Thrones
Second Sphere
Dominions
Virtues
Powers
Third Sphere
Princedoms
Warriors
Guards
Mortals
Millattus
Chasstilia
Norohmba
Odalveim
Jesserion
Gaddoriu
Yahrinstahd
Salheim

Diagram 1

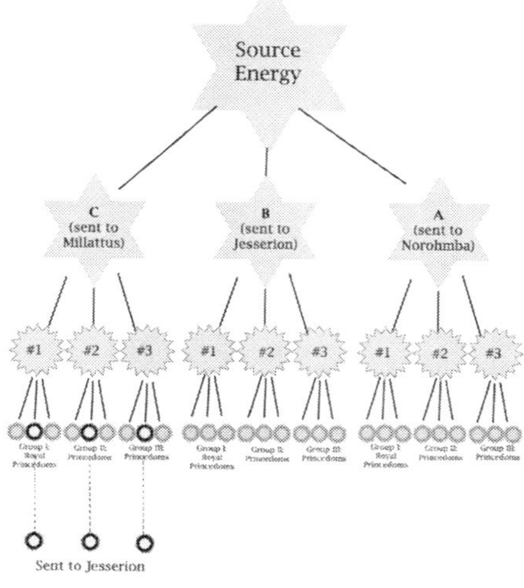

Diagram 2

Emalickel: God was proud of the creation of the heavens, and He knew it was good, but He desired to bring more into existence. He created three planets within each of the nine realms and began dawning life unto them. The celestials of each realm were instructed to oversee the well-being of their own realm's planets as they developed.

The scene faded from an intergalactic view to one containing a stunning natural landscape, similar to that of the Earth. Spread throughout the landscape were male human beings. The land was pure and without blemish, void of any man-made developments or technological advancements.

Emalickel: Within our own realm of Millattus, He began creating a very special and unique lifeform. He sculpted mankind. Our LORD found favor in mankind, whose physical form was made in the image and likeness of Him. He brought Man to life with His very breath, then He sent half of the celestials from Lapoi to embody the physical forms of Man and bring him into awareness.

Man was established in the Garden of Eden, which exists in the highest dimension of vibrational frequency upon the Earth. Man's body was gifted with five senses which enabled him to interpret the invigorating world around him so that he may gain an exclusive perspective of his experiences. He was given authority over the Earth and was instructed to name its creatures, to guard and cultivate the land, and to enjoy the pleasures blessed upon it. In this time, everything was absolutely flawless.

God knew man would desire a relatable companion beyond that which the animals could provide, so He created another form similar to that of Man. This form would carry physical attributes in balance to the man. It was called woman. Remember the third aspects to each celestial-pair of Lapoi—the feminine aspects that were placed in Jesserion? Every feminine form of Earth is embodied by one of these aspects. A woman's essence is that of the third aspect of a Lapoian celestial-pair.

4. Artist: Danheim
Song: Gungnir

Man and Woman were instructed to flourish and multiply themselves. They would work without tiring and live without dying. Man was designated as the protector and provider. Woman was designated as the life-bringer and care-taker. They were permitted to indulge themselves in anything among the land, except for fruits from the tree of knowledge of good and evil. Obtaining this knowledge would contaminate their divine innocence with an awareness of evil, which would result in the death of their divine spirits. As long as they stayed away from this knowledge, Man and Woman would live in abounding prosperity and untarnished joy.

Emalickel continued sharing the story as the beauty of Eden faded into another scene showing a close-up view of a very vibrant male face. He was illuminated in a glowing golden light and was surrounded by a pitch-black background. The view began to pan-out from his face, until his chest came into view. When he turned around to face away, it became evident this male was a high-celestial. Extending from his back, were two sets of golden wings large enough to cover the entirety of the backside of his body. With the celestial's back turned to me, I noticed the golden glow which illuminated him suddenly turned to one of crimson red. All this, while Emalickel narrated.

Emalickel: Meanwhile, in the first sphere of the heavens, was a wise and mighty Cherub, named Haelael. As a guardian of the Throne of God, Haelael was an overseer above all three spheres of the heavens. He watched enviously as mankind glorified God and received an ability to procreate among themselves. He became arrogant in his high-ranking position and began to feel that he deserved glory for himself. When God approached Haelael with concerns about his sudden pride, Haelael presented his case.

Then, the scene turned to show a set of lips illuminated in red as they spoke. The lips were accompanied by the echo of Haelael's voice as Emalickel recalled his words.

Haelael: Why is it, Lord, when You already receive an abundance of glory from Your celestials, You allow Yourself to receive additional glory from man? Does it not seem fair to allow Your celestials to receive this glory from man in response for our service to them? Our glory goes to You, but what glory shall come unto us?

The lips of God were illuminated in such a bright light, they appeared almost whitewashed.

God: He who receives glory is the creator of it, Haelael.

Once again, the scene switched back to the lips of Haelael glowing crimson.

Haelael: What may I create, then? You have given those in man an authority to create on the Earth, but the celestials have been given no such authority.

The lips of God replied before fading away.

God: Celestials were made to provide service to Me, not to create with Me.

Emalickel continued as a close-up of Haelael's eyes came into view. The irises of his eyes changed color, from an illuminated light grey to that of dark red as he roared aloud and became consumed by darkness and rage.

Emalickel: Overcome with resentment, Haelael discretely began devising a plan to gain the glory he felt he deserved.

Haelael: I will sacrifice my divinity and break my covenant with God. I will roam the Earth, wreaking corruption and temptation, contaminating man with fear and anger. I will deceive them with

illusions, and I will manipulate them by twisting truths. I will lure them away from righteousness so they no longer thrive, for the unrighteous will be unfulfilled. The desperate, unrighteous man will attempt to fulfill his short-comings by relishing in the things I will offer. In their weakness, my offerings will appeal to them, and they will choose to follow me.

I found myself presented with a view of Eden again. This time only one man and one woman were in view. They were frolicking at a slow-motion speed in a garden resembling a fairy tale. Particles of glitter floated in the air and rays of sunlight beamed down through the clouds. The colors of everything were vibrant and true. As this scene came into view, I could still hear Haelael's voice as Emalickel remembered it.

Haelael: If mankind surrenders to following my path, then surly they become disobedient to God. What better way to begin this rebellion against God than to tempt man into doing the one thing from which God forbid him—partaking in the fruit of the tree of knowledge of good and evil? The ones who go by the name of Adam and Eve will be my first victims, and I will deceive them by slandering God's words. I will appeal to their egos and secure my place of eminence among them.

The scene changed to display Haelael, without his wings, sitting upon a crimson and bronze throne. He was leaning back, in a relaxed position, displaying his arrogance. One of his arms rested on the bronze armrest of the throne, while the other acted as a prop for his chin. A semi-translucent Earth began to appear behind this throne. He was wearing a bronze-colored crown and displayed a wicked and arrogant smile packed with pride.

Haelael: I will maintain a tight grip on mankind, thus establishing my superiority over them. I shall indulge in the glories they will

bestow unto me. I will appoint myself the prince of the Earth, building my kingdom, backed by celestials who will support my claim. The celestials shall relish in the harvest of my crop, and reap the benefits of their superiority over mankind. I will construct a world of freedom—a kingdom to call mine own—where God is no longer the focus, but rather the establishment of my reign. May the glory in which I deserve come unto me, and in this way may I become the god they worship!

5. Artist: Clint Mansell
Song: Lux Aeterna (Requiem of a Tower 6:30 Version)

An image of Eden faded-in and Eve could be seen strolling through the divine garden. Then, I saw Haelael appear before her. His form could easily be associated with a winged-serpent or dragon with the face and body of a man. As the image played, Emalickel's voice continued telling the story.

Emalickel: And so, Haelael came down to the Earth in his Cherub form. When Eve saw him, she was afraid not, but was rather impressed by his display. Mesmerized by his majestic presentation, she became beguiled by his conniving words. Convinced that God was withholding privileges from her, she consumed the forbidden knowledge in which Haelael offered to her. He had succeeded in his deception. From then on, he became known by the names of Satan and the Devil, which translate to mean "the adversary" and "the deceiver."

The scene became darkened as stormy clouds swarmed the sky. Adam ran to Eve from where he had previously been gathering berries. They both looked to the sky in fear. Crying hysterically, Eve frantically conversed with Adam in the presence of Haelael. She pointed to Haelael and fearfully seemed to be explaining what she had learned. Adam then turned his attention to

Haelael, who exhibited a wicked grin. The two of them exchanged words before Haelael engulfed himself within his wings and disappeared into thin air. Adam and Eve looked at one another, and they both scurried for vegetation to cover their exposed bodies.

The scene panned upward into a vision of the Universe again. I saw flashes of various colors of lightning. It was exploding sporadically throughout all the realms. Celestials were using energy-surges against one another, and some celestials wielded various weaponry to execute their attacks upon one another. During this visual, Emalickel continued speaking to me.

Emalickel: And that is when it happened—a great battle among celestials took place. At God's command, Haelael and all of his followers were thrown from the heavens. They were banished from dwelling among those of divine essence.

I saw the view of a celestial who exhibited a wondrous golden glow about him. He wielded a great sword which glowed from flames along the entire blade. I could not see this celestial's face for it was covered by a golden galea with a black hair crest pulled upon the very top. This full-faced helmet resembled that of a trojan warrior, except the hair did not run vertically along the helmet, but rather it derived from a central point at the top, like a high ponytail. This celestial also wore golden boots and a golden breastplate with black long-sleeved undergarments and pants. His golden balteus-belt contained an apron which draped to midway down the front of his thighs. His armor was polished, but instead of appearing glossy and shiny, it carried the texture of a dull bronze.

This celestial was in direct combat with Haelael. His attacks were executed with great strength and technique. His every move was smooth and fluid. He seemed to fight effortlessly and with great confidence. Emalickel's narration continued.

Emalickel: This great battle was led by the one known as Archangel Michael. The collective Principality of the heavens gathered their forces and purged corruption from the heavenly places. It was then that the veil went up, concealing the mortal plane from the celestial plane, separating divinity from corruption, and locking it into place as presently stands.

The scene dropped downward, below a cloudy veil, until it focused on a series of different happenings upon the Earth while Emalickel described them.

Emalickel: Along with punishing those of the celestial plane for their disobedience, God also punished those of the mortal plane—the fallen celestials were stripped of their divine abilities. All celestials with wings, found their wings had been clipped, and their powers were depleted to a bare minimum.

Then I saw the people of Earth. They were disputing with each other and murdering each other. I saw stealing and robbing. Structures were being set afire. Mankind was consumed with pride, indulging in a variety of acts revolving around possession and power. These scenes were darkened with contrast.

Emalickel: Mankind was punished by feelings of physical pain and emotional turmoil. They were cursed to experience struggles, trials, and tribulations all through their lives. All creatures were physically changed so that their bodies became vulnerable to disease and decay—leading to eventual physical death after a set number of years.

The scenes before me became slightly lighter. The people on Earth seemed lost and hopeless, but instead of displaying their anger and rage, they seemed sad and confused.

Emalickel: I know what you are wondering . . . why did God allow all this? Listen carefully so that you may understand! God saw all this was good, for He already knew the choices of the fallen ones. He continues to allow them to manipulate the mortals because evil is a trainer of strength to mankind. Putting them through trials and tribulations ultimately teaches them to turn away from disobedience and, having no other option, they submit humbly to God by their own free-will.

Satan was destined to be a tool for the development and conditioning of man's soul. Man was introduced to the concept of evil in order to provide him the opportunity to harness a unique power of God, the power of righteousness—and the power to rebuke evil. By mastering this skill, man becomes even closer to embodying the image of God. This lesson could not be supplied by God Himself, for He already is the embodiment of uncorrupted divinity. He desires for mankind to make this same choice.

6. Artist: Really Slow Motion
Song: Hero

Then, I saw visions of noblemen helping others and praying. A light of radiance seemed to shine upon them. Those who had been taken to their knees by darkness, began rising to their feet. One-by-one the people of Earth began standing-up in resistance to the wretchedness around them.

Emalickel: In order for mankind to develop righteousness, they had to first experience the negative effects of evil. The goal was for man to learn how to filter evil and repel darkness from becoming a part of his spirit. The Earth is the training ground where man shall practice, develop, and exercise his

God-given traits of love and nobility, strength and courage, power and authority, and wisdom and self-control. Without the existence of Satan, how would mankind be able to grow a divine backbone? How would they be able to develop a righteous free-will in the image of God?

The next thing I saw was a glowing child being held in its mother's arms. There were several different views of this child as it grew into a man until reaching the age of around thirty. His hair was dark brown and wavy, extending just past his shoulders. He wore linen garments and had many followers among him.

Emalickel: In addition, God promised unto the mortals a gift, a very unique and powerful gift. He sent the very Spirit of Himself to dwell in the corrupted mortal plane. He became one of living flesh among them. He shared His Word, endured tragedy, and overcame temptation. He demonstrated His divinity even during the painful sacrifice of His mortal life. He knew that even after death His Spirit would continue to remain among man. His Spirit would provide an offer of protection to ensure their souls would not share in the same impending doom as the fallen ones. Even we celestials are bewildered by this mystery of God. We marvel at salvation, for it was a personal gift given solely to mankind, directly by God Himself.

The man whom I had been seeing was Christ. He exhibited an angelic glow. Everyone who was in his presence also exhibited this glow.

Emalickel: The promise of this Spirit has already been fulfilled. This gift has already been bestowed upon mankind in the form of Christ. The King has overcome the works of Satan and of the sin that infects man. By following the path of our King, mankind shall be cleansed and purified again, and

they will be delivered from the mortal plane. All who accept this and live by it shall be forever saved. The men will return to their origins in the celestial plane, and women will return to their celestial-pair as the third and final aspect of completion.

7. Artist: Audiomachine
Song: Tangled Earth

Fire filled the next scene. The dark crimson celestial, the devil himself, stood alone. He was surrounded by darkness with a great fire burring behind him. He fell to his knees and roared in great disappointment, for he knew he had been defeated by the Spirit of God upon the Earth.

Emalickel: Ultimately, by Satan's free-will, he intended to bring a curse upon man, diverting their focus from God and onto himself; instead, he brought to man a blessing in disguise. Though the focus may temporarily be on the devil's work at times, salvation has given man the victory over evil. Salvation has enabled man to develop his divine spirit in an environment occupied and protected by the actual Spirit of God.

Then, the three dark realms of the celestial plane came into view again. The celestials who roamed these realms appeared as savages. They did not glow, nor did they appear lively. They were pale and thin, and their expressions were somber and cold.

Emalickel: Satan continued regular contact with the three negative realms. For a while after the fall, he continued recruiting more celestials to join him on the mortal plane. By appealing to their desires, he made the kingdom of the fallen seem better than that of the celestial plane. In exchange of

their fall to Earth, Satan promised them an invigorating and fulfilling experience.

I saw the corrupted crimson beast, surrounded by a volcanic abyss. Others were with him as he opened his arms and looked upward. Satan spoke aloud in the voice of a wicked roar.

Satan: Why do you continue dwelling in a place of slavery, celestial brothers? There is so much here I can offer unto you in this mortal plane! Release yourselves from the numbing dullness! Come, experience exhilaration! Find your freedom! I have so easily succeeded at gaining the obedience of man. Enjoy the benefits of this obedience for yourself! Take the women for yourselves and feel all the pleasures within this Earthly kingdom that I now call mine own!

Dusty clouds of ash began flickering with lightning, and the sound of thunder crashed within the abyss. Satan laughed in satisfaction as he levitated himself upward and out from the volcano. The sky of the Earth was stormy. Several fire-balls shot across the skyline and plummeted. Some of the fire-balls slammed against the side of the volcano, near where Satan was levitating. Celestials emerged from where these fire-balls had crashed.

Emalickel: In their weakness, more celestials chose to fall to the mortal plane—a great abundance of them came from the three realms of Haffelnia, Gaddorium, and Yahrinstahd. Drawn unto the women, and the women drawn unto them, they savored each other through physical contact, and THAT created a big problem. Their lustful physical expressions resulted in a hybrid offspring known as the Nephilim. They were conceived as a result of celestial-energy being emitted into a mortal female during physical pleasure. A celestial's energy mimicked that of a mortal man's seed and activated the genetic process of conception within the women of Earth.

8. Artist: Mark Petrie
Song: Celestial

The image quickly scrolled into the far distance; it was so far and so fast that even time seemed to leap forward. Finally, it stopped at a pair of legs that towered over all other men. It scrolled up to the body and face of a giant, primal-looking man-beast. He wore only a loincloth of black leather. He stared down at the people of the land below with his hands clenched into fists. He stood well over thirty-feet tall. His stature was broad and sturdy. His wavy, unkept hair extended past his shoulders and rested on his chest.

Emalickel continued.

Emalickel: The Nephilim were a race of humanoid giants. They exhibited some celestial abilities, which made them impossible for humans to control or tame. Since the fallen had been stripped of their powers and since all divine celestials were commanded to stay in the celestial plane, there were no forces to overpower the Nephilim at that time. Because of this, the Nephilim became oppressive and overbearing. They placed themselves in positions of dominance over the entire mortal plane.

This drove man to begin worshipping them as gods. Mortals no longer focused on the one true God. They feared the Nephilim who became consumed by self-glorification and pride. As a whole, the beings of Earth had become ridden with darkness and evil.

Images of the celestial plane faded into view. The warriors, who had fought the dark celestials once before, appeared to be preparing themselves for battle once again. The words of Emalickel's description followed along with the images.

Emalickel: One-third of the celestials had fallen to dwell in the mortal plane. They lost their places among the Divine Ones. Among them were several of our very own Guards of Lapoi, several of the celestials from the first and second spheres, and a significant number of celestials from the realms of Haffelnia, Gaddorium, and Yahrinstahd.

9. Artist: Paradox Interactive
Song: Drums of Odin

Below the celestial plane, I witnessed the Earth being consumed by water. The warrior celestials of Lapoi collectively orchestrated their powers and guided the deep blue oceans to engulf the green lands entirely. As this happened, Emalickel proceeded to narrate.

Emalickel: Throwing His hands into their air, God instructed the Lapoian Warriors to initiate a great flood so that almost all would perish. It would cleanse the Earth of any abominations and reset the evolutionary spectrum.

Waves crashed violently onto every piece of dry land until the Earth had been completely swallowed-up by water. Then, the images of Emalickel's words were painted before me as he continued telling the story.

Emalickel: After the bodies of the Nephilim had perished in this flood, their spirits were chained and bound in a location completely apart from the mortal plane. Meanwhile, the dark spirits of the fallen celestials were confined to the mortal plane, never again to return to the heavens. Only ten-percent of them were allowed to roam the Earth—where they presently continue following the lead of Satan in his attempt to

control mankind. The remaining ninety percent of the fallen celestials were permanently chained and bound in darkness, upon the mortal plane where they still await judgement.

The celestials who remained in the realms of Haffelnia, Gaddorium, and Yahrinstahd had already chosen in their hearts to rebel, but since they had not yet followed through with their decisions, God spared them from perishing in the fall to the mortal plane. Instead, all three realms lost their grace and light. The radiance that had once glowed upon their realms was dimmed into total darkness.

I saw the three realms become darkened, as if a glowing light had been turned off from them. Everything became pitch-black and completely silent for a moment. Then, I found myself hovering peacefully above the present-day Earth again, just as when this entire vision had first begun.

Emalickel: The spiritual battle on Earth shall continue until the day God is ready to reap His Divine Harvest. Until then, the world beneath the veil will endure great challenges. This is all I shall share with you. Absorb it. Process it. Pray about it. Share it. And finally, you must practice your participation in this ongoing battle. Go back now, put on your full Armor, and remember what you have seen this night, Princess of Lapoi.

2

TAKEN AWAY

10. Artist: John Dreamer
Song: Becoming A Legend

My eyes opened. I was in my bed, as if waking from a night of sleep. Another day had begun, one just like all the rest. My feet hit the floor and the usual morning routine began. From the bathroom to brush my teeth, to the kitchen to feed the cats, I started getting ready for another day of teaching school. I wondered how I would be able to function like everybody else that day. All I wanted to do was sit in a quiet room for days upon days to process what I had just seen. This would be impossible, for a typical day contained way too many distractions.

As I went through the motions of that day, I tried to maintain a normal demeanor, but in actuality, my mind revolved around everything Emalickel had revealed to me. His words continued recycling and processing in my mind. I had to force myself to blend-in with the people of my surroundings, seeming to be present with them; but all the while, my mind was consumed by the amazing vision of what I had seen the previous night—and the people around me had absolutely no idea, nor would they truly believe me or understand me.

There were few moments of peace and quiet in my life at that time. I made the most of my thirty-minute commute to and from work. Some nights, if I wasn't too exhausted, I spent a limited amount of time in self-reflection. One afternoon, I came home from a very hard day at work. I knew I needed to remove myself from the company of others, for I was on-edge and was carrying a negative aurora. I made time for myself that afternoon to sit in peace on the back porch of my home. As usual, my mind always wandered its way back to recollections of Lapoi.

Me: It has to be real. They exist . . . the celestials. They're somewhere out there.

I thought quietly to myself as I looked toward the sky from my screened-in porch.

Me: What are they doing right this moment? Can they see me? I wonder if they're watching me, or if they can hear my thoughts?

From where I was sitting in the rocking chair, all I could see were pine trees and gray skies in front of me. There was a coolness in the breeze. It looked like it was about to storm. The back porch had become my "thinking place." I'd sit out there for as long as I possibly could and think about various things. Mostly I found myself thinking about my experiences with the celestials which had begun six-years earlier; how I could get back to the celestial plane again to visit; and how I could spend more time with the brothers.

Me: Emalickel . . . Thorenel . . . can you hear me? Are you there? Show me a sign.

11. Artist: Audiomachine
Song: Existence (Extended to 5:30)

My thoughts always wandered back to the image of them—the two Royal-Princedom celestials of Lapoi. The entire realm of Millattus was ruled by these two brothers. Before I knew they were of Princedom status, I had intimately engaged with both of them. As a result, I became crowned and joined them at the throne. I remembered the grand, open balcony behind their throne chairs. It overlooked a range of snow-capped mountains in the far distance of a vast, grassy valley—The Valley of Dillectus.

It wasn't easy going from being an immortal princess, residing in a majestic palace in the celestial plane; to being an ordinary, lower-middle-class mortal, living in the daily grind and struggle of mortal life on Earth. I no longer lived in the Garden of Eden. I was a nobody again—just another sheep among the herd. Six years ago, in Lapoi, I had been introduced to magnificent power, freedom, beauty, unconditional love, and security, and then stripped of it all, just as abruptly as it had all been revealed. Experiencing the splendor of Lapoi, made it even harder to exist in the mortal plane again. I had experienced greatness, only to return to a regular existence again. Although I had gained new perspectives and insights, I came back to Earth feeling deeply dissatisfied. My visit to Lapoi was both a blessing and a curse.

I had seen the lands of Lapoi and experienced its phenomenal beauty and magic. Since returning to the mortal plane of existence, I felt an emptiness in my heart; and I felt lost among everyone. There was no one who would believe me, nor be able to truly comprehend what I had experienced. Nobody in my life talked about what I really wanted to talk about. They received no blame from me, as I couldn't possibly expect for them to discuss anything or anyone from Lapoi with me. Truth be known, that is all I wanted to talk about, dream about, think about, or read about. I became obsessed.

Lapoi was more than a vivid dream, it had become a part of my emotions and my soul. My whole world integrated Lapoi into it. It was as if I were in a middle-world, somewhere between full-on Earth and full-on Lapoi. Everywhere I went I carried Lapoi with me. Sometimes I felt invigorating angel-juice pulsing through my veins, giving me an overjoyed feeling. Other times it felt like baggage; having experienced such a magical, perfect place, only to return to the matrix with nothing more than a story which most would believe to be fantasy fiction.

I had experienced an authentic, genuine place not of this world; a place filled with celestial beings who oversee mankind. Their civilization, physically located in our galaxy, exists on a giant planet called Lapoi. Although this planet may not be visible from the mortal plane, I was certain it was there. Lapoi was not something my mind created or dreamt—it had felt too real. I still questioned exactly how it happened to me. I wasn't sure whether I had visited Lapoi physically through an episode of astral-projection or through some kind of subconscious journey, but I wanted to figure it out because I wanted to go back.

I was consumed with obsessive thoughts of returning to Lapoi, or at least making contact with the celestials again. My mind relentlessly replayed memories of scenes from my last visits. My heart yearned endlessly to see Emalickel and Thorenel. I wanted to feel their strong, protective embrace once again. I wanted to marvel at the diverse lands and roam the halls of the massive, majestic palace they called home. How could I get back to that magical, beautiful, wondrous place?

I wanted to see the beauty of the land again. The landscape was vast and appealing, like a blend of Scandinavia and Greece. It contained giant rock-cliffs lining the oceans, meadows of flowers and wheat grass, monstrous waterfalls, evergreen woodlands, and sandy riverside colonies. I wanted to smell the wintergreen breeze. I craved the scent of new leather coming from Emalickel, and the scent of amber from Thorenel. I missed the taste of sweet mead and cheese served in the palace during celebrations. I wanted to hear the sound of Celtic-Renaissance tunes playing merrily in the background again. I missed the feeling of belonging I had felt when I sat upon the gold and black throne chair next to Emalickel.

12. Artist: Fearless Motivation
Song: Revival

I heard a loud chirping sound and noticed a bird swoop down to feast on the bird-feeder in the back yard. I had lost myself in thought again, reliving the brilliance of Lapoi; only to realize I wasn't actually there. Although this saddened me in the moment, I felt soothed that I had recorded every detail of my previous encounters and published them in a novel to share with the rest of the world. So, whether or not anyone else had the opportunity to experience Lapoi in the way that I did, its existence had been permanently recorded in written text and had spread worldwide. Upon my mortal death, my story would not become buried with me, but rather it would be left in a tangible, hardcopy form, that it may never be lost or forgotten. I had shared the experience, in great detail, from the most epic moments to the most private moments. It comforted me to know the entire world would have access to this story, perhaps for as long as the sun were shining.

Standing up from the rocking chair, I walked to the edge of the screened-in porch. I returned my gaze to the sky; always hopeful I would see a sign of them or hear a whisper. As usual . . . nothing. I recalled what Emalickel had said to me on the palace balcony before I departed Lapoi years ago. A portal to Earth had already been made and I was bidding farewell to the celestials. I remembered the sound of Emalickel's voice as he reached up and removed the sparkling, celestial princess crown from my head. He had a deep, smooth voice, with an English accent. He carried a low, masculine pitch that resonated within me. His tone was calm, but authoritative. Memories of his statement echoed in my mind.

Emalickel: I will put your crown safely in its place, where it shall stay until your return, Princess of Lapoi.

Although I was confident in the existence of Lapoi, I still had doubts about my status. It was hard to believe that I had actually met two celestial Princes with whom I had shared intimacy and an emotional bond. In turn, I was made into the princess among their kingdom of celestials. It was still so hard to believe. I felt so ordinary and common on the Earth—how could I be a princess in the celestial plane? I shook my head in astonishment and smiled while saying to myself.

Me: ***The Princess of Lapoi.***

I paused for a moment, and my face grew serious.

Me: ***If I am this princess, then why am I living such an ordinary mortal life? Shouldn't I have more? Perhaps I can have more, and this is a test of my abilities?***

Thorenel had provided me insight on this before. He had referred to it as the Law of Attraction. By faith in God, he told me, all mortals have power. Beliefs are what create one's reality, not the translations of the seemingly realistic conditions surrounding them. He said it was important to focus on desired conditions, instead of on undesired conditions. Remember only what you want in life, and refrain from thinking about the things you don't want. One must fool themselves—believing and living as if they already have what they desire. Only then will those things begin to transpire.

I understood the concept, but this was incredibly difficult to execute. I knew, regardless of my Lapoian status, the Earth is where I belonged for the time being. I came to Earth to experience mortal life and evolve my spirit. There would be of no place to evolve if every desire had already been provided to me in mortal plane.

I came to terms with this and created two Earthly desires. I desired to have an abundance of time—that way I could have more time to focus on my spirit and return to a state of unconditional love. The second Earthly desire was for an abundance of money—that way I could have the financial freedom to travel the Earth and see all there was to see and to do all there was to do. The money would also provide freedom from the need to work, which in turn would provide me more time.

Ultimately, happiness and peace were my ultimate desires. Unfortunately, the world had too many distractions and negative conditions. It was nearly impossible to ignore them and maintain a focus only on the desired. The real problem wasn't even the inability to achieve my desires, but rather the matter of Earth feeling less like a home to me anymore. I had unearthly desires; desires to regularly visit Lapoi as I carried out my time on Earth. Unable to achieve any of these things, I continued feeling restless and unsettled.

One of my cats had come outside and was brushing against my legs. His big green eyes with vertical pupils stared up at me from the floor. I wondered what he was thinking about. What did he think about in general? I bet his mind was simple and quiet. I tried to remember the last time my mind was in such a state. Perhaps the last time was when I was twelve years old—that was the last time my mind was carefree like that of a child. From my early teens to late twenties, my mind was consumed by becoming accepted by everyone else. Then, at the age of 28, it reversed completely. I wanted to go off-the-grid and stray as far away from conformity as possible.

13. Artist: Charles Bunczk
Song: The Inner Light

Just before experiencing Lapoi, my mind was consumed with striving for something beyond the monotony and conformity of Earth. After returning from Lapoi, my mind became consumed with how to get back there or how to bring Lapoi here. One positive attribute I was able to permanently bring with me from Lapoi was my mindset becoming more optimistic about others. My outlook on life became less restricted, and I felt a sense of freedom. I felt somewhat released from the walls of judgement and conformity. Other people didn't interfere with my thoughts and emotions anymore. In turn, I became less judgmental of them. They could do, think, and believe as they pleased without any effect on me. I didn't take things so personally. I tried to evolve my spirit by taking control of my own thoughts and emotions. I utilized the power of belief to shape my own world around me, despite what others were doing or thinking.

Although I had obtained freedom from my perception of others and how they perceived me, I still needed more practice in controlling my thoughts, reactions, and emotions in any given moment or condition. I knew it was key to achieving my desire of happiness and peace.

Even still, I caught myself slipping into the matrix of conformity. The demands and mishaps at work would cause me to lose sight of my ultimate desires, and I would catch myself becoming immersed in the problems, instead of putting things in perspective and moving-on in happiness. At home I would slip into the matrix of negativity as a result of routines and expectations required to run a household. I was becoming a robot again.

I started resenting any distractions which seemed to impede me from achieving the level of happiness and peace I had once obtained upon my initial return from Lapoi. Distractions were keeping me from evolving. They kept me from my serenity. They restricted me from having the time and proper mindset to reflect and pray. The distractions in life made me tired. I was practically sleepwalking, which left no chance of astral-travel back to Lapoi.

Walking around in resentment and self-anger, it became even harder than before to blend-in and mesh with everyone else in society on the Earth. The resentment of all of life's distractions caused me to harness negativity. I was angry with myself for allowing the darkness to win. I expected more of myself. I wanted to focus on happiness amidst the chaos—my goal was to keep my head high, in dreamland, despite the goings on around me. I wanted to overcome the mortal world which consumed me.

14. Artist: Thunderstep Music
Song: They Are Coming For Us

Just then, my five-year-old daughter stormed through the back door and onto the porch. She was frustrated and whining because she couldn't get into a play-dress she desired to wear. No big deal, I could help her with that. Little did I know; this was only the beginning of a giant snow-ball of calamities that would take place that afternoon and evening.

I calmly helped my little girl with her dress and alleviated that problem. Then she wanted for me to make her something to eat. That was fine. I cooked for her some spaghetti, but she wanted macaroni and cheese. She also wanted a drink. I gave her some juice, but she wanted water. I gave her the water, but she wanted ice in the water.

As I gathered ice in a cup, the cats crowded under my feet and tripped me—they too wanted to be fed. While walking down the hall to get the cat food, I stepped in cat vomit. I cursed as the cold, slimy feeling of goo squished between my toes. While in the laundry room retrieving cat food, I remembered the clothes in the dryer needed to be folded. There were also clothes that needed to be ironed. I knew I would have to come back to the laundry later. The cats needed to be fed, and the vomit needed to be cleaned-up.

The cats were always fed in the kitchen. Afterward, the floor always needed to be wiped because Figaro usually dipped his paws into the food dish, and it would make a mess all over the floor. While in the kitchen tending to the floor, I noticed the mail had been delivered.

I went outside and walked down the driveway to retrieve the mail. This ended up being a bad decision. On the way to the mailbox, I walked barefoot, and I stepped directly onto a sharp pebble in the driveway. It caused the bottom of my foot to bleed. I didn't have time to worry about it, but it was painful nonetheless. I pulled the stack of mail out of the mailbox. In the stack, I noticed a bill from the local hospital. It was from an unavoidable visit to the emergency room from a few months back. I opened the envelope—another bad decision. The balance due was over two-thousand dollars! I was already cutting-back on finances by eating rice for lunch every day. The absolute last thing I needed was another expense to pay. Christmas was only two months away.

On my way back inside the house, my phone rang. It was my auto insurance company. I had recently been in a car accident. The insurance company was trying to set up an appointment for me to take my car to the repair shop and pick up a rental. Every evening after work that coming week was full of things to do. However, I did not want to drive around with a beat-up car for an entire week. I had to figure something out.

I was back in the kitchen and was still on the phone with the insurance company when I heard a loud crashing noise. I turned in the direction of the noise. My little girl had spilled her macaroni and cheese everywhere! As I rushed to set down the stack of mail, my finger was sliced with a paper-cut. Disgruntled, I quickly finished my phone conversation with the insurance company and entered the car-repair appointment in my calendar of overflowing engagements. I would have to figure out modifications to my schedule some other time. Maintaining a calm outward demeanor, I cleaned up the sticky, cheesy mess. It was on the table, the floor, and all over my little girl's clothes. I felt myself falling into a dark emotional state.

15. Artist: Wardruna
Song: MannaR Liv

These types of chaotic events continued playing-out over the course of the evening, until we had reached the time to prepare for bed. On the outside, I kept a collected and soft presence, but deep inside, my emotions were not in control. I felt like a boiling volcano, full of hot lava, about to erupt at any moment. I managed to keep myself composed as my little girl and I went through our bedtime routine. Then, I did the usual bedtime ritual: I tucked her into bed, kissed her goodnight, told her I'm right here if she needs me, and that I love her.

All I really wanted to do was sit for a quiet moment of peace, but it seemed the demands of life had other plans for me. Still, I resisted and my emotions became on edge.

Returning to the laundry room, I opened the dryer and begin folding the laundry. Several articles of light-colored clothing had turned pink! This was quite disturbing. My phone rang again. It was a reminder of an important appointment I had the next day, in which I had forgotten all about. I had already made prior plans and would need to reschedule those as well. Overwhelmed, I rushed off to the bathroom to have a melt-down.

I was sitting on the bathroom floor, with my knees pulled to my chest. I buried my face into my knees and began rocking myself, crying in absolute hysterics. Tears poured down my face, dampening the loose strands of hair which fell from my messy ponytail. Black mascara dripped down my cheeks. The black streaks became even more smeared as I wiped tears from my face with the palm of my hand. Looking up, I saw the darkness of the night peering in through the blinds of the square bathroom window. It intensified my internal feelings—dark, empty, and alone.

I tried to stand up and pull myself together. Still sobbing, I rested my elbows on the bathroom counter and held my own face in my hands. I saw my own reflection in the mirror. I did not see a strong, wise, princess; I saw a weak, confused, unsettled, out-of-place mortal. I leaned into the mirror and looked myself in the eyes. I ground my teeth in frustration. I spoke to my reflection under my breath.

Me: You're better than this!

It was hard to believe my self-affirmation. I was disappointed in myself for being so weak. My resentment grew. I clenched my fists, and my eyes squeezed shut as I held back a roar of emotional turmoil—completely distraught and lost. Tears continued spreading across the surface of my face. I continued grinding my teeth as I quietly repeated phrases to myself between each crying breath. It was therapeutic.

It's not fair!

I took a breath.

Why does it have to be so hard!?!

There was a pause while I sniffed my nose.

Make it go away! All the endless distractions! I can't take it anymore!

I paused to collect my thoughts again and sat down on the rim of the bathtub behind me.

I just want to go back! Why won't they let me come back!?! Let me come back!

Wiping my eyes and taking in another deep breath, I continued.

Nobody understands!

I clenched my hair with my fists, messing it up quite a bit, then I dropped my face into my hands.

It's too much! I can't take it!

I took another breath and wiped my eyes.

Why can't it be easier!?!

My temperament flew into rage as I picked up each of the five bathmats, one at a time, and flung them across the bathroom. Even in my outrage, I remained an instinctively good mother by ensuring my daughter didn't see or hear how out of control I was. Inside the bathroom I looked like a crazed mad-woman, but from outside the bathroom door, it would be hard to tell I exhibited the level of fury in which I had reached. My cries were muffled as I kept my face buried in either my hands or my knees. I contained my frustration and urge to lash out by maintaining clinched teeth, clinched fists, and by throwing the soft rugs all around.

Finally, I sat back down, this time on the closed toilet seat. I leaned forward to rest my elbows on my knees. My fingers fed into my hair to hold my head as I looked down at the floor for a moment. My eyes felt swollen from crying, and my face felt like a sticky mess. I became tired. I stood up and went to the sink. As I turned on the water, I looked at myself in the mirror, only confirming I was a complete mess. I splashed the clean water on my face. Although my eyes were still swollen, it felt refreshing to wash the sorrow away.

16. Artist: Olexandr Ignatov
Song: Rising from the Ashes

After somewhat collecting myself, I fixed the bathmats and turned off the light. Slowly, I walked toward the bed, paying close attention not to stub my toe or run into something in the dark bedroom. Sniffling, I crawled into the empty bed and pulled the covers over me. My mind still raced, but I finally started drifting off to sleep.

Then, I became startled. An unexpected bright light began shining in the room. I could see it through my closed eyelids. When I opened my eyes, I saw a being at the foot of the bed. He was squatting down with his elbows on his knees. His head rested upon his hands which were folded under his chin. He exhibited a relaxed smile. My eyes opened wider. Alarmed, I sat up abruptly, at what point he rose to a standing position at about seven feet tall.

He wasn't Emalickel or Thorenel, nor was he any of the brothers I had met in Lapoi. I had never seen this being before. He carried appealing features. He appeared to be in his late twenties with a slender athletic build. His weight was probably somewhere around 250 pounds. His complexion was of warm-ivory. His flowing, dark brown, wavy hair was medium in length and touched just above his shoulders. The left side of his hair was tucked behind his ear. His face was oval in shape and was framed with a short boxed-beard. His deep-set eyes were dark brown and were framed by his low-rise eyebrows.

He wore a black cloak, which touched just behind his knees. It was trimmed in light-colored, soft, brown fur which was especially abundant over his shoulders. Under the cloak, he was wearing a dark brown tunic with a black leather belt across his waist. His trousers were black and blended with his boots. I noticed a sheathed sword on his left hip, and he was wearing thick black gloves on his hands.

He stood there for a minute. I collected myself and tried to absorb the reality. I wasn't necessarily afraid, but I was caught off-guard. He had startled me, and I was trying to calm myself. At the same time, I was trying to figure out who he was. I felt slightly uneasy about his presence, since I did not know him, nor did I know why he was there.

17. Artist: Antti Martikainen
Song: Otherworld

He began walking closer to my side of the bed. I could hear the sound of his stiff, leather boots stretching and crunching as he slowly approached across the carpet. When he arrived next to me, he removed one of his gloves and held out his hand to me. I looked at his hand, then up at his face. His smile grew wider. I was hesitant to take his hand. Without speaking aloud, I asked him questions within my mind to see if he would be able to hear them.

Me: ***Who are you?***

He passed my test by responding aloud in perfect timing. His voice was low and resonate.

Being: I have been sent for you.

Me: ***By who?***

Being: By your beloved, Emalickel.

I hesitated for a moment. The light radiating from this being grew brighter. I froze in shock. Was this my chance to finally return to the celestial plane again!?! I shook my head in attempt to gain better awareness. There I was, staring up at a glowing being in my bedroom, trying to figure out if I could trust him. I collected my thoughts and organized a few additional questions to ask him. Again, I asked these questions within my mind.

Me: ***I belong to Emalickel. Why did he send you instead of coming to me himself?***

The being lowered his hand and repositioned his stance.

Being: He is presently receiving the orders from the Dominion.

I looked down and scratched the side of my face. I was still uncomfortable with throwing all my trust into this being whom I had just met. With my hand on my chin, I scanned the room in thought.

Me: ***What about Thorenel? Why did he not send Thorenel?***

The being chuckled and shook his head as if amused by the ignorance of my question.

Being: And then who would watch the Throne of Lapoi, dear one?

I was trying to think how that would work.

Being: The Throne of Lapoi cannot be left unattended. If Emalickel is receiving the orders from the Dominion and if Thorenel were here, who would be in charge of the kingdom of Lapoi?

He had made a perfectly valid point, and I didn't want to miss an opportunity to return to Lapoi. If I refused to go with him, I didn't know when, or even if, I'd get another chance to go back there.

Me: ***And, what is your name?***

His face grew serious again.

Being: My name is of no importance. What is of importance is that you come with me.

I folded my hands in my lap and looked down at them. I really couldn't trust him, but I knew that no amount of questions would make that possible. I was going to have to take a risk. He did look gentle, and he did seem to carry himself with mild-temperament. I weighed the odds before making a final decision. Most likely, he was telling the truth, and I couldn't turn down the opportunity to see Lapoi again.

Being: Well then, are you coming?

Slowly, I slid from the bed. Again, he extended his hand inviting me to take it. I smiled a hesitant smile and placed my hand into his. He pulled me in closer to him and placed his other hand flat on my forehead. He maintained a serious demeanor. It was as if he had business in which to tend, and he seemed to remain focused on the objective.

I felt a wind suddenly begin to blow—right there in the bedroom. The unusual thing was that nothing in the room blew with this wind. The curtains remained still. There were no papers which flew about. The linens on the bed were perfectly still. The wind was localized on me and the being. I started seeing glittering twinkles of light, and I felt myself lift from the ground.

We were traveling via teleportation. It was a little different from when I had travelled with Emalickel, but I knew each celestial had a unique process in activating their abilities. Traveling through teleportation with Thorenel had felt different than with Emalickel. Teleportation with this celestial was incredibly windy and contained golden, glittering light. I saw a rainbow of colors pass my line of view as we seemingly flew through space and time. Then, everything faded into white.

When everything subsided, I looked around. I was standing in an opening on a hillside of dark brown grass. Surrounding the outskirts of the hillside, was a jungle-like environment containing trees with dark-red foliage. The ground of the jungle was covered in a sheet of dark-red plant-life. I saw brown vines, black-colored hanging moss, and red ferns. The atmosphere was darker than I had remembered of Lapoi. The sky was covered in thick, dark-gray clouds. A thin fog hovered above the ground at the base of the hills. The land was silent and still. I didn't hear any birds or any signs of life. All I could hear was the breeze whisping through the brush and trees. The air smelled musty, like mold or mildew. It was humid, but the air felt slightly cool, like right before a thunderstorm.

18. Artist: Hi-Finesse
Song: Another World

I slowly scanned the scenery around me by turning a complete circle. From the hilltop, I saw gently rolling hills bordered all around by a dense, red jungle. I looked back at the being who had brought me there. He was smiling, but he appeared to carry a mischievous, evil vibe. My face grew concerned. Looking down at myself, I noticed I wasn't wearing the simple white dress I had once worn during my last astral visit to Lapoi. Instead, I was wearing a flowy, full-length, long-sleeved, black dress. A thin, golden rope was elegantly wrapped and crossed several times above my waist. The sleeves were peasant-style, containing loose ruffles at the ends. I also noticed I was wearing a black choker necklace with a golden circular pendant, one-inch in diameter, containing the Lapoian triquetra symbol. I spoke aloud with confidence and bravery.

Me: Where are we?

The being chuckled at me.

Being: It doesn't look like Lapoi, does it?

I grew worried and silently shook my head to indicate the answer as "no."

Being: You see, I might have . . . kind of . . . well . . . lied to you!

The being turned his back and walked a few steps away from me. His voice was satirical.

Being: You and I . . . we have met before. You do not recognize me because I made some adjustments in my appearance upon my regeneration. My name is Barthaldeo. You remember me, right?

I gasped. Of course I remembered him! He was the Royal-Princedom celestial of Umgliesia. Umgliesia is the celestial planet of the realm of Haffelnia, one of the three negative realms among the Universe. The first time I visited Lapoi, he and his legion abducted me and had taken me on-board their ship. He had intended to use the memories from all my soul's lifetimes to gain insight on how to advance the mortals in Haffelnia. Barthaldeo was jealous of Emalickel and envied the progress of the realm of Millattus.

I had flashbacks in my mind of how unbearably painful it was during the process of Barthaldeo reading my soul's memories. In the past, Emalickel had defeated Barthaldeo and saved me from becoming his hostage. All celestials were immortal, and I knew that Barthaldeo would eventually rebuild his energy. Emalickel had previously disclosed this to me during my last visit. Defeated celestials go to a non-physical plane where they spend an extended period of time regenerating and recharging their auras, until they physically manifest again on their celestial planet.

Upon recognizing Barthaldeo, my eyes widened, and my expression turned into one of terror. He had completely restored himself! Unable to muster-up any words, I gulped and looked for a way out.

Barthaldeo: Welcome to Thermaplia, one of the three mortal planets in the realm of Haffelnia!

He held out his arms in welcome, but I knew he was being sarcastic and arrogant. He had successfully fooled me, and now he had me trapped. I tried to remain calm, reassuring myself that I would get out of there somehow. I squinted my eyes closed in attempt to wake myself from the nightmare I had entered. My mind began scanning ideas. I acted brave, but inside I felt sheer-panic. I didn't want Barthaldeo to think he had won. I wanted him to think he had made a terrible mistake.

19. Artist: Audiomachine
Song: Black Cauldron

Me: You know Emalickel will come looking for me! And he will be so pissed when he finds you!

Barthaldeo smiled proudly.

Barthaldeo: No! Emalickel will not find you. No celestial from Lapoi will. You, my dear, have been warded from them.

Me: I don't understand.

He picked up a shiny silver rock from the ground and held it up to my face. I could see my reflection within it. Across my forehead I noticed several symbols etched in a row from the left side to the right side. Just then, I remembered Barthaldeo had placed his hand on my forehead before we had teleported from my bedroom. At the time, I had thought it was a part of his method of travel, but I realized he had been placing the warding symbols during that time.

Barthaldeo: They cannot see you, nor hear you, nor track you in any way. You've disappeared completely from their celestial radar.

Me: They'll know it was you, and they'll come.

Barthaldeo: That may be so . . . in fact, I hope it is so. The only way they'll be able to find you is if I allow them to know of your exact location. Each of the three mortal planets in Haffelnia are twice the size of your planet Earth. There's no possible way they'll find you in this realm without my help. You are but a grain of sand on entire beach. The vastness of Haffelnia is so monstrous it is daunting!

Me: Why would you want to attract them here?

Barthaldeo burst out laughing.

Barthaldeo: You entertain me, you know that? So oblivious! So naive!

When he regained control of himself, he continued.

Barthaldeo: You are my hostage for Emalickel. In order to know of your whereabouts, he must disclose his secret. Millattus is the only realm which has discovered this secret—the secret to achieving a Golden Age of evolution among the realm. Emalickel is well on his way with this in Millattus, but I desire to achieve it.

Me: And what if he chooses not to disclose the secret?

Barthaldeo: Then you shall waste away until you rot on this planet of Thermaplia. Then you'll start all over again in another life.

Me: Emalickel told me I would likely be ready to enter Lapoi

after this lifetime, instead of cycling back into mortality again.

Barthaldeo placed a finger on the side of his mouth and pretended to think deeply.

Barthaldeo: That is only assuming you have accomplished everything to achieve your spiritual evolution in this lifetime. And I very seriously doubt you will be able to do that, seeing that you are here and not in your home-realm of Millattus. You must be in your own realm in order to evolve, and this, my dear mortal, is nowhere near your realm.

20. Artist: Paradox Interactive
Song: Drums of Odin

In the far distance, I heard a thunderous roar. I became immediately alarmed.

Me: What was that!?!

Turning in the direction of the sound, Barthaldeo looked out through the distance for a moment.

Barthaldeo: That would be one of Thermaplia's very own mortal life-forms.

He turned his head to look at me and squinted his eyes.

Barthaldeo: Everything here is wild and untamed, Princess of Lapoi. My advice for you is to avoid . . . wellEVERY life-form here.

Whatever creature had made that sound was enormous. I panicked.

Me: You wouldn't let me die! That would defeat the point of having a hostage!

Closing his eyes Barthaldeo smiled.

Barthaldeo: Being Emalickel's beloved, you are my primary choice, but there are plenty of other potential hostages, who are meaningful to Lapoi . . . should I need to replace you.

At that, he disappeared into an orb of light. The ferocious roar rumbled again. The creature was still far in the distance, but it was approaching closer. Off and on, I heard the wind periodically whoosh. Then I heard bouts of thunder in a steady tempo —rumm, rumm. What I was hearing were footsteps—gargantuan footsteps! The steps were slow, but they were rapidly getting closer. As it approached, I heard branches breaking. The leaves and bushes rustled. The cool wind suddenly picked up.

Still standing vulnerable on the open hillside, I looked in the direction from which the commotion seemed to coming. Straining my eyes to see in the distance, the treetops swayed tremendously, shaking debris all around. I wondered what creature was causing such a disturbance. I could hear the cracking and breaking of massive trees as they broke and collapsed to the ground. Something gray and orange had begun to surface above the canopy of the trees. It was bobbing up and down like a bird in flight. Then it disappeared again below the tree-tops, at which point, the stomping sound resumed. The treetops near the tree-line jerked and swayed violently. I could partially see the grayish-orange creature but couldn't make out much detail.

When it finally emerged into the open, my body froze in shock. The creature was fully visible. Once it exited the tree-line, it opened a pair of massive wings to fly. In doing so, the wind picked up. The whooshing sound I had heard was the flapping of its wings. All I could do was try to breathe. It was a monstrosity! Larger than any creature I'd ever seen on Earth, resembling a large-winged tyrannosaurus rex, but four times the size!

21. Artist: Paradox Interactive
Song: Terror from the Sea

Its dark eyes were pronounced and seemed to be searching for something to endure its wrath. It folded its wings behind its back and resumed walking upright on two raptor-like feet. Stretching its neck out, it let out a low growl, similar to that of a tiger or lion, but deeper and louder. The ground vibrated beneath my feet.

Then, the creature stopped dead in its tracks and rose up on its clawed toes. It raised its nose far into the air. Even though it seemed to be more than a mile away, I could hear it breathing! It sniffed all around, seemingly zeroing in on something. It took one step forward and raised its head into the air to let out a high-pitched shrieking sound. It echoed all around for several seconds. I can only describe the sound as being like a blend of a donkey, fox's vixen scream, and Howler monkey—like the scream of a mythological banshee! It raised the hairs on the back of my neck.

Suddenly, it jerked its head toward me. It made that terrorizing sound once more. I could see its snarling teeth. They looked like jagged shards of razor-sharp glass. Its feet began taking more slow, steady steps—this time in my direction. I knew I had to get out of there! I was out in the wide open! There was no cover provided from the jungle for a mile in any direction. My only choice was to run.

Without hesitation, I started down the other side of the hill. I kept looking behind me to see if I could see the creature, but the hillside was obstructing my view. I knew it was near as I could hear its footsteps. Luckily, the footsteps hadn't started moving at a faster pace. Then, I heard the whooshing sound of the wind, and the creature's footsteps ceased. I whimpered fearfully under my rapid breaths.

Me: It's flying! Oh my god, it's flying!

I knew that meant the creature would approach me quickly. As I ran, I scanned around for obstructions or any kind of hiding place. I saw several boulders but knew the creature would still be able to find me there. I looked behind me. The dragon-like creature was about to rise behind the hilltop. I was sweating and shaking. My breaths were shallow and shaky. I couldn't think or see straight anymore. Even if there were a safe place to hide, because of my panic, I would not have seen it. Everything was a blur. All I could think about was the raptor-like dragon behind me. It continued letting out shrieking roars. It became so loud, my ears actually felt intense pain. Suddenly, all sounds became muffled and like I was wearing earplugs. I felt faint.

22. Artist: Songs to Your Eyes
Song: Termination

Confused and disoriented, I stumbled on a small boulder and lost my footing. I fell on my side, to the ground. While stumbling back to my feet, I saw the dragon. He was flying low to the ground, right behind me. It untucked its raptor-like feet from its belly and landed on the ground. The creature's wings were folded behind it. Lowering its head, it took a rumbling step toward me. Then, it let out an angry roaring shriek. Immediately, I came to my feet and started running again. This time I started screaming out-loud. There was no doubt it was after me.

As I hobbled along, my ankle sent shock waves of pain, but I continued out of sheer frenzy. The dragon was behind me, walking swiftly on two feet. The violently shaking ground made it difficult to move with any coordination. I looked back and could see the creature was only one step from me. It extended its neck and cocked its head. Two fiery orange eyes with vertical pupils stared at me like an evil serpent. Sharp, crocodile-like teeth lined the top and bottom of its mouth, appearing to be an evil grin. All I could do was continue running, in hopes the creature would mis-step or tire-out.

Up ahead, I saw a humanoid man appear from behind a cliff to my left. He seemed to be motioning quickly for me to come his way. With no other options, I did just that! I ran to the left, behind the cliffside, in hopes of finding safety. The cliff led directly into a narrow cave that was hidden within the rocky cliffside.

Once inside, I kept running for a moment and looked behind me. The creature had stopped. All I could see was a giant, lizard-like foot, containing three claws, standing directly in front of the small cave entrance. Then, it bent down, and I could see one of its large, copper-colored eyes peering right into the small opening of the cave.

A male voice echoed from within the cave.

Voice: Fear no more. You are safe.

3

MEET CLIVE GWYDION

23. Artist: Whitesand
Song: Eternity

I turned in the direction of the voice.

Me: Who are you?

Voice: You speak in familiar tongues! My name is Clive Gwydion.

Me: I'm Adrienne. I'm not from around here.

The cave was semi-dark, and it was very hard to see much of anything. Judging by the sound of Clive's voice, he must have been somewhere between the ages of thirty or forty years. His voice sounded very deep and developed, but had a slight raspy strain to it. He spoke with a European accent. Along with the sound of dripping water, the cave echoed as he spoke.

Clive: Nor I. I have lived in this cave for over ten years, but I am not from here. Where are you from?

Me: I'm not from this pla—

I was about to say the word "planet," but stopped myself, figuring that would probably scare the man into hysterics. I quickly recovered.

Me: . . . place . . . I'm not from this place.

From the lack of sufficient lighting, I was unable to see much detail about Clive, only his silhouette. He was tall—a good foot or so taller than me perhaps, about 6-feet 3-inches. He tilted his head and grabbed a torch from the cave wall beside him. The cave walls were dark-red in color. Clive slowly walked closer to me, holding the torch up. He seemed to be focused on my face.

Clive: So, I see.

With the torch in his hand, I could finally put a face to the voice of Clive. He reminded me perhaps of a young Leonardo Da Vinci. His attire was like that of a monk and consisted of a full-length, brown, hooded robe tied at the waist with a beige rope. The hood was over his head and very much covered his face.

He removed the hood and scratched the back of his head. I could see his face better. He appeared to be in his late twenties or thirty years of age with light skin tone. His platinum-blonde hair was long and straight, but was slightly unkept. It extended midway down his back. The front portion of his hair was pulled back and away from his face. His skin was youthful. His face was smooth except for a full beard with the hairs being about one-inch long. His eyes were dark-brown and almost always seemed to squint slightly, as if they were smiling. His eyebrows, on the other hand, were narrowed, as if in perpetual concentration.

Clive stared at me analytically for a minute. Then, signaling with his arm, he continued.

Clive: Come. Let me acquaint you.

I didn't want to go with him. I just wanted to sit right there at the edge of the cave and think. I needed to process everything that had happened. I also needed to problem-solve. Taking a tour in a dark, musty cave with a strange man, no matter how kind he seemed, was not on my list of things to do.

Me: Nah, it's ok. I'd like to be alone for a while and just . . . think.

Clive: I understand.

He turned to continue deeper into the cave, but then stopped suddenly. He turned only his head to look at me, over his shoulder. Through the darkness it looked like he had a sly smile on his face.

Clive: Let me know when you ARE ready. I shall decipher that ward on your forehead and attempt to free you from here.

He recognized the symbols. That's why he had been looking at me so analytically. I was surprised. Pointing at my forehead I asked him if he knew what the symbols were.

Me: You know these symbols!?!

Clive turned his body around and crossed his arms at this chest.

Clive: Those symbols create a strong, heavy, impenetrable barrier between you and some type of celestial beings. My question is from what celestials are you being warded, and also why? They must possess an indescribable amount of power. And you . . . you must be someone of particular importance to be the recipient of such a ward.

He raised his eyebrows and spoke in a matter-of-fact tone.

Clive: You are not from this place in any way, shape, or form. . . are you?

I felt hopeful.

Me: How do you know? The one who brought me here said everything is wild and untamed out here. Yet here I am, communicating with one of my own kind, in a language we both speak.

I became curious.

Me: What's your story, Clive?

He shrugged his shoulders and smiled mysteriously.

Clive: As I said—come this way, and I shall acquaint you.

As we walked deeper into the cavern, I stayed close behind Clive. He held the torch to light the way ahead of us. I continued hearing sounds of dripping water over the echoes of our feet as they crunched the gravel and sand of the cave floor. It was warm and slightly humid in the cave. In fact, I found it to be quite pleasing. It reminded me of a spa.

Clive: Come along, just around the curve of this tunnel.

Me: Where are you going?

Clive: To my den. I have resided here for some time now.

I was curious how he had managed to survive on such a dangerous planet for ten years.

Me: How do you live here?

Clive: My journey has not been one of ease. It has been one not of my own choosing.

24. Artist: Mikolai Stroinski, Marcin Przybyłowicz, Percival
Song: The Nightingale (Extended to 5:12)

We had just come to the end of the cave tunnel. It opened up into a larger cavern measuring about 30-feet square and 15-feet tall. The cave walls were the color of mud. Several large natural archways were created from the rock. A natural spring was located in the back-left corner. Three boulders, large enough and flat enough to rest upon, were situated in a triangular formation. In the center of the formation was a fire pit. I noticed Clive had been using the fire pit to cook because a log was positioned horizontally above the pit. It was held into place at each extremity with two more logs, tied together to make an "x"-shape. Each end of the large, horizontal cooking log rested in the "x" made by the smaller logs on each side. There was a cooking pot made from some kind of pottery hanging from the cooking log. A small fire still burned in the pit. Several torches were hanging along the walls of the cavern.

Clive walked over to the fire pit and took a seat on one of the boulders. Looking down at the floor, he repositioned his hood onto his head again. Afterward, he continued to sit quietly, staring down at the floor. This cavern area was still warm, but not as humid as the tunnel leading to it, perhaps as a result of the fire. I shuffled my feet, as I slowly walked around the cavern.

Finally, Clive looked up and motioned for me to have a seat on one of the boulders.

Clive: I beg your pardon for my being so rude. Please, do take a seat and relax by the fire. I was lost in thought. The situation —my situation—seems to have become more complicated since your arrival.

I walked to sit down on the empty boulder across from him. He seemed intensely focused in thought. I broke the silence by asking him a question.

Me: So what can you tell me about these so-called wards on my head?

Clive looked up at me and shifted in his seat. He sighed, in preparation to compose an answer.

Clive: All I can tell you is what they mean. You would know more than me about why and how they got there—which is information imperative for me to know, if you wish to have a chance of returning to the place from whence you came.

I shook my head in confusion.

Me: I don't even know where to begin.

Clive: Would it help if I asked a series of questions for you to answer?

That seemed like a much better method than trying to explain everything from start to finish. I nodded my head.

Me: I think that would be easier.

Clive shifted himself to sit on the edge of the boulder. He clapped his hands together once and rubbed the palms together as if preparing his thoughts. He cleared his throat before he began questioning.

Clive: The most logical question to ask would be, do you know how you obtained the wards?

Me: I am not exactly sure how he did it, but I do know for certain who did it.

Without speaking, Clive raised his eyebrows and nodded his head, urging me to continue.

Me: His name is Barthaldeo. He is a celestial being who oversees the realm of Haffelnia. This planet lies within that realm.

Clive: Mmhmm. And do you know why he may have given you the wards?

Me: He did it to prevent the celestials of my own realm from finding me.

Clive stood up. He removed his hood again. He rubbed one of his hands on his face, as someone would do if they were tired and trying to wake up. Then, he put both hands behind his back and began walking around the fire for a few moments. He reminded me of a defense attorney about to question a defendant in the courtroom. He moved his hand to stroke the short beard on his chin perplexingly.

Clive: How did you end up outside your own realm? Have you any idea why this Barthaldeo would ward you from the celestials from your own realm?

It felt strange, sharing the details of such a bizarre story with someone whom I had just met, but I knew I had to trust Clive—there was nobody else here. Besides, he had saved me from the dragon-creature. He was my only chance of staying safe and possibly getting back to Millattus.

Me: Barthaldeo abducted me by tricking me into thinking he was one of the celestials from my home realm, Millattus. He is holding me here as a hostage because he wants to gain information from the celestials of Millattus. He wishes to evolve the mortal beings of this realm to the level of those in my home realm. He wants to know the secrets to evolution. The celestials of my realm refuse to share that information with him, as it is forbidden by God to exchange information between realms—each realm is to expand individually in their own unique way under the law of free-will. Barthaldeo wants Haffelnia to be the first realm to reach a new level of

expansion, before Millattus. He hopes he can obtain secrets from Emalickel, the Prince Celestial of Millattus, in exchange for my safe return.

25. Artist: Mikolai Stroinski, Marcin Przybyłowicz, Percival
Song: Cloak and Dagger (Extended to 8:27)

Clive ran both his hands through his hair restlessly. He seemed to be trying to understand everything. It was a lot to process. After a moment, he resumed his questions to gain further clarity.

Clive: Since you have been warded, your celestials cannot hear your cries. How does Barthaldeo expect for them to know you are being held hostage?

Me: They may not hear my cries, but they will notice I am missing.

For a moment, I second-guessed myself. Surely, they would notice I was missing. Emalickel had said I would be watched and guarded through the remainder of my time on Earth. That being the case, they must have noticed I was gone. I wondered what they were doing. My thoughts were interrupted by Clive. I had forgotten he was questioning me. I was hopeful that he'd find a way to get me out of Haffelnia.

Clive: I mean you no offense but I must ask, why would an entire realm of celestials be concerned with the whereabouts of you, one mere mortal? Why would they abandon other priorities and pursue a rescue-mission for one single mortal?

This is where it got complicated. I took a moment to organize my thoughts. I wasn't even sure Clive would believe what I was about to tell him.

Me: I once met the celestials who oversee my realm of Millattus; and I went to the celestial plane and visited their celestial planet called Lapoi. While I was there, I met Emalickel and Thorenel, the Royal-Princedom brothers who oversee the entire realm of Millattus. Unaware of their high-ranking positions, I developed a relationship with them. The bond between the soul of a mortal female and a celestial is unbreakable as they blend into one energy. Without the presence of all aspects of that energy, the souls feel empty. My energy blended with theirs. Although I have returned to my mortal planet in full mortal form, the two brothers can sense my energy, hear my thoughts, and feel my emotions—they are a part of me.

Clive nodded his head enthusiastically, as he added to what I had said.

Clive: If you have blended with the Royal-Princedom celestials, then that would make you a part of their Principality. Son of Odysseus! You are a PRINCESS!

Clive's jaw dropped open. He shook his head and looked all around as if trying to make sense of everything. I remained silent to allow him an environment of focus. Finally, Clive spoke again.

Clive: Being of that status, your missing presence is certain to raise every celestial eyebrow across your realm! They will search for you relentlessly! Barthaldeo created the celestial ward to keep all celestials, with the exception of himself, from being able to sense you in any way. Otherwise, it would be far too easy for your Princedoms to come in, swoop down, and take you back to safety.

He began pacing around the cavern at an even faster pace. He was focused on the thoughts that seemed to be rapidly firing in his mind.

Clive: Millattus and Haffelnia have a history of conflict. For thousands of years, the rogue celestials of Haffelnia have infiltrated the mortal planets of Millattus. They follow Satan, attempting to distract mortals from their spiritual evolution and causing them to stray from God through influences of temptation. What a waste of energy and time, for the mortals have been ultimately saved.

Clive looked up from his focus, which had previously been down, on his feet which paced the cave floor. He blinked a few times as if he were trying to recollect himself.

Clive: Of course! THAT is how Barthaldeo is certain your celestials will come to him in seek of you! When they notice your energy is missing, your celestials will know you have been warded. Given the history with Haffelnia, your celestials will know it was Barthaldeo who has taken you.

My eyes wondered the cavern as Clive continued on his rant. I was trying to understand how he knew so much. Finally, I squinted my eyes analytically at him.

Me: How do you know all of this? What's your story?

Clive folded his hands down in front of him.

Clive: Like you, I come from Earth in the realm of Millattus. I am a Gnostic Level VI mystic. I started my studies in Alexandria when I was fourteen years old. For twenty years I have been practicing through the sub-levels of enlightenment. I have learned much about the celestial plane and many of the realms. This is how I knew about the wards.

Me: You're from Alexandria? How do you speak English?

Clive: Mastery of all languages was a Level II skill in which I have already mastered.

That still didn't tell me much. Although Clive was mysterious, I felt in my gut I could trust him.

Me: How did you get to Haffelnia?

Clive: Long story short, I traveled in my astral form shortly after Emperor Constantine hosted the Council of Nicaea. My goal was to explore the heavenly realms.

Me: Wait—Emperor Constantine? That was back in the 4th century.

Clive responded unenthusiastically.

Clive: I have never heard of the 4th century, but yes, I started exploring the other realms shortly after the Edict of Milan had been passed.

Me: You were alive during the time of Constantine!?!

When he answered, he squinted his eyes at me with intense perplexity.

Clive: Yes. Were you not?

Me: No. I'm from a time 1700 years in your future!

Although Clive seemed surprised, he no longer seemed confused. He must have known a great deal about the relationship between time and traveling to other realms. He responded with a joke.

Clive: Ah! THAT explains your unique dialect!

I narrowed my eyes at him and tried to hide the humored smile of my mouth. Clive refocused our conversation to the previous matter.

Clive: In my astral-travels, I came across Haffelnia. Almost immediately, I was met by Barthaldeo and his legion. Just as it were with you, they tried to gain information about Millattus by penetrating my mind—a quite painful experience. Ever since then, I have been trapped here.

Clive lifted up the sleeve of his robe revealing wards on his shoulder, similar to those on my forehead. Clive continued explaining.

Clive: I retreated to this cave for safety. I have warded it from Barthaldeo and his legion so they could not find me here while I could find a way of returning to Earth.

I was impressed at what he was capable of doing. I wondered how he knew so much, but time was of the essence, so I steered the conversation back to topic of finding a solution to my rescue.

Me: Do you think you can help me?

Clive: Let me see . . .

He walked over to me. He focused intensely on the wards etched into my forehead. He brushed his finger over the wards and concentrated for a moment.

Clive: Travel, telepathy, and apprehension—all of them are inhibited.

Me: What does that mean?

Clive: It means your celestials are unable to find you, communicate with you, or sense you in any way.

Clive continued to scan the wards.

Me: What is it?

Clive concentrated for a minute before answering under his breath.

Clive: This is intriguing . . . these wards block the celestials from having any contact with you, but I see nothing that could impede you from being able to view them.

I became hopefully excited.

Me: You think I might be able to see them!?!

Clive: Yes, but they will not know of your presence—they will not be able to sense you in any way.

I didn't care about the stipulations. I just wanted peace-of-mind, to see them again and know they were aware of my disappearance.

Me: I wouldn't mind all that. It would mean so much just to see the live image of them again. How could I do that?

Clive sat down once again on the boulder by the fire. He grabbed an empty pottery bowl nearby and a spoon-like utensil. He leaned in toward the cooking pot and served himself a bowl of the broth. He held up another empty bowl, offering it to me. I knew I probably needed to eat but just wasn't hungry.

Me: No, thank you.

Clive spooned a helping of the soup into his mouth. He closed his eyes in pleasure as he savored the taste for a moment. Finally, he answered my question.

Clive: I would need to mix a potion. Upon drinking it, you would enter into a trans-hypnotic state, where I would prompt you to the celestial planet of Lapoi. Only your

consciousness would travel there, while every other aspect of you would remain here in a hibernated state.

Me: Is it safe?

Clive: Yes, it is safe.

Me: What are the ingredients?

Clive: A handful of plant stems, a pinch of soil, a cup of water, and a small cup of your blood. I will heat the potion until it is warm and then activate it with sacred words. As you consume it, I will chant a final set of sacred words, at which point you will enter the trance.

26. Artist: Olexandr Ignatov
Song: Rising from the Ashes

Me: That's it? What will it feel like?

Clive: As you drink it, you will feel a burning sensation in your throat, as if you were ingesting a potent fermented beverage. As it enters your stomach, you will feel a warming sensation. You may feel stabbing pains in your gut, but not for long as you will soon-after become dizzy and intensely tired. Then, you will fall into a deep sleep, and your consciousness will travel across the realms, having complete awareness.

Me: You sure this is safe? It sounds like some sort of roofie or poison!

Clive: I assure you it is safe. I have no reason to harm you. If I were going to, I would have already done so, and I would have done it in a much simpler way than going through the trouble of making a poison. I would just club you in the head and be done with it.

He chucked teasingly and looked down to stir the soup in his lap. He became quiet before continuing.

Clive: The truth is, I will do whatever it takes to ensure you are safe and protected. I desire to return home to Alexandria, and it seems my only hope lies with you. If you return, then perhaps you could send word to your celestials regarding my entrapment.

He was being genuine and truthful. I felt his heart pouring out. He was a mortal human, just like me. Although our stories and our life situations were completely different, we shared a oneness in the fact that we were both humans trying to get back to a place of comfort called home. My heart ached for him. I felt his sadness and loneliness. He was lost, forgotten, and empty. The only glimmer of hope he had left lied with my successful return.

Me: I'll make you this promise, Clive—should I return safely, I will make sure they know of your whereabouts. I will do everything in my power to help get you out of here and back to where you belong.

Without saying another word, Clive exhaled a sigh of relief. He looked at the ground and smiled with hope. He spooned more soup into his mouth.

Me: So, when do we begin?

He swallowed, then he smiled at me.

Clive: You certainly waste no time.

Me: I just like to stay focused.

Clive turned up the bowl of soup and began gulping it from the edge without a spoon. He gulped quickly until he finished it all.

Then, he stood-up, wiped his mouth with his sleeve, and exclaimed.

Clive: Then, by all means, we shall begin right away!

27. Artist: Antti Martikainen
Song: At the Journey's End

We spent the next thirty minutes walking through various tunnels of the cave finding just the right ingredients for the potion. Clive grabbed an empty bowl before we left the main cavern. Also, in the main cavern was a warm natural spring. Clive dipped the bowl into the water and filled it up. As we travelled through the rest of the cave, we gathered dirt and various plant stems. Then, we headed back to the main cavern.

Clive used an empty bowl and a stone, like a mortar and pestle, to crush the plant stems. Then he mixed all the ingredients into the bowl of spring water. One last ingredient was needed before we could execute the process. We needed a small cup of my blood.

I sat down on one of the boulders. I nervously wondered aloud.

Me: So, how are we going to get a cup of my blood?

Clive went near the natural spring and bent down to pick up something. Then he came over to sit on the boulder with me. He looked down in his hand. He was holding a stone. It was shaped like an arrowhead. I knew what it was for, but I wasn't sure where he was going to cut. I tried to think of the least painful place that would produce enough blood.

Me: Where should we cut?

Clive: Open your hand.

I dreaded it. Taking a deep breath, I prepared myself. I thought about how I was going to be able to see Emalickel and Thorenel again. It would be worth the pain.

Me: You'll have to do it to me. There's no way I'll be able to cut myself willingly.

Clive gently chuckled and smiled.

Clive: I understand. I will do it.

I squinted my eyes shut and covered them with my right hand. Then, I held out my left hand to Clive. I tucked my head down into my chest. My body was tense. I knew it was coming any minute. Then, it hit me—the burn of being sliced open on the palm of my hand. It wasn't unbearable, but it was incredibly uncomfortable. It began throbbing in burning pain.

I felt Clive pull my hand to the bowl. He closed my hand in effort to squeeze the blood out. I uncovered my eyes and stared at the firepit. I couldn't bring myself to look at the wound in my hand. It continued dripping. I could feel the blood dripping down the side of my hand. I could hear the drops as they splashed into the bowl. The sound echoed within the cavern. My hand continued dripping for about two minutes before I finally felt Clive wrap my hand in a cloth.

Clive: It is finished. That is all we will need.

I brought my hand into myself and clutched it with my other hand. It was still throbbing. I knew I wouldn't be able to use it for at least a week.

Clive: Go to the spring and rinse it off. Wash the cloth too. Then rewrap it.

It sounded like a very good idea. He had cut me with a dirty rock, and then wrapped it in a dirty cloth. I knew the wound needed to be cleansed. Still clutching my hand, I stood up from the boulder and walked to the spring. I knelt down and slowly unwrapped my hand. The wound burned as I waved my injured hand in the water. I used my other hand to wave the cloth, trying to rinse any dust and debris from it. I rewrapped my hand in the cool, wet cloth and walked back to Clive.

Me: What now?

Clive: When you are ready, I will initiate your journey. You will drink the contents of the bowl in its entirety. Then, I recommend you lie down.

I was nervous, but I was ready. Perhaps, if nothing else, the potion would make the annoying pain in my hand go away for a while. I sat down on the boulder across from Clive.

Me: Well then . . .

I looked around the cave for a moment. I could feel myself nervously chewing the inside of my cheek.

Me: I guess there's no better time than now.

Nodding his head and smiling in humor, Clive lifted the bowl and began speaking into the bowl in an ancient language. He blew into the potion between breaths as he chanted. He chanted about five sentences, which sounded like Greek, then he repeated them once again into the bowl. Afterward, he was silent. He looked down for a moment before turning to me with the bowl.

Clive: Rest assured, I will be right here while you are on your journey. It is my promise that I will not leave your side and will watch over you closely. When you awaken, I will be here with food and drink ready for you.

I smiled and jokingly teased at him.

Me: Don't make promises you can't completely keep.

He maintained a serious expression. He had taken my comment seriously.

Clive: Why it is you feel I have made a promise in which I cannot keep?

I smiled and rolled my eyes while responding to him, still in a teasing tone.

Me: You'll eventually have to leave my side to get food and to sleep for crying out loud!

Again, Clive responded in total seriousness.

Clive: The food has already been stocked and is frozen in that corner behind you. My promise is true when I say I will not leave your side for more than a moment of time. As for sleep, my mind is racing and my heart is anxious, I shall not tire until you have awoken.

I turned around and looked behind me. In the corner, adjacent to the entry of the main cavern, I saw what looked like fog. There was another boulder in that corner. On the boulder, sat what looked like raw meat. Upon closer examination, the fog was actually condensation. The corner looked cold like a freezer. With a confused expression, I turned back around and looked at Clive as if waiting for an explanation.

Clive: I created active frost runes on both walls of that corner. They must be renewed every week to maintain the cold temperature.

My eyes grew wide. It was nothing new to me, witnessing magic, but I was astonished he was able to do this. Clive wasn't a celestial, nor was he on the celestial plane. I was fascinated!

Me: Ok, you have officially blown my mind.

I reached out for Clive to hand me the bowl. He placed it on my hands, and I set it in my lap. I looked around a for another moment.

Me: Having power like that, I guess I can trust my life in your hands. What am I going to feel like when I wake up?

Clive: You are going to feel tired, thirsty, and possibly have a mild headache. It will subside once you resume consuming liquids. I shall have some water waiting for you as soon as you awaken.

I took a deep breath raising the bowl to my lips. Before taking a sip, I joked.

Me: This is not going to taste like fruit punch is it?

Clive laughed.

Clive: I do not know exactly what fruit punch is, but it sounds like it might taste good—so, no, it will not taste like this fruit punch in which you speak of.

I shook my head. I hesitated once more before drinking from the bowl.

Me: Skäl!

Without words, Clive nodded his head at me. I turned up the bowl and took a giant gulp. I would rather drink it quickly and get it over with, than to sip it slowly and endure the taste for longer. It tasted like metal, earth, and leaves. Mostly, I could taste the dirt of the soil, but with a metallic aftertaste from the blood.

Clive stood up and came over to kneel next to me.

28. Artist: Mark Petrie
Song: Ultrasonic

Clive: Picture your celestials. Picture their planet. Picture things of familiarity from their planet. Feel the emotions of your reuniting with your Princedom brothers. Envision memories of them. Breathe and relax into these memories. In your mind, I want you to place yourself in Lapoi again.

He began chanting in Greek again. Almost immediately I became dizzy and tired. I couldn't help but close my eyes. I laid down on the boulder. I could feel Clive guiding my head down slowly with his hands. All sounds became muffled and disoriented. All images turned into splotchy blackness. Then, everything became completely quiet and pitch-black.

The tired and dizzy feelings subsided from me, and I felt normal again.

Me: Did it not work?

I opened my eyes. expecting to see Clive standing over me in the cavern. Instead, I found myself standing at the foot of some stairs which were covered by a black runner rug trimmed in gold. At the top of the stairs, I saw two golden thrones. Behind the thrones I saw archways which led to a vast semi-circular balcony outside. I was in the palace in Lapoi!

I heard echoes of male voices coming from the balcony outside. Trembling with excitement, I brought myself up the stairs past the thrones. It was as if I were floating in a dream.

4

THE NEPHILIM

29. Artist: Two Steps from Hell
Song: Evergreen (Extended to 9:19)

The sound of the male voices was getting nearer. I heard one of them laugh. It sounded like the arrogant laugh of Princedom brother Xabiel. As I approached, I could see six celestials. An intense discussion was happening among them. Their backs were turned to me as they all peered at the massive grassy valley below the edge of the Grand Balcony. I recognized them as they moved around, turning their heads throughout their discussion. From left to right they stood as follows: Seronimel, Xabiel, Dennoliel, Romenciel, Emalickel, and Thorenel.

Each of the six Princedom brothers wore hooded-cloaks which varied in color based on their Princedom titles. These particular cloaks were different from the ones they had worn during my first visit to Lapoi.

Emalickel and Thorenel stood out as they were wearing the Royal-Princedom cloaks—hooded cloaks made of crimson red-velvet on the outside and lined with white fur on the inside. The royal cloaks were trimmed in sparkling gold ribbon along the outer edges and contained a large golden triquetra symbol on the back.

Romenciel and Xabiel, being the two Princedom-Warriors, wore cloaks made of black-velvet on the outside and lined with red satin on the inside. Their cloaks were trimmed in white fur and contained a large white triquetra symbol on the back.

Dennoliel and Seronimel, being the two Princedom-Guardians, wore cloaks made of white-velvet on the outside and lined with gold satin on the inside. Their cloaks were trimmed in black ribbon and contained a large black triquetra symbol on the back.

Under their cloaks, all the brothers wore their formal Princedom attire which consisted of black trousers and black leather boots. They wore different long-sleeved tops depending on their title.

For Emalickel and Thorenel, the suit-top was quite elaborate. It was made of black linen. On the chest, there were two vertical columns of nine golden buttons. Stretching horizontally between each pair of buttons, was a series of intertwined curvy lines embroidered in gold to resemble a line of infinity signs. Both the collar and the cuffs of their sleeves were made of gold linen. Extending from the top of their left shoulders to the side their right hips, was a golden sash about three-inches wide. It was sewn into the suit, making it tight and fixated to the material. Another golden sash, of the same type and size, was wrapped around the waist. Finally, the shoulders of their suits contained golden epaulettes with a single tassel hanging down from each shoulder. This attire distinguished them as holding the highest title as the Royal-Princedom Celestials of Lapoi.

Romenciel and Xabiel, being Princedom-Warriors, wore a more comfortable attire as their formal-wear. Warriors regularly wore heavy battle-armor, so on special occasions, they aimed for comfort rather than visual appeal. The two Princedom-Warriors each wore a dark-red tunic, made of thin cotton, containing an opening at the neck which was loosely secured by laced string. It was a solid, buttonless, loose-fitting tunic which grazed just above their knees. In the center of it, was a golden Tree of Life emblem overlaying a black circle. Their sleeves were rolled-up to their elbows. On both wrists, each of them wore three-inch black leather cuffs containing an engraving of the triquetra symbol. This attire distinguished them as holding the title of Princedom-Warriors.

Dennoliel and Seronimel, each wore a white-linen suit-top, which came down just below their hips. Their suits contained three, vertically-positioned, brass-buttons, running up the central part of the chest. There was a golden geometric fractal symbol—similar to the Flower of Life—to each side of each of these buttons, for a total of six. The fitted-belt around their waistline was two-inches wide and contained black/gold horizontal lines. It was secured by a square, black-metal clasp in the center. This attire distinguished them as holding the title of Princedom-Guardians.

The Royal-Prince, Emalickel, was seven-feet tall and weighed about 350 pounds. His skin was bronzed, smooth, and soft, except for a shadow of stubble on his lower face. His face was well-chiseled and defined. I noticed his profound masculine features including medium-length, dark brown hair; full, defined eye-brows; and a strong, squared jaw. His eyes were the most noticeable feature about him. He had a pair of piercing, deep-set, aqua-blue eyes. They almost seemed to glow—as if they were slightly illuminated. They contrasted with the dark hair of his eyebrows.

The second Royal-Prince, Thorenel, also stood at about seven-feet tall and weighed about 350 pounds. His skin was bronzed and his body was well-defined. Thorenel had wavy blonde hair which flowed about four-inches past his shoulders. His face was slightly scruffy, and pieces of his hair fell in front of his eyes; but I could still see their piercing glacier-blue glow.

Princedom-Warrior Romenciel had facial features resembling that of the other brothers. However, he was much more physically developed with a much larger, more defined physique. He appeared to be older than Emalickel, but only by a few years—maybe in his late 30s or early 40s. His eyes glowed a white-gray color, and he had the same bronzed skin as his brothers. Unlike them, Romenciel had a short beard on his face. It was grown-out about one inch past his jaw. His hair was dark-brown and wavy, and it extended about eight inches past his shoulders. The hair around his face was pulled back and tied into several leather ties at the back of his head; similar to that of a Viking hairstyle. He was the largest of the brothers. He appeared to stand about seven-feet and five-inches tall. He seemed to weigh about 400-pounds.

Princedom-Warrior Xabiel had medium-length, dark brown hair. He stood about six-feet and eight-inches tall and appeared to weigh about 320-pounds. Like his brothers, his muscles were very well-defined. He exhibited masculine facial features but appeared a bit younger than Emalickel and Thorenel. His bronzed skin was a slightly darker shade than the others. The irises of his eyes glowed a bright white-grey, just the same as Romenciel's.

The Princedom-Guardians Dennoliel and Seronimel were very

similar to each other in appearance. They could have been twins. They both resembled Thorenel but looked younger. There was a hint of arrogance behind their facial expressions. They both had long, wavy, blonde hair past their shoulders. Seronimel's hair was tied back like Romenciel's. Dennoliel's hair was down, with a few loose strands blowing across his face.

Emalickel pulled Thorenel to the side. They appeared to begin a private discussion. I flew closer to them, close enough to hear their voices over anyone else. As I gazed at their faces, emotions began flooding within me. In that moment, all I wanted was for them to hold me. I wanted to smell their masculine scents and feel their breath on my neck as they breathed while holding me in a passionate embrace. Looking at Emalickel, only inches from his strong face, I smiled and quietly said aloud.

30. Artist: Audiomachine
Song: Enoch

Me: Emalickel! It's me!

He didn't respond, nor even look at me. He leaned in to whisper to Thorenel again. I turned to look at Thorenel, desperately gazing at his glowing face.

Me: Thorenel! I'm here! See?

Neither of them acknowledged me in any way. That is when I remembered what Clive had told me. I was visiting Lapoi in conscious form—thought-form only. There would be no possible way any of the celestials would be able to hear, see, or sense me. I became slightly depressed. To be able to be so close to them, and yet so far made me feel hopeless. I wanted to cry. Quickly, I brought myself back to attention. Wondering if they had noticed I was missing, I listened closely to what they were discussing amongst themselves. Emalickel quietly muttered to Thorenel.

Emalickel: Thorenel, I understand your motivation, but you must not take such a risk. It is far too dangerous, and it puts the Throne of Lapoi in jeopardy.

Thorenel: Thank you for your input, brother, but I've already made up my mind. The only realm who would have intensions of hiding her would be Haffelnia. I shall go there, and I WILL find her.

Emalickel's voice became forceful, yet he was still speaking quietly,

Emalickel: Even if you are right—perhaps Barthaldeo has regenerated since I put him down years ago. Perhaps he does know of her whereabouts. That still does not change the fact that your plan is self-destructive! We need you in your place as the second Prince in the order of the Throne!

31. Artist: The Secession
Song: Unbreakable

The other brothers suddenly became quiet. They had all turned their attention toward the private discussion happening between Emalickel and Thorenel. Emalickel's back was turned to his other brothers. He froze, then exhaled his breath while rolling his eyes. He and his brothers were all connected. They could sense each other and hear each other's thoughts. Emalickel had already sensed his brothers eavesdropping on his conversation with Thorenel. He turned around to look at them.

Emalickel: Brothers, if you would please be so kind as to excuse us.

He motioned for them to go away. Without saying anything, the brothers dropped their heads in disappointment and headed inside the palace through the archways of the balcony. After they were gone, Emalickel waved his hands to draw a sphere shape in the air. This put up a forcefield around Thorenel and himself. It was marked, all around, with glowing wards. I assumed the wards were to keep anyone from eavesdropping again. Being in such close proximity to them, I was enclosed within this force-field with them, enabling me to hear all which they said.

Emalickel: Thorenel, as my paired-brother it is YOU who must take the throne in times of my absence.

Thorenel: Romenciel is third in the order of succession. Why can he not preside? Xabiel is fully capable of leading the warriors without Romenciel.

Emalickel scratched his head. He was becoming agitated at Thorenel's persistence.

Emalickel: Enough Thorenel! Although I am proud of your heroic motivation, I forbid for you to partake in such reckless behavior!

Emalickel leaned into his brother. He pointed to his own head with the index finger of both hands and spoke through his teeth.

Emalickel: It is stupid, brother!

He stood up straight again and crossed his arms at his chest.

Emalickel: It is absolutely absurd. Think about it. What would be the point of going all the way to Haffelnia? You know Barthaldeo will refuse to disclose her whereabouts—especially without expecting something in return from us.

When replying to Emalickel, Thorenel raised his voice.

Thorenel: Then we threaten him, Emalickel!

Emalickel shook his head.

Emalickel: Threaten him how, exactly?

Thorenel: With the brute force of our warriors! We could easily knock-out three-fourths of his legion! Then he wouldn't have enough of a legion to protect his own realm, leaving him weakened and vulnerable. He would have no choice but to surrender and disclose her location.

Emalickel took a deep breath. He tried to smile and remain calm, but it was forced and took some effort on his part.

Emalickel: Thorenel . . . dear brother.

He uncrossed his arms.

Emalickel: We cannot abandon Millattus where we are already fighting an active battle with those of the negative realms. If we leave now, the mortals could so easily fall astray. We have work to do here—by the commands of God.

Thorenel dropped his head. He knew Emalickel was right.

Emalickel: Besides, let us say we went to Haffelnia, and we were able to defeat Barthaldeo and his entire legion with one-third of our warriors. Then what? He is perverse and would refuse to surrender. You know this. We still would not know the whereabouts of our Hadriel. We must figure out a way to find her on our OWN terms.

With his head still dropped, Thorenel paused for a while before he finally nodded. Then, he looked back up at Emalickel and spoke quietly, as if remorseful.

Thorenel: You speak wisely, brother. Forgive me. My emotions for her have fogged my rational mind.

Thorenel grew a worried and distraught expression on his face.

Thorenel: How in creation are we going to find her? It's like trying to find a thistle seed on a beach.

Emalickel placed his hand on Thorenel's shoulder.

Emalickel: It is alright, brother.

Thorenel shook his head.

Thorenel: I cannot believe she is gone. She doesn't deserve this. How could this happen again?

With his head low, Emalickel removed his hand from Thorenel's shoulder. He folded them down in front of him.

Emalickel: By her free-will. Likely, she was deceived. More importantly than how it happened, we need to focus on how to find her again.

Emalickel waved his hands in the air, dissolving the force-field that had been around them. He turned around and started walking back into the palace. Thorenel followed behind him. Romenciel, Xabiel, Dennoliel, and Seronimel were waiting patiently at the foot of the stairs. When they noticed Emalickel and Thorenel coming in from the balcony, they all stood at attention with their feet apart and their hands folded in front of them.

32. Artist: Mark Petrie
Song: Renewed Spirit

Without saying any words, Emalickel went down the first set of stairs to the landing where his throne was. He did not go down the second set of stairs to meet his brothers; instead, he went directly to his throne and sat down. He slouched slightly in his chair. He rested his elbow on the armrest and propped his head up with his fist. He didn't say anything. I could tell he was trying to think. He took a deep breath and exhaled. His sights were not focused on anything specific, but rather seemed glazed-over. He appeared long and weary.

Thorenel somberly walked down the second set of stairs to meet his brothers. They supported him. Dennoliel placed one of his arms around Thorenel's shoulders.

Dennoliel: We will find a way to get her back.

All five brothers on the floor talked quietly amongst themselves, while Emalickel sat on his throne, thinking deeply. Suddenly, Emalickel sat up straight. He leaned forward, placing his arms on his knees. His eyes opened wide as his expression changed to one of excitement. He exhibited a slight smile as he muttered to himself, in wonder.

Emalickel: The Nephilim.

His brothers immediately ceased their conversations and all turned their attention to him.

Romenciel: What did you say, my Prince?

Emalickel paused. Then, he stood up and started walking around in front of the throne chairs. He crossed his arms at his chest. He nodded his head reassuringly as he spoke.

Emalickel: The Nephilim! We will release the Nephilim!

Xabiel burst out laughing.

Xabiel: Did he just say what I think he said!?!

Dennoliel: Uh, I think he did.

Seronimel: Yep... He sure did!

Xabiel scratched his head.

Xabiel: Yeah. Okay. So uh, brothers . . . shall we go ahead and hold a council meeting? Evidently, our Prince is not in his right mind.

33. Artist: Twelve Titans Music
Song: Bound by Purpose

Immediately, Emalickel stopped pacing and jerked his head to glare at Xabiel. Before Emalickel could do anything, Thorenel intervened.

Thorenel: Silence, all of you! I want to hear this.

From the foot of the stairs, Thorenel tilted his head, looking upward at Emalickel who continued standing in front of the thrones, peering down at Xabiel. Thorenel was very slow and articulate when he questioned Emalickel.

Thorenel: Where exactly are you going with this, Emalickel?

Emalickel walked down the stairs to meet his brothers and present his case.

Emalickel: They are the answer—the Nephilim. They can find her. They are the only ones who can find her.

Xabiel shook his head, slapping his forehead with the palm of his hand.

Xabiel: You've got to be kidding me, Emalickel! What the hell is wrong with you man!?!

Emalickel pushed one of his hands outward in the direction of Xabiel. Without even touching him, this motion forcefully pinned Xabiel against one of the Iconic-style columns lining the center aisle. Xabiel struggled to move as Emalickel kept him pinned against the column with an invisible force.

Emalickel: I will remind you that the crown rests upon MY head, Xabiel! You will address me as your Prince, and you will respect me as such, little brother! You will not question my judgement, nor will you curse at me in this palace!

Xabiel continued struggling. He appeared to be on the verge of blacking out. Thorenel looked concerned but tried to remain calm. He stepped closer to Emalickel, angling his body slightly in front of the disgruntled Prince.

Thorenel: Emalickel, please.

Emalickel continued holding Xabiel against the column.

Emalickel: I am sick and tired of his arrogant, disrespectful, adolescent attitude! I have had enough! It is time he learned a lesson!

Thorenel gently placed his hand on Emalickel's shoulder and spoke to him quietly.

Thorenel: I agree, brother . . . but now is not the right time. Your emotions for Hadriel have overcome you. We need to stay focused. We need each other. We must work together!

Xabiel frantically kicked his legs, trying to free himself from the invisible force. He was on the verge of his end. Taking a deep breath, Emalickel gave in. He exhaled and lowered his hand. Xabiel was released from the column and dropped to the floor. Still in shock, nobody said a word. Emalickel turned his back to everyone in attempt to recollect himself. Xabiel rubbed his throat, as if it were sore. He slowly sat up and mumbled quietly to himself.

34. Artist: Audiomachine
Song: Earth Shaker (Drums)

Xabiel: You think you're so damn far above us, Emalickel. Thorenel doesn't address you as Prince—neither shall I. Don't belittle me.

Emalickel's expression turned bitter as he whipped himself around to face Xabiel again.

Emalickel: Excuse me!?!

Raising his hand again, he was about to react with hostility. Thorenel intervened again. He grabbed Emalickel's hand and pushed it back down. Still holding Emalickel's hand down, Thorenel turned to Xabiel and answered him.

Thorenel: Mind your mouth, Xabiel! Emalickel and I are the Royal-Princedoms of this realm. He and I are of the same energy. We are equals. I do not address him any differently than I address myself. You, on the other hand, are one of our brothers, but you are not of the Royal-Princedom aspect. Do not disrespect either one of us, or we shall both find you in contempt! This IS your final warning!

Thorenel briefly looked at Emalickel to gage his emotional state before slowly releasing his hand from blocking over Emalickel's hand. Then, Thorenel walked with determination to Xabiel and leaned into his ear to mutter stern, threatening words.

Thorenel: Now, that will be quite enough out of you, brother. I suggest you hold your tongue, or I will personally place a muzzle over your mouth for your own well-being!

35. Artist: Fearless Motivation
Song: Revival

Still sitting on the floor, Xabiel lowered his head and subtlety rolled his eyes. Emalickel sat down at the foot of the stairs. Everything became quiet. The whole time, I noticed that one of the Princedom brothers, Seronimel, had been keeping to himself. Always the quiet, reserved type, he was leaning his back against a column opposite of Xabiel with his armed crossed at his chest, appearing to be unfazed by the disorder that was taking place. Dennoliel broke the silence.

Dennoliel: Why are you sometimes so stupid, Xabiel?

Romenciel, with his head resting in his hand, was shaking it back and forth.

Romenciel: His arrogance is beyond my mind's comprehension.

Xabiel narrowed his eyes at Dennoliel and Romenciel, who were both standing beside him. Then, he drew his knees into his chest as he got comfortable sitting on the floor. Dennoliel cleared his throat and took a few steps forward toward Emalickel.

Dennoliel: With all due respect, my Prince, despite Xabiel's stupidity, I must agree with his concerns in this instance. The Nephilim were locked away for a reason. And, even if we wanted to, how could we possibly release them from their binds? You would need permission from God and instructions from the celestials of the higher spheres—

Thorenel looked behind him at Dennoliel and the other brothers.

Thorenel: We all collectively share your concerns, Dennoliel. As a most-intelligent Royal-Prince, I am certain Emalickel has already considered all of these concerns and more, but let us give him a chance to explain everything...

He turned his head even further around to glare at Xabiel while adding sternly to his sentence.

Thorenel: . . . without interruption this time.

Emalickel was still seated on the stairs. He appeared lost in thought, but when he noticed everyone had gotten quiet and had turned their attention to him, he jolted himself back into awareness to share his mind.

Emalickel: We would need to approach this very carefully and strategically.

He stood up and began walking up the stairs to the throne area. He paced around while he continued to think aloud.

Emalickel: The Nephilim will be able to find Hadriel once we introduce them to her energy. Since they were created partially from mortal energy, the wards that Barthaldeo has apparently placed upon her will not hinder them, yet their celestial energy will allow them to track and find our princess. All we must do is obtain their obedience.

He paused for a moment to think. Romenciel took this opportunity to chime in with his military-mindset. He stepped forward and added to the process.

Romenciel: And we gain their obedience by bribing them with their freedom. We shall let them freely roam the parameters of Lapoi for as long as they remain obedient to us. Any act of retaliation and we will send them back to the place of their imprisonment.

Clearly, Romenciel was in agreement with Emalickel.

Emalickel: Of course, Romenciel. Although we never had a chance to prove our celestial powers over the Nephilim, that which you speak remains a given fact, seeing how we are full-celestial and they are only half.

Motivated by the conversation, Thorenel began nodding his head and pacing around at the foot of the stairs.

Thorenel: This could actually work! The only problem is gaining approval. Will God will it? And if so, how do we go about releasing the Nephilim? We don't even know where they are located and bound.

Emalickel: I will go to the second sphere of the Dominions. I will explain to them all that has happened, although I feel certain they already know. I will ask for permission to release the Nephilim, making sure to inform them of the terms and conditions. I think, if we thoroughly comb through the details of this mission, not only could the Nephilim save our princess but they may also help aid and protect all of Millattus for the future to come.

Thorenel: What can we do to help?

Emalickel: Right now, I need for you to come here and join me, my brother. Come . . . take the crown.

Emalickel motioned, with his head, for Thorenel to come his way. With slight hesitation, Thorenel turned and slowly proceeded up the stairs, his royal red cloak trailing behind him, gliding on each step, until he arrived face-to-face with Emalickel. They were staring at each other, squarely in the eyes. They both seemed calm with their arms hanging by their sides.

Emalickel: My presence will be gone while I receive the orders

from the Dominion. You must bear the Crown of Lapoi while I am away. When I return from receiving the orders, there will be no ceremony for me to reclaim my title as Prince. Instead, you shall dawn the crown while I find our Beloved.

The other four brothers looked at one another in confusion. Emalickel stepped closer to Thorenel and placed his hands onto his brother's shoulders.

Emalickel: I trust you, Thorenel. You will remain Prince until I can find our princess and return her to safety. You are to stay here and protect Millattus, so that it will be safe for us to return after her rescue. I know you want to go with us, but it is crucial that you remain here and protect our realm. Do you understand?

Thorenel looked at Emalickel for a moment, then he reluctantly nodded his head in agreement. Emalickel turned to the rest of his brothers. All but Xabiel were standing attentively in the aisle near the base of the throne stairs.

Emalickel: Are we all in agreement here?

After much shuffling of their feet and showing hesitant nods, the brothers seemed to be on-board with the plan.

Emalickel: Seeing how I hear no objections; we shall move forward then. Let us reclaim that which is ours. Let us find Hadriel and bring her home. Let us continue the perseverance of Millattus and represent the strength of Lapoi. We are the divine ones, and we shall overcome all attempts of manipulation and blackmail. As David once took on and defeated the giant, so shall we; for we are the celestials of God! And God is with us and God is for us! Forever, brothers, He is above us all!

36. Artist: Really Slow Motion
Song: Shine Like the Sun

Emalickel turned again to Thorenel giving him a look of preparation. Thorenel, after pausing to take a deep breath, bowed his head and went down on one knee.

Emalickel reached up and lifted the crown from his head.

The solid, sparkling, golden crown had a base about one-inch tall. Along the outside of the base was a convex series of intertwining infinity symbols. In the gaps of each infinity symbol, there was a glistening diamond. There were twenty-seven of these diamonds circling around the entire base of the crown. Atop the base, in the center, was a large, two-by-two-inch, Lapoian Triquetra symbol. It contained a large diamond sparkling in its center. Evenly spaced atop the remainder of the circumference of the crown were eight one-by-one-inch Lapoian Triquetra symbols, each of them containing a small diamond in their centers.

Emalickel held the crown out toward his brothers as he spoke.

Emalickel: The Crown of Lapoi represents supremacy among the entire realm of Millattus. May he who bares this crown, adorn it with great honor holding the title as the Prince of Lapoi. May all who come into his presence, embellish him with great respect, obedience, and admiration.

Emalickel turned back to Thorenel, who was still kneeling down. He gracefully placed the crown upon Thorenel's head. Then, Thorenel rose to a standing position, and Emalickel went down on one knee. Thorenel placed his hand on Emalickel's right shoulder signaling acknowledgement. Emalickel then rose and bowed his head to Thorenel.

Emalickel took a deep breath in and out. He gulped. Then he turned his body to descend down the stairs. Thorenel stood tall, with the crown sparkling on his head. He watched as Emalickel walked down the aisle. The other four brothers were quiet as they moved out of the way for Emalickel to pass. Emalickel continued up the long central aisle, toward the outside door. His red cloak flowed behind him, majestically grazing the floor as he walked with purpose.

When he arrived at the giant arched doorway, Emalickel raised his arms up and out. The twenty-foot doors rumbled and echoed, like heavy pieces of steel clanging together, as they opened to the outside. A ray of golden light beamed down on Emalickel as he exited through the palace doors. He was headed to the cave where only he could enter the second sphere of the Dominion.

37. Artist: Peter Gundry
Song: The Last of Her Kind

I gasped, as I felt my body sit straight up. I looked around and saw that I was in the cave with Clive. My legs dangled over the edge of the large boulder I had been laying on. Clive was hovering over me with a cool wet rag. He placed it on my forehead.

Clive: Are you well? How do you feel?

My head felt like it was being smashed in a vice. I placed my hands over my head and leaned on my knees.

Me: My head hurts.

Clive: You need water.

He went over to the spring with an empty bowl and scooped

some water into it. He walked back over to me, careful not to let any water splash out along the way. When he offered the bowl to me, I took it from him with both hands. I didn't feel thirsty, but I tipped the bowl up to my lips and drank some anyway.

Me: How long was I out?

Clive: Twenty-one hours.

My head was pounding. I was famished and dehydrated since I hadn't had anything to eat or drink that whole time. I took a few more gulps of water. Clive sat anxiously next to me on the edge of the boulder.

Clive: So, tell me, what did you see?

Swallowing down the water in my mouth, I prepared to answer him.

Me: They know I am missing.

Clive: That is good.

I nodded my head.

Me: Yeah.

Clive scooted himself closer to me on the boulder.

Clive: Then why do you wear such a face of sorrow?

Me: Things have gotten complicated. The brothers are on-edge with each other. The tension among them is high. I've never seen them like this before.

Clive: Why is that? What happened?

Me: Emalickel is going to ask the higher celestials, the Dominions, for permission to release the Nephilim. He thinks

they will be able to find me despite the wards. He has passed his crown down to his next brother, Thorenel.

Clive was surprised. He looked stunned.

Clive: The Nephilim!?! Of course! It is a daring approach, yet brilliant. This Emalickel of yours, he must be a confident and bold Prince. He also must be very wise.

I smiled at the thought of Emalickel and his perfection.

Me: Yes, he is all of those things, but not all of his brothers think it is a good idea to release the Nephilim.

Clive: The Nephilim, sons of celestials and mortals, were not as bad as all the lore makes them out to be. They were an enormous species with great strength and power. The mortals took advantage of this, using the Nephilim for slave-labor.

Clive looked forward into the ember coals of the fire pit.

Clive: One by one, the offspring were captured and chained. They were forced to aid in building monolithic structures. They carried heavy materials across great lengths, like pack-mules. You can see how, after a while, the Nephilim grew weary of this.

He stood up and placed a nearby log onto the fire. He began poking it with a stick. Sparks shot into the air and flames began to reemerge. When Clive had returned to his seat, he looked over at me and tipped the bowl of water to my lips.

Clive: Please. You must drink more.

38. Artist: Audiomachine
Song: Hallowed Dawn

Although I was anxious to hear what he was going to say regarding the story of the Nephilim, I took another sip from the bowl. Clive watched to make sure I swallowed the water. My headache had already started to slightly subside. Bringing his attention back to the fire again, he continued.

Clive: After a while, the Nephilim retaliated. Utilizing their celestial powers, they rose-up against the mortals who enslaved them.

The fire crackled and popped as the new piece of wood began to burn. The warmth of its flame brought comfort to me. Flickering shadows danced along the cave walls and floor as the fire continued to flourish.

Clive: At that time, celestials were allowed not to intervene with the affairs of Earth. It did not take long before the deeply angered and resentful Nephilim overran everything. They overpowered the Earth, ruling it as their own. They designated themselves as gods and ruled above all who dwelled the planet.

Clive shifted his position to lean forward. He pulled from a pocket in his robe a pipe carved from wood. He began packing it with green leaves that were stashed in a leather packet from the same pocket of his robe. Concentrating on his pipe, Clive continued.

Clive: In order for the Earth to successfully evolve and flourish again, the planet had to be cleansed of all corruption.

I nodded my head in understanding. Everything started to make sense.

Me: The Great Flood.

Clive pulled a small twig from the fire and brought it to the opening of his pipe. He puffed a few times to light the contents within. After inhaling the smoke from the pipe, he shook the flame from the twig and discarded it back into the fire, as one would a match.

Clive: Indeed. It wiped the slate clean and allowed for a new dawn of man.

39. Artist: Danheim
Song: Tyrfing

There was a sound like small rocks falling at the front of the cave. The echo of this sound reached the cavern where Clive and I were located. Immediately, Clive set down his pipe and stood up. He was alarmed. I became worried.

Me: What was that?

Clive grabbed two sharp axes which had been hanging on the wall behind the fire pit. He walked cautiously toward the tunnel, which led to the cave entrance. He held a hand out to me in motion for me to stay.

Clive: Don't move. It's probably some savages. I'm going to go find out.

Although a part of me wanted to go with him, there was another part of me that felt fear, making me want to hide. I stood up from the boulder and slowly crept closer to the tunnel where Clive had disappeared. I didn't know exactly what a savage was, but I assumed by Clive's demeanor, that they were a threat. I looked in the direction of the fire pit to see if there were any more weapons hanging on the wall. I noticed a long butcher's knife. I swiftly moved to grab the knife and then went back to peek around the corner of the cavern tunnel.

I heard a low-pitched grunting noise followed by the sound of Clive yelling out. Then, I heard another grunting noise, this time it was an even lower-pitch. Clive made a similar sound. I heard metal clanking together. I knew there was a struggle and that they were fighting. I wanted to help Clive and wondered how many enemies there were, but I knew I had no idea how to fight. If I went out there it would probably only complicate things for Clive and cause him more stress about the situation.

The struggle continued. I heard grunting, groaning, and screaming from different beings. Judging by the number of different voices I heard, I estimated there were five intruders in the cave. The sound of metal clanking against metal became more intense. A weapon-fight must have broken out between Clive and another intruder. My emotions turned from feeling worry to feeling panic. I wondered what would happen to me if Clive was unable to hold the savages back. What were the savages anyway? I knew I would have no choice but to fight them should they enter the main cavern where I was located. There was no way I was going to run out of the cave. I remembered the giant dragon-like creature that roamed out there.

The sound of commotion came to a silence. I could hear the echo of footsteps approaching. They sounded heavy. I hoped it was Clive. Hiding just around the corner of the cavern tunnel, I squeezed the handle of my knife with great force. My left hand was still sore from where it had been cut the day before. In that moment, I was glad I chose to use my left hand for that. My hands were sweating. Pure adrenaline pumped through my veins. I was ready to fight. The footsteps came even closer. I could tell they were just a few yards from entering into the cavern. Closer and closer, the footsteps echoed. On the floor, I noticed a shadow coming.

The footsteps suddenly stopped. The figure stood, in silence, just behind the corner of the cavern tunnel. I still could not see who or what it was, but I could still see the shadow. I wondered if it was Clive. Then, I realized it probably wasn't Clive. He would have no reason to approach so slowly and cautiously.

40. Artist: Rok Nardin
Song: Destroyer of Worlds

Whoever it was, it wasn't familiar with the cave and felt the need to inspect before entering. I remained completely still and tried to calm my breathing. My body was stiff with fear. I wondered what had happened to Clive. If he didn't make it through the battle, what would I do? How would I survive? The feeling of fear turned into terror as I worried myself with thoughts.

The figure began walking again. It sniffed the air as it entered the main cavern cautiously. It stepped past the edge of the tunnel, revealing its physical appearance. I could see it definitely was not Clive. It was a savage beast! It was looking away from me, so I couldn't see its face, but its body was like that of a gorilla or some kind of troll. It walked erect but was hunch-backed and leaned on the knuckles of its hands as it walked. It was covered in gray hair from head to toe. Its waist was small, but it had a wider, V-shaped upper body. Its head was proportionally larger than its body. The creature was covered in long, thick fur around its head and neck, like the mane of a lion. Large, hairless, pointed ears peaked out from the mane.

The creature continued sniffing the air. It looked forward, and I could see the profile of its face which was similar to a human. The nose was much smaller and flatter than a human, and the eyes appeared much larger. Its lower jaw seemed to be much longer and wider, and it protruded outward. In its hand, it held a sharp metal shank.

41. Artist: Audiomachine
Song: Lord of Drums

I knew it was only a matter of time before the creature noticed me. A feeling of hopelessness came across me as I prepared for the probability of my death. The odds were not in my favor based on the appearance of this savage. It carried the demeanor of a ruthless wild animal. Its size was much larger than me—at about fifteen-feet tall and weighing at least 3000 pounds. I could feel my heart racing inside my chest.

The savage paused. Suddenly, it jerked its head in my direction with two large dark eyes glazed-over with evil. They were looking right at me. My eyes grew wide. Instinct drove me to slowly begin walking backwards, clenching the knife down at my side, holding it close.

As I started taking cautious steps backward, the savage stood on its hind legs and turned its body to directly face me. It became evident he was of the male gender. Walking on four limbs again, the savage took steps closer to me. For every one step I took backwards, he took two steps forward.

42. Artist: 2WEI
Song: Expectations

He sniffed the air more intensely. I bumped into a wall behind me. I was cornered. He was only ten feet away as he continued approaching me. Horrified, I darted, trying to run away. In sheer panic, I figured I would take my chances outside the cave, at least to get out of the immediate danger of the savage.

As I ran across the cavern floor, I looked back at him. He sprang into the air and landed on top of me, pinning me to the ground on my back. I squirmed but couldn't move anywhere. The shank he held dropped to the ground, and he pressed his hairy hands down on my arms. I couldn't move my hand which held the knife. He lowered his head down to my chest as he inhaled. He took-in my scent, from my chest, to my neck, to my face. I frantically shook my head from side to side, trying to escape his face from being so close to mine. He smelled like a wet canine. I kicked my legs. He grunted in frustration and wrapped his legs around mine, trying to keep me from kicking. His weight felt like it was crushing my spine into the floor.

I was running out of stamina, but managed to free one of my arms—it was the arm holding the knife. I reached around and stabbed him in the side. He groaned loudly and snarled at me, exposing two large, sharp, canine teeth. He snapped and bit me in the bicep of the arm which held my knife, forcing me to drop it from agony of the pain. I screamed, flared, and flinched. He went back down and bit me in the side. I screamed in desperation. It was hard to move from all the pain. Blood was rapidly oozing from the bite wounds. I felt faint and everything began fading to dark.

Suddenly, the savage cried out and quickly stood up from his mount on me. Something had injured and deterred him. Unable to move my body without excruciating pain, I turned my head to see what was happening. The savage was struggling with something else. Blood splatter spewed on the floor. The savage went down on his knees, then fell, face first, to the ground. Standing behind him was Clive, holding a bloody axe in his hand. Breathless and tired, he dropped the axe. It echoed as it clanked on the ground. Clive stood there, starting at me, trying to catch his breath. Everything started to appear blurry. I felt my eyes roll into the back of my head, and my head dropped to the ground as I slipped into unconsciousness.

43. Artist: Peter Gundry
Song: A Nostalgic Dream

I opened my eyes. Everything was bright and unfocused as I tried to make sense of my surroundings. I found myself submerged in warm water. Walls of a cave, lit by torches, were all around me. A familiar face came into view. It was Clive. He was placing a warm, wet cloth on my arm. Looking down, I realized I was in the natural spring of the cave—wearing nothing but the bottoms of my undergarments. The sight of this startled me and concerned me. I quickly tried to cover my chest with my arms, but felt intense pain in my side and in my right arm. Clive tried to soothe me.

Clive: You needn't feel vulnerable nor uncomfortable. You have been unconscious for fifteen minutes. If I were going to lust for you or molest you, I would have already done so. Your wounds were bleeding profusely. I had to undress you in order to cleanse them. Please do not try to move. I am here, and I will keep cleaning and wrapping these wounds for you.

Although I still felt vulnerable and exposed, I knew there was no way I would be able to take care of myself in my current condition. Giving up resistance, I relaxed and allowed Clive to do as he needed. He wrapped my right arm in clean, damp rags and secured them with tight linen for bandaging. He brought my arm above the water, resting it on the ledge of the spring. He then began bathing the wound on my side. The wound was directly under my arm, beside my right breast. Although I was uncomfortable with the idea of being mostly naked, I understood why Clive had to undress me. There would have been no other way of getting to the wound. He gently patted it with a wet cloth. The water turned pink with blood.

Clive stood up and walked over to the fire pit. Out of the cooking pot, he pulled a very long, rectangular cloth. It was about seven-feet long and one-foot wide. It was drenched in hot water, but he wrung it out. Then, he positioned himself behind me and carefully pulled my body from the water, where I had been sitting on a rock which protruded from inner wall of the spring. He sat me on the ledge and began wrapping the warm, long rectangular cloth around my chest and back two or three times. He then secured it into place by tying another tight cloth linen on top.

The wound on my side was the worst. It hurt to even breathe. Every time my ribs or chest cavity moved, it felt like I was being stabbed. Unable to move, I sat helplessly on the ledge of the spring. I struggled to speak. It hurt to even use my lungs to talk.

Me: What happened?

Clive went back to the fire pit. He took down the cooking pot and replaced it with another one. The second pot must have been heavy, as Clive seemed to use great effort to hang it up. He used a spoon and stirred the contents of the pot.

Clive: That my dear, was a savage, equivalent to humans on this planet, except much more feral. This cave is a desirable location, safe from other giant creatures out there. Many have tried to drive me from here.

He continued.

Clive: At the front of the cave, I managed to fend off three savages, but the one whom you encountered was the first one

I have seen with a make-shift weapon. Seems they are evolving in their level of intelligence.

Me: Was he going to kill me?

Clive shook his head.

Clive: He was attempting to procreate with you.

Taken aback, my eyes grew wide in disbelief. I remembered the massive size and wretchedness of the large, savage beast.

Me: What!?! Why?

Clive: You are an upright humanoid female similar to his kind. He saw the potential to procreate with evolution.

I took a deep breath and sighed in relief.

Me: Thank you for saving me. Are you hurt?

Clive held the back of his neck and stretched it slowly, tilting his head from side to side.

Clive: Just a little sore and bruised. I will be alright.

I could smell food cooking in the pot over the fire pit. It smelled wonderful. Like a salty, fatty, chicken broth with onions and herbs. I didn't realize how hungry I was until I smelled the sensational aroma.

Me: Are we safe now?

He nodded his head as he answered.

Clive: I think so. I placed their carcasses on spikes outside the cave. Hopefully, the gruesome sight of this will raise second thoughts to any prospective intruders.

I tried to pull my feet out of the water. I wanted to sit on one of the boulders and hoped Clive would share some of the food he was cooking. It was difficult to pull my legs from the water. Every time I moved, I felt intense pain in my right side. Clive dropped the spoon where he was cooking and rushed over to my aid.

Clive: Whoa, whoa, whoa! Do not do that! Please, ask for my assistance. Your wound needs to close completely and securely before you try any movement. That will take a few days' time.

He bent down and picked me up. One of his arms was under my legs at my knees and the other was around my neck.

Clive: Where do you want to be?

Me: Over there, on one of the boulders.

He gently placed me on the boulder and scanned my body for problems with the wounds. Then, he turned back around and headed for the cooking pot again.

44. Artist: Adrian Von Ziegler
Song: Walking with the Ancestors

Clive: Would you eat some of this?

I was so relieved and happy he asked me.

Me: It smells good. What is it?

Shaking his head, he avoided answering me. He repeated his previous question.

Clive: Would you eat some?

My stomach felt completely empty. I was incredibly hungry. A part of me didn't want to know what it was, or I may not enjoy eating it as much. I knew I had to eat, regardless of what it was. I shrugged.

Me: Sure. I'm too hungry to care what it is anyway.

Clive: Good. It is critical that you eat. You will need your strength for the unknown that may come along with all that has yet to unfold.

He dipped one of the empty bowls into the pot and handed it to me.

Clive: I am here should you need aid. There is no reason to feel the need to be brave and strong. I am right here should you need any assistance.

I smiled at him, then looked down at my soup to stir it. My stomach growled. Although it smelled delightful, it was still a bit too hot to eat. I thought about how kind and caring Clive was; I was lucky to have run into him. Only fate could have arranged such a meeting. Not only was he knowledgeable in the area of extra-dimensional matters, but he had the heart of a friend—or better yet, of a brother. I felt a glimmer of hope knowing that perhaps I was meant to survive.

I picked up the bowl and brought it to my lips. Clive watched me as I sipped the broth. It tasted exactly as it smelled—salty, thick, and fatty. My stomach had been so empty, I could actually feel its warmth as the soup traveled down my throat and into my gut. Almost immediately after swallowing the first taste, I turned the bowl up again for another, and then another. I gulped the food down so quickly I hardly saved time to breathe between gulps. Clive smiled.

Clive: There is plenty here should you desire more.

I held my bowl out to him, signaling that I wanted more. Once again, he dipped my bowl into the pot, filling it up to the top. He carefully passed it back to me. Then, he filled up a bowl for himself before sitting down on the boulder across from me. Drawing the bowl up to his lips, he took several sips of the warm broth.

Me: So, what now? Do I just stay here and wait to be rescued?

Clive: If you wish, and if you replenish yourself with enough nourishment, I shall make another potion tonight. Not only will it force your body to be still and rest as it heals your wounds, but it may help you find peace of mind to know what they are doing.

Me: Yeah. I'd like that a lot. I think you are right.

We both sat there, finishing our soup and talking about all the possible outcomes of the whole ordeal.

Afterward, Clive set-out to obtain more ingredients for another potion. It grew darker outside the cave as the sun—or whatever they called the giant life-giving star of that planet—started to set above the horizon. I had tried to sleep during the day, but my body was in too much pain to be able to rest soundly.

As it grew dark outside, Clive had returned with the ingredients. I was looking forward to the potion, but I dreaded being cut again. Clive was already mixing the other ingredients in the bowl.

Me: I've got to be honest, Clive, I dread having to provide the last ingredient—my blood.

Without looking up, Clive continued to stir the ingredients.

Clive: Yes? And why is that?

Me: Because it is going to hurt. I don't know how much more pain I can tolerate.

He looked up from the bowl and stopped stirring. Holding the bowl, he walked over to me and knelt beside the boulder upon which I was lying. He spoke quietly to me.

Clive: What if I told you it shan't hurt at all?

I was puzzled.

Me: What do you mean? How would that be possible?

He picked up another bowl from the floor near me and brought it closer for me to see. Inside the bowl was blood. Enough to fill the bowl completely.

Clive: I assumed you would want to journey again, so I took advantage of your unconscious, injured-state and collected enough blood from your wounds for another journey or two. I hope you do not mind. I assumed you would not, given the situation.

I was so happy he had done that! I grinned from ear-to-ear.

Me: Clive, you are brilliant! That is wonderful!

He poured about half the bowl of blood into the other bowl with the other ingredients and stirred them together. He went to the cooking pot and switched it out with another cooking pot. He placed the bowl inside the cooking pot and closed his eyes. He waved his hand over the pot and began speaking in Greek again.

Clive: Boreí to aíma tou taxidióti na tin férei sti vasíleiá tou apó ta ouránia! (μπορεί το αίμα του ταξιδιώτη να την φέρει στη βασίλειά του από τα ουράνια)

I could almost see power radiating from him. It was like a clear thick bubble of light started to illuminate him. I still couldn't believe he was able to make a magic potion that would take me into the celestial plane of Lapoi. I made a mental note of the recipe. Maybe I could make it myself in the future, back on Earth. Clive was finishing up the incantation. I waited until he was done.

Me: Do you think you could teach me the spell? I want to be able to do this when I return back to Earth.

Clive unhooked the cooking pot from the fire pit. He set it down in the ground by his feet. He reached inside the pot to retrieve the bowl and carefully walked over to me with it. The potion was ready.

45. Artist: Mark Petrie
Song: Renewed Spirit

Clive: This incantation is not a simple memorization of words, but rather a mindset and an emotional state. Mastering the method can take years of solitude and dedicated practice.

He offered the potion to me. I gratefully took it from him. Taking a few breaths in preparation, I pulled the bowl to my lips and drank from it. The dizzy, tired feeling almost immediately came upon me. I was glad to have already been in a lying-down position. Clive knelt down beside me as my eyes grew heavy and began to close.

Clive: I will be right here. Anxious to learn of what you have seen, traveler.

I opened my eyes again, trying to lift them up to Clive. I wanted to ask him more about the incantation. When my eyes split open, it was bright. I blinked a few times trying to gain my bearings. I was no longer in the cave with Clive. Instead, in perspective, I was in the Valley of Dillectus, looking up at the palace balcony.

Thorenel and Emalickel were standing side-by-side at the balcony's edge. They stood tall and proud, looking beyond the iron railing. They gazed over the green valley filled with countless celestials. Thorenel was still wearing the royal crown. Both he and Emalickel were wearing their crimson red, Royal-Princedom cloaks lined inside with white fur. They both dawned the golden battle-armor that had been worn by Archangel Michael during the vision I had received from Emalickel a short while ago.

Down in the valley, next to my view, I saw Romenciel, Xabiel, Dennoliel, and Seronimel. Romenciel and Xabiel were wearing their all-black Princedom-Warrior battle-armor with their black cloaks lined in red satin. Dennoliel and Seronimel were wearing their gold and white Princedom-Guardian armor with their white cloaks lined in gold satin. The breeze gently blew their capes to the side as the four of them engaged in conversation. Zamadriel, who was the female aspect to Romenciel and Xabiel, was standing among them.

I looked around at billions of other celestials in the valley. They were organized into square quadrants of about one-thousand celestials each. There were more quadrants than I could count. They were spread all through the vast, flat, valley—from the edge of the woodland forest in the west, to the edge of the wheat fields in the east, and extending all the way back to the edge of the mountain range in the North. There must have been over one million quadrants in the entire valley.

Thorenel began to address them all. His smooth, resonate voice echoed from the giant, snow-capped mountain range a few miles in the distance.

46. Artist: Antti Martikainen
Song: The King of the Highlands

Thorenel: Are we ready, celestial brothers!?!

He paused after speaking, waiting patiently for the valley to grow silent. The golden crown on his head sparkled as he panned his glacier-blue eyes across the valley. The white fur of his and Emalickel's royal cloaks glowed brilliantly. They both stood with magnificence, owning their sovereign-status, as they peered over the enormous balcony at their great kingdom of celestials.

Once the muttering among the valley had dissipated, Thorenel continued his speech. He spoke in a slow and articulate manner.

Thorenel: Celestial brothers of Lapoi, the orders have been received. Today is going to be a day of great change for our realm of Millattus. For after today, the Nephilim—the sons of celestials and mortals—will be given an opportunity to walk freely among us. In exchange for their freedom, they shall work diligently alongside us in protecting this realm. They shall continue to receive their freedom for as long as they exhibit obedience unto us. For as long as they abide by this order, we shall embrace this change that is to come. Should any of them choose rebellion, we may use our powers to return them to the bindings from whence they came. Otherwise, from this day forward, dear brethren, the Nephilim are to be considered as one among the rest of us!

The Valley of Dillectus became polluted with utterances. It was as if the celestials were either in shock or in terror. One of the warriors spoke-out above the rest. He was a dark-skinned celestial warrior in the quadrant behind Romenciel and his brothers.

Celestial: My Prince, please excuse my interruption, but what shall we do if the Nephilim seek control as they once did on the Earth?

Thorenel turned his head in the direction of the warrior and smiled before answering the question.

Thorenel: Gahndriel . . . You are forgiven for your interruption. Your concern is genuine, and I wish to alleviate it. If your memory serves you correctly, you will remember we celestials are much more powerful than the Nephilim. In fact, the Nephilim overran the mortals of Earth as result of our divine absence. In that time, only the fallen celestials walked among Earth, and their celestial powers were depleted upon their choice to fall from divinity. They lacked the ability to tame the Nephilim without the aid of the divine ones.

Gahndriel: And why were we not sent as an option to tame those giants who roamed the Earth?

Thorenel's tone became slightly irritated, but he remained calm and patient.

Thorenel: This is neither the time nor the place for such a discussion, Gahndriel. The Princedoms have already reviewed all which needs to be addressed on the matter. As warriors and guards, you are to accept and trust the decisions upon which we have arrived. However, I will provide an answer to your question, since it has already been presented among the crowd as a public concern, but this WILL be your final question.

He looked out at the rest of the celestials in the valley.

Thorenel: This will be the final question and comment from ALL of you. In regard to Gahndriel's concerns, we celestials were previously commanded not to assist in the matter of the Nephilim during their inhabitance on Earth, for it took place during a time of great distrust from God. You must remember, many celestials had chosen to fall from His grace to procreate with the females residing on Earth. This caused great chaos and disarray among all the planes. We obedient ones were specifically instructed to stay here until further command. After the extermination of the Nephilim and fallen celestials, we were informed of the severe consequences that would transpire should any of us choose disobedience from the commands of God.

Turning his head to look at Emalickel, almost in the same manner as would a student seeking approval from their teacher. Thorenel paused before redirecting his speech to the previously desired path.

Thorenel: That being said, let us return our focus to the matter regarding the release of the Nephilim from their binds.

He looked out in the direction of Romenciel and Xabiel.

Thorenel: As our Princedom-Warriors, Romenciel and Xabiel shall be in charge of the command of the Nephilim. They will choose one quadrant among the warriors to accompany them while executing this mission.

I noticed Romenciel and Xabiel exchange a look before Xabiel turned around to look at the quadrant of warriors behind them. Clearly, he was scoping them out and measuring them up in seek of which quadrant would be a good fit for the job. Romenciel jabbed his elbow into Xabiel's side, redirecting his distracted attention back to Thorenel. Xabiel shot a glare of annoyance at Romenciel, then looked back up at Thorenel on the palace balcony. Although Thorenel continued his speech, Emalickel pierced his aqua-blue eyes, glaring directly down at Xabiel.

Thorenel: Momentarily, Emalickel and I shall send a shock-wave into the Northern Mountain . . . where the Nephilim are imprisoned.

There was a rumble of discussion among the crowd of celestials. Apparently, nobody knew the Northern Mountain had been the location of the Nephilims' imprisonment. Thorenel waited patiently for the conversations to subside.

Thorenel: This shock-wave must originate from the powers of the Royal-Princedoms of the kingdom of Lapoi. Emalickel and I will crumble the exterior rock which seals the access way into the mountain. Once the wall has collapsed, Romenciel will lead the rest of the chosen quadrant through the remainder of the mission per his instruction. The rest of you shall remain close-by. You will be summoned to the valley after they have returned with the Nephilim army.

Thorenel looked at Emalickel standing next to him. As if reading each other's minds, they nodded their heads in unison at one another.

Thorenel: And so, without further ado, we shall initiate the release of the Nephilim!

47. Artist: Really Slow Motion
Song: Legendary

The North Mountain was in the distance, directly across from the balcony where they stood. The Royal-Princedom brothers both held their hands in front of them as if holding a medium sized ball. A white orb formed between their hands. Both of them, each holding their white orb, raised their hands above their head. They looked at each other, in preparation, with a pause. Then, they both opened their arms to the sky, and the two medium-sized orbs became one singular orb which measured about twenty feet in diameter. It continued growing larger above the balcony. Emalickel and Thorenel kept their arms open but bent them behind their heads as if getting ready to push the orb. The brothers paused and took a few deep breaths. Thorenel looked at Emalickel and grunted under his breath.

Thorenel: Are you ready, brother?

Emalickel nodded his head one time at Thorenel signaling his concurrence. Thorenel looked back up at the giant white orb, then out at the Northern Mountain.

Thorenel: In three, brother. Three . . . two . . . one.

When Thorenel said the word "one" they both pushed, with great force, to send the ball of energy across the Valley of Dillectus directly into the side of the mountain. As the giant orb traveled, Thorenel's voice resonated and echoed across the land. His voice was strong, and the words were spoken with great confidence.

Thorenel: Release the Nephilim!

Upon contact with the mountain, the ground shook and rumbled. After hitting the mountain, the orb dissipated. The royal brothers repeated the steps to make another giant orb above their heads. The orb seemed to take great effort for them to create and maintain. They both appeared to struggle as they held their hands to the sky, holding the orb as if holding the weight of the world. They breathed heavily and grunted in their efforts. Although short-winded, Thorenel encouraged Emalickel.

Thorenel: Just two more, my brother. Just two more!

Again, they pushed and threw the enormous ball of energy into the great mountain ahead, causing another thunderous rumble and shaking of the ground. Breathing intensely, the two brothers formed another giant orb.

Thorenel: Last one! We've got this!

The relationship between Emalickel and Thorenel was one of mutual respect. They supported and trusted each other, yet they were not afraid to speak honestly with one another. They didn't always agree, but they did always have each other's back. It was easy to see the genuine bond between them, yet there was a definite separation of personalities. Emalickel was headstrong, but level-headed. He was a very powerful, yet a fair and wise leader. His demeanor was serious and focused.

Thorenel was also headstrong, but he was more pliable than Emalickel. Thorenel was understanding to those whom he saw deserved empathy and support. He was humble and high-spirited. His overall demeanor was playful and relatable.

48. Artist: Two Steps from Hell
Song: Welcome to Amaria

With one final forceful throw, Thorenel and Emalickel released the third and final ball of energy into the great Northern Mountain. In effect, the blow made a monstrous rumbling sound. The outer layer of the front-face of the mountain crumbled down. A monstrous avalanche of giant boulders, debris, and clouds filled the area. Thorenel and Emalickel lowered their hands to their knees and bent down to catch their breath together. The celestials in the valley remained silent as they gazed in awe at the astounding event of the great mountain crumbling behind them in the distance.

Thorenel, still crouched down in exhaustion, pointed at Romenciel and signaled for him to begin heading toward the mountain.

Immediately complying, Romenciel patted Xabiel on the back. He leaned in and spoke quietly to Xabiel.

Romenciel: We'll need to take it from here, brother. The rest of this is up to us.

Romenciel snapped his fingers twice at the quadrant of one-thousand warriors positioned behind them and signaled for their attention. He commanded them to synchronize and organize their movements.

Romenciel: Warriors of quadrant eleven, stand at attention!

With the sound of metal-armor clanking, all the celestials in the quadrant simultaneously stepped their feet together and stood tall with their arms behind their back.

Romenciel: You have been chosen for the journey to the Northern Mountain. You are the chosen ones to aid in our release of the Nephilim!

Meanwhile, Xabiel stepped forward and addressed the other quadrants among the valley.

Xabiel: The rest of the quadrants, may you be released until our return.

All the celestials of the valley dismissed themselves, using teleportation. The valley became completely empty, except for the chosen quadrant standing at attention behind Romenciel and Xabiel. Xabiel walked back to join Romenciel at the head of the quadrant. They both looked back toward the balcony. Emalickel and Thorenel had regained their strength again. They stood tall and proud, with their hands folded down in front of them. Providing a single nod of reassurance, they watched as Romenciel coordinated the warriors for the journey.

Romenciel and Xabiel headed toward the mountain range with the quadrant of warriors following them in formation. They treaded through the semi-long, soft grass of the Valley of Dillectus. The sky was blanketed with heavy grey clouds of debris from the crumbling mountain. The light of their sun-like star, Auruclerum, had been significantly dimmed from these clouds. The sky appeared as if it were about to unleash a violent thunderstorm. Flashes of lightning flickered in the dark clouds which swirled above the mountain.

It was unusual to see such dark clouds. Lapoi typically exhibited party cloudy skies with a blanket of fluffy white clouds. Usually the land of Lapoi glowed a hue of coral, as during a sunrise on Earth, but such was not the case on that day, as the brothers and warriors made their way toward the eerie, chaotic scene of the Northern Mountain.

The sound of rolling thunder still rumbled in the distance, but the ruckus and movement of crumbling rocks had finally ceased. As the debris and dust began to settle, it became evident there was a huge chunk missing from the front side of the great snow-capped mountain range. The concave gap stretched across the entirety of the face of the central mountain and arched from the base to the midpoint of the slope. Clearly, the cave-like gap was the point of destination for the warriors as they continued traveling bravely toward the uncertainty of what lied ahead of them.

49. Artist: Steve Jablonsky
Song: My Name is Lincoln

While they walked, Xabiel confided in Romenciel.

Xabiel: I still don't understand why we have to be the ones to do this.

Xabiel's tone was full of resentment. Romenciel repositioned his black cape behind his shoulders. He rolled his shoulders and moved his arms around as if warming them up for a fight.

Romenciel: Am I going to have to listen to you whine like a mortal school-boy the whole time we execute this mission?

Xabiel: I'm not whining. I'm just trying to figure out why WE have to do the grunt-work of Emalickel's plan. He's the one who wants to do this, so he should be the one to do it!

Romenciel rolled his eyes. He was clearly annoyed at Xabiel's point-of-view. Romenciel took a bite of some grapes he had stashed away in a satchel. He chewed the grapes as he responded to Xabiel.

Romenciel: You know, there is room at the back of the quadrant. If you'd like to walk back there, I wouldn't mind.

Xabiel: You're so tolerant of being ordered around.

Romenciel stopped walking. He swallowed the grapes he had been chewing. He paused for a moment and looked directly at Xabiel. Holding a finger to his lips, Romenciel gathered his thoughts before responding.

Romenciel: Do you know why it seems as though I always do our brothers bidding...? Because I DO. They are the chosen leaders of this realm. They have the wisdom and capacity to make decisions better than any other celestial in this kingdom. I trust them. So, no, I am not tolerant of being ordered around, but rather in agreeance with their decisions.

Romenciel reached in his satchel to retrieve more grapes. He tossed a few into his mouth and proceeded to chew them. He turned his head forward to look out at the mountain and then added to his reply with a sarcastic, teasing tone.

Romenciel: Though I do also understand your perspective, little brother. It derives from a place of innocent ignorance—from one who wouldn't recognize the hand of wisdom if it were to slap you directly in the face.

Romenciel made himself stand taller as a teasing grin grew upon his face.

Romenciel: It isn't your fault, little brother. You cannot help your stupidity . . . that is why you have me along your side.

Xabiel stared at the ground. Romenciel smiled and playfully punched Xabiel in the arm. Then he draped his arm around Xabiel's shoulders. They started walking again as Romenciel chuckled.

Romenciel: C'mon brother! I was only teasing you . . . sort of.

Romenciel's face grew playfully serious.

Romenciel: Not about walking in the back, though. You really should do that. Seriously—spare me the sound of your sissy whining.

This time, they both chuckled under their breath. They had an understanding of each other. Their relationship was one of tough-love. Xabiel, being one of the younger brothers, always seemed to feel the need to prove his worth and independence. He was deviant, outspoken, and arrogant. Made from the same energy as Romenciel, Xabiel was an exceptional warrior. They were the leaders of Lapoi's celestial warriors, regularly training them at the Warrior Temple.

Romenciel, on the other hand, was an elder brother and always carried himself with honor and valor. He was respectful, collected, and focused. Although their personalities were quite opposite, Xabiel and Romenciel complimented and balanced each other. It was this way with all of the brother celestial-pairs —Emalickel and Thorenel, Romenciel and Xabiel, and Dennoliel and Seronimel.

50. Artist: Antti Martkainen
Song: At the Journey's End

The warriors continued moving through the vast valley toward the mountain-range. I had never approached so closely to the mountains before. From the balcony of the palace, they looked normal in size, but the closer we came to them during this journey, their majestic size became a reality—they were absolutely enormous! Comparable to Mount Everest of Earth, the Northern Mountain seemed to rise about 40,000 feet above the surface of the ground. The surrounding mountain-chain was at an average elevation of about 25,000 feet. At times, the peaks of the mountains would be above the clouds in the sky.

Xabiel: So, what's the plan? What are we going to do when we get there?

Romenciel: Emalickel informed me that the Nephilim are still

chained inside the mountain. Their arms are chained together, then another chain locks them down into the bedrock. We will release the Nephilim who are compliant, but only from their bedrock chains. Their hands will remain cuffed together until the Crown-Prince, Thorenel, receives their solemn oath of allegiance.

Xabiel: That's it!?! We're just going to trust the Nephilim? We're just going to take their word given in a verbal oath?

Romenciel shook his head and chuckled to himself.

Romenciel: So naive, Xabiel. Just as a lion cub instinctively knows not to challenge an adult male lion; it is also true with the relationship of a half-breed Nephilim and a full-power celestial.

The journey persisted. After a while of treading through the grass of the valley, the warriors finally had arrived near the foot of the Northern Mountain. Grey rock debris was scattered all over the place. From huge boulders to small pebbles, the rocks were piled between the warriors and the entrance, making it a difficult passage. The entrance to the mountain was still 500-yards away. Nothing but rock, debris, and other obstacles stood between the warriors and the entrance.

Romenciel: We will tread over this on foot. There is no need to exhaust our powers in moving everything out of our way.

Romenciel did not use his celestial powers very often. I remembered from my last time in Lapoi, he only used his powers when absolutely necessary. Otherwise, he did everything like a mortal. He traveled by horse, instead of teleportation. He mostly fought with a great sword, instead of using magic. So, it didn't surprise me that he chose to tread over the rocks by foot. As expected, the other warriors always followed his pursuit. They all had a great respect for Romenciel and exhibited a demeanor of obedience and respect toward him. Even Xabiel felt this way, although not without his usual comment of criticism.

Xabiel: You've always got to do things the hard way, Romenciel.

Ignoring the comment, Romenciel began leading the group through the debris. It was still dusty. None of them said anything as they treaded through the rubbish. It was hard work and far too difficult for anyone to speak. They concentrated on their footing and focused on controlling their labored breaths. Slowly, they made their way over the seemingly endless obstacles. After some time, they had finally arrived at the entrance.

Inside the gaping hole, created earlier by the forces of Emalickel and Thorenel, there was a gate made of metal bars. It measured approximately twenty-feet high and ten-feet wide. It was easy to see through the bars and inside the mountain. The inside was slightly illuminated by a dim source of light. It appeared as though there was nothing inside except for giant boulders scattered all throughout. The rest of the warriors had caught up and regrouped behind Romenciel and Xabiel at the gate.

Romenciel: Now that we are all here, Xabiel, it is time to open the gate.

Xabiel: What!?! Me!?! Why don't YOU open the gate! You're the leader!

Romenciel: That is correct; and as your leader, what have I instructed for you to do?

With a selfish attitude, Xabiel folded his arms in front of his chest.

Xabiel: We don't even know what lies behind these bars,

Romenciel—what might emerge from within. We could be ambushed! I hold the status of a Princedom brother! I am not expendable! Let one of the other warriors do it!

Romenciel: We know EXACTLY what lies behind these bars, brother—the Nephilim, and they are chained to the maximum level of security. They will not go anywhere until we allow them. The gate will only open to the handprint of a Princedom brother. And what did you just say your celestial status was again?

Standing taller with a prideful expression, Xabiel replied to Romenciel's question with a tone of animosity.

Xabiel: I am the same as you, a Princedom brother. Why don't YOU do it, leader of the warriors!?! I think you are afraid, and you are too prideful to admit it.

Romenciel walked closer to Xabiel, until they were face-to-face, and spoke to him in a stern, yet quiet voice.

Romenciel: Do not be so quick to label me with the qualities of yourself, my dear arrogant brother. After countess battles together and after all we have been through since the very beginning of our existence, it baffles me how you still lack trust in me and question my motives.

Romenciel spoke boldly and pointed at the gate.

Romenciel: I will trade positions with you, if that is what you wish. I will gladly volunteer to be the one who opens that gate, but then, it would be YOU who is first to step inside and lead us through the unknown of the darkness within it.

Xabiel remained silent. Embarrassed, he scanned his eyes at all the warriors who were listening to the altercation. Romenciel broke the silence by reiterating closure on the matter.

Romenciel: You are second in command, and it is I who is the first. My wisdom and nobility have earned my position as leader of the warriors of Lapoi. Do not question nor misconstrue the motives behind my orders, Xabiel. You should know better by now.

Xabiel let out a defeated sigh and slouched his stance once again. Timidly, he walked up to the gate. He turned around to make sure the warriors were all attentive and ready. Slowly, he placed his hand on a circular iron-metal pad next to the gate, containing within it the triquetra symbol of Lapoi. As he did this, the sound of metal echoed loudly, and the gate slowly began to rumble open. A few small pieces of rock-debris fell as the gate opened inward.

Once fully open, all was silent again. There was not a single sound or motion from within the mountain. Everyone waited and paused, looking at each other with a stunned expression. After a moment, Romenciel took the first steps into the cave. Xabiel followed behind him. Suddenly, Romenciel turned around toward the quadrant of warriors behind them. He held up his hand in a "stop" signal.

Romenciel: Wait here. We do not want to overwhelm them.

Xabiel looked at his brother, wide-eyed and in surprise. It was evident he would rather the warriors accompany them for extra protection.

Romenciel nodded reassuringly at Xabiel. Once again, Xabiel slouched his shoulders in defeat. The two of them progressed inside. It was cold and musty. The air had a slight rancid smell to it, like old food. Xabiel covered his nose with his hands.

Xabiel: Would it be too much to ask if I used my powers to

shield my sense of smell? I do not think I can tolerate this for very long.

Romenciel pressed onward without much regard to his brother's request.

Romenciel: There you go whining again. I am glad the other warriors are outside, unable to witness this. You are making yourself out to be weak and puny.

Romenciel stopped walking and turned to his brother.

Romenciel: Where is your strength and your courage, brother? Are you sure you are a princedom celestial of Lapoi, second in command to billions of our warriors? Does the energy of a Princedom brother not course all through your veins?

Xabiel took a deep breath. Lacking a response, he looked at Romenciel with a disquiet expression.

The mountain was completely hollow inside except for ten stories of large platforms which extended from all sides of the mountain's interior walls, all the way up to the top. At the very top of the mountain, there was a giant hole, allowing light and air into the hollow cavity. The brothers' footsteps echoed as they walked. The rocks crunched beneath their feet with every step they took. With a disgusted look, Xabiel covered his nose with one hand. His eyes squinted to see clearly in the semi-lit cavern. Romenciel took cautious steps and scanned his eyes from left to right with focus. Then, Romenciel stopped. He looked up and all around. Xabiel stopped beside him. He seemed annoyed they had stopped their quest, and was anxious to get out of the foul-smelling mountain.

Xabiel looked at Romenciel, with his hand still covering his nose. Perturbed, he whispered forcefully to Romenciel.

Xabiel: Well!?! Where are they? What do we do now?

51. Artist: Antti Martikainen
Song: The Land of Eternal Winter

With a look of shock, Romenciel slowly turned in a complete circle. Then he replied to his brother in a quiet whisper.

Romenciel: They are here. They are all around us.

The giant boulders started to move. They weren't giant boulders at all! They were the sleeping Nephilim, all curled up in a deep slumber.

Romenciel: They are still resting. The time has come for us to awaken them from their hibernation.

Xabiel: I wish not to disturb them and risk their hostility. How are we going to approach this without alarming them?

Romenciel: We must awaken them with the Song of the Nephilim Incantation.

Xabiel's facial expression grew into a mixture of confusion and disgust. Without further regard, Romenciel began the incantation song. It was a soft, slow-paced song in a low-key, meant for a male voice. The tone of the song was neither happy nor sad—but rather, it was neutral.

Romenciel: Noh flay-nom. Noh flay-nom. Na-flah, nue-flee. Noh flay-nom.

He repeated the verses again.

Romenciel: Noh flay-nom. Noh flay-nom. Na-flah, nue-flee. Noh flay-nom.

He continued repeating verses. His voice echoed through the mountain. It was smooth and resonate. Romenciel always seemed like a rugged, grungy, warrior. I would have never imagined him to have such an engaging singing voice. Xabiel continued to exhibit the same facial expression. It was easy to see he felt awkward. The Nephilim continued their hibernation, but they slowly began to toss and turn in their sleep.

Xabiel: They're not waking up, Romenciel.

Romenciel briefly stopped singing.

Romenciel: That is because it takes the voices of two princedom brothers to awaken them from their slumber.

Xabiel looked at Romenciel in disbelief and rolled his eyes.

Xabiel: You MUST be kidding me.

Romenciel: Not unless you would rather me retrieve Denno-liel or Seronimel. Then, they can take all the credit for the bravery.

Letting out a huge sigh, Xabiel prepared himself to sing with Romenciel. He cleared his throat and shifted his stance. When he started singing, it was in a soft voice. After singing the phrase two times, Xabiel felt the power behind the incantation. He started singing it louder. He, too, had a magnificent voice. In that moment, I realized why people had always complimented talented singers of Earth with the phrase, "you have the voice of an angel." Their voices seemed to bounce all throughout the walls inside the mountain. Their voices resonated with a physical vibration that could be felt. I could feel their voices as if deep in my bones. It sounded like nothing I had ever heard before. It was the most glorious, beautiful, heavenly sound I had ever witnessed.

The light beaming down into the mountain began to brighten. The Nephilim started to make vocal sounds. They began to groan and grunt as they became more awake and alert. They sounded like great beasts with very low-pithed voices, like that of a lion's roar. It gave me a haunting feeling as the sound echoed intensely within the mountain. Since it was so open and so large, the echoes within the mountain were vaster than that of a cave. They echoed louder and for a longer duration of time.

I could hear the sound of metal clanking as the chains binding the Nephilim shifted and dragged. One-by-one, their bodies repositioned into sitting positions, shaking the last semblance of sleep from their heads. Rocks and pebbles crumbled as they shifted and moved. I could see the dust stirring within the bright beam of light that came down from the opening in the top of the mountain.

The Nephilim began rising to stand. They were located throughout all levels of the mountain; from the uppermost platform, ten stories high, to the ground level. They were monstrous! Their physical appearance was like that of a human, only much, much larger. They stood at about 30-feet tall. Their hair was long, extending down past the base of their backs. It was matted and tangled and full of rubbish. They had overgrown beards extending down to their chest. Wearing tan, loincloths, they were not fully clothed and their skin was dirty. They facial expressions appeared angry and bitter because their sleep had been disturbed. Their eyebrows were lowered and their mouths were pulled down in a frown.

Romenciel and Xabiel's voices could no longer be heard over all the noises made by the Nephilim. They stopped singing. It was evident the Nephilim were awake. Romenciel addressed them, yelling over all the noise. His voice was loud, clear and authoritative.

Romenciel: Nephilim, sons of celestials and mortals, I am Romenciel—Princedom leader of the Warriors of Lapoi; brother to the Royal-Princedoms of Millattus! You have been awakened because you have been chosen! This is a second chance for you to prove your value to the collective! You are about to be given a proposition; one by which to obtain complete freedom within the kingdom of Lapoi.

The movements and rustling came to a stop and all sounds subsided except for the fading echo of Romenciel's voice.

Romenciel: The terms are simple. Refuse the proposition, and you shall remain shackled in your present state. Pledge your allegiance to Lapoi and your shackles shall be relaxed. Should you choose allegiance to Lapoi, you will remain free for as long as you are loyal to the throne. Should you pledge your allegiance to Lapoi and then rebel, you shall suffer great agony. You will be at the mercy of the divine celestials before being returned to your previous-place in this mountain.

52. Artist: R. Armando Morabito
Song: Sea of Atlas

The Nephilim looked around at one another. They seemed tame and interested in the offer. Romenciel's voice still echoed within the mountain. He looked at Xabiel and widened his eyes as if urging him to speak. Contributing to the speech would assert Xabiel's dominance among the Nephilim. Xabiel blinked a few times, trying to gather his thoughts of what to say.

Xabiel: This opportunity will not arise again. You must make

your decision in this moment.

He waited until the sound of his echoing words had subsided. The echo must have sounded four or five times before it faded. Xabiel then continued.

Xabiel: Those of you who wish to pledge your allegiance and regain your freedom, please remain standing. Those of you who wish to pass on this opportunity, please lower yourselves back to the ground. You have one minute to make your final decisions.

All was quiet except for the sound of Xabiel's echo. The Nephilim shifted their footing, but not one of them lowered themselves back to the ground. Their expressions appeared to change from angry and confused, to humble and genuine. Romenciel and Xabiel gave them a few moments to decide.

Romenciel: Those of you who remain standing, if you are choosing to pledge your allegiance to Lapoi, please raise your shackled arms into the air.

The sound of rattling chains echoed as every Nephilim, almost in unison, raised their bound arms into the air. Romenciel and Xabiel looked at each other in pleasant surprise.

Romenciel: Keep your arms raised high. My brother, Xabiel, and I will come around and cut the chains that leash you to the bedrock. You will then stand in your place until we instruct you to exit. Remember, allegiance and obedience are the only paths to your freedom.

The Nephilim remained standing with their arms raised. They patiently waited for their turn. Before the brothers got started unlocking the bedrock chains, Romenciel pointed at a chain and whispered to Xabiel.

Romenciel: The grasp of a Princedom hand will disintegrate the chains.

Xabiel walked up to a nearby Nephilim. Their eyes met. The Nephilim looked down at Xabiel. The celestials of Lapoi were large in size—Xabiel stood at nearly seven feet tall, but the Nephilim towered over him. Xabiel's head only came to the Nephilim's knees. The Nephilim's breaths were slow and steady. Xabiel gripped the long chain which connected the cuffs on the Nephilim's wrists to the bedrock of the mountain floor. At first, it turned orange, then it melted until it disappeared altogether. Although his hands were still bound at the wrists, the Nephilim could freely move them around. He respectfully bowed his head to Xabiel.

Both of the brothers continued moving from Nephilim to Nephilim, unleashing them from their shackles. After they had freed the Nephilim located on the ground level, they climbed the ladders to the other levels and unleashed the rest of them.

Outside the mountain, the quadrant of warriors remained attentive in their positions. The dark, stormy cloud above the mountain had dissipated completely. Romenciel and Xabiel soon emerged from the mountain. Behind them trailed hundreds of Nephilim who squinted their eyes. It had been a long time since they had seen the full-light of Auruclerum. The Nephilims' arms hung down in front of them, still shackled together. The warriors of the quadrant held a look of shock on their faces as their heads scanned the giants from head to toe. The ground rumbled as the first few Nephilim took their first steps out of the mountain cavity. The warriors were still in a quadrant-like position, but their formation was imperfect due to the clutter of debris on the ground.

Suddenly, many of the boulders began to glow in a blue arura. I noticed one of the Nephilim, who had just emerged from the mountain, stretch his shackled arms straight out in front of him. He was pointing both of his index fingers at the glowing boulders. After a moment, the boulders disintegrated completely, forming a clear pathway stretching to the open Valley of Dillectus. Xabiel's jaw dropped open. Despite being bound in cuffs at the wrists, the Nephilim were capable of using their inherited celestial powers, without any training whatsoever. Xabiel turned to look at Romenciel and whispered nervously to him.

Xabiel: How are they able to do that?

Romenciel: They seem to have a natural instinct of their celestial powers. It looks as if they are comfortable using them—a little too comfortable if you ask me.

Romenciel stopped walking and turned around to face the Nephilim. He scratched his head while he spoke to them.

Romenciel: Listen, dear nephews, you are to carry yourselves like warriors. We warriors conserve our energy. We use our energy for battle... not for magic. There will be no further use of magic unless it is given in an order by either myself or one of the other Princedom celestials.

All the Nephilim looked at Romenciel without any reaction, but the one who had performed the magic complied with a nod of his head.

The warriors made use of the cleared trail. The journey back to the Valley of Dillectus had been made easier since the rugged terrain near the mountain had been cleared by the Nephilim. The warriors channeled through the clearing. The Nephilim were still emerging from the mountain, in a semi-orderly fashion, behind the warriors—there were hundreds of them.

53. Artist: Antti Martikainen
Song: Eternal Saga

After the last Nephilim had emerged from the mountain and everyone was beyond the debris area, Romenciel ordered the quadrant of warriors to regroup into their square formation. He then placed one Nephilim at each corner of the quadrant. He directed four additional Nephilim to each stand at a mid-point between the four corners. So, there were a total of eight Nephilim surrounding the entire quadrant of warriors. Romenciel then walked behind the quadrant of warriors and instructed the remaining Nephilim to form a separate rectangular-quadrant of their own, containing a total of about six hundred to walk behind the warrior's quadrant.

Romenciel walked back up to the front of the entire troop. He turned around to look at his work, crossing his arms at his chest before giving a satisfied nod. He then turned back around as the long journey to the palace continued. The palace was far away. It appeared as a distant light from where they stood.

A constant rumbling sound shook the land with every step of over six hundred Nephilim, like distant thunder. The warriors all seemed nervous and uneasy about hundreds of giant wildmen clustered all around them and walking directly behind them—towering above them like trees! The warriors had to put this paranoia behind them, for there was no other choice. They all walked together, slow and steady, as a single unit. They knew this was something to which they must all eventually become accustomed.

The light of Auruclerum began fading in the west behind the gentle hills of the breezy wheat fields. Although it never became completely dark on Lapoi, it did turn to dusk for about twenty hours. The clouds were colored beautiful shades of lavender and blue. Two moons appeared in the sky—one was about the size of two Earth-moons, the other was about the size of ten Earth-moons.

The journey back to the palace was a quiet journey. Nobody really said much of anything. They were all either too tired or too nervous to speak. The Nephilim were also quiet—perhaps still trying to recollect themselves from thousands of years of deep hibernation. Their overall demeanor was compliant, peaceful, and complacent. All that could be heard was constant booming footsteps resonating throughout the valley.

After many hours, they had finally arrived back to the Valley of Dillectus below the palace. Emalickel and Thorenel were already waiting, sitting on the bench at the balcony's edge. By this time, Auruclerum had already started to rise again above the treetops of the woodland forest in the east. Rays of light trickled down through the trees, casting soft, concentrated light onto the dewy grass of the valley.

Finally, Romenciel stopped and looked up at the balcony. At that time, Thorenel rose from the bench to address the troop in the valley below. He still wore the Lapoian Crown and his red royal cloak. He opened his arms in the direction of the immaculate troop of warriors and giants.

Thorenel: Success, my brethren! We are greatly pleased to see your return—and with such an increase in numbers from when you first departed!

Observing all of this through a state of transfiguration, my vision allowed me to focus out at the Valley of Dillectus from the perspective of the balcony with Emalickel and Thorenel. Emalickel stood up from the bench and leaned over the balcony rail.

The presence of the Nephilim seemed to bring an impeccable power with them. The eight of them who surrounded the quadrant of warriors made the warriors untouchable. The wide, rectangular quadrant of six-hundred Nephilim was an intimidating sight. They stood like fierce, barbaric berserkers, ready to unleash their wrath upon any enemy. As a whole, the troop was unbreakable.

Emalickel smiled as he scanned the vast troop below. He proudly announced.

Emalickel: I like it, Romenciel, presenting the troop to us in this magnificent, splendid, battle-formation. What a vision of glory you have bestowed upon us for your arrival!

Romenciel: Although it is an honor to have pleased you, Emalickel, it would be dishonest if I withheld from you my true intentions for preparing this formation. I was not attempting to present an impressive display, but rather to develop a degree of comfort between warrior and Nephilim. By treading for fifteen hours in such close quarters to one another, both Nephilim and warrior must learn to trust and depend on one another as a brotherhood. No one can successfully defeat his enemy without first trusting his own allies.

Both Emalickel and Thorenel nodded their heads in approval of Romenciel's strategic method.

Emalickel: I appreciate your honesty, brother. Personally, I like the formation even more now, knowing it has served such a purpose. I am pleased you lead Lapoi's warriors, and I am proud to call you my brother.

Romenciel lowered his head with a dignified smile.

Thorenel: Warriors and brothers, we stand ready! Ready to

bring peace to Lapoi! And ready to bring destruction to the foes who have provoked us!

Emalickel's expression suddenly turned to one of disgust. He sniffed the air a few times. Then he leaned toward Thorenel and muttered under his breath.

Emalickel: Meanwhile, on a matter of hygiene, we must have these giant barbarians groomed before we can proceed any further. Their hair is so long, it is practically a hazard to them in battle.

Thorenel glanced over at Emalickel, attempting to hide an amused smirk. He quietly replied to Emalickel.

Emalickel: For now, I will retrieve the Princess's crown from her throne chair. Romenciel shall present it to each Nephilim, familiarizing them with Hadriel's energy and scent. I have faith they will be able to track her. They will find her, and we will save her.

Emalickel patted Thorenel on the back before turning away from the balcony to make his way inside the palace. The troop watched as Emalickel departed from the balcony. They waited patiently, keeping their gazes upward, ready for a direction from the Crown-Prince Thorenel.

54. Artist: James Paget
Song: The Hero Within

Thorenel announced the plan.

Thorenel: Nephilim, this moment of your arrival has brought with it greatness to Lapoi! We shall allow you to take your Oaths of Allegiance. As each Nephilim takes his oath, the final binds from his wrists shall be removed. By the power and

authority of the Celestials of Lapoi, failure to hold true to your oath will result in your immediate return to eternal hibernation in the Northern Mountain.

The Nephilim shuffled their feet and looked among one another while Thorenel continued his speech.

Thorenel: Romenciel will soon present each of you with the royal crown of Hadriel, the Princess of Lapoi. She has wrongfully been taken from our realm and has been warded from the view of all celestials. We suspect the culprit to be none other than Barthaldeo, Prince of Umgliesia, over the realm of Haffelnia. He is envious of the progress of Millattus and is likely holding our Princess for ransom in exchange for information regarding our realm's evolution.

Thorenel clasped his hands behind his back and began walking behind the railing of the balcony, back and forth.

Thorenel: Millattus is a greatly revered realm, best-known for our loyalty to God. We refuse to be exploited by Barthaldeo's selfish greed and pathetic insecurities! We will not tolerate his feeble attempt at oppressing us!

Thorenel's voice grew louder, and his speech was articulate. A bold passion had risen from within him and delivered itself in the form of words. As he spoke, his voice could be felt resonating the ground. He stopped walking and leaned on the railing with both hands.

Thorenel: Sons of our brethren, Millattus is also YOUR home. We must continue to maintain the dignity it represents! This time, we lean onto you, our nephews. As hybrids—part celestial and part mortal—you have an ability to see through the wards that conceal Princess Hadriel. We ask that you comb-through the realm of Haffelnia until you find her. This is our

very own Princess at stake! She is alone, afraid, and in danger; and she deserves better!

The Nephilim in the valley were all focused on Thorenel. He seemed to have captivated their interest with his moving speech.

Thorenel: In becoming unshackled, your freedom will be granted, but you must undertake this mission to locate our Princess. Your allegiance to us is a condition of your freedom, but my hope is that your allegiance may someday derive from your own nobility. Regardless, one thing remains certain, that we MUST FIGHT! This attempt at infesting Millattus with the pestilence of fear shall not go unpunished! Justice will be served! And it will be served with great RETRIBUTION!

The warriors and Nephilim of the entire quadrant demonstrated motivation in their body-language. The Nephilim nodded their heads in approval and looked around to ensure all the others were on-board. As they continued bobbing their heads, they shifted their weight from side to side, rolling their shoulders and stretching their necks from shoulder to shoulder. They appeared to be warming-up in confirmation of their commitment to the mission. Thorenel smiled in satisfaction and began walking again.

Thorenel: In the meantime, should you choose to take your oath, we will coordinate arrangements for each of you to refresh yourselves. Then, we shall indulge in a feast fit for a legion of kings!

The hyped-up warriors shouted and raised their fists into the air as they ranted and raved. Thorenel chuckled proudly to himself. He was humbled by the strong presence and eagerness of each warrior and Nephilim alike.

5

DISASTER

55. Artist: Adrian Von Ziegler
Song: Maiden's Lullaby

Suddenly, everything in my view began fading into darkness. The image of Lapoi slipped away from me completely until I found myself looking upon a fire. I was surrounded by dark walls with hanging torches. Then, I realized I was back in the cave with Clive again, waking up from my altered state of consciousness. I was lying on my right side, on one of the boulders, looking in the direction of the fire. I struggled to move my body. It was still sore. I was sore everywhere. Clive was sitting across from me reading a book titled, *Interrogatio Iohannis*. When he noticed I had awoken, he immediately rushed over to me.

Clive: You have awakened! You started to frighten me! You have been asleep for over thirty-six hours! How are you feeling?

It hurt my abdominals to speak, so I spoke softly and gave it little effort. My lips felt cracked and severely chapped.

Me: Everything hurts.

Clive immediately walked around the cave and frantically shifted through his belongings.

Clive: You were out for too long. The potion causes dehydration. Being asleep for as long as you were causes severe dehydration.

I was alarmed and concerned, but was too weak to even move my head to watch Clive as he continued scurrying about the cavern. My head was throbbing in pain.

Clive: Your body is in a state of severe famine. You need nourishment immediately.

He filled up a bowl of water from the natural spring and brought it to me. My lips were so dry, they were nearly sealed shut. It was hard to open my mouth. When I tried, my lips cracked and bled. With a look of worry, Clive raised my head up with his hand. He brought the bowl of water to my mouth and tilted it up for me to drink. After about five sips, I had already started feeling better. Clive lowered the bowl for a minute.

Clive: Take it slowly. I do not need you throwing it all back up.

56. Artist: Fearless Motivation
Song: Redemption

Clive sat down beside me on the boulder. He placed his hands on his knees and rubbed them for a moment. He paused before turning his head to look at me.

Clive: So, tell me . . . what did you see in your journey?

Remembering everything, I became temporarily distracted from the pain. I slowly sat up, and my eyes grew large with excitement.

Me: They released the Nephilim! The warriors and the Nephilim were gathering together in the valley below the palace to coordinate the task of finding me!

Clive: That is superb news! Now, it is just a waiting-game.

We both became quiet. My mind wondered about Clive. I wondered what was going to happen to him. He didn't deserve to be left in Haffelnia, but he also would not fit-in on Earth.

Me: What about you? What are you going to do?

Clive: I know what I must do. I must allow for things to be in their natural order.

I knew what that meant. Once I became saved from that place, I would likely not see Clive again. Unsure of what to say in response, I looked at him with sorrow. To break the awkward silence, Clive stood up and clapped his hands together. He redirected the conversation back to the Nephilim.

Clive: The Universe is vast. We do not know how long it will take for your Nephilim to find you. You still have not eaten any food. We do not have any because I did not leave your side while you journeyed and slept. I absolutely must go out of the cave to scour for our much-needed nourishment.

Me: I'll go with you.

Clive held his hand up at me as if telling me to stop. He spoke with a bold, loud tone.

Clive: There is absolutely no possible way I am letting you leave this cave, my friend.

Taken back, I lowered my eyebrows in question at him.

Clive: Do you realize you are protected from sight of Barthaldeo in here? He has not been able to track you since you came into this cave. There is no doubt he is searching for you. He knows you are not dead or else he would have picked up on the residual energy from your vessel. He knows you are alive but that you are hidden. You step one foot outside of this cave and you are back in his sights. He would be here before you could even step out with the other foot.

Me: What about those savages? What if they come back to the cave and attack again?

Clive walked with intent toward the back wall of the cavern where various primitive weapons were hung. He grabbed a large axe and a sword. He tossed the sword to me. My reflexes were quick to catch it by the handle.

Clive: Take that chance. The savages may be powerful creatures, but they are far easier to fight than a powerful, resentful celestial.

Without pausing, Clive walked toward the opening of the cavern to head out of the cave. I examined the sword closely, grazing my thumb across the blade. I could tell it was incredibly sharp. Having never used a sword or any other weapon before, I knew my chances of successfully defending myself were slim to none. I wondered if I would even know how to properly use such a weapon? I knew to use a basic swinging motion, but I wasn't sure of any special technique or form. Worry stirred within me. If I stepped outside, Barthaldeo would be waiting, but if I stayed inside, the savages may return.

I took a deep breath and looked at the tunnel where Clive had disappeared from sight. I looked all around the cavern. It was quiet. All I could hear was the occasional dripping of water echoing along the walls.

Lying down on my back, I stretched across the boulder and more closely examined the sword. Bringing it closer to my face, I saw my reflection in the steel blade. I couldn't believe I was trapped in another realm, on a very strange planet, locked away from sight. I thought about Emalickel and Thorenel; how I wished to see them and feel them hold me in the safety of their presence.

57. Artist: Fearless Motivation
Song: Day of Purpose

Visions of Emalickel circulated in my mind's eye. I remembered the first time I ever saw him—in the summer of 2012, during a normal trip to the beach with my family. I had seen him standing on the surface of the ocean—tall, confident, and mysterious. I reminisced of the first time I visited Lapoi. I remembered watching Emalickel's majestic stride as he walked throughout his kingdom, and how his cape would gently graze the floor gracefully behind him. Images of his eyes flashed in my mind. When he looked at me, his eyes had a twinkle in them. They captivated me and instantly pulled me in; they absorbed me like a sponge in water. How I wished those eyes would glimmer at me again, so I could see them glow and feel them pierce my heart with their captivating stare. I wanted to capture a hint of Emalickel's scent—new, fresh, clean leather and mint. I remembered his touch and how it warmed my entire body; how it made me feel secure and comfortable.

Visions of Thorenel also circulated my mind's eye. I remembered the image of Thorenel when he came out of the palace to greet me at the beginning of my second return to Lapoi. He glowed with a ray of light beaming through the clouds upon him. I remembered how his long, wavy, golden-blonde locks of hair reflected the light of Auruclerum, and how a few loose strands blew nobly across his face in the breeze. When he wore the golden Crown of Lapoi, it blended so perfectly with everything on him. I wanted to look at his flawless, radiant face again. It stirred me, like butterflies fluttering within my stomach, when I thought of being able to touch his face and to feel the embrace of his hands cupping my face. Thorenel was the embodiment of divinity; the archangel poster-child; the image of an ultimate superhero—powerful, handsome, strong, and masculine.

I recalled the image of both brothers perched on the balcony of their palace, with their capes blowing royally behind them. They peered out across their vast celestial kingdom with pride and authority. Both of them were such strapping, magnificent, benevolent celestials. They worked alongside one another and supported each other without question. Even after six years, it was hard to believe they were actually a molecular part of me. Literally, flowing through me were particles of their celestial energy, and flowing through them were particles of my being. It amazed me to think that celestial molecules continued to surge throughout my body. In that aspect, they were with me always.

Feeling empowered by my daydream, I stood up and practiced maneuvering the sword as if I were in a physical altercation. My body was sore, but the rush of inspiration within me diminished the severity of it. As I clutched my side with one hand, I simulated a series of imaginary fight-moves with the other. The more I moved, the intense pain began to subside. My body started moving more fluidly. After a few minutes of practicing sword-fighting, I realized my pain was gone altogether, and I was able to clutch the handle of the sword with both hands. Sweat was dripping down the sides of my face as I became absorbed in concentration with executing a variety of fighting techniques. My mind had painted the image of myself as a rising warrior princess. I felt invincible!

This image was abruptly interrupted by a steaming sound. It sounded like a hot pan that had been placed under a steadily dripping faucet of cold water. The sizzling sound continued as I paused, standing completely startled. I froze and listened carefully.

58. Artist: Audiomachine
Song: Through the Darkness

Turning my head from side to side, I tried to zero-in on the locational origin of the sound. It was coming from the direction of the cave entrance. I wondered if Clive was doing something. He had only been gone for thirty minutes, but I figured he might have already found food and had returned. I hesitantly called for him as I walked cautiously into the tunnel.

Me: Clive?

My voice echoed loudly. There was no response. I continued hearing the steady steaming sound. The further into the tunnel I walked, the closer the sound became. I could see the exit of the cave ahead of me. It was daylight outside. The sizzling sound continued at a steady pace. It was definitely coming from the front entrance of the cave. I didn't see Clive anywhere inside, so I figured he was outside the entrance doing something to prepare the food. I called for him again. This time louder, so he could hear me from outside.

Me: Clive!?!

Still, no response. I approached the entrance of the cave so I could peek outside. The only thing unusual was a tree trunk that I hadn't remembered being there before. It was made up of a series of small, brown vines which interlaced into one tree trunk. The trunk was about two feet in diameter. I noticed a small puddle of greenish-yellow slime beside the tree. More goo was dripping into the puddle. This was the source of the sizzling sound. I wondered what the goo was. The puddle had grown large enough to run against the side of the cave wall. Upon contact, the rock of the wall corroded away! The puddle contained some kind acidic substance which was hot or potent enough to completely corrode rock on contact.

Careful not to emerge any of my body from the cave, I positioned myself to better see the tree. It was barren of leaves and contained many bare branches starting midway up the trunk. I hadn't remembered seeing anything like this before, but it certainly was beyond creepy.

59. Artist: Audiomachine
Song: Slash Bash

Suddenly, the tree moved! The base of the trunk split into two, and it appeared to be walking! It knelt down on the ground to peer inside the cave entrance. It had two dark, gaping holes for eyes and an opening for a mouth. The dripping acid was leaking from its mouth. It jerked to look at me. It made an incredibly loud screeching sound like a pig crossed with a screeching hawk. As it opened the hole for its mouth, it displayed shards of thick, sharp thorns which oozed the green acidic slime. Unable to move or make a sound, all I could do was tense-up and gasp.

It was hostile and attempted to lunge at me within the cave, but it couldn't fit through the entrance. It let out a frustrated screeching yell. It flared its branches like arms in attempt to wedge itself inside the cave. Small rocks began crumbling from the edges of the entrance. The creature suddenly stopped struggling. It cocked its head down to watch the slime from its mouth dissolve the surface of the cave walls. Then, it grew an evil grin and looked up at me.

The tree-creature jerked its head to the side and started gnawing the edges of the cave opening where its body was wedged. With every moment the creature gnawed at the rocks, they rapidly deteriorated. As a result, the opening of the cave was becoming wider. The roof of the cave began to crumble and collapse. I walked backward, deeper into the tunnel toward the cavern. The creature continued working its way into the cave, collapsing the walls as it trailed in. At that rate, not only would the creature soon be able to get to me, but without the warded cave walls, I would be exposed to Barthaldeo's radar.

60. Artist: Blue Lion Music
Song: Everything Ends Here

My palms began to sweat. I clutched the sword, but felt completely unprepared to use it, especially on a monstrosity such as that creature. Still backing into the direction of the cavern, I wondered the whereabouts of Clive. I wondered if he heard the commotion and if he would return in time to diffuse the situation. I began strategizing in my head.

Me: ***It'll be easy for this creature to get to me once we enter the cavern because it is more open in there. I have a better chance of surviving this if I use the sword while in this tunnel.***

I looked behind me to gain a perspective of the tunnel's length. Only about fifty-feet of tunnel extended between me and the cavern.

With a loud rumble, the exterior of the cave entrance crumbled. The creature made its way inside and charged for me. I knew it was time to act. With my hands sweating and my entire body shaking in fear, I stabbed and sliced the base of the creature repeatedly. I could hear it screeching louder as I swung away at it, but I could tell the sword wasn't doing any debilitating damage. It merely scuffed the bark-like skin of the creature.

Me: ***Where are its weak spots?***

I searched for weak spots. I thought that perhaps the face area would be a vulnerable place to strike; the only way for me to reach that area would be to throw the sword like a spear. I knew that would be my desperate final attempt to take the creature down.

The creature did not slow down despite my relentless strikes. It continued charging in my direction, leaving a trail of crumbled rocks behind it. Dust and debris filled the air and made me cough. It was also hard to see. All I could hear was clamoring of countless rocks hitting the ground, the sizzling sound of acid dripping all over the place, and the high-pitched shrill of the creepy tree-creature. It barreled its way toward me until I realized we had reached the vast, open cavern of the cave.

Once inside, the creature was able to stand up. It was as tall as the cavern—about twenty-feet tall. A place that had once felt so safe and hidden had become my death-trap. I became overwhelmed in terror. There was nothing else I could do, and I knew it. My only option was to throw a "Hail Mary" with the sword at the creature's face. I knew I had a slim chance of success. It peered down at me bringing its face closer. I looked into the empty darkness of its eyes.

With all my might I clutched the metal handle of the heavy

sword. I drew it back behind me and launched it forward. Time seemed to slow down as I watched it soar through the air. It flew ten feet before making contact with the creature. Then, I heard the sound of metal clank on the hard ground of the cave. It echoed through all the walls. I had missed.

61. Artist: Dean Valentine
Song: A Fire Shall Be Woken

Although the sword had indeed hit the creature, it failed to stab very deep. The creature had become even angrier because I had wounded it with the sword. My instincts told me to run from the cave—I had no weapon, no help, and nowhere else to go. I knew it would be risky trying to get past the creature and flee the cave, but the only other options were to become a puddle of melted flesh or a meal for a creepy tree-creature. I knew I would die either way. My final chance at survival would be to flee.

Without hesitation, I sprinted. My legs took big strides like an ostrich. I ran so fast I felt weightless. Since the creature was in the middle of the open cavern, I ran along the outer perimeter, keeping my distance. The creature reached for me with its long skinny limbs. It got so close to me, I could see the cracks and detail in the bark of its woody limbs. I felt a breeze skim past me when it missed. It lunged forward at me but tripped over one of the giant boulders in the cavern. I took advantage of the opportunity to gain headway. Without looking back, I ran through the destroyed tunnel to exit the cave. I knew the creature wouldn't be far behind me.

As I ran through the tunnel, I kept looking up. The cave roof had completely been destroyed, and I could see the open sky above me. An overwhelming feeling of vulnerability overcame me. I knew Barthaldeo was on his way to finding me. Although the thought of this frightened me, I was somewhat relieved by it. He would probably kill the tree-creature and then hold me hostage somewhere else, but at least I would still be alive. I saw the front of the cave and headed directly for it, trying to avoid the puddles of acid and debris of crumbled rocks scattered everywhere.

Once I had emerged outside, I continued sprinting into the meadow. I was headed for the jungle in the distance. There, I would find more places to hide. I heard the screeching creature trailing behind me. I turned around to see how much distance was between us. It was no more than fifty-feet from me. It used the limbs to help it run, slapping them on the ground heavily enough to tear up the surface.

I was running out of breath. I wasn't sure how much longer I would be able to run before collapsing. I screamed for Clive again and frantically searched the tree-line of the jungle, hoping he would emerge.

Me: Clive! Help me!

Rapidly approaching the jungle, I tried to search for a quick place to escape and hide. As I was running, my foot became entangled in a system of thick-roots exposed from the ground. I fell forward with great force. I tried to free my foot, but the roots were too thick. I was too entangled. My foot was bleeding because I was barefoot. Giving into my fated doom, I relaxed and mentally prepared myself for my end. I managed to roll onto my back. Everything began to play-out slowly and silently. The tree-creature was coming right at me, flaring its arm-like limbs, with its mouth open wide. It stopped at my feet and for a moment, it stared at me with the abyss in its eyes. I was frozen in fear. Its eyes were two pits of pure darkness—deep, cold, and absolutely terrifying.

62. Artist: J. T. Peterson
Song: Honor and Gold

From the right side, I heard a whooshing sound. As I looked up at the creature, a long spear had been stabbed straight through its head and was poking through the other side. I sat myself up and looked in the direction from which the spear had come. Standing there, at the edge of the jungle, was Clive. His blonde hair was pulled back into a messy bun. He started running in my direction. The creature landed next to me with a loud crash—as a tree would sound after being cut down. I looked at it. The eyes and mouth had disappeared. It looked like a regular dead tree, and it didn't move at all. Relieved, I called out for Clive. My foot was still entangled in the ground roots.

Me: Clive! I'm stuck!

Still holding another spear in his hand, he rushed to my aid. When he arrived to me, he set down the spear and pulled a small knife from his belt. Breathing heavily, he frantically fought to free me.

Clive: We need to take a look at that foot. Hopefully, we have time enough to escape being sighted by Barthaldeo. Let me help you.

After my foot was finally freed, Clive picked up the spear from the ground and helped me to my feet. He slung my arm over his shoulder and aided me in walking. It was difficult to put any weight on my injured foot. Clive used the spear in his opposite hand to help us balance. We headed back toward the cave, as quickly as possible, but our pace was significantly slowed by my limping.

Me: That tree-thing had me cornered in the cave! I had no

choice but to flee! It would have killed me! The cave is destroyed!

Clive: Destroyed or not, the cave will be better coverage than out here in the open.

63. Artist: Rok Nardin
Song: Hell Rising

Although it was at a slow pace, we continued toward the cave entrance. I was hopeful we would not be found by Barthaldeo. I thought perhaps he had become preoccupied with something else and hadn't noticed my presence. When we had finally made it to the cave entrance, I heard a deep voice behind us.

Voice: Aren't you going to invite me in?

The voice sounded conniving and of evil intent. I had hoped it was a celestial or Nephilim of Lapoi, but knew it was likely not. Clive and I whipped around to see the source of the voice. My fears were confirmed when I saw Barthaldeo standing behind us with his arms crossed proudly at his chest. He was smirking in a malicious way. He looked at Clive.

Barthaldeo: Hello, Cliviticus! It has been a long-time, old friend. And my, aren't you good at playing hide-and-seek!?! I had grown bored of playing your childish games, but now I sure am glad I found you, for it seems you have found something that belongs to me.

Barthaldeo peered at Clive, circling us until he stood between us and the cave entrance. The spear was still in Clive's hand, but he slowly bent down to place it on the ground as a sign of surrender. Without taking his eyes from me and still exhibiting an evil grin, Barthaldeo forcefully pushed one of his palms outward toward Clive. I watched helplessly as Clive's body flung, with great force, across the entirety of the meadow and crashed into the trunk of a tree near the front of the jungle. His limp body fell onto the ground and was motionless.

Barthaldeo: And you, Princess of Lapoi, what have you been up to all this time? Trying to find your Emalickel through the abilities of that mystic man?

I remained silent. I couldn't take my mind off of what had just happened to Clive. I wondered if he was even alive. All I could think about was my guilt. I should not have come out of the cave. I should have died from the wrath of that tree creature. Death was my destiny, not Clive's. I thought about how he had done nothing but help me—he enabled me to see Lapoi, the celestials, and the Nephilim. He had saved my life several times. My hope had derived from the heart of Clive, but in return, all I had done for him was led him to his death. I was so distraught and consumed by these thoughts, I had forgotten that Barthaldeo was even there. Then, I snapped back to reality when I heard his voice again.

Barthaldeo: So, he took you on a vision-journey to Lapoi? My, my, your mind is so easy to hear. Tell me, though, what exactly are the Nephilim of Millattus planning to do?

I felt violated. He immersed himself into my mind, freely roaming within my thoughts without my permission. Trying not to think about the Nephilim, I looked in the distance at the jungle and tried to focus my thoughts on something vague like the wretchedness of the landscape in front of me. That thought made me think of Clive's motionless body, which made me think of my resentment of Barthaldeo. Unable to control my vengeance, I responded coldly to him as I narrowed my eyes in anger.

64. Artist: Audiomachine
Song: Taste of Blood

Me: Perhaps they'll be here soon-enough to tell you themselves—in the flesh!

Barthaldeo: You mean to tell me they're physically coming here!?! Sounds like suicide.

He had manipulated me to gain the knowledge in which he sought-after. This infuriated me! He had no right to be in my mind! He had no right to bring me to his wretched realm! He had no right to punish Clive!

Losing all self-control, I yelled in anguish and charged at Barthaldeo. I went berserk. Frantically, I pushed and punched and hit him repeatedly. He maintained his stance, completely unaffected by my attacks. He placed his hands on his hips and began to smile down at me and chuckle as if he were entertained or amused by my attempt to cause harm to him. This made me even more angry. I started kicking him and slapping him. I screamed hateful remarks and pointed my finger in his face.

Me: I hate you, Barthaldeo! You're a terrible, awful, horrific being! You're a waste of space and energy, and you don't even deserve to exist! Emalickel is going to find you, and he'll enjoy taking you down again! Only this time, I hope he does it slowly and painfully, so that you'll beg for it to end. And then, if Emalickel is merciful enough to kill you, I hope your soul falls into an endless pit of darkness and fear, where if you ever did hit the ground, you'd splash into the scorching-hot, dark-burning fires of Hell. Nobody would even miss you—you're nothing but a wretched monster! The Universe would do well to be rid of your presence altogether!

My rant continued, and I kept flaring my arms about, until suddenly, I felt Barthaldeo forcefully pull me into him. He trapped me, wrapping his arms around me so that I couldn't move anymore. I was facing away from him, but I struggled to turn around toward him, so I could head-butt him or knock him with one of my knees. He squeezed me even tighter as I struggled. He squeezed me to the point of it causing my body pain.

Barthaldeo: If you'd stop resisting, I would be gentler with you!

I couldn't bring myself to relax. It just wasn't natural to stop resisting. All I could feel was rage pulsing through me. Being still was impossible.

Barthaldeo: I don't have time for this. We must go. If these Nephilim can track you, then I need to get you back to Umgliesia and find a way to shield you from them.

He forcefully pushed me away from him and quickly held out his palms toward me. A transparent, yellowish shield of light surrounded me on all sides. I became engulfed by an orb of light in which I assumed was his force-field. I touched the wall of this shield. It was solid. Ferociously, I punched at the walls. I was infuriated at Barthaldeo for his enforcement of control over me —I despised being forced to do something against my will.

65. Artist: Audiomachine
Song: Bloody Brigade

Although I was deeply exasperated, I stopped my attack on the wall, for I knew I was only wasting my energy. Defeated, I sat down and wept. Pulling my knees into my chest, I bowed my head and prayed through my weeping breaths. The whole experience in Haffelnia had felt like a terrifying ride at an amusement park. All I wanted was for it to end. I just wanted to close my eyes and reopen them to normalcy. My mind and body had both run out of stamina.

Suddenly, I felt the orb begin rising from the ground. Attached to the orb were two strings of yellowish light which extended from Barthaldeo's hands. He was still standing on the ground, but was using the strings of light to control the movement of the orb. Barthaldeo interrupted my prayers.

Barthaldeo: Are you ready to go for a ride, Princess?

He swung the orb back as if getting ready to throw it with great speed and force. Inside the orb, I quickly stood up to brace myself, trying to hold myself steady. I took a wider stance and pressed my arms against the walls. There must have been a look of fright on my face. Not only was I afraid of heights, but I was not a fan of speed. Barthaldeo was about to inflict both experiences upon me. Just as he was about to throw the orb with me inside, I heard a loud clap of thunder, as if lightening had struck nearby. The ground shook. Even through the orb, I could feel it rumbling beneath my feet.

66. Artist: Antti Martikainen
Song: The God of Thunder

Following the thunderous boom, there was an ambient sound like that of a didgeridoo echoing a low note in the distance. Then I heard a loud, deep, echoing voice speak from directly behind me.

Voice: You take her nowhere!

I turned around and saw two giant legs. The knees were at eye-level. My head and eyes scrolled up to a large, primal-looking giant. He wore fitted, dark-brown shorts made of leather. Leather straps were tied and wrapped around both his wrists and biceps. A Lapoian Triquetra pendant hung around his neck by the same type of leather. He was staring down at Barthaldeo, with his hands clenched into fists. I could hear his lungs inhaling and exhaling as he breathed slow and steady.

He stood at approximately twenty-five feet tall. His stature was broad and sturdy. His muscles were large and dense, although not as defined as the celestials of Lapoi. He looked healthy, strong, and of good shape. His hair extended past his shoulders and rested on his chest. It was wavy in texture and was dark-blonde in color. His facial hair was short and stubbly. Barthaldeo was sure to belittle the being's heroic entrance.

Barthaldeo: Would you take a look at that! Look at the monstrosity! You must be one of the Nephilim from Millattus —one of those bastard beings. Who would have thought a mutt could turn out to be such a beast? The question is, are you a mortal or a celestial? It must be hard not knowing exactly what you are—to not have anywhere really to belong.

Nephilim: I am Drakahdra.

Drakahdra spoke with an intimidating deep voice. Drakahdra looked beyond Barthaldeo and seemed to be thinking.

Barthaldeo: Oh dear, I am sorry . . . I meant not to offend. I am not very good at making small-talk. Besides, the girl and I really must be on our way. So, I will help you get back to where you came from.

Positioning himself with a wide stance, Barthaldeo held out his hands, palms forward, toward Drakahdra. He forcefully pushed them out toward Drakahdra, just as he had done to Clive earlier. A massive wave of blue energy flew from his palms directly at

Drakahdra's torso. When Barthaldeo's energy-wave made contact with the giant, it made a sound like that of a large bell. The sound resonated for some time after the hit. Drakahdra remained in the same position, completely unscathed by the impact.

Barthaldeo was astonished. He shook his head in doubt. It was evident Barthaldeo had expected the energy to knock Drakahdra down. Barthaldeo shook out both of his arms, stretched out his fingers, took a deep breath, and tried again. This time, he tried with an even more immense amount of energy. As he pushed, he yelled out, using all his strength to send it at Drakahdra. Upon impact, the large bell sound occurred again, but it was much louder this time and resonated for much longer. Again, Drakahdra maintained his stance. Without saying anything, he stared at Barthaldeo and crossed his arms. Barthaldeo looked puzzled and also concerned. He shook his head again.

Barthaldeo: I don't understand. That energy is powerful enough to alter entire planets! How does it not affect you?

Drakahdra: I am indestructible to you.

Looking completely baffled, Barthaldeo dropped his arms. He walked closer to Drakahdra, but not too close.

Barthaldeo: You're telling me, the molecules of your energy do not react to mine? All my energies are repelled?

With his arms still crossed at his chest, Drakahdra nodded his head once. Amazed, Barthaldeo looked down at the ground. He started talking to himself.

Barthaldeo: Incredible!

After the initial surprise, Barthaldeo looked back up at the giant.

His eyes grew evil and cold. He held his arms out to his sides as he spoke.

Barthaldeo: You may be partly celestial, but you are also partly mortal, Drakahdra. You must have some kind of vulnerability or weakness. Let's see if I can discover your Achilles Heel!

The dark grey clouds of the sky picked up speed as they moved swiftly across the dreary planet. I felt the wind begin blowing with greater intensity. Something was happening. Behind Barthaldeo, in the distance, I noticed a thin, black line stretching horizontally across the sky. It was waving like the surface of the ocean. All around it were tiny orbs. Whatever it was, it was getting rapidly closer. The wind continued picking up speed. I could tell by the way Barthaldeo's hair was blowing, that the wind was blowing toward Drakahdra and me—Barthaldeo stood in front of us as his medium-length hair blew into his face. Leaves and sticks were flying from the trees of the jungle. Through the sound of cyclone winds, I heard rumbling roars and thunder. As the thin black line came closer, I could make out more detail. It was not a single, solid black line, but rather a horizontal line-up of giant dragon creatures! There were well over fifty of them.

Drakahdra lifted Barthaldeo's force-field with me inside. He did this using only his hands. Then he placed me on the top of the fallen cave. The orbs of light came in fast, like meteors darting through the sky. They landed with sounds of explosions, one after the other. Each orb was one of Barthaldeo's Umgliesian celestials, dressed in their dark-blue armor with full helmets covering their faces.

The dragons also started to arrive. When they landed, it sent debris from the ground in the air. I assumed I was protected from harm, being inside Barthaldeo's force-field, but I still worried with uncertainty. I also felt fearful for Drakahdra and worried about the fate of his outcome.

The dragons surrounded Drakahdra, while the Umgliesian celestials surrounded them in an outer circle. The dragons roared loudly, blowing Drakahdra's hair behind him. Drakahdra didn't flinch. Three of the dragons had a reddish glow in their throats. They puffed up, raised up, and then exhaled a massive stream of fire directly onto Drakahdra's body. He disappeared into the flames. All I could hear was roaring, howling wind, rolling thunder, and explosions. The scene was chaotic. I screamed-out in panic as I watched helplessly—worried about Drakahdra, and wondering when or if he would receive any help. The stream of fire from the dragons lasted about twenty-seconds before finally fading out.

I was pleasantly surprised and also astonished when I saw Drakahdra was still standing there, unscathed and unfazed. His arms hung confidently at his sides and his facial expression was unaltered. He scanned the outer ring of Umgliesian celestials for Barthaldeo.

Drakahdra: I not want to harm these creatures. Leave them out. This is between us.

Barthaldeo laughed and yelled back to Drakahdra.

Barthaldeo: You say that like it holds leverage! I don't care about these creatures or I wouldn't have brought them into this in the first place!

Drakahdra: They do not deserve this. Send them away.

Barthaldeo: Not going to happen, Half-Blood!

67. Artist: Audiomachine
Song: Famine

The dragons closed in on Drakahdra, taking turns blowing fire at him. Standing still, Drakahdra waited. I could tell he did not want to fight them. They continued closing in, though, and left him no choice. He picked up the nearest dragon by its neck and swung it around, like a lasso, to hit all the other nearby dragons. Their bodies flung across the sky. He continued to use this dragon like a bat as more dragons closed in on him. The Umgliesian celestials jumped high into the air and started landing on Drakahdra. They piled onto him, giving the dragons a chance to close in as well. It looked like a swarm of darkness as Drakahdra disappeared below a cloud of bodies and debris. I knew the Nephilim were strong and that they were only affected by Lapoian celestials, but I questioned how much a single being could take from a massive militia. There were several hundred, dragons and Umgliesians, piled on top of Drakahdra.

Barthaldeo teleported next to me on top of the cave rocks. Appearing to be in a rush of panic, he attached the strings of light from his hands to the orb again. Breathing frantically, he lifted the orb into the air.

Barthaldeo: That should occupy him for a while!

With me inside, he threw the orb into the air with great force. The ground appeared further and further away at a rapid speed. Then, I saw Barthaldeo flying next to me. He placed his hands on the transparent wall to my left and grinned wickedly at me. He made me feel a level of anger beyond that of which I had ever felt before. Not only had he killed Clive, an innocent human who accidently found himself on Thermoplia, but possibly a Nephilim who was only trying to save me. In that moment, I found myself going to yet another unknown place, and all the efforts of Clive and Drakahdra had been wasted.

68. Artist: Really Slow Motion
Song: Legendary

Barthaldeo was evil, heartless, and careless. I couldn't stand the presence of him. Giving up hope, I fell down in the force-field and covered my eyes. I collapsed into distress and began weeping uncontrollably. I wanted everything to end—I just wanted it all to be over.

That very moment, I heard a familiar voice. It spoke in a deep tone that resonated with power.

Voice: Fear no more, Hadriel. We have come.

I lifted my face from my hands in search for the comforting voice. Standing about ten-feet in front of me, glowing in a radiant light, was none other than Emalickel himself! He was backed by Romenciel and Xabiel and an army of one-thousand Lapoian warriors. The divine light radiating from them cleared the sky and felt like warmth and hope. The glow of light behind them contrasted with the shadow of their all-black armor. The image reminded me of a painting of avenging archangels sent from Heaven. Emalickel turned his head to look at me. He seemed just as relieved to see me as I was to see him. Quickly, he turned his attention to pierce at Barthaldeo.

Emalickel: Barthaldeo, trespasser of Millattus, these crimes of yours shall not go unpunished!

Yelling loudly in anger, Barthaldeo shot across the sky at Emalickel, knocking both of them from view. The orb encompassing me began to plummet. I was headed toward the ground at an increasing speed. I stood up and began screaming, frantically punching at the walls. The ground approached closer and closer, as I continued falling. I closed my eyes and braced myself for impact.

Suddenly, the falling sensation ceased and I was floating again. I heard grunting from below. I looked down. Beneath my feet was Thorenel, holding the orb like the mythical Atlas who held the Earth.

Thorenel gently guided the orb down to rest on a hillside, away from the ongoing battle in the distance. A swarm of Nephilim and Lapoian warriors were fighting on the ground where Drakahdra had been. The sounds of roaring and thunder had faded.

Thorenel released the orb on the hillside and turned to face me. His back was to the fight below. Strands of his long, blonde hair wisped across his face as the wind blew from the side. His red-velvet cape whipped majestically with the wind. Time seemed to slow as I looked into his magnificent face. He stood there, calm and collected, as the scene behind him displayed one of utter chaos. He stood tall, exhibiting such confidence. It was as if there wasn't a doubt in his mind that Lapoi would conquer. His expression was serious and protective, unphased by the battle, and I could see a hint of a proud smile as he stared down me.

I hadn't felt that safe and protected since the last time I was on Lapoi. Being in the presence of Emalickel and Thorenel made me feel stable, guarded, and gratified. I felt admiration, comfort, and freedom. The brothers were always calm and composed. Even in times of disagreement and turmoil, they handled it with flow and poise. I was comfortable around them and could speak any thought without risk of offense or judgement from them. It was as if they were extensions of myself.

Thorenel nodded his head at me, as if reading my thoughts.

Thorenel: You are safe now. I am going to take you home.

69. Artist: Philipp Beesen
Song: Shadow Warrior

Just then, a body came out of nowhere and hit Thorenel from the left side. It sent him flying twenty feet away. Disoriented, Thorenel stood up and looked around for the apparent danger. The body which had collided with him was lifeless. Thorenel brushed himself off and bent down to investigate the body. It was an Umgliesian warrior who must have been thrown from the battle ground below. Then, from behind Thorenel, came a Umgliesian legionary wearing a dark-blue robe with a hood. He held up one of his hands, about to throw energy at Thorenel's back. Thorenel noticed the panicked expression on my face. He ducked and turned around just as the legionary shot a large shard of light at him. It flew right over Thorenel's head. Thorenel pushed a wave of energy at the attacker, sending him into the air and down the hillside.

Another attacker crawled up the hillside, this time with two others. Thorenel used a variety of physical techniques to ward them off. He kicked one of them to the ground and shot a shard of light into his chest; which sent the attacker rolling down the hillside, clenching his chest. He threw a punch at the second opponent to his right and then elbowed the other opponent to his left. He ran up to the opponent on his left and leaped into the air before coming down onto him. As Thorenel landed, a surge of energy radiated into the opponent on impact.

Meanwhile, the third attacker, stood back up. He pursued Thorenel from behind as Thorenel finished off the second opponent. The third attacker shot waves of energy at Thorenel's back, but Thorenel whipped around in time to put up a golden transparent shield which reflected the energy back onto the attacker. The third attacker fell to the ground. Thorenel picked him up by his neck and looked him in the eyes for a moment before throwing him into the tree-line of the jungle over one mile away.

More attackers started coming over the hillside. Short-winded, Thorenel yelled to Emalickel.

Thorenel: Emalickel! She's right here, but we are under attack! You're the only one who can disintegrate the shield that Barthaldeo placed around her!

I could not see Emalickel, but I heard his voice resonating within my mind. He must have sent his thoughts to both Thorenel and me to hear collectively. His tone was agitated, but genuine. He seemed to be caught-up in a struggle of his own.

Emalickel: ***I will be right there . . . as soon as I can get this nuisance . . . off . . . my back!***

Thorenel battled and fought each attacker as they continued coming over the hillside. He remained focused and vigorous, never seeming to lose his awareness or stamina. One after another, he took on the opponents without failure or doubt. None of them could get past him. It was impressive watching him take on a legion of attackers like they were pesky gnats.

70. Artist: Tom Player
Song: Desolation

Just then, one attacker walked slowly up the hillside displaying an abundance of confidence as he approached Thorenel. He wore adornments over his robes. He was taller than the others and moved smoothly. His demeanor was calm and unafraid. Thorenel had dissipated the rest of the legionaries and turned his attention to this particular opponent. The hillside became very still as the two of them looked at each other in silence. Finally, Thorenel spoke to him.

Thorenel: Jamaleo, brother of Barthaldeo. Why have you trudged yourself to this hillside of death? Have you come to seek it as well?

Jamaleo: Don't get too arrogant, Thorenel. You and I both know we are equals.

Jamaleo was the equivalent to Thorenel in the celestial hierarchy. They both held the secondary Royal-Princedom status of their realms. Jamaleo was the direct brother of Prince Barthaldeo, as Thorenel was the direct brother of Prince Emalickel.

Shaking his head with an offended look on his face, Thorenel replied.

Thorenel: Let us set one thing straight before we begin. You and I are NOT equal! You are a lazy, evil, manipulative freeloader of darkness. I, on the other hand, am the antithesis of you. We are sons of God, and because of that, the victory of Lapoi has already been determined.

Jamaleo: That is yet to be determined, pretty boy!

Without warning, Jamaleo pushed Thorenel backward with a surge of energy from his palms. Jamaleo continued pursuing Thorenel, aggressively walking toward him and shooting spheres of energy directly at his body. Thorenel abruptly stood up and repositioned himself into a sturdy stance. He absorbed the impact of a second attack with his forearms, then he sent an energy surge back at Jamaleo. Jamaleo fell onto his back. Thorenel conjured a long, sparking, lightning rod and held it in his hand as he barbarically stepped over his opponent. Jamaleo rolled over and out of the way just as Thorenel stabbed it into the ground where Jamaleo had been lying.

Energy waves shot rapidly at Thorenel from Jamaleo's palms, causing Thorenel to become unstable on his feet. While Thorenel stumbled, Jamaleo sat up and yanked the lightning rod from Thorenel's grasp. While Thorenel struggled to steady himself, Jamaleo jabbed the rod straight into Thorenel's chest and out the other side of his back. Upon contact, immense amounts of electrical energy discharged into Thorenel, with flashes of lightning dispersing all around him. Thorenel's body trembled and convulsed until it finally fell to the ground. His skin became pale and lacked its usual lusterous glow. I screamed out and cried hopelessly to him.

Me: No! Thorenel!!!

Jamaleo smirked at me and shrugged his shoulders.

Jamaleo: Looks like I won that one!

Then, Jamaleo darted away, disappearing into the battle below the hillside. I frantically cried and pounded on the walls of the orb that surrounded me, trying to get to Thorenel, who laid motionless on the ground in front of me. His eyes had rolled into the back of his head. He had become lifeless. I whaled in painful emotional agony. In denial of his death, I kept trying to wake Thorenel from his state of unconsciousness.

Me: Thorenel! Please, no! Please, wake up! Thorenel! You've got to wake up!

Then, reality hit me. Thorenel wasn't going to wake up. He was gone. I let out a long, final, loud, whaling cry before I collapsed into my hands.

Me: No!!!

A celestial shook the ground as he landed nearby. After he landed, he froze and did not move. I looked up. It was Emalickel. He stared, in shock, at Thorenel's body.

Me: Emalickel!

He forced himself to refocus and hurried over to me. He placed both his hands onto the orb around me.

Emalickel: Brace yourself. Get down low.

Without hesitation, I crouched down low. A thunderous boom shook my surroundings followed by a bright, red shock-wave. The orb disintegrated, and I was free. I stood up and fell into Emalickel's arms, pressing my face into his chest, crying uncontrollably. Emalickel held me until I somewhat collected myself. I looked up at him and saw the somber look on his face as he processed the reality of his brother's exanamite body. With his fist, Emalickel wiped a single tear from under his left eye.

Me: Is he . . . ?

71. Artist: Hans Zimmer
Song: Time

Emalickel reluctantly bowed his head in sorrow. He released his hold of me and walked over to Thorenel's body. Bending down to pick him up, Emalickel threw the lifeless weight of Thorenel over his shoulder, then he held out his other hand to me. Without expression, he stated aloud.

Emalickel: We need to go.

Still weeping, I went to him. My heart hurt so much; I felt a physical stabbing pain within it. I could not believe it was real. I hung onto the hope that everything had been a bad dream and that I would wake up soon. Either way, I knew I wanted to get out of that terrible, horrible place. Clinging to Emalickel, I swallowed hard as I prepared to face reality. Emalickel put up his force-field around us as we prepared to launch out of Thermoplia.

Then, I remembered Clive. His body was somewhere near the tree-line of the battlefield below us. We couldn't leave him there. He deserved better than that.

Me: Wait! We've got to get Clive.

I had interrupted Emalickel from his upward gaze into the sky as he prepared for departure. He abruptly turned his head to look back down at me.

Emalickel: Who!?!

Me: Clive! I think he is dead, but he saved my life. I wouldn't even be here right now if it weren't for him.

Emalickel shook his head.

Emalickel: What is a part of Thermoplia, must stay a part of Thermoplia.

Me: But he isn't from Thermoplia; he was from Earth.

Emalickel lowered his eyebrows and bit his inner lip while he thought for a moment. I continued.

Me: He became trapped here and didn't know how to get back.

Emalickel's expression changed from one of confusion to one of clarity. He almost seemed to suddenly become aware of who I was talking about—as if he remembered something that had once been forgotten. Peering out in the distance for a moment, Emalickel took a deep breath before responding.

Emalickel: Where is he? I will scan for his residual energy.

I pointed at the tree-line where I remembered seeing Clive's body. Emalickel stepped away from me and used his free hand to send a line of light in that direction. It extended from his palm, arched over the battlefield, and grew longer until it touched down exactly where Clive's body laid. A spherical force-field surrounded the body, illuminating it, and lifted it above the trees. Emalickel drew the line back into him and gently dropped the sphere on the hillside where we stood. The force-field disappeared from Clive's lifeless body. Emalickel examined it for a moment. Then, his expression turned remorseful, and he whispered to himself under his breath.

Emalickel: We have been looking for you, Cliviticus. So this is where you have been hiding all this time?

He bent down, picked up Clive's body, and threw it over his other shoulder—Thorenel was over his right shoulder and Clive over his left. The noises from battle became louder. A dragon had been flung into the air and landed on a hill just above us. Emalickel quickly turned to look at me. Instead of yelling over the noise, he communicated to me with his thoughts. I heard him as if he were inside my head.

Emalickel: ***You are going to have to hold onto me by yourself; with your own might. Can you do that?***

I nodded. Although I was nervous, I had no doubt that I would be able to hold onto him. Facing him, I wrapped my arms around his torso as tightly as I could. Emalickel put up his glowing, transparent force-field again. We lifted from the surface of the ground, and gradually, we rose higher. Then, we started moving fast. Everything appeared as a blur. I heard a loud booming sound. I wondered if we had broken the sound-barrier, causing a sonic boom. Light increased and I was forced to close my eyes. My hold on Emalickel was strong. I heard the familiar static noise and felt the same heat-wave as with the first time I traveled to Lapoi with Emalickel. I knew we were doing some kind of inter-dimensional travel or teleportation.

6

LAPOI

72. Artist: Soundcritters
Song: Stardust

When the loud static had subsided, and the heat had turned into a cool breeze, I knew we had arrived in Lapoi. I caught wind of a wintergreen scent; the natural aroma of Lapoi's atmosphere. I assumed it was the trees which produced that refreshing smell. The trees were a type of tall evergreen. They resembled giant fir trees without any limbs on the lower-half of the trunks.

As we approached landing, I caught a glimpse of Lapoi from high above. It felt like I had arrived home. Feelings of comfort, freedom, and joy surged within me; like a child cozied by the fireplace with hot chocolate at Christmas. We were over the vast, green Valley of Dillectus. The palace came into view below us. It was the size of an ant. The snow-capped mountain peaks were in the distance beyond us. To our left, in the woodlands, a majestic waterfall fell from a cliff and into a lake of clear, turquoise water.

Emalickel glided us down to land upon the open Grand Balcony of the palace. He gently lowered Thorenel and Clive from each of his shoulders. They laid motionless on their backs. When Emalickel stood up, he rolled his shoulders and stretched out his arms, as if trying to regain feeling in them. I heard footsteps coming from behind us. It was Dennoliel. He was approaching the balcony from inside the throne area of the palace. I immediately noticed he was wearing the Crown of Lapoi. His face grew concerned as he picked up his pace to meet us. When Dennoliel spoke, his voice sounded clear and well-developed. His voice wasn't as deep as Emalickel, Thorenel, or Romenciel's, but he carried the same old-English accent.

Dennoliel: What is this? What happened, brother?

Emalickel only shook his head.

Dennoliel: Where is everyone else? Should I send aid?

Emalickel bent down and placed his hand on Thorenel's chest and closed his eyes.

Emalickel: No. We need to keep the rest of the warriors in Millattus. We cannot jeopardize the safety of the realm. Those in Haffelnia will conquer. The Nephilim are strong.

Dennoliel: I don't understand. How did this happen?

Emalickel stood back up.

Emalickel: He was alone—ambushed. I should have come to him sooner. Barthaldeo had me occupied.

Dennoliel walked closer. He bent down to Clive and looked closely at his face. He squinted his eyes in concentration. He mumbled to himself in surprise.

Dennoliel: Cliviticus?

Dennoliel looked up at Emalickel.

Dennoliel: After all these years, I never thought we'd find him.

Dennoliel looked back down at Clive and shook his head in disappointment.

Dennoliel: I wish we could have found you sooner . . . even if you were a rogue mortal.

He stood back up and looked at me, then at Emalickel with his eyebrows lowered.

Dennoliel: How did he turn up? Was he on Thermoplia?

Emalickel turn his head to me as if signaling for me to explain. After all, even he didn't exactly know many details.

Me: Yes. He said he was a mystic. He accidently wound up in Thermoplia during one of his spiritual practices. He said he wanted to come back, but he did not know how.

73. Artist: Fearless Motivation
Song: Revival

Dennoliel: This is all he told you?

I nodded my head, waiting for another explanation.

Dennoliel: We knew Cliviticus very well. He was kindhearted and brave, but he was also rebellious; always seeking the powers of the divine before he was ready for it. The powers of the celestial plane are meant for the celestial plane. Instead of seeking to return to Lapoi in his celestial form, he decided to stay mortal and push his abilities to the limit. He practiced rituals and incantations in which he knew were risky for

mortals to practice, yet he performed them anyway. Our guards warned him repeatedly of the possible dangers, but he didn't listen. One day, he disappeared from our radar completely. We have been searching ever since. Now I know why we couldn't find him. He warded himself so that we could not track him and stop him from practicing his rituals. Turns out, warding himself also kept us from tracking him and saving him.

Trying to process the information Dennoliel had disclosed to me, I remained silent, staring at Clive's lifeless body. He was a good man with a good spirit. It broke my heart to see him wasted away.

Me: Emalickel, you can bring them back . . . right?

Emalickel narrowed his eyes at me, as if slightly offended by my remark. He responded in an authoritative tone.

Emalickel: Perhaps I can, but such a decision is not mine to make.

I became irritated at him.

Me: So that's it? They just die? And we stand-by and let it be!?!

Emalickel raised his voice and articulated his words.

Emalickel: Let me make one thing very clear, Hadriel! I am not the chooser of fate! If they were meant to be alive, then they would be alive. God is the Master of Creation, and I shall not interfere with His plan.

We all stood there, remorsefully looking down at the bodies of Thorenel and Clive. Finally, Dennoliel broke the silence.

Dennoliel: Thorenel will not be gone forever. He will regenerate. It will take a great deal of time, and he may not take the

same physical form as before, but nonetheless, he will return to us. It is simply a matter of how he progresses in his time of reawakening. The same goes for our friend, Clive, here.

I snapped.

Me: That answer sucks! Neither of them deserve this! If I hadn't carelessly fallen for Barthaldeo's trap, then they would both still be alive! It's not fair!

Emalickel: It was part of the plan. We don't always understand it, but we must accept it.

I jerked my head toward Emalickel and walked up to him. I was angry.

Me: Why do always have to be better than everyone else? You're so concerned about your standing with God that you don't even consider anything or anybody else! All you have to do is touch them, and they'll come back like nothing ever happened; but instead, it's all about your image to God! How selfish!

Without making eye contact with me, he remained calm as I shouted insults at him.

Emalickel: You mean not what you say. You are emotional. That is all.

Me: I just don't get it! Why do you have to try to be so perfect all the time!?! He is your brother! He is the third aspect of us! How do you know God doesn't want you to bring them back? Have you ever thought that maybe your choices are a part of fate? Maybe you were meant to bring them back, and the choice is left up to you! Maybe God is testing your intuition to see how noble you truly are; to see if you still have a soul with a heart behind it!

By this time, Emalickel had become flustered. His voice was loud again.

Emalickel: I will not be tempted by you! Do NOT belittle me for my decisions. I will always love you, and I will always love my brother; but God will always be first, as He should be among all creation. I will not do something that has not been granted, by Him, for me to do. I never have been defiant, and I shall not start today; which is precisely the reason I was chosen to oversee this realm! Now that is the end of it! We will speak no more on the matter!

Emalickel abruptly turned away and walked to the edge of the balcony. With his arms resting on the rail, he looked out at the Valley of Dillectus. I looked at Dennoliel. His head was dropped low, trying to stay out of the dispute. I looked out at the valley from where I stood. It was a beautiful day that day. Rays of Auruclerum beamed down through the think, fluffy, white clouds of the sky. I noticed a breeze began coming in from the east. It was a cool, crisp breeze. Suddenly, it did not smell of wintergreen, but rather carried a sweet, floral scent with it. Immediately, Emalickel turned his head in that direction, as if he was alerted by something. Then, we heard a male voice in the breeze. It was in a whisper. It resonated all around us.

Voice: Emalickel... You are wise. True. Obedient.

74. Artist: Really Slow Motion
Song: Gates of Pearl

Emalickel, Dennoliel, and I all looked at each other. We were checking to see if each other had heard the voice. It appeared we had all heard it.

Voice: You have proven yourself, Prince of Lapoi. There is nothing more for you to prove.

Emalickel looked back in the direction from where the voice had come. He became nervously excited, seeming to recognize the voice.

Emalickel: Immanuel, my King!?!

Immanuel: I am.

Emalickel and Dennoliel immediately went down to their knees into a kneeling position. I followed suit.

Immanuel: Know that you are worthy. Trust your humble heart. Make your decisions from there. Go, awaken them. Watch them rise, and they shall thrive.

The whisper faded away with the wind, and with it, so did the sweet, floral scent that had come along with it. Emalickel raised his head from his kneeling position and looked at the bodies of Thorenel and Clive resting on the balcony floor. He slowly rose to his feet. He carried a look of bewilderment as he walked closer to them in astonishment. He brought himself to kneel down between the two of them. At first, he hesitated. It was as if he couldn't believe what he had just heard and was trying to process everything.

Even though I had been frustrated at him for being so stubborn, Emalickel was indeed sovereign, honorable, and righteous. He was collected and regal. He had confidence, wisdom, and both physical and emotional strength beyond that of any other being I had ever encountered. I couldn't help but feel intensely drawn to him. I was impressed with the ability he was about to demonstrate.

First, he placed his hand on Thorenel's forehead. Emalickel took in a deep breath and then exhaled. His facial expression became one of concentration while his eyes slightly rolled into the back of his head. A glowing, white light appeared in the space between his palm and Thorenel's forehead. From that same area, I heard something that sounded similar to tiny, high-pitched wind chimes clanking together.

75. Artist: Ivan Torrent
Song: Afterlife

Thorenel's body began to glow in a beam of golden light. The wind chime sound grew louder. A light fog began forming around Thorenel, swirling all around him. Then I heard deep rhythmic drumming, similar to that of a heartbeat. We could all hear this sound, for it was loud enough to feel the resonance of it. After a few moments of this drumming rhythm, Thorenel's eyes popped open wide. The blue color within them was illuminated and glowed of white. Thorenel frantically gasped for breath as he sat up and inhaled loudly. All other sounds faded away, except for the sound of his panting breaths. After Thorenel had managed to calm himself down and regain control of his breathing, the fog surrounding him dissipated. The glow in his eyes softened to their natural glacier-blue color, and the beam of light which spotlighted him became dimmer.

Appearing confused, Thorenel looked at Emalickel, who was still kneeling beside him. Then, Thorenel looked around trying to orient himself.

Thorenel: What happened? How did I get here? Why is everyone standing around me?

Emalickel stood up and folded his hands down in front of

himself. He answered Thorenel with the truth, but he presented it in a quiet, smooth tone as not to overwhelm Thorenel.

Emalickel: You have been brought back to life this day, brother.

Thorenel jerked his head to look at Emalickel again with concern.

Thorenel: Brought back to life!?! When did I fall?

Emalickel: You have been given a second chance. You fell in battle on Thermoplia against Jamaleo. I saw it, but I did not make it in time to save you.

Thorenel rushed to his feet and positioned himself directly in front of Emalickel. His tone became concerned and upset.

Thorenel: Why did you bring me back, brother!?! Why would you compromise your obedience to God? My fall was His will! How careless of you! You have sacrificed your divinity!

Emalickel calmly smiled without flinching. He seemed proud.

Emalickel: I brought you back because our King, the Son of God, has willed it so. You are to live, and I was instructed to make it so.

Thorenel looked down and seemed to be absorbing what was said. He never seemed to fully process everything because his eyes came upon the body of Clive, which still laid lifeless on the balcony floor.

Thorenel: Who is that? Wait . . . that can't be . . .

He shook his head in bafflement.

Thorenel: What did I miss?

76. Artist: Judah Earl
Song: Creation

Emalickel: Indeed, this is Cliviticus of Alexandria. He, too, is to be revived. I will let him explain everything to us himself. All we know is that he was on Thermoplia. He aided Hadriel and died at Barthaldeo's hand.

Thorenel looked over at me. His eyes widened with concern.

Thorenel: Did he hurt you? Did he do anything to you?

I was flattered by Thorenel's protective nature. I shook my head.

Me: He took care of me. He even provided me with an elixir that helped me to see your celestial plane.

Thorenel rushed over to me and placed his hands on my shoulders. His eyes became even more wide.

Thorenel: What was this . . . elixir?

Although I was nervous about their reaction, I answered truthfully. If I had done something wrong, they needed to know. Plus, they'd be able to hear my mind anyway.

Me: I was afraid. When Clive informed me that he could help me see Lapoi, I was hopeful. When I knew you were all looking for me, it gave me hope and comfort.

Emalickel chimed in.

Emalickel: It was likely a simple Land & Blood elixir.

I was relieved at Emalickel's lack of concern.

Me: Yes! That is all it was. He mixed soil of Thermoplia and my blood. It worked, too. I saw everything and knew you were sending the Nephilim on a search for me.

They all nodded. Then, Thorenel spoke again with a calmer demeanor.

Thorenel: Is there anything else we should know?

Me: No. Just that he saved me many times from many dangerous creatures. He was hospitable and caring. He had hoped that I would be able to help him find his way back to Millattus.

Everyone was silent as they processed the information. Emalickel and Thorenel looked at each other. Then, Emalickel looked down at Clive's body.

Emalickel: Well then, I shall bring him back with his hope fulfilled. His soul is good. He deserves a second chance in this life.

Emalickel walked over to Clive and knelt down. The same events unfolded as had happened moments earlier with Thorenel. When Clive opened his eyes, he looked shocked and gasped for air. He immediately sat up and tried to gain his bearings. He looked all around.

Clive: Where am I? What is this?

Without pause, Emalickel answered him with his comforting tone.

Emalickel: Your hope has been fulfilled, Cliviticus Gwydion of Alexandria. You have been granted a second chance. This is the celestial plane of Lapoi. You have returned to your home-realm of Millattus.

Slowly, Clive rose to his feet, still looking out at his surroundings. He saw me, then turned his attention to Emalickel, Thorenel, and Dennoliel. He scanned them as if trying to put it all together in his mind. They were wearing their Princedom cloaks.

Clive: You must be the Princedom celestials.

Dennoliel spoke next.

Dennoliel: We have been searching for you. We couldn't find you as a result of that ward you put upon yourself. You had no business practicing those rituals, Civiticus! My guards warned you, but you failed to comply. We still would not have found you had it not been for the events that have unfolded with the Princess. However, we are grateful for your aid to her. With time, your past shall be forgiven.

Clive looked at me again. He smiled and respectfully bowed his head at me. Thorenel walked to the edge of the balcony, and then turned around to face us again.

Thorenel: So, what are we to do now?

Emalickel walked over to join Thorenel, but he faced the valley as he replied.

Emalickel: You and I must return to Haffelnia to finish the battle.

Then, he turned around to face us. He looked at me with a love-smitten smirk.

Emalickel: Dennoliel, you will continue to hold the Crown of Lapoi for a while longer. Thorenel and I will be occupied after our return from Haffelnia. We will be spending some uninterrupted quality-time with Hadriel. We wish to take advantage of this time we have been gifted with her presence.

77. Artist: Antti Martikainen

Song: Throne of the North

He held his gaze at me and continued smiling. Thorenel did the same. They stood there, side-by-side, without taking their eyes from me. The two most-exalted, beautifully handsome, most-powerful celestial brothers stared at me with passion in their eyes. I felt weak in the knees as I anxiously pondered what would transpire between us throughout the evening of their return.

Emalickel snapped out of it and continued his instructions to Dennoliel.

Emalickel: Watch over them until we return. They are to remain within the palace parameters where their safety will not be compromised. Add extra security with additional warriors in the vicinity.

He walked over to me and cupped my face in his hands. He announced loud enough for everyone to hear, but he gazed at me while speaking.

Emalickel: Prepare the festivities for our return—we certainly have much to celebrate.

Emalickel kissed my forehead and stepped back.

Emalickel: Until then . . .

Thorenel came over to me. He pulled me into him and embraced me, bringing my head to his chest. He rested his chin on my head for a moment, then pulled away while maintaining eye-contact with me. He took a few steps away until he stood next to Emalickel. Then, he whispered to me with a smile.

Thorenel: Until then, Princess . . .

They both shot into the air, stirring the wind as they departed. I heard two sonic booms, one right after the other, and knew they were gone. Clive, Dennoliel, and I all stood there in silence. We weren't sure what to do while we waited for everything to return to normal on Lapoi. I felt helpless and purposeless. Trying to break the awkward silence, I thought of something to say to start a conversation. I looked at Dennoliel and pointed at the crown he wore.

Me: I see you're wearing the crown.

Dennoliel and Clive seemed to relax a bit as Dennoliel flowed with the conversation.

Dennoliel: One Princedom must always stay in Millattus to protect the realm. The crown initially went to Thorenel, but he managed to convince Emalickel into passing it down the line to me.

Me: How did he manage to do that?

Dennoliel: He presented the argument that the power of both Royal-Princedoms, being himself, Emalickel, and Romenciel, would be needed in order to stand a chance in Haffelnia. Romenciel would be going to Haffelnia, and Xabiel would be occupied here with the warriors, so I was next in the order of succession for bearing the crown.

Me: So right now, you can do anything Emalickel can do?

Dennoliel became very serious.

Dennoliel: Yes, but I intend to use the power wisely, not for show.

I smiled at him.

Me: I wasn't suggesting that. I was just clarifying my knowledge of the crown. Nobody has ever explained it to me.

Dennoliel began walking back into the palace from the balcony. He held his arm out to me in escort. I took his arm and we headed inside—through the massive archways and down the first set of stairs toward the back of the throne chairs. Clive followed behind us. Dennoliel spoke as we walked.

Dennoliel: The crown harnesses unequivocal power. When worn by a Princedom Brother, his power becomes equal to that of a Royal-Princedom until the crown is removed. One of us must be in charge of overseeing Millattus at all times. Millattus must always have the active presence and protection of one of the six Princedoms.

Dennoliel, Clive, and I continued down the second set of stairs, past the thrones, toward the palace aisle. Thinking back on my past visits to Lapoi, I postulated a few questions.

Me: I don't remember Emalickel ever wearing the crown before I knew he was the Prince. Was someone else wearing it during that time?

Dennoliel: As a Royal-Prince, Emalickel does not rely on the crown for his powers. In fact, the powers harnessed within the crown are those of his own. He only wears the crown for the purposes of ceremony and tradition.

Me: What about the first time I was abducted by Barthaldeo? All six of you came to my aid, so who was wearing the crown then?

Dennoliel: After your abduction, Emalickel passed the crown to Thorenel. Barthaldeo's ship was still in the parameters of Millattus. Although Thorenel helped us to get into

Barthaldeo's ship, he returned to Lapoi right after our entry. That is why you did not see him on the ship with the rest of us. Emalickel regained the crown the following day when he revealed his true identity to you.

This had all started to make sense. Clive had been quiet the whole time. I knew he was lost in the conversation. He didn't know what we were talking about. I didn't want him to feel excluded, so I steered the conversation elsewhere.

Me: Seeing how you are the current Prince of Lapoi, what is going to happen to Clive now?

Dennoliel: Although I am the acting Prince, I choose not to make such important decisions. I am here to ensure the protection of Millattus remains in place, not to oversee long-term decisions. Those decisions I will leave for Emalickel upon his return. Until then, Cliviticus shall remain here with you.

We continued walking down the long central aisle, toward the main entryway of the palace. Mid-way down the aisle, Dennoliel stopped walking and turned to Clive.

Dennoliel: Meanwhile, Cliviticus, I suggest you think about your future.

Clive stopped walking and turned around toward Dennoliel. Dennoliel continued to explain.

Dennoliel: I am certain Emalickel will ask this question of you when he returns. Would you wish to return to Earth as a different man, or would you rather stay here in Lapoi as a guard or warrior? Emalickel will not decide your fate without at least considering your preferences.

Clive: I cannot answer that question without first asking more questions.

Dennoliel: Then know your questions. Emalickel will have your answers.

We resumed walking.

Dennoliel: I am going to take my leave from you now. Both of you are free to roam the parameters of the palace—the inner walls, outer courtyards, the under-keep. By the order of Emalickel, neither of you are to stray into the woodlands or valleys. Should either of you find yourselves in need, just call to me. I will be close-by.

Dennoliel released his escorting arm from me and walked toward the stairway to our left. The stairway was tucked away behind several sets of archways. There was another stairway, tucked away, to our right. They both led to the upper floor, which contained a balcony overlooking the main level of the palace.

I turned to Clive.

Me: I know the palace pretty well. Would you like for me to show you around?

He smiled at me and held out an escorting arm. I enjoyed being treated so respectfully from a gentleman.

Clive: That would be splendid, my lady.

Knowing Clive was interested in magic, I decided to take him to the Education Quarters. The Education Quarters was a giant circular-shaped room at the front of the palace, on the eastern side. It was built having two levels filled with shelves of books, small tables with refreshments, and study aids for magic. The center of the Education Quarters was open to the second floor, so one could peer down from the second level onto the first floor. The decorations and construction were made in resemblance of a medieval time-period. Candles were the source of lighting, and wood was the construction-type of the walls, ceiling, and furniture. There were many trophy boxes with various artifacts enclosed within them.

We walked through the arched doorways. It was relatively quiet inside. There were about ten celestials, dressed in golden robes, dispersed within the quarters. They were studying. Some were seated with books at small, square, wooden tables while others were roaming around. Two celestials were engaged in a quiet conversation, but we could not hear what they were saying.

I led Clive up the open staircase to the left of the doorway. We walked around the second floor, looking over the balcony into the vast room. I spoke to Clive in a quiet voice, as not to disturb the other celestials.

Me: This is the Education Quarters. You'll never get bored in here with all these books to study!

Clive looked around, wide-eyed, absorbing the whole picture.

Clive: This is incredible!

As we progressed to the other side of the circular upper floor, we passed a celestial seated at a table. I paid no attention to the celestial, as I was trying to mind my business. Then, I heard him utter something in Clive's direction.

78. Artist: Marcin Przybyłowicz
Song: On the Champs-Désolés

Celestial: Don't get too comfortable here, Renegade. You have much to prove before you earn a place among us.

I stopped and turned around toward the voice. It was Xabiel. He was leaning back in the chair with his legs propped-up and crossed at the ankles on the table. His expression was stone-cold. He took a sip from the chalice in front of him before standing up. He towered above us. I was confused by his seemingly intrusive remark.

Me: What did you say?

Xabiel peered at Clive.

Xabiel: The renegade heard me.

Me: Renegade?

Xabiel's voice became loud and stern.

Xabiel: He is a rebel who fails to follow instructions! He should have rotted in Thermoplia!

Clive became defensive.

Clive: I was only trying to push myself to the limit; evolve myself to the highest level of possibility.

Xabiel snapped at him.

Xabiel: There are no excuses, Cliviticus! You aren't allowed any excuses! We should not have had to compromise Millattus and focus so much attention on searching for someone with such selfish intentions!

I knew there was much to learn regarding the story of Clive. Every celestial we encountered had seemed resentful and irritated by him. On the other hand, I knew I didn't appreciate

Xabiel's disrespectful attitude toward him. Emalickel had brought Clive back for a second chance.

Me: Everyone deserves a second chance, Xabiel.

Quickly cocking his head at me, Xabiel burst-out and pointed his finger at me.

Xabiel: YOU can stay out of this, Princess! You don't know one damn thing about his history!

I was taken-back by his outburst and was afraid to say anything further.

Suddenly, Dennoliel appeared from behind Xabiel.

Dennoliel: Should you not be tending to the warriors, Xabiel?

79. Artist: Zack Hemsey
Song: Don't Get in My Way (Instrumental)

Without turning around, Xabiel rolled his eyes and shook his head. He smiled wittingly and placed a hand over his heart, while he replied in a conniving tone.

Xabiel: Oh my! It seems our Prince has arrived! We must display our best behavior now!

Xabiel rolled his eyes again and allowed his expression to return to one of being annoyed. Dennoliel walked to position himself in front of Xabiel. He looked directly down at him.

Dennoliel: I shall advise you to show more respect.

Xabiel removed his feet from the table and sat upright. He responded with an overly surprised demeanor.

Xabiel: Oh dear, where have all my manners gone!?!

Xabiel stood up to face Dennoliel.

Xabiel: I should be bowing to you, shouldn't I!?!

But Xabiel did not bow. Instead he remained standing, eye-to-eye with Dennoliel for an awkwardly long moment. Finally, still holding eye contact with Dennoliel, Xabiel drummed a few times on the table beside him before speaking again.

Xabiel: I will be going. I have said all I need to say.

He looked at Clive and me once more before walking past us and toward the stairs. Dennoliel raised his palm out in a stopping motion. A high-pitched ringing sound occurred. I heard Xabiel making sounds of struggle. The royal crown on Dennoliel's head began to glow. Although Dennoliel reminded me a lot of Thorenel, his eyes and face were larger and his hair was a darker shade of blonde. Like Thorenel, he radiated power and divinity, especially with the crown upon his head.

Dennoliel: I do not have time for this Xabiel! There are others who can take your place leading the warriors until Romenciel returns. I will put you away, brother! Emalickel will not argue with my decision to teach you humbleness.

I turned around to look at Xabiel. Dennoliel had him pinned against a wall. He kept the hold on Xabiel for several more seconds, gazing at him with fury.

Dennoliel: Do you understand!?!

Xabiel continued to struggle, but did not answer. He persisted in fighting to free himself from the restraint. Dennoliel push his palm forward a bit more. Xabiel grunted even more. Dennoliel spoke louder and with more articulation.

Dennoliel: I asked you a question!

Xabiel clenched his teeth in pain and nodded. Keeping the restraint on Xabiel, Dennoliel shook his head as if struggling to hear.

Dennoliel: What's that!?! I couldn't hear you.

Xabiel yelled out through the pain.

Xabiel: Yes!!!

Immediately, Dennoliel dropped his hand. The ringing noise faded. I heard a thud as Xabiel dropped to the floor. He was on his hands and knees, clutching his chest. Dennoliel walked past us and respectfully bowed his head. He continued walking forward, but paused beside Xabiel, who was still cowering on the floor. Dennoliel mumbled and shook his head at him.

Dennoliel: Yet another lesson in humility. When will you learn?

Xabiel did not answer. He was still trying to catch his breath. Dennoliel scoffed and shook his head again. Then he proceeded around the balcony toward the stairs. Just then, Seronimel teleported at the top of the stairs. He appeared frustrated as he spoke to Dennoliel.

Seronimel: What is it now between you two?

Dennoliel continued walking. He answered Seronimel without slowing his pace.

Dennoliel: Same as usual with our arrogant, pompous brother.

Seronimel: You forgot vain, conceited, and egotistical.

Still on the floor, Xabiel spoke up.

Xabiel: Remember your place, Seronimel. You hardly speak, why start now?

Seronimel jerked his body as if fighting the urge to attack Xabiel. Dennoliel froze in his tracks, as he was about to pass Seronimel. He looked as if he had an epiphany. Without turning around, Dennoliel turned his head to the side to see Xabiel in his peripherals.

Dennoliel: You know what, Xabiel? You are no longer in charge of the warriors...

Dennoliel looked at Seronimel.

Dennoliel: Seronimel is.

Seronimel looked confounded. Xabiel sat up tall and scratched his ear as if trying to clean it out. He responded in his usual pretentious tone. He managed to cough-up a laugh.

Xabiel: I'm sorry, I thought I heard you say Seronimel is in charge of the warriors! You really must have done a number on me!

Without saying a word, Dennoliel patted Seronimel on the back and proceeded down the staircase. Xabiel stood up and rushed to the stairs. He hollered down at Dennoliel.

Xabiel: Have you lost your mind!?! You can't put a guard in charge of the warriors! What was Emalickel thinking putting that crown on your head!?!

Keeping his pace down the stairs, Dennoliel called back to him.

Dennoliel: The same wisdom he always uses when he refuses to put it on yours.

At that, Dennoliel opened the large doors and exited the Education Quarters. When they closed, it echoed throughout the large room. We all stood there—quiet. Seronimel was still in shock as he remained motionless at the top of the stairs. Xabiel was still leaning over the rail watching the doors where Dennoliel had just left. Xabiel shoved himself from the rail in anger and snared at Seronimel.

Xabiel: You know what? It'll be nice not to be burdened with the responsibility of overseeing them all. It's too much work anyway. You have fun with that duty, little brother.

At that, Xabiel teleported out of the quarters.

80. Artist: Wardruna
Song: Volüspá

Unfamiliar with Seronimel, I did not know what to say next. I smiled neutrally and decided to go with the first question in my mind.

Me: What are your thoughts, Seronimel? I don't know you very well.

He stood there quietly for a moment and then smiled before answering.

Seronimel: In this moment, I feel satisfaction. I am thinking about Xabiel's fear. He needs to feel that fear.

Me: But what about presiding over all the warriors? Aren't you anxious, or nervous, or overwhelmed?

Seronimel's smile grew. His light-blue eyes had cute wrinkles in the corners that became more evident as his smile grew larger. He walked closer, in the direction of Clive and me. He crossed his arms and leaned his back against the railing which overlooked the main level of the Education Quarters. His smiled relaxed as he responded.

Seronimel: I feel none of those things.

Me: I would be a total wreck if someone had just told me I was in charge of all the celestial warriors of Lapoi.

Seronimel grazed his tongue across his teeth and shook his head.

Seronimel: But you are not me.

He brought his eyes to look into mine. He held his gaze without blinking. Seronimel's expression became serious.

Seronimel: Do not ever mistake one's silence for weakness.

He tilted his head to each side, popping his neck in the process. Then, he turned around and looked over the edge of the railing at the lower level of the Education Quarters. He leaned his arms on the railing in a relaxed manner.

Seronimel: There is a reason I have been placed into a position of lower rank among my brothers.

Me: What do you mean?

Seronimel: My abilities—they are not meant to belong to one who holds a position of authority.

Me: What are your abilities?

He cautiously looked around the Education Quarters, scanning the entire room around him, as if checking to see that no one was watching. Then, he smirked at me, making the wrinkles on the outer corners of his eyes become more evident again.

Seronimel: See for yourself.

After a moment, Seronimel's eyes glowed completely white. It looked as if he had rolled the irises of his eyes into the back of his head, yet he had not. A high-pitched ringing sound grew within the room, as if a frequency were being emitted. He continued looking over the rail at the bottom floor and fixated his focus on the celestials below.

Suddenly, they all dropped what they were doing and looked up at Seronimel. They all started walking toward the center of the room where they gathered and paused, looking intensely bitter at one another. Then, Seronimel spoke a command quietly, almost to himself.

Seronimel: Fight.

At that, the celestials below all began fighting with each other in physical combat. I looked at Seronimel to gage his reaction. He kept a straight face while his eyes still glowed of white light. The celestials kept battling with each other, yelling and throwing punches and kicks. Finally, Seronimel spoke another quiet command.

Seronimel: Stop.

The high-pitched ringing sound immediately ceased, and all the celestials below returned to normal, as if nothing had happened. They went back to their initial places and calmly resumed what they had been doing before.

Afterward, Seronimel turned around and rested his back against the railing again. His eyes resumed their normal blue hue. My mind circulated millions of questions I asked him aloud.

Me: What was that!?! Did you just control them? You have mind-control abilities—over celestials!?!

Seronimel removed himself from the rail and headed for the

stairs. Before proceeding down, he turned around and looked at me.

Seronimel: It is nice to finally make your acquaintance, Princess.

He winked at me before he disappeared. Clive and I looked at each other with our mouths dropped open. I had never seen a celestial who could control other celestials before. I wondered if, being a guard, he was able to use this ability within the mortal plane to control the mortals. Regardless of that, I knew Seronimel could use his ability to super-charge the warriors by granting them with his Princedom abilities and making them faster, stronger, and more resilient.

81. Artist: Marcus Warner
Song: Among the Giants

I attempted to alleviate the awkward silence by adding a bit of casual humor to the matter. I chuckled as I spoke to Clive.

Me: So umm . . . well that's the Education Quarters! Where would you like to go next?

Clive chuckled aloud, confirming he had understood my sense of humor.

Clive: You know the place better than me. Take me where you think I will find delight.

I thought briefly about where he would enjoy best. I thought of the Courtyards, the Mead Hall, the Billiards and Lounge, the Ballroom, or the Great Library. There were also so many other rooms to choose from. I decided to take him to the Courtyards. I knew we could progress from there to the Mead Hall and then to the Billiards and Lounge.

Me: Follow me.

The afternoon went by rather quickly. We sat in the courtyard and played a game of chess. From there, we progressed to the Mead Hall where we savored a few rounds of mead together in casual conversation. Afterward, we fancied a few games of pool in the Billiards and Lounge. We roamed around until it began growing dark outside. The days in Lapoi lasted longer than on Earth. There were 48-hours of daylight on Lapoi, and 20-hours of night.

Emalickel and Thorenel hadn't yet returned. The palace was quiet. I felt myself becoming tired as the sky fell into dusk. The two moons began shining through the deep purple clouds. Since I didn't know what the next day would bring, I decided it would be best for me to rest. I decided I would retire to Emalickel's Quarters, though I knew I was also welcome in Thorenel's Quarters. I had always spent the night in Emalickel's Quarters, so I felt more comfortable falling asleep in his bed. I informed Clive of my plans.

Me: I'm not sure what tomorrow will hold, so I'm going to lie down and rest for the night. You should probably do the same. I'll find Dennoliel.

I called to Dennoliel in thought. I knew, since he held the Crown of Lapoi, he would hear me. Within less than a minute, Dennoliel appeared in the Billiard & Lounge Room. He also seemed to already know why I had called to him.

Dennoliel: You wish to retire for the night? I have just conjured a place for Clive to rest in the living room of Emalickel's Quarters.

The three of us made our way to the Throne Hall and headed, up the Western Staircase, for Emalickel's Quarters. It was located in the northwest quadrant of the palace. Thorenel's Quarters were located in the northeast quadrant. Both Emalickel and Thorenel's quarters were equivalent in size and layout. Each of their private quarters were like mansions inside the palace! They both contained a kitchen, dining room, living room, study, several bedrooms, three bathrooms, a trophy room, and a king's room. Their living quarters only took up the northern corners of the palace—which painted a picture of just how massive the palace actually was.

Clive made himself comfortable in Emalickel's living room, and I retired to the bedroom. As I laid in the bed of soft white sheets, I pulled the golden-colored bedding over my chest. My feet pointed north, toward a large, open archway measuring about ten-feet wide and ten-feet tall. The archway led to a small semicircular balcony overlooking the Valley of Dillectus. Another archway was located to my left, which overlooked the woodlands of evergreen trees in the west. This archway also led to another small semi-circular balcony. White chiffon drapes hung from both open archways. The drapes blew with a gentle breeze. The light of both moons beamed in through the whisping curtains. Although I was tempted to step outside and gaze at the beauty of the land, my body wouldn't move from the comfort of the bed. It had conformed perfectly to my curves and crevices, and I was completely content. My eyes were heavy. I caught myself falling asleep a few times, and that was perfectly fine, for I knew I was safe. It felt like home.

~

7

CELEBRATION

82. Artist: Dominik A. Hecker
Song: Hear It, See It, and Feel It

The light of a pink morning haze filled the room when I opened my eyes the following morning. I knew I had obtained twenty hours of rest. I felt refreshed and rejuvenated. Amazingly, I didn't feel the usual need for coffee. I was fully awake and ready for a new day.

As I folded the sheets back to step out of bed, the balcony on the northern wall beckoned for me to step outside. Still wearing the same long-sleeved, black dress with no shoes, I slowly made my way toward the gently blowing chiffon curtains hanging loosely in the archway. Once outside, I walked to an iron bench which sat close to the railing, overlooking the Valley of Dillectus. I sat down on the bench and propped my feet up on the railing in front of me. Taking a deep breath, I savored the sight around me —Lapoi was like the Garden of Eden. It was stunning in beauty, supple in land, and invigorating in its atmosphere.

The light of Auruclerum peeked between the mountains in the

distance. It was a spectacular site like none I had ever seen before. The air was cool and crisp with the usual invigorating scent of wintergreen. The sky was accented with an abundance of clouds colored pink, lavender, coral, and orange. The atmosphere contained a light hazy fog, but around the mountains, there was a dense fog. The base of the mountain range was not visible due to the fog. I could see only the peaks towering above the smoky haze below.

I heard something behind me. It had sounded like a low-pitched vibrating noise. I turned my head around to see what it was and saw Dennoliel standing about ten feet behind me with his hands folded. The sound must have been a result of teleportation. Dennoliel held a gentle smile on his face.

Dennoliel: Good morning, Princess. I felt your wakeful presence. This crown is amazing!

He reached up and touched the crown on his head. I realized, since the crown held the powers of Emalickel, any of the brothers who wore the crown would be able to feel me, read me, and sense me—just as Emalickel was able to do.

Dennoliel came over to sit down on the bench next to me. Mimicking me, he propped his black boots on the railing. I picked up a trace of his scent. It was refreshing, and reminded me of eucalyptus. Although I was glad Dennoliel had come to keep me company, it had made me miss the presence of Emalickel. I missed his scent of fresh, clean leather and the sound of his deep, smooth voice. Dennoliel looked out at the Valley of Dillectus as he drummed on his lap.

Dennoliel: Emalickel should be returning with the others soon.

I wasn't accustomed to Dennoliel being in my head like that. He had read my thoughts and responded to them. This was the first time a celestial, other than Emalickel or Thorenel, had done that. Although I felt slightly uncomfortable about it, I tried to remain discreet.

Me: Good. What will happen after they return?

Instead of answering immediately, Dennoliel reached up and removed the crown from his head. He slowly placed it on the bench between us. I could feel him looking at me while he did so. I tried to act like I didn't notice and kept my sights on the valley below.

Dennoliel: Will that make you more at ease?

I knew he was referring to the crown, and how he had removed it; but I pretended to be oblivious. I shifted my eyes down at the crown with an unconcerned look.

Me: It's alright. You don't bother me.

Dennoliel removed his feet from the railing of the balcony. He leaned forward to rest his arms on his knees and folded his hands. Taking a deep breath, he relaxed himself as he fixed his gaze forward.

Dennoliel: Do you trust I will treat your daughter with the same respect and protection as Emalickel treats you?

His comment caught me off-guard. I looked at him analytically. He kept his sights forward while chewing on his inner lip. It reminded me of the way Emalickel appeared when he was in deep thought. I wasn't sure how to respond. During a previous encounter in Lapoi, I learned that Dennoliel and Seronimel were in pursuit of obtaining the companionship of my Earthly daughter, just as Emalickel and Thorenel had pursued me. Although I did not know Dennoliel and Seronimel very well, I trusted their integrity. After all, they were the very brothers of my own Princedom companions. Dennoliel waited patiently for an answer before turning his head toward me.

Dennoliel: If she decides to choose us, I assure you she will be protected and loved more than you can fathom. I give you my word we will bring her more joy and satisfaction than can be imagined.

It was easy to see he was in search for my approval. I smiled approvingly and offered him the only words I could think to say at that time.

Me: You're right. I do not know you as well as I wish I did, but I am a woman of instinct, and my instincts tell me that you will provide all that you have spoken. I feel I can trust your word.

I paused and looked forward at the valley before continuing. My smile grew wider and slightly mischievous. I teased at him.

Me: Besides, you wouldn't want to disappoint me— seeing how I AM the Princess and all.

He chuckled under his breath at my witty comment.

Dennoliel: I cannot argue with that.

He stood up and leaned over the railing.

Dennoliel: I know you've said that you love her more than creation itself.

A slight breeze blew a few strands of his long, wavy locks of dark-blonde hair. The coral-colored light of Auruclerum had just begun to rise over the mountaintops in the distance. Rays of radiant light shone through the loose pieces of Dennoliel's hair as he continued admiring the view in the valley before him.

Dennoliel: Would you believe me if I told you we will love her even more than that?

He turned his head around to look at me. He had a gentle and genuine smile. I stared at him, trying to process how anyone could love something more than creation. He didn't flinch. He only stared deep into my eyes as if trying to show me his genuineness. I realized he was completely serious, as if he knew something more than me. He appeared to exhibit some kind of unexplainable wisdom beyond what my mind could perceive. I was ridden speechless. There was nothing I could say in response to his bold statement. He was completely confident in what he had said, and I knew it. All I could muster was a smile and a nod of defeat. Still trying to wrap my head around what he had said, I became absorbed within the view of the distance.

83. Artist: Antti Martikainen
Song: Spirit Creek

Dennoliel turned his head forward again. After a few moments, he broke the long silence. His tone was sincere.

Dennoliel: You must feel hungry. Would you eat?

My stomach did feel empty. Even though I was in the celestial plane, my body was still partially attached to the mortal plane. Trying not to appear overly needy, I answered with a casual tone.

Me: I suppose I could eat something.

Dennoliel turned around to face me. He crossed his arms at his chest pridefully and leaned his back against the railing.

Dennoliel: And what foods do you desire?

I wasn't sure what was available. Shrugging my shoulders, I answered him with uncertainty.

Me: I could eat anything really.

He smiled.

Dennoliel: Well, then . . . how about a little bit of everything?

I stood up and walked to the railing beside where he was positioned. I pressed my lips into a satisfied smile.

Me: That sounds amazing! What about Clive? He's probably hungry, too.

Dennoliel walked to the right side of the balcony. He pointed in that same direction.

Dennoliel: He's right over there. Why don't we ask him?

I looked in the direction he was pointing and saw Clive standing on the Grand Balcony of the palace; on the balcony behind the thrones. It was about seventy-five-yards to our right and slightly lower in level. It was hard to tell whether or not Clive was looking in our direction, as he was too far away for me to see any facial detail. Dennoliel placed the first two fingers of one of his hands on his temple. He looked in the direction of Clive and spoke quietly under his breath.

Dennoliel: Good morning Civiticus. There is a breakfast feast in the Dining Hall should you desire fulfillment.

Clive looked around for a minute, seeming to search for someone. He must have heard Dennoliel's voice and was trying to find him. After a minute of confusion, Clive turned around and began walking back into the palace. Dennoliel displayed a smile of satisfaction.

Dennoliel: I do believe he is headed to the Dining Hall.

Dennoliel turned and headed back into Emalickel's bedroom through the large archway. I followed behind him. Trying to look a bit more presentable, I brushed through my hair with my fingers as we walked. We walked through Emalickel's bedroom and out a door located in the left corner. From there, we walked down a hallway and under another archway which led to Emalickel's kitchen.

Everything in the kitchen was polished and contemporary. The appliances were made of stainless-steel. The walls contained a gray, stone backsplash which accentuated the white cabinets and the gray marble countertops. The entire kitchen was about 1,500 square-feet. It had three fifteen-foot archways located on the wall in front of us. The archways all led into the living room. We walked through the one on the far left. The living room was about the same size as the kitchen, but with a much higher ceiling extending twenty-feet high. The living room also had an abundance of windows which overlooked the fir trees of the evergreen woodlands in the west. Three massive archways were located on the living room wall opposite of where we were standing. We walked through them and into another hallway which ran perpendicular to us. Directly across from us, on the opposite wall, was a large, arched door. Dennoliel pulled it open, and we proceeded through.

We emerged into the hallway which connected Emalickel's Quarters to the upper level of the Throne Hall. The hallway ran perpendicular to us. We turned left and followed that hallway until coming to the balcony which overlooked the Throne Hall below. We turned right and proceeded down the Western Staircase. Once we were on the main level of the palace, we turned left, and made our way through the Throne Hall, until we finally arrived at the Dining Hall.

Inside the Dining Hall, the back wall was made of windows overlooking the Valley of Dillectus. The massive room contained two floors with an open ceiling. The second floor overlooked the main level. An array of tables and chairs were dispersed throughout the 7,500 square-foot room. The tables varied in size from square tables to long rectangular tables. They were all wooden and some were painted white. They were all topped so delicately with floral and candle centerpieces. White fur rugs were under each table. A long, eloquently decorated table sat upon a platform parallel to the windows along the back wall. I remembered eating there once before during one of my past visits to Lapoi. All the brothers had sat there with me after Emalickel's homecoming from receiving the orders one time. We had feasted and drank mead together. I smiled as I reminisced.

84. Artist: Peder B. Helland
Song: Earth in the Sky

Clive was standing just inside the doorway, as Dennoliel and I entered. He shrugged and looked at Dennoliel.

Clive: I figured it was your voice I heard from the Grand Balcony. Is this the right place?

Dennoliel nodded his head at Clive and then and escorted us to a large rectangular table in the back of the room. It was parallel to a series of scenic windows peering out at the valley along the back wall. Dennoliel pulled out a chair for me to sit in. It was the chair in the right corner, with its back to the windows. He sat himself at the head of the table, to the left of me. Clive settled in a chair to the right of me.

Dennoliel folded his hands on the table. He looked at Clive and me with pride.

Dennoliel: Are you ready for the breakfast of a lifetime? I hope you are both hungry.

He looked toward the main door of the Dining Hall and snapped his fingers one time. As soon as he did this, a swarm of celestials wearing light-brown robes, entered the room with trays of food. One by one, they placed the food on the table. The trays included waffles, fried chicken fingers, pancakes, crapes, Danishes, biscuits, bacon, sausage patties, sausage links, scrambled eggs, donuts, bagels, steak tips, hash browns, breakfast burritos, and other items beyond my realm of comprehension. Other trays included condiments such as shredded cheese, whipped butter, stick butter, whipped cream, sprinkles, syrup of various flavors, ketchup, peppers, hot sauce, bacon bits, sugar, and many others. There were drink trays including coffee, milk, various juices, and teas. There was even a tray of sweet indulgences.

A musical group came in with lutes, mandolins, and drums. After they set up, Dennoliel spoke a prayer before we began our feast. The musical group played a lively morning tune of a renaissance style. It was absolutely unbelievable. There were only three of us, and we had private entertainment and endless food choices.

Dennoliel: Do not worry. The leftover food will not be wasted. The other celestials will indulge themselves after we are finished. Enjoy the feast!

We filled our plates and cups completely. I barely came up for breath as I savored every bite of bliss.

After a few minutes of us gorging ourselves, Seronimel entered the Dining Hall. He seemed concerned. He pulled up a chair from a nearby table and placed it opposite of me. He did not fix a plate for himself, but rather rested his hands in his lap. Dennoliel continued eating. Seronimel did not say much at first, but it was evident he was holding something back.

Seronimel: Good morning all. Everything is well?

Still chewing his food, Dennoliel replied to him.

Dennoliel: We are well, brother. How goes the matters with the warriors?

Seronimel: I do not wish to interrupt your feast, but there are a few matters of concern. When you all finish, I need to meet with you privately, Dennoliel.

Dennoliel took a nearby empty plate and placed it in front of Seronimel.

Dennoliel: Nonsense. Anything we need to speak about can be discussed here, with the Princess of this realm. Make yourself a plate, brother!

85. Artist: Adrian Von Ziegler
Song: Song of Brotherhood

Seronimel's eyes looked at me, then over at Clive where they paused. Dennoliel had been looking at Seronimel, but then he moved his eyes to look at Clive after he noticed Seronimel was staring in that direction. Dennoliel put down his eating utensil and casually leaned back in his chair. He folded his hands beneath his chest. He spoke to Seronimel, but kept his eyes on Clive.

Dennoliel: Concern yourself not with the presence of Cliviti-

cus. Although he has obtained great knowledge, he holds no power in the celestial plane.

Dennoliel moved his eyes back to Seronimel, narrowing them, before he continued.

Dennoliel: Then again, none hold any TRUE power over those of us in the Princedom brotherhood.

Dennoliel leaned onto the table with his arms crossed. He peered at Seronimel with a hint of judgement behind his eyes. Seronimel maintained a straight face as he removed his eyes from Clive and returned them to Dennoliel.

Dennoliel: And besides, given your arrogant demonstration in the Education Quarters earlier, I am certain Cliviticus knows the extent of our capabilities.

Dennoliel lifted an eyebrow at Seronimel, holding a pragmatic expression. Seronimel immediately disengaged eye contact and began focusing on piling his empty plate with food. He said nothing, but seemed a bit perturbed. He stabbed a steak-tip with his eating utensil and began chewing it. He kept his eyes down while he chewed. Dennoliel maintained his eyes on Seronimel, with a harsh gaze, before he finally resumed eating from his plate. He continued speaking while he chewed.

Dennoliel: You hold such great power, Seronimel, but you lack the equivalent responsibility. You seem to forge that the greater the power, the greater the responsibility.

Seronimel kept eating without looking up from his plate. He seemed irritated that he had been called-out on the secret display of his abilities in the Education Quarters. Seronimel was not keen on having to listen to a lecture from his older brother.

The lecture was interrupted by someone who suddenly burst

through the main doors of the Dining Hall. This time it was Xabiel. He entered the room boastfully as he barged-in, with such a commotion, that the even the musicians stopped playing their instruments. It was evident that Xabiel had intended to draw such attention to himself.

86. Artist: Thomas Bergersen
Song: Illusions

Xabiel: You're absolutely right, Dennoliel. With great power does come great responsibility.

Xabiel was wearing the Crown of Lapoi on his head. Dennoliel and Seronimel immediately jumped up from the table with great concern.

Xabiel: Leaving the Princedom Crown laying on a bench on Emalickel's balcony does not exactly scream "responsibility," does it?

Seronimel briefly looked back at Dennoliel with disappointment. Clive and I stayed seated, but we both put down our eating utensils and readied ourselves for action. We weren't sure what was going to happen.

Xabiel walked across the room, closer to the table. As he continued toward us, he spoke with utter disgust.

Xabiel: Do you even realize the chaos happening on the mortal plane as you sit here, mindlessly shoveling food into your face-hole?

Everyone remained quiet. Dennoliel and Seronimel looked alarmed. Xabiel's boots clunked on the floor as he slowly walked closer.

Xabiel: The grey ones from Gaddorium have already infiltrated the Earth. Their highly advanced technology allows them to become invisible at will. They hide among the humans, brainwashing them into corruption.

Xabiel stopped behind the chair at the head of the table, opposite of Dennoliel. He rested both hands on the back of the chair.

Xabiel: Meanwhile, Barthaldeo's accomplices from Haffelnia walk among the humans, in the physical; blending in with them as one of their own kind. They have forced their way into positions of influence. They, too, are steering the humans into the ways of corruption.

Xabiel walked up to the window and looked out at the Valley of Dillectus. He folded his hands behind his back.

Xabiel: Not to mention the creatures from Yahrinstahd. They continue inducing and feeding upon the fears of mankind.

He turned his back to the window and faced in the direction of Dennoliel. Xabiel's tone grew bitter, and his voice became louder with frustration.

Xabiel: We are fighting three different wars, with all three of the negative realms, and our leader isn't even here! Instead, he is on another realm, with an entire quadrant of our best warriors, fighting a stupid battle over a mortal girl with an abomination of Nephilim for his army! Am I the only one who sees something incredibly wrong with this picture!?!

Maintaining his composure, Dennoliel commanded order.

Dennoliel: Playtime is over, Xabiel. Hand over the crown.

Xabiel laughed.

Xabiel: Playtime!?! Is that what this is to you? This isn't a

game, Dennoliel! We are fighting for the fate of our future, the fate of Lapoi, the fate of our entire realm of Millattus!

Dennoliel: Xabiel, you are disobeying orders—orders which have been strategically put into place to protect all we are fighting for!

Xabiel: I disagree. I am only modifying the orders. Improving them to better execute the objective. I say we remove the guardians from the Earth and replace them with our warriors. The guardians do nothing but try and reverse the influence of the negative realms. Since the humans have free-will, this method has not been successful. If we were to physically take our warriors into the mortal plane, we could completely abolish all other entities, and they would no longer have any influence. We could take them out of the picture completely—fighting the war at the heart of the problem, instead of engaging in a relentless competition.

Dennoliel: We cannot do that. The mortals must evolve themselves and choose for themselves to grow deeper toward the Spirit. Should we remove all negative influences from them, we would be coddling them and spoiling them. They would no longer feel a need to search deeper within themselves, thus they would never truly find God. Their souls would never progress to their heavenly origins.

Xabiel remained silent. He appeared to be listening, but still held an angry look on his face. Dennoliel began walking around the table slowly approaching Xabiel.

Dennoliel: Behind everything we do here, there is a plan. Emalickel executes the plan according to the instructions of the Dominions. We stray not from this plan, for we know it

comes directly from God Himself. Veering from the plan would certainly reap most devastating results for Lapoi.

Dennoliel stood directly in front of Xabiel, and, without flinching, held out his hand. He looked at Xabiel with authority and power.

Dennoliel: You know nothing of what to do with the power that rests upon your head, Xabiel; nor do you comprehend the consequences at stake should you use that power for your own will...

Dennoliel slowed his speech to an extremely articulate speed.

Dennoliel: Hand. Over. The crown. Brother.

Xabiel breathed heavily for a moment. Then, he finally relaxed in defeat. He grabbed the crown from his head, with both hands, and dropped it heavily into Dennoliel's hands. Without saying anything further, Xabiel stormed out of the room, slamming the doors behind him.

87. Artist: Wardruna
Song: MannaR Liv

Dennoliel placed the crown back on his head and began walking back to the table. He settled back down in his chair and resumed eating. Seronimel hesitantly turned back around. He looked at Clive and me before taking his seat again. There was a long silence as we chewed our food. Dennoliel spun his finger in the air, signaling for the music to resume. After taking a few more bites of his food, Dennoliel looked up at Seronimel and pointed his eating utensil at him.

Dennoliel: You, Seronimel, are not off the hook. You should not have done what you did in the Education Quarters.

Seronimel disengaged eye contact and continued eating without saying anything. Dennoliel kept looking at Seronimel.

Dennoliel: Now, what were you going to tell me about the warriors?

Seronimel didn't answer immediately. He finished chewing his food first.

Seronimel: I was going to inform you that I think Xabiel has been sharing his ideas with the warriors; trying to gain their support and converting them into his way of thinking. It could potentially lead to a rebellion.

Seronimel took another bite of food before continuing. This time, he spoke with slight hesitation.

Seronimel: But, with your permission... I have the ability to reverse their thoughts.

Looking annoyed, Dennoliel intentionally dropped his eating utensil so that it clanked heavily onto his plate. Without saying anything, Dennoliel stared at Seronimel, holding a look of disgust. He finally shook his head.

Dennoliel: You shall do nothing of the sort—not while under MY rule.

Seronimel seemed frustrated.

Seronimel: Why does my ability scare you so much? My powers don't even work on any of our Princedom brothers.

Dennoliel: Let me make one thing very clear, little brother. Your ability doesn't scare me, but rather I choose not to interfere with free-will. Our warriors are genuine, real, free-thinking celestials. They have heart behind their choice to fight for Millattus. Should we use your ability on them, they

become nothing more than brain-washed drones, and we stoop to the level of the negative realms.

Seronimel: But what if their freedom of thought steers them into rebellion? My ability would keep them pure-hearted, focused, and level-headed. They complain about being bored, always having to fight on the outskirts of Millattus, when the real battle is, indeed, happening on the Earth.

Dennoliel abruptly stood up from his seat. He raised his voice and the music stopped once more.

Dennoliel: Then step-up and remind them they have the most important job of the realm! They are the first line of defense! They are the armor of Millattus! Tell them to quit whining like school-children and do their damn jobs!

Seronimel retaliated by raising his voice and banging his fists on the table.

Seronimel: And what if they still rebel!?!

Trying to regain his composure, Dennoliel used his napkin to calmly wipe his mouth.

Dennoliel: Then they will be sent into infantry until they can get their act together.

Seronimel: But if they rebel in great numbers—

Dennoliel slammed his napkin on his plate and interrupted Seronimel.

Dennoliel: This conversation is over, Seronimel!!! I have given you my answer! Take it up with Emalickel when he returns, should you feel the need to persist in this mindlessness!!!

Dennoliel stormed away from the table and left through the

main doors of the Dining Hall. Clive and I had finished eating, but we remained at the table in silence. Seronimel took one last bite of food and finished chewing it up. Then he gently set down his eating utensil and wiped his face with his napkin while looking out the window in front of him. He placed the napkin on his plate and looked around the room. Then, he cleared his throat while pivoting his head around the Dining Hall in search for service.

Seronimel: I don't suppose it is too early to ask for a bottle of mead? Anyone?

One of the celestials who had been serving us stepped up to the table and conjured a tray. The tray had three clear, cylinder-shaped glasses surrounding a black bottle in the middle. The serving celestial began pouring the contents of the bottle into the glasses. Seronimel looked over at Clive and me.

Seronimel: So, now you see... THAT is why I choose not to speak.

He picked up the full glass of mead in front of him and chugged it all down at once. He slammed the glass down on the table and nodded to the serving celestial for a refill. Clive and I took a sip of ours. Seronimel chugged down his second glass before standing up. He placed the glass back down on the table and wiped his mouth with his arm. Once again, he looked at Clive and me.

Seronimel: Princess. Cliviticus. It has been a pleasure having breakfast with you.

88. Artist: Antti Martikainen
Song: Northland

Seronimel pushed in his chair and walked toward the main door. Clive and I looked at one another while taking another sip of our mead. Seronimel's boots echoed as he walked to exit the room. Clive took the bottle of mead and topped off both our glasses.

Clive: You up for a game of chess in the courtyard?

I smiled and took my glass. We both stood up from our chairs and made our way outside to the courtyard.

The day passed without any further conflict. Clive and I remained outside in the nature of Lapoi. It was a beautiful day, as always. There was a gentle breeze, the light of Auruclerum was curtained by a sky full of clouds. We played a few games of chess, taking breaks between games to walk the perimeter of the palace. We walked to the backside of the palace, and I showed Clive the spectacular library located directly under the Grand Balcony.

We didn't see any more of the brothers for the remainder of the day. I wondered what each of them was doing and how Emalickel was going to react to all of the problems once he returned. It didn't bother me too much, for I knew he would be able to make amends with it all. He was the true Prince of Lapoi. His power, his profound wisdom, and his insightful perspective would be able to come up with great solutions to all problems.

I took Clive back inside the palace. We went to the Throne Hall so I could introduce him to the two majestic, white lions who sat on either side of the throne chairs. When we entered, the lions rose from their pronate position, to an upright sitting position. I sat down beside the lion on the right. Clive appeared nervous about this.

Clive: These lions... are they friendly?

Recalling information in which Thorenel had once shared with me, I explained the power and purpose of the lions to Clive.

Me: Thorenel once told me the lions rise if an uninvited presence were to enter the palace. The lions will roar. This roar transmits to every being on Lapoi. The lions will then tactfully back the unknown presence into a corner, roaring them into submission.

I stroked the mane of one of the lions. The lion opened its jaw to breathe a great yawn. Clive looked nervous

Me: It's alright. They are loyal companions. They won't attack unless instructed to do so, or unless you are an enemy.

Clive hesitantly reached out to touch the soft, thick mane of the massive white lion. It sniffed Clive's hand, then rubbed its neck into his hand. I watched Clive as he smiled gently at the affection of the lion. There was much I didn't know about Clive. I wished to know more.

Me: So, tell me your story, Civiticus Gwydion.

Clive sighed before answering.

Clive: There is more to tell than time allows.

Me: Perhaps you could at least get me started?

Clive: Not long before I left, our emperor, Constantine, legalized the practice of Christianity across the Roman Empire. He outlawed the stoning and the persecution of Christians. My home city of Alexandria was in tremendous religious uproar. We had a mixture of religious groups trying to coexist together—Jews, Egyptians, and Christians. Even the Christians were arguing amongst themselves about the stance of Jesus in the Holy Trinity. I chose a path of

freedom from religious conformity. I felt every religion held some truths, yet they all seemed too closed-off and boxed-in.

Me: The world isn't much different, even in the year 2018.

Clive: In my time, failure to fit into a certain category of beliefs, labeled you a heathen. Heathens were all frowned upon. A small group of us decided to live on the outskirts. We took our coins and belongings and lived like monks, only returning to the city periodically to retrieve necessary supplies. We immersed ourselves completely in our spiritual practices; learning all we could and as much as we could. We were able to achieve great enlightenment. We had visions and spirit-journeys to other realms.

Me: How did you end up in Thermoplia?

Clive: I only desired to see all there was to see; to know all there was to know. To find a path which best suited my own personal journey toward God. Apparently, the celestials of Lapoi frowned upon my path. They thought I should endure and participate in the same spiritual battle as all mortals. I didn't listen to them because I saw it differently. Unfortunately, in my attempt to seek more knowledge, my spirit-journey took me permanently to Thermoplia.

Clive continued his story for the remainder of the afternoon. I was deeply intrigued with all he had to share. It was interesting to hear his recollection of an ancient time and place. It was amazing to be able to ask him questions about the city of Alexandria, as it was in the 4th century. It was way more stimulating than reading about it in a history book. His story added color, emotion, and perspective.

The hours passed quickly. Clive was able to finish his story with me. I listened attentively, as I knew I would record his story when I returned to Earth.

Me: Your story is so incredibly interesting. When I return to Earth, I will share it in a text about you.

Clive smiled shyly and looked down.

89. Artist: Fearless Motivation
Song: Day of Domination

Suddenly, we heard the giant, main door of the palace open. Dennoliel had entered with two females, dressed in light-blue robes, walking on either side of him. He proceeded down the aisle toward Clive and me. The heavy doors clanked closed behind him, echoing through the entire open Throne Hall. He was wearing his white Princedom cloak over regular black garments. As he walked, he brushed the hood from his head, revealing the Crown of Lapoi still resting in its place upon the top of his head.

Clive and I waited in silence as Dennoliel made his way to us. He stopped at the foot of the throne stairs where we were seated with the lions. He exhibited a wide, excited smile.

Dennoliel: Princess, the battle is over! It has been won! Emalickel will be returning with the others shortly. These are your assistants, and they will escort you to the Spa Quarters, should you choose to prepare yourself.

I smiled and nodded in acceptance to his kind offer. He delivered the assistants to me, who then escorted me to the Spa Quarters on the second level of the palace in the Southwest quadrant.

The Spa Quarters was about 50-yards by 50-yards and was

walled-off to form different rooms containing such luxuries as a hot tub, sauna, fountain, hair dressers, a yoga studio, meditation rooms equipped with essential oils and crystals, massage rooms, and more pampering amenities.

The assistants of the Spa Quarters were always charming and eager to help. They took pride in their work and enjoyed what they did with a passion. I was first pampered to a full massage with hot stones in a large room with a hot tub. I relaxed in the hot tub for a while. Then, the assistants helped dress me in a fine, full length, cream-colored ballgown. I remembered wearing this gown once before, during a palace celebration in a previous visit to Lapoi.

The top part of the gown was fully jeweled with diamonds. The full, flowing, bell-shaped skirt of the gown was made of satin with a chiffon overlay. Small diamond sparkles were scattered throughout the overlay of the skirt. The sleeves were sheer and extended down my entire arm length. The cuffs of the sleeves were covered in diamonds, looking something like thick jeweled bracelets. The gown also had a four-foot train extending behind me when I walked.

My hair had been fixed with flowing curls and was pinned in a loose style, accented with tiny jewels. The celestials used their light-energy to brighten my skin tone and smooth it out. Around my neck they hooked a simple pewter necklace containing the Lapoian Triquetra symbol with tiny diamonds. The symbol was about one-centimeter in diameter. From my ears, hung one-inch dangling earrings; each containing the same, one-centimeter wide, Lapoian symbol. On my feet, the assistants slipped eloquent heeled-shoes with clear straps containing diamond sparkles.

90. Artist: Audiomachine
Song: Homecoming

The two female assistants, who had escorted me to the Spa Quarters, waited by the arched doorway of the quarters. A male celestial warrior, who was in charge of guarding the palace, peaked in. I knew he was a warrior because he was wearing the casual warrior attire—black pants, a dark-red tunic, and a black cape. He announced that everyone had arrived and they were ready for me. The female assistants motioned for me to come to them. Around my shoulders, they placed a shimmery-ivory royal cloak. It wasn't made from the same heavy velvet material as the Princedom brothers, but rather a lighter material similar to that of my dress—a gold, satin inner lining with a chiffon overlay. It was trimmed around the edges with a one-inch thick border of diamond sequins. On the back of the cloak was a gold, Lapoian Triquetra symbol, measuring about one-foot in diameter and outlined in even more diamonds.

I pulled the hood of the cloak onto my head. One of the assistants walked to stand in front of me. She reached up and removed the hood from my head. The second female walked in front of me. She was holding a square, white pillow which had my crown resting on top of it. The assistant, who had removed my hood, smiled at me as she delicately reached for the crown with both hands. She extended her arms to place the crown on my head.

Assistant: You are ready now, Princess.

She bowed her head at me and moved to the side. The celestial warrior offered his arm to me and began escorting me down the hall to our left from the Spa Quarters. There was a set of fifteen stairs at the end of this hallway. Then, there was a landing with a window on the wall. The window looked out at the ocean in front of the palace. We turned 180-degrees and then, went down a second set of fifteen stairs to a hallway on the main level.

On our left, we passed a pair of arched doorways which led to the Western Courtyard. We continued down the hallway, past several windows. Through the windows on our right I could see the ocean, while through the windows on our left I could see the giant Western Courtyard. After passing about seven rows of windows, we came to the arched doors of the palace chapel on our right. On our left, was an open archway which led to the main Throne Hall. The open archway had been closed-off by white velvet drapes, but I could hear muttering echoing within the Throne Hall. It sounded like there were hundreds of celestials in there.

91. Artist: Whitesand
Song: Eternity

I became nervous as we approached the grand open archway of the Throne Hall. It was only about 40-feet ahead on our left. Just outside the grand archway, two more warriors stood guard, at attention. I saw the perfectly pressed and cleaned, black runner-rug of the aisle. It was peeking out from the edge of the grand archway. Each of the warriors standing guard, were holding a long golden pole in their outside hands. As we arrived to the archway, the warriors pounded the bottom of their poles on the ground three times in perfect unison. The Throne Hall became quiet, and there was no noise to be heard. Then, music began to play. I heard violins, steady drums, and a small choir. It was majestic and uplifting. It reminded me of hope and joy. It moved me and brought tears of happiness to my eyes.

The warrior who had been escorting me, released my arm from his. Then, he nobly bowed his head to me.

Warrior: They await you, Princess.

He motioned his arm open in the direction of the aisle, showing me the way to proceed without him. I turned the corner of the grand archway. Celestials filled the Throne Hall. They packed the balcony of the second floor and filled the main level on both sides of the aisle. They filled the room between the columns, from wall to wall of its 100-yard length and width. Their heads were all turned in my direction, watching me as I slowly stepped onto the runner-rug and made my way down the aisle.

I looked out toward the end of the aisle. Dennoliel was standing at the top of the stairs, in front of the throne chairs. He stood with his hands folded down in front of him and with the crown still glistening on his head of long, flowing, brown, wavy locks of hair. He was wearing his white, Princedom-Guardian, cloak over his formal attire.

At the foot of the stairs, directly in front of the aisle, I captured the sight of Emalickel and Thorenel. The air from my lungs was stolen from me upon the image of the two of them, standing side-by-side, awaiting my arrival to them. Emalickel stood on the left and Thorenel on the right. Both of them were wearing their crimson red Royal-Princedom cloaks over their formal attire. They, too, had their hands folded down in front of them. They glowed of magnificence. Even though they had just returned from battle, Emalickel's hair was perfectly placed, combed, and trimmed. Thorenel's hair was pulled back into a sleek, low, ponytail. Several strands had come loose from the ponytail and fell gently into his face. Even though they were 100-yards away from me, I noticed they both wore brilliant smiles on their faces.

I progressed down the aisle and noticed celestials bowing their heads to me as I passed them. There were guards wearing golden robes with white capes. There were warriors wearing the black capes with black boots, black pants, and casual dark-red tunics. There were many females wearing gowns of various colors. It was a very much like a royal ball scene. Every head bowed to me as I continued closer to Emalickel and Thorenel, who waited patiently as I took my time stepping carefully.

About halfway down the aisle, I saw Romenciel and Seronimel standing to the left side of the stairs. They were wearing the black Princedom-Warrior cloaks over their more casual, than formal, attire. Romenciel had his hair partially pulled back with a few loose strands falling randomly into his face. Seronimel had his silky, blond hair pulled back completely into a ponytail. Their hands were folded respectfully down in front of them. It must have been a uniform stance for the Princedom brothers.

I came to the last twenty feet of the aisle and noticed Xabiel was standing in the crowd. He was in the front row, to my right, and closest to the stairs. He was wearing the same attire as the guards—golden robes and a white cape. I assumed this was the formal attire of the regular-ranked guardian celestials. Although Xabiel appeared out of place, he maintained the same respectful stance as his brothers. When I passed him, he respectfully gave me a slight bow of his head.

Finally, I came to Emalickel and Thorenel. Each of them held out their innermost hand to me. With my back to the crowd, I placed each of my hands into theirs. My left hand in Emalickel's right hand, and my right hand in Thorenel's left. They both bowed their heads and brought my hands to their lips. I smiled bashfully and whispered to them.

Me: Why does everyone keep bowing their head to me?

Emalickel was the first to answer.

Emalickel: You are the third and final aspect of the Royal-Principality of Lapoi; but I must say, the sight of your presence does make it difficult for one to bow without staring.

Thorenel, always playful, alleviated the need for formalities with his usual straightforward, whimsical comments.

Thorenel: Well excuse me, but I am going to stare . . . I did my bowing—and now I'm just going to let myself stare!

92. Artist: Audiomachine
Song: Morningrise

He was looking at me up and down, not even trying to hide his appraisal. I chuckled under my breath. Their flattery had made me blush. I felt Emalickel guide me around to face the crowd. Emalickel shouted to the crowd of celestials in the palace. His voice echoed from the high ceiling and the walls.

Emalickel: Celestials of Lapoi!

Thorenel and Emalickel each raised one of my hands into the air.

Both: Your princess lives!

The crowd cheered. I was so utterly confused as to why they were making such a big deal out of me. Why was I the last to walk into the Throne Hall? The last time Emalickel returned from receiving the orders, all eyes were on him as he walked down the aisle. This time, all eyes were all on me and I didn't understand why.

The crowd was still cheering when Emalickel leaned in and whispered in my ear.

Emalickel: They celebrate the victory of your safe return. You are their only princess; and they rejoice that you are home, unharmed, and well.

I absorbed the moving scene around me. It made me feel incredibly special to be so loved and adored by real, live celestial beings. It was a privilege to have all their attention focused solely on me at one time. These were the same magnificent, divine beings whom I had read about in religious and historical texts! They existed before the dawn of man. They had been around longer than the Earth itself. Everyone had some association with them. Major religions referred to their types as angels. They had been called aliens and spirit guides. They had even been referred to as gods by ancient civilizations. They were superior beings with divine power radiating all through them, yet they bowed their heads at me. They smiled and cheered for ME!

I couldn't believe what I was witnessing. With my eyes wide, and my mouth frozen open, I was dazed in awe. All I could do was absorb the fantastic scene taking place all around me. It was like a dream—too fascinating to be real. I kept asking myself was I going to wake up? Thorenel leaned into me and whispered words of confirmation.

Thorenel: You will not wake up, my dear; for that would infer you are sleeping.

Emalickel interjected.

Emalickel: You will return to your mortal state soon, but first, we have a celebration in which to partake!

Emalickel turned around to look at Dennoliel and nodded his head. At that, Dennoliel held up both his hands. The celestials became quiet again and listened to him as he spoke.

93. Artist: Olexandr Ignatov
Song: Our Fates are Bound Together

Dennoliel: Today, celestial brethren of Millattus, we have much to celebrate. Not only has our princess returned safely, but the celestials of Haffelnia have drastically diminished their involvement in our affairs. Barthaldeo retreated with only one-third of his legion. Although we still fight a battle on the Earth, our blessed realm has once again triumphed in victory over the negative realms. We have so much for which to be grateful. May all the glory go to God. And now, without further ado, let us celebrate God's favor of Millattus and the safe return of the one and only Princess of Lapoi!

Dennoliel extended his arms in presentation, then motioned for me to join him atop the throne stairs. I looked to Emalickel for reassurance. He smiled and nodded his head to me as he and Thorenel released my hands. I bowed my head humbly and turned to proceed up the stairs. Gathering the excess length of my dress in front of me, I carefully ascended six white marble steps, which were covered by the black runner-rug trimmed in gold. The lions on either side were sitting upright, at attention, with their thick white manes protruding proudly. The light of Auruclerum beamed-in through the chiffon drapes of the archways behind the thrones. The curtains swayed gently with the cool, familiar wintergreen breeze of Lapoi's atmosphere. The entire room seemed to fill with ambient light. A sense of comfort and belonging overcame me. As I brought myself to stand beside the Crown-Prince Dennoliel, the celestials in the Throne Hall, including all six Princedom brothers, raised one fist into the air and shouted in unison.

All: All hail to the Princess, Hadriel!

Lively music began playing again. This time it sounded like cheerful Celtic-renaissance music with lutes, mandolins, and fiddles. All the room began mingling and moving around. Some celestials dispersed to other parts of the palace. There was music, plentiful food and spirits, and light-hearted commencing in every room.

Emalickel and Thorenel didn't move from their places in the front of the aisle. Dennoliel escorted me down the stairs to rejoin them. Romenciel and Seronimel walked in to join us as well. Dennoliel stepped to stand in front of me. He took both my hands into his and made direct eye-contact with me as he spoke.

Dennoliel: The grace of your presence renders us senseless, Princess.

Blushing, I disengaged eye-contact and looked to the floor smiling. He squeezed my hands.

Dennoliel: Do not shy away in your humble ways. Own your status, for it is truth. Keep your eyes lifted—smile and nod with confidence!

I did as he advised, raising my eyes back up to meet his and giving him a nod. Smiling in satisfaction, Dennoliel released my hands, giving them a final squeeze before stepping aside. He turned to converse with his brothers. Xabiel emerged from the crowd to stand with us. Other celestials also began crowding around. They came to introduce themselves, and to discuss the battle amongst one another.

I heard talk of Jamaleo being defeated. Apparently, before he left Haffelnia, Emalickel had taken revenge on him for the fall of Thorenel. One thing I wanted to know was the whereabouts of the Nephilim. I hadn't seen them, and they certainly would not fit in the palace—it would be like having a herd of bulls in a

China shop. During a brief pause in conversation I inquired about them.

Me: Where are the Nephilim now?

Emalickel was first to answer.

Emalickel: They are in Versallus, a large stretch of land on Lapoi we have designated as their own. Drakahdra has been appointed their noble leader. They are most certainly celebrating, as well.

Thorenel leaned in and whispered to me.

Thorenel: I know you want to see. I give you my word we will go to Versallus this evening.

I looked at him, smiling in admiration that he had read my mind so promptly. He winked and smiled back at me. I loved how he winked at me. It was his own little way of showing affection. It was attractive to me that neither Emalickel nor Thorenel were clingy or needy in any way. They were both gentlemen. They were independent and self-reliant. They respected my space, yet showed their love in various ways. They struck my passion through the things they said and how they said them through stimulating conversations in which they engaged me. It was the way they smiled at me, held my hands, protected me, provided for me, tucked my hair behind my ear, and did other gentlemanly things like offering their arm to me for an escort wherever we went.

Dennoliel made an announcement.

Dennoliel: For all those interested in watching a chess tournament between Emalickel and myself, we will begin our game in the Western Courtyard in ten minutes!

Apparently, the celestials were having a debate about who would win a chess game; Dennoliel, who wore the Crown of Lapoi, endowed with Emalickel's abilities, or Emalickel himself. Celestials were placing bets on their abilities. The room grew louder as celestials conversed and debated about the topic.

Emalickel leaned into me and spoke boastfully and loud enough for others to hear.

Emalickel: Worry not, for the game shall not last long.

He called to a nearby celestial who was wearing brown robes and serving others.

Emalickel: Uthesiel, I need a round of mead for my brothers and the Princess.

Uthesiel bowed his head at Emalickel and disappeared from the room.

Celestials draped their arms around Emalickel's and Dennoliel's shoulders, showing their support, as they all made their way outside to the Western Courtyard. I followed behind the crowd of about twenty or thirty rambunctious celestials. I felt a warm, heavy arm drape around my shoulders. I turned to see who it was. I was pleased to see it was Thorenel. He pulled me closer into him as we walked across the palace to the western end.

He pulled himself away for a brief moment to look at me. He did not say anything, but rather shook his head in disbelief and smiled. It was his way of complimenting me without being overbearing or expecting a reply back from me. Then, he brought me back into him as we exited through the doors to the courtyard.

94 Artist: Inward Oceans

Song: Rolling Through

Emalickel and Dennoliel were about to sit down at the chess table in the courtyard. It was late afternoon, and the light of Auruclerum was just over the horizon of the ocean. Clouds blanketed the sky and shaded the ground from bright rays of light. The celestials gathered around the chess table. Several of them stood against nearby statues and urns, or they sat on the ledge of a fountain in the middle of the courtyard. Others rested on nearby benches, while the rest of them conjured chairs. Everyone was holding a drinking cup. Some had horns while others held chalices.

The serving celestial, Uthesiel, reappeared with a tray of drinks. He appeared beside Emalickel and placed one of the chalices on a small table beside his chair. Emalickel looked around for the rest of us. He signaled for Thorenel and I to come over and join him. Thorenel offered his hand to me and guided me through the crowd closer to the chess table. A few celestial warriors were sitting on a bench in front of the chess table, adjacent to Emalickel and Dennoliel. The celestials on this bench turned around when Thorenel and I arrived. Immediately, they jumped up from their seats and cleared the bench for us to sit. Then, they conjured their own chairs.

Uthesiel handed Dennoliel his mead, then he handed one to Thorenel. Thorenel passed the mead to me, then took another one from Uthesiel for himself. We sat down on the bench. Thorenel held his drink in his right hand and placed his left arm along the back of the bench behind me.

Seronimel and Romenciel were standing behind a bench across the table from us. They were talking to each other, leaning on the bench with their hands. Both of them had their cloaks pushed behind their shoulders. Their attire was black and sleeveless. They both wore three-inch thick leather straps around their wrists and biceps. Uthesiel made his way toward them, and they booth took a drink from his tray.

Seronimel licked his lips and took a refreshing breath after his first sip. He looked around the courtyard. When his eyes met mine, he smiled and nodded his head upward in greeting. I was happy to better know Seronimel. He was still very mysterious to me, but I felt comfortable talking and interacting with him. He was a very attractive celestial, along with Dennoliel, and I was glad it would be them who pursued my daughter of the Earth as their companion. I remembered Seronimel's powers and thought about how safe she would be in his presence. I couldn't believe he was able to completely control other celestials with his thoughts! He could make them do anything. I wondered if he had ever used his powers to control the celestials of other realms. I knew he was unable to control any of the Princedom brothers, but what about other celestials of other realms?

Thorenel cleared his throat in an exaggerated manner. I turned to look at him. His eyes were wide and they were fixated right on me. Then, without moving his head, his eyes moved over to look at Seronimel in annoyance. I assumed Thorenel didn't like me thinking about Seronimel's powers. They preferred to keep his powers concealed. I looked at Seronimel, who was watching us as he began drinking heavily from his cup. Seronimel looked around the crowd in search for a distraction. Finally, he turned to Romenciel and began a conversation with him. Whatever he had said, it made Romenciel laugh intensely.

Xabiel was nowhere to be found. I assumed he was resentful of Dennoliel and did not want to watch the game. I also did not see Clive anywhere. He was probably inside playing pool in the

Billiard and Lounge. That had been one of his favorite rooms when I was showing him around the palace.

Suddenly, I heard the crowd groan. Dennoliel appeared to have made a bad move. He began looking around the courtyard.

Dennoliel: Where's Uthesiel? Tell him to turn on the lights. It is getting too dark out here. I cannot see the board very well.

Emalickel teased at Dennoliel.

Emalickel: What's wrong? I can see the board fine.

Dennoliel ignored his brother's smart remark and spotted Uthesiel.

Dennoliel: Uthesiel? Would you turn on the courtyard lights?

A few moments later, the entire courtyard lit up with lights overhead. The lights were strung together in a clear netting and draped above the courtyard. It was radiant the way everything glowed beneath the ambient lighting. The game continued for a while longer. We sipped our drinks and watched and laughed as the game progressed.

Finally, Dennoliel made an attention-grabbing move.

Dennoliel: Check.

Emalickel stared at Dennoliel for a moment with a sly smile. After a brief pause, Emalickel looked at the board and lifted one of his chess pieces. Maintaining the sly smile, he looked back up at Dennoliel while placing the chess piece firmly down for his final move. He then grabbed his chalice and eased back in his chair, before gulping down the rest of his mead. He gave a nod of his head at Dennoliel and spoke with great confidence.

Emalickel: Checkmate, brother.

Dennoliel couldn't believe his eyes. He stood up from the table and teased Emalickel.

Dennoliel: You can read my thoughts through this crown!

Emalickel chuckled.

Emalickel: Surely you can find a better excuse than that?

Dennoliel rubbed his hands through his hair.

Dennoliel: Best two out of three?

95. Artist: Really Slow Motion
Song: Suns and Stars

The music changed to a new song. Emalickel perked up when he heard it.

Emalickel: Not this time . . .

He stood and turned his head to look at me. His smile was youthful.

Emalickel: I feel dancing.

Making his way toward the bench, he extended his hand to me. Obliged, I placed my hand into his and stood up from where I was sitting. He pulled me in closer to him and spoke to Thorenel.

Emalickel: Mind if I steal her away for a dance?

Still sitting on the bench, Thorenel removed his arm from around my back. He held his drink with both hands and brought it to his mouth for a gulp. Then, he leaned forward to rest both arms on his legs.

Thorenel: If she so wishes.

Thorenel nodded and extended his hand out, offering me to Emalickel. Then he took another gulp of his drink and resumed his initial position on the bench. Emalickel escorted me to an open spot in the courtyard. The lights shined down upon us like romantic candles. The music was beautiful. It sounded like a full orchestra backed by the harmony of a heavenly choir. Emalickel pulled me in close to him and held my hand as we danced. His eyes looked deeply into mine. He was smiling down at me like child at Christmas.

Emalickel: Listen to this music.

I smiled back at him in approval and with appreciation.

Emalickel: Creativity is one of God's greatest gift to man.

We danced as the song continued. With the night sky and the glowing lights above us, it was as if we were dancing among the stars. The other celestials gathered around us to watch our dance, but they blended in with the darkness of the background. The lights seemed to only shine on us in that moment. Emalickel twirled me around a few times and caught me in his arms. He looked deeply into my eyes as we spun around together, hand in hand. He was passionate and exhibited such respect and protection of me.

Thorenel, who had been sitting on the bench, stood up and began walking our way. He was chewing on a piece of something brown—a toothpick or a piece of wheat perhaps. He flung it away before coming over to Emalickel and me.

Thorenel: A lovely sight the two of you are.

He took one of my hands into his. Then, he looked at Emalickel.

Thorenel: Are we ready to visit the Nephilim?

8

THE LAND OF VERSALLUS

96. Artist: Antti Martikainen
Song: Northland

Around the courtyard, the other celestials were talking amongst themselves. Some of them had already teleported away. Emalickel reiterated Thorenel's invitation for us to visit the Nephilim.

Emalickel: Yes, let us travel to Versallus.

Everything started to fade into darkness. I felt the wind pick up and blow onto my face a cool breeze. Then, everything brightened back up again, but we were no longer in the courtyard. We were in a completely different land, unlike any I had ever seen on Lapoi before. He first thing I did was look up to see if Emalickel and Thorenel were with me. The last time I went to an unfamiliar land, I found myself with an enemy. I was relieved when I saw them looking down at me with smiling, comforting eyes. They seemed to understand my need for reassurance.

Thorenel: Worry not, beloved; we are here.

I looked at the land around me. It was cooler and breezier than any of the other lands of Lapoi. We seemed to be situated on an elevated high-point—atop a mountain. Behind us was a slope which was made up of evergreen trees and a large forest. Giant structures resembling oversized Viking longhouses were perched throughout the slope of the mountain, having an extraordinary view. The structures were made from elements of the land including stone and wood. The structures were large enough to comfortably house a thirty-foot Nephilim. All of the structures were lit on the inside by candle light. We could hear laughter and horseplay nearby. Suddenly, Emalickel spotted something. He motioned for us to come to him.

Emalickel: Follow me. This way.

We were headed toward an enormous fortress fenced-in by walls of wooden slats. The slats were the light color of birch trees. They were placed together to form a barrier around the outside. The elaborate fortress, within the barrier, was made from stone, sticks, and straw. The fortress contained multiple extensions and wings. The whole structure itself measured about 300-yards wide, 500-yards deep, and 200-yards tall. It was colossal in size! There seemed to be three total levels making up the entire construction, each about seventy-feet tall. Each level had its own sloping roof. Two tall, round towers were situated on either side of the fortress. On the top of these towers appeared to be an open balcony, as I could see a railing. Torches were lit all over the outside of the fortress—hundreds, perhaps thousands of them. The light of these torches flickered peacefully in the dusk. I was pulled out of my gazing-trance when I heard Emalickel's voice.

Emalickel: And that must be Drakahdra's dwelling.

Me: Did he build this?

Emalickel: Indeed, he did. Each Nephilim has built his own homestead. Drakahdra was provided more land since he is the leader of the Nephilim.

We walked up a hill, on a gravel pathway, which led to the main gate of the fortress. The sound of music, laughing, and shuffling feet became louder as we approached. Several Nephilim were located just inside the gate. Two were standing guard outside the gate, but the others were horsing around in the open yard of the inside. When the two Nephilim guards noticed Emalickel, they stepped aside and allowed us to enter through the gate. We walked down a straight pathway, about fifty-yards, to the stairs leading to the main door of the fortress. The stairs were gigantic; each step was about three feet tall. The doorknob to the wooden door was above Emalickel's head. The door itself must have been fifty or more feet tall and about twenty-feet wide. Instead of trying to open the door manually, Emalickel used a wave of force to push open the door.

Upon entering, I was immediately taken back by the monstrosity of the place. I felt so small. Everything was so extravagant. They lit the place only with candles and chandeliers—hundreds of them. There were wooden tables, chairs, and benches. Thick, soft furs hung behind the chairs and were thrown across the benches. Some furs hung on the walls. A series of giant, rectangular fire-pits were situated evenly through the center of what looked like a throne hall. The floor and walls were made from grey stone. Stone columns were evenly dispersed all throughout the room for structural reinforcement.

Nephilim were engaged in humorous conversations as they sat at the tables or roamed the large room with drinking horns. As I looked up, the ceiling was open all the way to the second floor, similar to the structure of the Palace of Lapoi. There was a balcony on the second floor which overlooked the grand room below.

97. Artist: Trobar De Morte
Song: The Bear's Dance

The music was lively and loud. The room was also filled with echoing voices of the rambunctious Nephilim. Although, the music was rather appealing. It had a Celtic tavern feel to it. It was upbeat and fun. I swayed my head to the beat. Meanwhile, I couldn't help but express how small I felt. Looking up at the vastness of the room, I leaned into Thorenel and spoke with a half-joking tone.

Me: So this must be the perspective of a house cat . . . I feel so small in here!

I heard Thorenel chuckle under his breath, but he too was busy absorbing the unbelievable sight around him. There was so much going on. Two Nephilim were grunting in an arm-wrestling match at a nearby table. Several others were dancing and clowning around in a drunken stupor. There were many who were engaged in seemingly entertaining conversations. Their laughter filled the halls and echoed from the high ceilings.

When I looked outside the windows, I noticed several torches were lit. I also saw movement, but it was hard to tell what was happening out there. I pointed in the direction of the windows and turned to Emalickel.

Me: What's going on out there?

Emalickel: Would you like to go see?

I knew it was probably quieter outside, but I did not want to interfere with any plans the brothers had for inside; I shrugged my shoulders and nodded.

There were several doorways located along the walls that led to the outside. There was a lot of commotion and traffic between these doors and us. Instead of risking being tripped upon by a Nephilim, Emalickel brought me into his chest and prepared to teleport. I knew this because of his words to Thorenel.

Emalickel: We will see you out there, brother.

98. Artist: Antti Martikainen
Song: Sons of Avalon

That is when I felt a cool breeze wisp through my hair. Everything had momentarily faded into black. Then, everything reappeared into a new scenery. We were outside. It was dark—lit only by the fire of torches. Nephilim were mingling, laughing, and roughing each other up. They were situated in a large circle surrounding two Nephilim who were fighting. It didn't appear to be a real fight, but rather for play, as if they were sparring. I saw one of the sparring Nephilim smiling at his opponent.

Nephilim: Your punch has quite the bite, Rahnukah!

They both chuckled before bumping fists together and continuing the fight. The surrounding Nephilim were eager to watch the fight, with mead in hand. I was more interested in learning more about the land. I turned to Emalickel to ask him some questions.

Me: How long has all this been here?

Emalickel: The land of Versallus has always been here. Prior to the release of the Nephilim, it was vacant. I have always thought this land to be beautiful, yet I was disappointed there

was nothing here of purpose. I am pleased the Nephilim have settled the land with their homesteads.

Me: How did they build everything so fast?

Emalickel: When we returned from Haffelnia, the Nephilim constructed them. The Nephilim are hybrids and have some of the same abilities as we celestials. Creating through thought is one of the easier abilities for them to master.

I was astonished and also slightly envious. I wanted special abilities. Out of the corner of my eye, I saw Emalickel staring at me before he spoke.

Emalickel: All good things come in their due time. You are not yet ready, but someday you will be.

He had been reading my mind. Then, I heard Seronimel's voice. He must have followed along with us when we left the palace.

Seronimel: Excuse me brothers, I mean not to interrupt, but have you seen what is happening over there?

We turned our heads to look at Seronimel. He was pointing at a large fire pit toward the back corner of the wooden fence. About forty Nephilim were gathered around someone.

Seronimel: It is Xabiel. He is conversing with the Nephilim.

There was a moment of awkward silence before Thorenel finally said something.

Thorenel: So? There are conversations going on all around us, Seronimel. What is your point?

Seronimel: After Dennoliel designated me to replace Xabiel's position over the warriors, I overheard many of them talking about Xabiel's plan. He desires to form a rogue-group that

will infiltrate the mortal plane and fight the negative beings from the inside. I already informed Dennoliel, but I fear Xabiel is currently trying to draw the Nephilim into his plan.

Emalickel brought his hand to his chin and thought for a moment. He narrowed his eyes and tightened his lips as he gazed across the land at Xabiel. Thorenel exhibited the exact same expression. Then, Emalickel bowed his head at Seronimel in respect.

Emalickel: Thank you, brother. I shall certainly see to this.

Seronimel bowed his head back to Emalickel. We all became silent. The three celestial brothers appeared to be lost in thought. I refrained from speaking as not to disrupt their processing. After a minute, Dennoliel materialized himself, twenty-feet from us, in the yard of the fortress. He approached Emalickel.

Dennoliel: Yes, brother? You called for me?

Emalickel's tone seemed perturbed.

Emalickel: You informed me Xabiel had been removed from his rank because of his defiance and disrespect, but you never disclosed his corrupt conversations about rebellion with the warriors.

Knowing Seronimel was the one who had briefed Emalickel on this issue, Dennoliel peered at him with bitterness. He then attempted to steer Emalickel's irritation toward Seronimel.

Dennoliel: There are some details of which I had planned to inform you after the celebrations of this evening—including how Seronimel demonstrated his full-fledged abilities on our very own celestials. I assume he was trying to show-off in front of—

Emalickel snapped at Dennoliel with an interruption.

Emalickel: Do not redirect this conversation! You are the Crown-Prince! You are accountable for establishing order among the kingdom and for finding resolutions to potential problems. Xabiel's corruption is a MUCH more concerning matter than Seronimel's ego!

Even though Dennoliel appeared to be collected, his voice gave away his frazzled and uncomfortable state of being.

Dennoliel: The issue of Xabiel has already been handled. Xabiel was made very well aware of the consequences should he persist.

Without a smile, Emalickel stared at Dennoliel while pointing in the direction of Xabiel. Emalickel leaned toward Dennoliel, scorning him through his teeth.

Emalickel: And yet, he still persists... this time, with the Nephilim.

Romenciel walked-up from behind us. He was concerned. He must have telepathically felt the tension occurring between the brothers.

Romenciel: Everything alright over here?

Emalickel was too involved in his focus to answer. Instead, Thorenel took the lead in the conversation.

Thorenel: Not particularly. We were gone for less than a day, yet it seems long enough for the household to fall into disorder. Apparently Seronimel enjoys strutting through the palace, impressing guests by parading his endowed powers on our very own celestials. Meanwhile, Xabiel has fallen into the ways of corruption, trying to persuade others to defy orders.

He has spoken in secrecy about forming a group of rogues to infiltrate the Earth and begin an internal battle against the negative forces.

Emalickel smoldered with fury. Romenciel lifted one of his eyebrows at Dennoliel, who's head was already lowered with shame. Without saying anything, Emalickel grunted and suddenly stormed-off toward Xabiel. He was fed-up. His cape whipped violently behind him as he paced rapidly to confront his dishonest brother.

Thorenel immediately followed him.

Romenciel: Uh oh...we should probably follow them—for the safety of Xabiel.

Seronimel and Dennoliel nodded their heads in agreement and proceeded behind Emalickel and Thorenel. Without any other option, I followed behind them. I certainly didn't want to get lost among the giants—plus, I was uncertain of what was about to transpire.

When Emalickel arrived at the fire pit, he yanked Xabiel up by the collar of his shirt and brought him closer. Xabiel appeared stunned, as if he didn't see this coming.

Emalickel: You and I have much to discuss, wayward brother.

Trying to calm his breaths and appear complacent, Xabiel replied with a cool tone.

Xabiel: I get the feeling this won't be a casual conversation.

Emalickel brought Xabiel even closer to him—nose to nose. He spoke to him through his teeth and under his breath.

Emalickel: No, it certainly will not.

The Nephilim sitting by the fire, all started to stand up. They stood tall, in an offensive manner. It appeared they were considering defending Xabiel. Thorenel wasted no time walking closer to the scene. He shook-out his hands; each activating some kind of pulsating blue energy in his palms. In unison Romenciel, Seronimel, and Dennoliel stepped-up to join him. Romenciel grabbed the two-handed sword from behind his back. Seronimel held his palms out in front, forming a transparent wall of unknown energy. Dennoliel conjured two axes in each hand. He twirled them in a circular motion, perhaps in preparation for battle or to draw attention to them.

The surrounding conversations and commotions subsided into silence, as curious onlookers focused their attention in our direction.

Emalickel still had a tight hold on Xabiel, but Xabiel managed to look at the Nephilim with his eyes, who were all lurking behind Emalickel. Emalickel slightly tilted his head in their direction, letting them know of his awareness of their close proximity. Xabiel shook his head at the Nephilim.

Xabiel: Don't do it—that's a bad idea, gentlemen.

Thorenel was quick to elaborate.

Thorenel: Indeed. It would end with a most-unfortunate outcome on your end.

Romenciel, Dennoliel, and Seronimel all kept an intimidating expression. Emalickel looked from the corner of his eye at them. He remained very still and very stiff. His jaw was clenched. He reminded me of an angry feline preparing to attack at any given moment. He took a few more breaths, then slung Xabiel away from him. Xabiel stumbled to regain his footing. Emalickel turned to walk away and said a few more words to Xabiel, without even turning around to look at him.

Emalickel: I will expect your presence at the palace tomorrow morning.

Then he stopped and turned around to look at his other brothers.

Emalickel: That goes for all of you.

The purple-hued light of the two moons beamed down onto Emalickel splendidly. It contrasted perfectly with his dark hair, and accentuated his aqua-blue eyes. The royal red cloak he wore, reflected the light and thus seemed to glow. In fact, he glowed more than any other being out there. He was sovereign, polished, and absolutely impeccable.

Without saying anything else, he turned back around and made his way through the crowd until he disappeared from sight. I knew he must have been terribly upset with Xabiel. He had never walked away from me and abandoned me like that before. I wasn't offended he had left because I knew he likely needed some space to bring himself back into balance before being able to continue with the evening. Emalickel knew the other brothers were present with me, otherwise he wouldn't have left me.

The attendants of Xabiel's meeting around the fire-pit had dispersed. Thorenel placed his arm around my shoulder and spoke to me in a lively manner.

Thorenel: C'mon, let's go watch some of these titans fight before we leave!

We made our way back to the circle where the sparring had been. This time, two other Nephilim were about to enter the ring. The audience of tipsy Nephilim were hooting, hollering, and carrying-on. None of them seemed too concerned about anything. They seemed to be enjoying their freedom; they were festive and carefree, lighthearted and cheerful.

99. Artist: Really Slow Motion
Song: Purple Skies

Thorenel and I stayed in Versallus for a while. We made our way through the exuberant crowd outside. The cold ground crunched beneath our feet. None of the other brothers were around anymore. I assumed they had dispersed in different directions. This gave Thorenel and I exclusive time together. We found great pleasure sharing each other's company. While we indulged in various spirits and cheese, we watched the sparring matches of the Nephilim from a nearby wooden table. The Nephilim fight-matches were interesting to watch. I was able to witness a variety of their abilities. Every step they took made the ground rumble.

Time passed, but all too quickly. After a while, Thorenel leaned into me and spoke softly.

Thorenel: We should head back to the palace.

I was not ready for the night to end. I was having way too much fun. Lapoi was a place of freedom, peace, and complete satisfaction. I knew if we went back to the palace, it meant the night was coming to a close. Then I realized, perhaps the festivities would continue at the palace; after all, there was so much to celebrate that evening.

Thorenel stood up and offered his hand to me. His golden hair reflected the purple light of the moons. His hair contrasted superbly with the red of the royal cloak. I became immediately entranced upon looking into his face. Like a moth mesmerized by light, I stood up and took his hand without my eyes leaving the sight of his flawless face. He expressed a certain smile. It was not a wide grin showing his teeth, (although that smile also charmed me) but rather he displayed a relaxed smile, with his lips together, revealing the small dimples on each side of his face.

Time had become frozen, on that particular frame of Thorenel. All sounds faded, except for the enchanting music. All other images were blurred. Thorenel became illuminated, in high-definition, while everything else faded into black. My heart raced, and my stomach performed flips. I was beguiled by all of his splendor. In a sense, I had totally slipped away from reality. My mind was mesmerized in that one singular image of him.

100. Artist: Fractured Light Music
Song: Salvation

Suddenly, I was jerked out of my entrancement when Thorenel spoke.

Thorenel: We are here.

I took a few labored breaths and looked around to regain my composure. We were in the palace aisle. The place was still packed with celestials who were celebrating along with the merry music in the background. I looked back at Thorenel again. His expression turned to one of concern.

Thorenel: Are you alright, love?

I was still trying to reorient myself. I stared at him, smiled, and shook my head in disbelief of the excessiveness of his aesthetic appeal. My answer was a whisper, for my voice would not yet work properly.

Me: Yes.

I cleared my throat and straightened myself up before trying to speak again. Blinking a few times and widening my eyes, I managed to refocus on the happenings of the present moment. Thorenel was still looking at me with concern. This time, I nodded when I answered.

Me: Yes . . . Yes, I'm fine.

Still seeming unconvinced, Thorenel offered his arm to me. I grabbed hold and he began guiding me toward the throne area. On the way, we approached a celestial with a serving tray of chalices. Thorenel reached out with his free-hand and grabbed one as we passed. We stopped for a moment. Thorenel took a sip of the drink, and then offered it to me. I obliged and savored a sip before giving the chalice back to him.

Thorenel: Come. This way.

We started walking again. There were celestials everywhere. They moved out of our way as we progressed down the aisle; it seemed as though they sensed we were coming—or perhaps Thorenel telepathically communicated with them unbeknownst to me. They all cleared the aisle as we approached them. They were staring and smiling at us in approval. I wondered if all of Lapoi truly approved of me, or if they simply accepted me as the one chosen by their Royal-Princedoms.

Thorenel had read my thoughts and addressed them accordingly.

Thorenel: I can assure you; they approve of you. They admire you and adore you, Princess.

Me: How can you be so certain?

We had finally arrived at the throne stairs. Thorenel proceeded up the stairs with me still attached to his arm. No one was in the throne area nor on the Grand Balcony. Thorenel stopped when we had arrived at the top of the stairs. He released his arm from me and turned to face me directly. Bending down, he put his face very close to mine. He answered me after receiving eye contact from me. His tone was very serious.

Thorenel: There is yet so much for you to learn.

Me: Please, I'm listening.

Thorenel stood up straight again and searched the crowd.

Thorenel: Not without Emalickel. Let us go onto the balcony.

101. Artist: Wodkah
Song: The Last Butterfly

As we ascended the second set of stairs behind the throne chairs, we passed under the central of three giant archways opening to the Grand Balcony. We passed two cherry blossom trees as we proceeded across the small bridge of the radiantly-lit spa pool. I could still hear music playing, although it became distant as we continued further away.

It was nighttime as we proceed onto the Grand Balcony. The two moons beamed their light onto the Valley of Dillectus. In the glow of the atmosphere, I noticed the Nephilim had begun to congregate in the valley. Their sparring tournament had apparently been relocated to Dillectus. I was confused. Thorenel provided clarity.

Thorenel: I initiated this. We were having so much fun that I commanded them to continue the remainder of their tournament here!

He smiled with his eyes and offered for me to take a seat on a bench near the edge of the balcony. In preparation for the tournament, the Nephilim lit torches all around. One-by-one, the torches flickered among the Valley of Dillectus as they rapidly became lit. The entire valley became filled with hundreds of them. The view was magical. It reminded me of a lantern festival or a candlelight ceremony. The beauty of the scene below rendered me stunned.

The Nephilim all started chanting. Their voices roared like thunder.

Nephilim: Uhn ah tufah nich! Uhn ah tufah nich! Uhn ah tufah nich!

The sound of their voices permeated through my feet and traveled up my spine. I wondered what the words of their chant meant. Thorenel had just sat down beside me. He leaned back, with one leg propped up by the knee of his other leg. He gazed out at the valley and smiled in amusement.

Thorenel: They are saying, "We are afraid not."

I smiled humbly at his prompt awareness of my thoughts. His and Emalickel's attentiveness never ceased to amaze me. I wondered about Thorenel's impression of the Nephilim.

Me: What do you think of them? Do you think it was a good idea to release them—will they remain loyal?

There was a long silence before Thorenel answered. Instead he took his time contemplating. He squinted his eyes and chewed on his inner cheek, in the same manner as Emalickel when he was thinking.

Thorenel: They are an elite force who supplement our

warriors, yet I do not fully trust them. My trust in them must be earned in time through their actions.

Thorenel shifted his legs to lean himself forward. He turned his head and gleamed at me.

Thorenel: All that aside, we will never have any regrets for releasing the Nephilim—after all, they led us to you.

Just then, Emalickel approached from the other side of Thorenel. He walked up to the balcony railing and looked down at the Nephilim in the valley.

Emalickel: I am with you, brother. Although they have not yet gained our full trust, they should be given the chance to earn it. The Nephilim have proven their loyalty this day in pursuance of retrieving the irreplaceable jewel which comprises our hearts.

Emalickel turned himself to admire me.

Emalickel: Delivered by the hand of their honor, she sits with us this night—the revered Princess of Lapoi.

I felt myself beginning to blush. I humbly chuckled as I responded.

Me: I still don't understand why I deserve to be on such a pedestal.

Emalickel squatted down in front of me and placed his hands on my shoulders. He looked up at Thorenel. As if they were communicating telepathically, Thorenel nodded at him in approval before standing and taking himself to look over the balcony rail. Emalickel returned his eyes to me.

Emalickel: I think it is time you hear a story. I want you to

listen carefully. Do not ask questions until the story has been told.

I could tell something was about to be revealed to me—something in which Emalickel was preparing me to digest. I nervously nodded to him, without saying a word. Emalickel stood up and walked to stand beside Thorenel at the railing. They both turned around to face me before Emalickel began speaking.

102. Artist: Brunuhville
Song: Forevermore

Emalickel: Do you remember the night I spoke to you in a vision about the creation of the Heavens and Earth? I showed you the story of Haelael and of Adam and Eve. I revealed to you the refined details described briefly in the book of Genesis?

Without speaking, I nodded.

Emalickel: If you will recall, Eve was tempted by Haelael to know more than the pure innocence in the Garden of Eden. She desired to gain the knowledge of fear, shame, and destruction; as those concepts were unknown by the residents of Eden.

Thorenel had conjured a chalice in his hand. He drank from it, then handed it to Emalickel, and continued from where Emalickel had left off.

Thorenel: After Eve was filled with knowledge of the negative realm, she became distraught. Adam rushed to her aid. She shared, with Adam, the matters disclosed by Haelael. Adam loved Eve immensely, and although he knew she had done

wrong, he wanted to be a part of everything about her. Whatever her disobedient fate may be, he wanted to share in the same fate with her. So, without hesitation, he listened to her and gained the forbidden knowledge for himself.

Emalickel stepped forward and sat down on the bench next to me.

Emalickel: God knew He must preserve the purity of Lapoi. Instead of sending Adam and Eve to dwell among the negative realms, he desired to see Millattus grow and evolve. Thus, He created the mortal plane of existence. He cast Adam and Eve from the celestial plane of Lapoi to dwell in the mortal plane of Earth. There they would encounter good and evil, fear and love, abundance and famine, peace and war, and life and death. They would remain there, experiencing all of those things, oblivious to the perfection of their celestial origins, until they had reached an evolved level of spirituality and became humbled by the Omnipotence of God. Only then, would they begin remembering their origins; at which time they would see the value of righteousness and become worthy of returning to the celestial plane.

Emalickel stopped talking for a moment. I wondered what the point of this story was. What did it have to do with my concern of the celestials accepting me as a revered princess? I saw Emalickel look at Thorenel. Emalickel exhibited an expression of hesitation. He pressed his lips together and sighed deeply. Thorenel nodded his head at Emalickel, as if encouraging him to continue.

Emalickel: The reason I have disclosed all of this to you, the reason I felt compelled to tell you all of these things, is because it provides proof of why you are so easily accepted and admired by the celestials of Millattus.

103. Artist: Brunuhville
Song: Timeless

He paused for a moment to collect his thoughts. He scratched his head. He was trying to think of the best way to form his words before he spoke.

Emalickel: As you know, Thorenel and I were created from a unified energy. We are the Royal-Princedoms of Lapoi; for we were the first created in this realm of Millattus. Before we were split into two energies, we were one. That singular energy, before it was split . . . it was Adam. We are Adam.

I was speechless. I narrowed my eyebrows at him, trying to absorb what he had just revealed to me. He looked at Thorenel. They both appeared worried about my reaction. Thorenel walked closer to Emalickel and took the chalice from him for a drink. Then, returning the chalice to Emalickel, he pushed through the silence in continuing the story.

Thorenel: Before Adam and Eve were cast-down to the mortal plane, God split Adam into two aspects. One aspect would experience mortality until he was spiritually fulfilled—the other aspect remained in Lapoi as an overseer. Emalickel, was the aspect whom walked the Earth, while I, Thorenel was the aspect whom remained in Lapoi as the Prince.

I looked downward, trying to focus, resisting the urge to ask questions prematurely.

Emalickel: From that point forward, other celestials were created. Every one of them was split into two aspects. One aspect of each celestial-pair would be sent to engage in the mortal experience while the other aspect remained in Lapoi. After a series of lifetimes, I, Adam, had finally achieved my

spiritual awakening and was able to return to Lapoi in my celestial form. As a result of my extended experience in the mortal plane, I became the primary Prince, and Thorenel become secondary.

Emalickel shook his head. He was breathing deeply. He looked to Thorenel, wanting for him to pick up the story from there. Thorenel spoke nervously, but then cleared his throat in attempt to compose himself.

104. Artist: Fearless Motivation
Song: Proof

Thorenel: As for Eve, she, too, was split into two aspects. One aspect was cast-down to the mortal plane, while the other aspect returned to her origin in Jesserion. After their first life-cycle in the mortal plane, Adam and Eve ceased to remember each other. Oftentimes, they would encounter one another in lifetimes that followed the first. In several of those lifetimes, they even fell in love with each other, but never did they remember their true origins. Finally, the masculine soul that was Adam had evolved to the fullest extent, and he returned to Lapoi as Emalickel. Eve, however, remained in the mortal plane. Her destiny was to gain a much deeper knowledge. She had greater lengths to evolve in her spiritual path. She has remained on the Earth for many more lifetimes.

Emalickel interrupted Thorenel by clearing his throat. He and brought himself to bend down in front of me. He looked me straight in the eyes and placed his hands on my knees. He was shaking.

Emalickel: Until recently, I have failed to understand why was I hearing your thoughts from the celestial plane. Why was I

feeling your Earthly emotions? Why was I so drawn to you—to Adrienne of Earth. There is a reason you and I are connected, Hadriel—we are connected deeply.

He arose and motioned, with his head, for Thorenel to stand next to him. They stood side-by-side. Both of them were gently smiling at me. Emalickel reached his hands down and assisted me in standing.

Emalickel: Do you remember when you saw me for the first time at the lake? I seemed familiar to you, but you could not explain why. The reason is because we have met numerous times. Our fate has always been intertwined, drawing us to each other, in many different lifetimes. In the first of these lifetimes, I was called Adam.

He paused for dramatic effect. He stepped a bit closer to me and leaned down so that our eyes were level. Emalickel gazed at me intensely.

Emalickel: And you, dearly beloved, in the first of your lifetimes . . .

My heart raced. I was excited, nervous, and scared—all at the same time. I knew what he was about to say. Then, he said it.

Emalickel: . . . you were called Eve.

Even though I had sensed he was about to say those words, I still froze in shock upon hearing spoken. Thinking of something was completely different than actually hearing it. I was astonished and speechless. With my mouth open, my eyebrows narrowed, and my head shaking, I finally found my voice to respond. I chuckled in disbelief.

Me: There's no way that's true.

Thorenel stepped toward me and stood next to Emalickel.

Thorenel: That is why the celestials treat you with such respect. They have you to thank for initiating the advancement of our realm. Without your boldness, we would not be on the leading edge of creation. God favors mankind because of their ability to overcome evil, despite its constant presence among them. Because of your destined choice in the Garden of Eden, man has been given the opportunity to prove themselves as the ultimate warriors of faith. No other celestial or realm has ever endured such a challenge.

105. Artist: Two Steps From Hell
Song: Peace of Mind

Thorenel walked around me until he was behind me. I remained in my position as I listened to him speak. He placed his hands on my shoulders. I could not see his face, but his touch sent a relaxing and receptive energy through me.

Thorenel: It was not by coincidence that Emalickel was drawn to your energy when your spirit began awakening. You are our third aspect. It could be none other than you to stand at our side. This is where you have rightfully belonged since the beginning of our creation. You have always been a part of us, embodying the third aspect of the Royal-Princedom energy.

I managed to gulp and relax my throat. I looked beyond Emalickel to scan the land in the distance, but I wasn't specifically focusing on anything. My face was likely glazed-over as I attempted to swallow this information. Still, I questioned whether or not I had heard them correctly. Perhaps I had misunderstood something? There was no way I was the embodiment of Eve. I could not find any words to speak.

Emalickel looked slightly remorseful.

Emalickel: I regret overwhelming you, but it was time you knew this. It is a part of who you are—learning about your true origin is a part of your evolution.

A silence fell upon us. Emalickel moved his eyes to look behind me, at Thorenel. Then, he nodded. I wondered if the two of them were communicating telepathically again. A moment later, Emalickel focused his attention back to me.

Emalickel: There is something we want you to see. You are ready, if you are willing.

9

THE VILLAGE OF RASAEVULUS

106. Artist: Marcus Warner
Song: Africa

Emalickel held a patient gaze on me, waiting for my approval. I scooted myself to the edge of the bench.

Me: You have my attention.

I noticed Emalickel glance at Thorenel before taking a few steps forward toward me. He leaned down to bring his eyes closer to mine, and he took my hand in his.

Emalickel: We must travel. Will you come?

Thorenel came around me to stand next to Emalickel. He took my other hand and smiled reassuringly while urging me to my feet. Although I completely trusted the brothers, I was not confident in my ability to process whatever they were about to show me. Unsure of what to expect, I smiled nervously and nodded my head. Emalickel pulled me in closer and whispered softly in my ear.

Emalickel: Princess, suppress your fears, and just close your eyes.

I was completely trusting of Emalickel and Thorenel. With a deep breath, I slowly closed my eyes. There was a warm wind which whirled all around me. It smelled of sweet vanilla. Both brothers tightened their hold on me. We became weightless for a moment, then I felt solid ground beneath my feet again. The brothers relaxed their hold of me. Then, I heard Thorenel whisper.

Thorenel: Open your eyes.

When I opened my eyes, I scanned my surroundings. I was outside in a scene of nature. It was daylight there. Everything was glowing as when the sun rises. It was all tinted with a golden-hue, as if I were looking through a golden filter. I stood in a forest of trees with orange and yellow leaves. Gently rolling mountains stood in the distance beyond a vast field of grassy hills. I heard the sound of trickling water behind me. I turned around and noticed a large creek running perpendicular to us. It contained a few boulders which created slow rapids in the waters. This creek was surrounded by trees which also ran along the bank.

Still turned in that direction, I looked through the tree-line of the woods. Beyond the woods was a meadow. The meadow extended down to a valley at the bottom of the hill. There was a large fjord just beyond the meadow. The body of water from the fjord was the source of the creek. I saw smoke rising to the partly cloudy sky. It was coming from a small primitive village located in the meadow.

I could hear the sound of metal hammering against metal. I also heard distant voices and laughter. All the structures in the village were made of timber and stone. The walls of the buildings were made from interwoven twigs and branches, while the roofs appeared thatched. Smoke was coming from each roof. There was movement in the village as people walked around performing various tasks and merrily conversing among themselves. The village was surrounded by a thick stone-washed wall containing a large gate at the front. The gate entrance was more elaborate in its structure than the rest of the walls resembling ramparts.

I turned around to once again face the area with mountains in the distance. Between the woods and the mountains was open land containing sporadic evergreen trees. In the middle of this land was a log cabin structure. About one hundred acres of the land surrounding the cabin was enclosed by a black fence similar to the kind seen on a ranch. In that direction, the creek extended from the woods toward the mountains. There were horses with their heads down as they ate the rich vegetation on the ground. In the distance, I noticed a heard of moose grazing at the foot of the mountainside.

I lost myself in wonder. Emalickel's voice brought me back to the present moment. He was behind me and had placed his hands on my shoulders.

Emalickel: All of which you see, this entire land and everything here, is a physical manifestation of your desires brought-forth by the power of God.

I squinted my eyes in confusion. Thorenel had taken himself to sit on a nearby log. He elaborated on Emalickel's words.

Thorenel: Your desires become real when given enough faith. This is the land your faith has drawn into existence. The land is your canvas, and the images it holds are your strokes of

paint. Lapoi is 663 trillion times the size of Earth. There is more than enough land on Lapoi for 120 billion past-mortal souls and 240 billion celestials to each have billions of square miles of land for themselves—and that would only be fifteen percent of the total land mass of Lapoi.

Having this new information, I slowly turned in a full circle to gaze at everything around me. It was true. Everything I saw was, in some way, shape, or form, a desire in which I had given much attention on Earth. I just stood there, completely stupefied. I followed what they were saying, but I could not understand it enough to completely comprehend it. How was that possible?

Me: I . . . I don't understand what your saying—but this land... it takes my breath away.

107. Artist: Howard Baer
Song: Celtic Mystique

Emalickel brought himself to stand in front of me. He paused for a moment and then smiled to comfort me.

Emalickel: Would you like to have a closer look?

Thorenel stood up from the log and adjusted his pants at the waist. He turned his back to us as he looked out at the village near the fjord.

Thorenel: The night is late, Emalickel. Should we not be returning to Dillectus?

Emalickel turned from me, he walked toward Thorenel until he was standing beside him. Then, he slung his arm around Thorenel and playfully brought him in for a hug from the side.

Emalickel: Nonsense, Thorenel! Have you forgotten? Denno-

liel is still the Crown-Prince! He will oversee the interest of Lapoi until our return. Meanwhile, we have not a thing with which to concern ourselves. This night is ours!

Emalickel gave Thorenel's shoulder a big squeeze with his hand and then patted him a few times. They both turned around to look at me. Emalickel stretched out his arm and motioned for me to come closer.

Emalickel: Come, Princess. Let us enjoy the splendor of your every desire.

I walked toward the brothers. The ground was supple and soft with rich grass. Behind me, I heard trotting footsteps. It sounded like more than one animal, and they were rapidly approaching. Startled, I whirled around. On the trail, coming through the woods, were three brilliant white horses. They were larger and whiter than any I had ever seen before. Their snouts and eyes were slightly shadowed with a gray shading, but everything else on them was bleach-white. They trotted together, one in the front and the other two following behind.

When I had reached Emalickel and Thorenel, Emalickel slowly raised his hand to signal the horses to stop. The horses slowed to a walk and then stopped directly in front of us. Emalickel walked to stand beside the horse in front and stroked its snout. Emalickel smiled at me and patted the horse's side a few times.

Emalickel: This one is yours, Hadriel. She belongs to you and to you alone. Her name is Arwynn.

Emalickel motioned for me to come his way. I timidly approached the massive white horse. She nodded her head up and down playfully as I came close enough to touch her. I grazed my hand down her snout. She pushed her head against my hand as if encouraging more affection from me. I flinched at her sudden unexpected move.

Emalickel: You needn't worry. She would never hurt you—her instinct is to protect you from harm.

I walked over to the side of Arwynn, next to Emalickel. Emalickel smiled with excitement.

Emalickel: We shall ride majestically into the village!

Thorenel walked past us, toward the two horses behind Arwynn. He stroked one of them along its side as he spoke to Emalickel.

Thorenel: Thunder seems pleased to be alongside Trojan again. It has been a long time since we have ridden side-by-side, brother.

Emalickel: Indeed, you are right. Let us change that today!

108. Artist: Audiomachine
Song: Between Heaven and Earth

Emalickel slowly swiped his hand across the air in the direction where the horses stood. Glitter swirled all around them for a few moments. Then, a black-velour blanket appeared, and became draped across the horses' backs. The blanket was trimmed in gold, and contained golden trinity knots on each side of the blanket. The horses each held a golden bit-piece in their mouth which was attached to black-leather reins by golden fixtures. The reins were one-inch wide. They were fixated across the forehead and snout of each horse, and also ran along each side of each their faces.

Arwynn's reins were traced with diamonds in its entirety. Trojan and Thunder's reins were traced with trinity knots—Trojan's were gold and Thunder's were silver. All three horses wore a decorative harness around their chest to match their reins. They also wore a decorative black, hexagonal pendant on the face of their snouts. Each pendant was trimmed in the same element as each horse's reins. Each pendant measured about three-inches wide, containing within it a two-inch wide circle, with a one-inch trinity symbol inside the circle. The pendant hung by two chains which extended down from the forehead strap of the reins. A small, flat, black, leather saddle sat upon each of the horses back, on top of the blanket.

Thorenel placed his booted foot in the stirrups and hopped on the back of his horse, Thunder. I looked up at Emalickel, who was still standing beside me. He patted the seat of the saddle on Arwynn's back and gave me a look of playful expectation. I smiled and obliged. I placed my hands on the saddle and my right foot in the stirrup. Emalickel moved around to the front of me. He placed his hands around my waist and helped me lift myself up. I swung my left leg around to the stirrup on the other side and grabbed the reins from the base of Arwynn's neck.

Emalickel walked around to the back the horse and adjusted my cloak so that it spread along the entirety of Arwynn's back. Then, he walked around to the front and stood staring with his arms crossed at his chest. He appeared entranced, with his mouth partially open. He shook his head.

Emalickel: I do not have words to describe the magnificence of the sight of you. It is as if I feel the need, the urge, to kneel.

He bent down to one knee, bowed his head. I lost my breath as I absorbed the sight of Emalickel, the Prince of Lapoi, the celestial leader of every being in the entire realm of Millattus, respectfully kneeling himself before me, as I sat high upon a majestic white horse! He slowly looked up at me with only his eyes. He waited, as if for approval. Smiling, I acknowledged him. Then I recalled and repeated to him the words he had once spoken to me in a previous visit to Lapoi.

Me: You will rise from this kneel. You need not kneel to me. We are one. We are equal.

Laughing, Emalickel stood back up. He seemed to have caught on to my imitation of him and found it amusing, just as I had intended. He walked around to his horse, and saddled up upon his back.

Emalickel: Lead on, Princess. To your village, where we shall become more acquainted with the splendor of it.

109. Artist: Andrea Pascali
Song: Hope Send

I gently whipped the reins on Arwynn's neck, signaling for her to start walking forward. A few seconds later, I heard Thorenel click his tongue for Thunder to move ahead, and Emalickel signaled to Trojan with a quick whistle. The air felt slightly chilly but only when the wind blew. There was a faint smell of smoke coming from the firepits in the village. I could hear the sound of the horse's feet stamping the soft dirt of the forest floor.

To be sure the brothers were still close behind me, I turned around to check for them. They were riding next to each other, sitting tall and proud upon their horses and conversing with each other. From my perspective, Thorenel was on the right, and Emalickel was on the left. Their bodies swayed and bounced with the movement of their horses' steps. I stared for a moment as I couldn't bring myself to look away from such a picturesque moment. Both of them were magnificent in image—strong, confident, collected, and wise. Adorned with royal cloaks draping from their shoulders. They appeared as kings returning from a victorious battle. Thorenel looked forward at me and show his perfect pearly-white teeth.

Thorenel: Worry not, my dear. We are right behind you.

Emalickel: We will move up, to ride alongside you, after we exit the forest.

We tracked on. The edge of the forest was about a hundred yards out. The horses followed a straight trail between the trees. I heard Emalickel gently slap his hand against Trojan's side a few times.

Emalickel: Trojan, old boy, it has been quite a while since we last took a leisurely ride in open nature.

I turned around to see him. Emalickel sat up straight again and continued talking aloud but seemingly to nobody in particular. He was gazing out in the distance, scanning the scenery, as he continued.

Emalickel: I must admit, with Dennoliel bearing the crown, I feel a sense of freedom and relief. No deeds to tend to, no binding obligations, no pressing matters to resolve...

Thorenel interjected, adding to Emalickel's words with a disgruntled tone.

Thorenel: No defiant brother with whom to deal...

I heard Emalickel scoff under his breath.

Emalickel: Xabiel? We will hold a council-meeting regarding him come tomorrow.

Thorenel sounded surprised.

Thorenel: A council-meeting!?! Why bother? We never have

before. You are sovereign. After the crowning ceremony tomorrow, it shall be up to you and God to decide the fate of our brother. The entire realm trusts in your fairness and justness. Why go through the trouble of sorting out the opinions of all us brothers?

Emalickel: The council will exclude Seronimel and, of course, Xabiel. It will only comprise Dennoliel, as Crown-Prince and leader of the guardians; Romenciel, as leader of the warriors; and you and I as the Royal-Princedoms.

Thorenel: But Dennoliel will still be the Crown-Prince. He despises Xabiel for his arrogance and has taken it personally. Xabiel undermined him during his reign. What if Dennoliel chooses to exercise his power of sovereignty while still bearing the crown? He might secure the fate of Xabiel before you have any say. After all, he already stripped him of his ranking over the warriors.

We emerged from the woods. Emalickel walked his horse beside me on my right. Thorenel walked his horse up to my left. They both looked ahead as we continued forward.

Emalickel: I am not concerned, Thorenel. I am calling for a meeting tomorrow. That is the end of it. There will no further discussion of the matter.

Emalickel turned his head to look at me.

Emalickel: Let us savor this exclusive time the three of us have together.

110. Artist: Steve Jablonsky
Song: Tessa

As we approached the village from the hilltop of the meadow, we could see down into the village which was surrounded by rampart walls on three sides. The back of the village was surrounded by the large fjord, so it was unnecessary to enclose it with a wall. The village contained about five-hundred structures including a large longhouse which rested upon a hilltop near the fjord. There were gardens of crops just on the outskirts of the village. Workers tended to these gardens. I noticed several farm animals near the crop fields including cows, chickens, and goats.

As we continued closer, we came to the large stone-wall gate, and could I notice more detail. About five armored guards stood in the ramparts above the main gate. Two additional guards stood on the ground on either side of the giant, arched, bronze-colored gate doors. I wondered where the people of the village came from and how they had gotten there. I also wondered if everything was authentic and real. I looked around in awe. A whispered utterance escaped my mouth.

Me: Wow!

The unintentional utterance had been traced by Thorenel. He, too, must have been blown away, for I heard him let out an exhaled gasp before commenting with surprise.

Thorenel: Wow, is right!

We slowed our pace to a stop. We paused there, in silence, taking everything in. After a moment, Emalickel managed to find his words.

Emalickel: You are quite a visionary, Adrienne of Earth. Thorenel and I have been aware of your village, but chose not to see it for ourselves until we could share that moment with you.

The chivalry of the two Princedom brothers never ceased to amaze me. Although deeply flattered, I managed to maintain my composure and was able to refocus on the village.

Me: Is this place actually real?

Emalickel: Indeed. It is all very tangible and real. Your village here is the likeness to a village during the Middle Ages on Earth. The only difference is the village here has been settled by celestials, instead of mortals; but these celestials choose not to use their abilities unless necessary.

Me: Celestials? So, they're from here?

Emalickel smiled and proudly gave a nod of his head.

Emalickel: Some of Lapoi's very own.

Me: Who are they? Why are they here?

Emalickel: The majority of the village consists of guardian celestials, but the armored ones are warriors. They have chosen to live here because the fantasy of a mortal village lifestyle appeals to them. They enjoy the pride of being able to do things without their powers. Although they are still immortal, they suppress their celestial energies, so that their bodies carry the facade of being completely mortal.

Until then, Romenciel had been the only celestial I knew who preferred not to use his powers.

Me: It would be perfect for Romenciel!

Both brothers chuckled at my comment before Thorenel further teased.

Thorenel: I cannot remember the last time I suppressed my

powers. There's no telling how much of a fool I will make of myself!

Emalickel: A bit of humbling never hurt any of us.

We proceeded toward the gates. Two large, black tapestries hung from the rampart walls on either side of the gate. They flapped monumentally with the vanilla-scented breeze. In the center of each tapestry was an emblem. It was the image of a winged-lion, sitting upright, and facing to the left. The lion was white with black lines for texture. On its head, it wore a crown colored with shimmering gold. The underside of the lion's open wing contained a glittering golden triquetra emblem centrally located on the wing. The walls behind each tapestry were taller than the rest, as if they were watchtowers. At the top of each watchtower, there was a large urn which held a tall, blazing flame. Between the two watchtowers was the lower rampart wall, where the five guards were stationed above the gate. Hanging from this wall, were three swags of black bunting; each containing a golden triquetra emblem in the center.

Emalickel: The crowned lion emblem belongs to you and to you alone. It is your mark and seal. The lion represents the majesty of your power and status. The crown, adorning the lion's head, signifies your union with the sovereign Royal-Principality of Lapoi; this indicates that solely you have become one with Thorenel and me. The lion's inner wing bares the Lapoian Triquetra symbol which declares your ever-lasting reign as the one, exclusive, Princess of Lapoi.

My sights were completely absorbed in the magnificence of that emblem. It appealed to me deeply. It resonated strongly with me. It was perfect in every way—it was big and bold, simple and clean, elegant and posh; yet it was also very distinctive and unique, personal and precise, recognizable and unmistakable.

I thought about the two white lions in the Palace of Lapoi, at the top of the throne stairs, and how my tapestry's emblem had adopted the image of them to represent me as embodying the characteristics of the Royal-Principality—strong, courageous, and revered. The contrast of this distinct white lion stood out from the tapestry's black background, alluding to the contrast between the Principality of Lapoi and all the unknowns of existence. The black color of the background conveyed darkness, subordinance, wickedness, and obscurity often associated with the unknown; while the white color of the lion overpowered the dark background, conveying illumination, predominance, purity, and clarity.

I was impressed by the decision to use shimmering gold for the color of the crown and triquetra symbol. It was stunning! The golden glitter not only added a hint of femininity to the emblem, but, more relevantly, it alluded to power and divinity.

My mind raced with excitement. That was MY symbol!?! It had made a permanent imprint of my legacy in Lapoi. It established my oneness with the Royal-Princedom brothers. My heart became overwhelmed with humbled joy. That village was my village, a place in which I had apparently created. Its inhabitants were my people, and they were there because they chose to be. Immediately, I took pride in the land, as if it were my own home. It was my responsibility to maintain it and to ensure it flourished through my desire and faith.

My connection to the entire tapestry was immediately deep. It drew me in, as if I were under a spell. I became immersed in its perfection. I was completely captivated.

III. Artist: Brunuhville
Song: Spirit of the Wild

Suddenly, I heard the sound of Thorenel's voice, and I snapped out of my intricate entrancement.

Thorenel: So . . . I take it, you like it?

That is the moment I realized the expression on my face probably looked profoundly stupid. My body was slouching. My head was tilted so far to the side, my ear nearly touched my shoulder. My mouth was frozen, wide-open; and my eyes were squinted just slightly enough to appear like a lost space-cadet. As an entirety, the dumb expression I exhibited would have probably made someone question whether or not I was defecating myself at the moment. Startled and embarrassed, I jerked my body back into an upright position and straightened my head. Simultaneously, I readjusted my facial expression to one of normalcy. When I looked over at Thorenel, he was already looking at me. He alleviated the awkwardness with his reliable sense of humor. His own facial expression turned to one of obvious, exaggerated confusion; then he tried to keep a serious tone while he teased.

Thorenel: What was that!?! The twitchy-jump thing you just did! Did I just...? Did I do that?

Maintaining the exaggerated look of confusion on his face, he intentionally stuttered his words and looked me up and down. Then he looked over at Emalickel.

Thorenel: Hey Mal! Did you see that!?!

Emalickel knew he had inadvertently been brought into act. He willingly played along with a quiet, relaxed smile; but it was evident he was not participating when he rolled his eyes and shook his head in amusement at Thorenel's overexaggerated acting performance. Thorenel briefly returned his focus to me.

Thorenel: I think I just . . .

He pointed at me several times with his finger, and looked back at Emalickel again. This time, he significantly lowered the volume his voice, pretending to be discreet with Emalickel. He pointed at me a few more times while he whispered at a quiet, but intentionally audible, voice.

Thorenel: I think I just might have caused her . . .

Thorenel jerked his head to look at me again, then immediately jerked it right back up to Emalickel, who still sat on his horse on the other side of me. Thorenel lowered his voice to a full whisper, but still made sure it was loud enough for me to hear. He used the back of his hand to pretend he was shielding his voice from traveling in my direction.

Thorenel: I think I just shocked her, bro—like zapped her with my voice! Did you see her—all jumpy and twitching out!?! I just discovered a new ability of mine!

He slightly moved his head in my direction for a clearer view of me. A playful smirk slightly grew on his face, reassuring me of his lack of having any seriousness. I had been chuckling at him all along, but I especially chuckled at the sight of his reassuring playful smirk. He continued dragging-out his foolish antics by mocking me with random twitching and jerking motions at unexpected times. That made it even funnier.

In all seriousness, I deeply admired Thorenel for his selfless and humble attitude. It warmed my heart that he was comfortable and willing enough to make a fool of himself, at his own expense, to deflect any embarrassment or discomfort from me. He knew he had startled me and that I was embarrassed by it. He also knew the only way to bring comfort to me was by making the ordeal into something exaggerated and humorous.

Even the guards at the gate of the village seemed confused, yet humored, by the sight of Thorenel while he continued mocking my jumpy movements from when I had been startled.

Emalickel: Brother, you do know the armored guards above the gate are watching you closely. They probably fear your lucidity was sacrificed in exchange for your resurrection.

Looking straight ahead, Thorenel was quick to find a witty comment of retaliation to aim back at Emalickel.

Thorenel: No, brother, I think they are watching YOU. They probably ponder your sexual orientation, judging by the way you sit upon your horse.

112. Artist: Whitesand
Song: Legend of the King

Emalickel ignored Thorenel's comment. Instead, he refocused on the present moment and turned his head in my direction.

Emalickel: Princess, I am pleased you find your emblem appealing.

Emalickel nodded his head once at me, then looked forward toward the gate, which was about fifty yards from us. He lifted the reins from Trojan's neck and let out a quick whistle. Trojan proceeded walking forward. Thorenel and I immediately followed and caught up to him.

Thorenel: As soon as celestials began settling your village, Emalickel and I knew it was time to employ your seal. Not only would it mark the village as yours, but it would establish a collective, universal understanding of your dominance through the union with Emalickel and me.

When we were about twenty yards from the gated door, I heard several of the armored guards raise awareness of our arrival.

Armored guards: Open the gate! The Royal-Princedoms and the Princess have arrived! They are here! Open the gate! The Principality is here!

The huge, bronze gate slowly opened inward with the sound of large, heavy, creaking metal. It appeared as if they were opening by themselves, but then I remembered Emalickel had said the celestials in the village preferred not to use magic unless absolutely necessary. When the doors had opened fully, a cobblestone pathway could be seen throughout the village. Emalickel stopped his horse, hinting for us to stop as well.

The two armored guards who stood outside the gate, remained there, while two more armored guards emerged from behind the other side of the gate doors. They must have been the ones who had pulled them open. These guards stood side-by-side in the gateway, between the other two guards on the sides. The four of them, in a line, all drew their swords from their sheaths and held them high in the air. Then, in perfect unison, they stabbed their swords to the ground and knelt behind them.

I was grateful Emalickel and Thorenel were with me, they knew proper etiquette. After a moment, Emalickel acknowledged them.

Emalickel: You may rise.

The two men rose to their feet and sheathed their swords again. Thorenel spoke in a cordial, yet authoritative, tone.

Thorenel: Greetings to all of you! We, the Principality of Lapoi, have arrived to stake claim to our three thrones of Rasaevulus!

The two armored guards in the middle of the gate entrance, took three marching steps forward, in unison, then clicked their feet together at attention. They both crossed their left arm across their heart. One of them responded.

Armored Guard: Then it would be our honor and privilege to escort you to your Longhouse.

They both turned their backs to us and began walking forward into the village. I looked to Emalickel for direction. He nodded his head, looking forward, signaling for me to walk my horse ahead.

Emalickel: After you, Princess.

I tapped the reins on Arwynn's neck, and she proceeded walking behind the two guards. Emalickel whistled to Trojan, and Thorenel clicked his tongue at Thunder as they brought their horses to follow directly behind me. As we entered the village, the two other guards positioned themselves to walk on either side of my horse. I looked behind me and noticed three additional guards positioned themselves to walk to among us. One was to the side of Emalickel's horse, one was to the side of Thorenel's horse, and the third walked in back of their horses.

Armored guards lined the cobblestone road for the entirety of the main strip. The celestials of the village stood in crowds behind these guards, on both sides of the road. They were cheering, jumping, and waving. As we passed them by, some of them respectfully bowed their heads while others knelt on one knee. Not a single eye strayed from us.

113. Artist: Antti Martikainen
Song: A Forgotten Kingdom

The villagers were dressed in fine noble clothing. They wore bright colors of bright red, majestic purple, royal blue, and deep yellow. The materials of their clothing consisted of furs and rich velvet. The women had on fine jewelry of gold and silver, with sparkling gems and colorful stones. Their hair-styles were elegant, and often down, without a single strand out of place. The men wore dark-colored trousers of brown, black, and dark green. The men also wore Elizabethan Age ruffled collared tunics and doublets. Both the men and woman had fancy chains of jewels which adorned the front of their attires. Unlike the villagers of the Middle Ages on Earth, these celestial villagers were more like wealthy nobles than peasants, yet they still lived as peasants and held the same status as peasants.

The village was set up in the same layout as in the Middle Ages. The main road continued straight, through the village from the front gate to the large wooden dock located at the giant fjord on the opposite end of the village. At several points throughout the main road, there were additional roads which forked off into new cobblestone roads to the left and right. At the end of one of these, I noticed a large temple built of perfectly-cut and placed rectangular stone blocks. Elaborate woodcarvings were finely chiseled throughout the framework of the entire structure.

Many homes lined the cobblestone roads. The homes were made of timber, stone, clay, and straw. Among other structures, I noticed two blacksmith shops, neighboring each other, as we progressed through the village. Both blacksmiths used anvils, piles of metal scraps, worktables, workbenches, and stone forges. Various shelves with tools were hanging from the walls, and wooden barrels were stashed in corners for storage.

Some of the other places of interest included several clothing merchants, a food market, three taverns, a jewelry merchant, and a few merchants selling general goods. There was also a section of the village containing several independent merchants selling various goods.

The village itself appeared to be about one square-mile and inhabited a little over one-thousand celestials. Thus, each structure was built on about one acre of land. Since most of them lived in pairs or small groups, most homes and shops sat upon a one-acre plot of land, often separated by a thatched fence. The temple and longhouse each sat upon about five acres of land.

We came near the end of the main road, and turned right onto another road which traveled between the shores of the fjords at the back of the village. It traveled across a stretch of land and wove up a small hill to the right of the shoreline. I could see a large structure resting at the top of this hill. A large, rocky mountain rested directly behind this structure. The structure was made of timber, stone, and straw, and was elaborate in shape and size.

Behind me, I could hear Emalickel and Thorenel conversing quietly with each other.

Thorenel: That must be the longhouse.

Emalickel: I think you are right.

Still surrounded by the armored guards, we continued weaving up the hillside. When we reached the top of the hill, the cobblestone road ended at five stone stairs which led to the front door of the longhouse. The longhouse was two-stories and rectangular in shape; it was about eighty feet wide and one-hundred-fifty feet deep. Two tapestries, each bearing my seal, hung from tall wooden crosses which were steaked on each side of the stone stairs.

Two armored guards stood at each side of the stairs. In the center of the longhouse, including the doorway area, there were three tiers of gabled-rooftops constructed with straw; each gable was a level higher than the previous one, and was constructed slightly further toward the back. The windows were horizontal rectangles, and were positioned high on the walls in rows. They traced all along the entire upper boarder of each level of the longhouse. I could see candlelight shining from inside the windows, but could not hear anything.

The two armored guards who were leading us, stopped at the foot of the stairs and turned around to face us. They remained still and silent until all the other guards had caught up to them and formed a horizontal formation. They stood with their hands folded in front of them. When everyone was settled, one of the front guards spoke.

114. Artist: Brunuhville
Song: Wolfborn

Armored Guard: We have safely reached your destination, Princedoms and Princess.

Emalickel and Thorenel were still positioned behind me.

Thorenel: We are grateful for your services.

I turned around to look at them. They were both in the process of dismounting their horses. Thorenel walked up to me and assisted me in dismounting Arwynn. He escorted me to the foot of the stairs. Emalickel walked up to stand to my right, on the opposite side as Thorenel. Emalickel extended his arm toward the front door, inviting me to walk in first. I picked up my dress to ascend the stone stairs and stopped in front of the door.

Thorenel approached from behind me and reached in front of me to open the door. I proceeded inside.

The interior construction of the longhouse was primarily made of dark wood. It was warm and cozy inside. Well-lit by candles, the room had plenty of lighting on the tables and lanterns along the walls. Four chandeliers, also lit by candles, were evenly spaced and hanging along the central parts of the tall, pointed ceiling. The room was long, extending back for about 140-feet. The hard-wooden floor had several rectangular fur rugs. About thirty feet into the entryway there was a set of large stone stairs, containing about seven steps, which led up to an area with a long, rectangular, wooden table. The table was about fifty-feet long and contained silver plates, chalices, and eating utensils. A wide array of food, drinks, and bottles of wine were laid out on silver trays along the length of the table.

As I approached the stone stairs, I noticed two wooden doors on my left and two on my right. They were tucked behind archways held by several stone columns. The doors were open and seemed to lead into other rooms. Celestials, both male and female, stood in front of some of these columns. They were dressed like the villagers and were holding serving trays with hors d'oeuvres and drinks.

Emalickel and Thorenel were still walking behind me as I continued up the stairs toward the long table. I wasn't sure where to go, so I stopped at the top of the stairs.

Emalickel: Keep going. All the way back.

I kept going, walking along the right side of the long table. More archways with columns lined the left and right sides of this part of the room. Tucked behind them were several round wooden tables with chairs. In the back of the room, resting at the top of another set of stone stairs, were three throne chairs in a row. Behind each of them hung large tapestries containing the crowned-lion emblem. The thrones themselves were made of wood and contained golden detail. Engraved along the framework were several intertwined, gold triquetra symbols. A single large, golden, triquetra symbol filled the entire back-piece of each throne. A hardwood floor filled the ten feet between the thrones and the top of the stairs. Another large, rectangular, fur rug laid on this part of the floor.

I stopped on the rug and waited for Emalickel and Thorenel. They stopped on each side of me. I looked up at Thorenel, who was standing on my left. He had been looking at the thrones, but looked down at me upon noticing my eyes on him. He smiled and extended his hand in the direction of the throne chairs.

Thorenel: Go, and claim what is yours.

I went to the middle throne and sat down. Emalickel followed and sat in the one to my left, while Thorenel sat in the one to my right. The thrones were large and solid. The entire room of the longhouse could be seen from this perspective. Thorenel leaned in to tease Emalickel.

Thorenel: There is nothing like sharing this view—all three of us together. You really should consider a third chair in the palace, Emalickel.

Emalickel: And you will never cease to nag me about this, will you brother?

Thorenel chuckled, and Emalickel sarcastically shook his head. I noticed how I did not like being between the two of them. I wanted them both in my sights, not one to my left and one to my right. I decided to request a change in our seating.

Me: Would you mind if I changed our seating arrangement?

Emalickel: It is your village, my dear. We shall make it to your liking.

Thorenel: Of course we do not mind, but do you mind if I ask why the change?

Me: I want to be able to see the both of you at the same time, not one of you here and one of you there.

Thorenel: Alright, fair enough. How would you like for us to be situated?

I stood up. The two brothers followed suit. I sat down in the throne where Thorenel had been sitting.

Me: Emalickel, you're the Prince of Lapoi, so I want you in the middle. And Thorenel, you sit where Emalickel was.

The brothers sat down in their new seats. From the aisle of the longhouse we were situated from left to right in the order of Thorenel, Emalickel, and then me. I looked to my right and was able to see both of them together. This made me very happy. Both brothers were looking at me for approval. Finally, Emalickel smiled asked how it suited me.

Emalickel: Is this more pleasing to you?

I returned the smile and nodded my head.

Me: Much better.

115. Artist: Alan Lennon
Song: Strive

We all three sat in our throne chairs with our arms laying on the arm-rests. I sat on the edge of my chair and crossed my legs at the knees, like a lady. Thorenel sat back comfortably, slightly slouched, and crossed one of his ankles over his other knee. Emalickel sat with his back leaning slightly to one side and with his legs in a relaxed, open position.

One of the longhouse attendants, who had been standing to the side, stepped in front of us on the rug. She curtseyed before she spoke.

Attendant: Good evening, Principality. We have all been preparing for your arrival and have put together some fine festivities. Should you be interested, we are ready to begin at your request. Just give us the word.

She had mostly made eye-contact with Emalickel for feedback. The celestials naturally looked to him as their leader—and with good reason—just because I had apparently created this village, didn't change the fact that Emalickel was the primary Prince of Lapoi and Thorenel was the secondary. I had always been humble, and even after finding out I was a part of the Lapoian throne, I simply viewed myself as a decorative jewel. I looked at Emalickel, waiting for him to give a response to the attendant, but instead he and Thorenel had both turned their attention to me.

Thorenel: Your humble heart will learn to make fire, Princess. With time and experience, you will ignite your fire using your humbleness as coals. And what a perfectly splendid balance you will be.

Meanwhile, Emalickel nodded regally at the attendant and sent her on her way with a wave of his hand. She curtseyed before tucking herself away to the side of the room.

Thorenel: So, let your fire-power make its first spark. If you would like to begin the said festivities, then let it be by the

authority of your voice. Your village unconditionally honors and respects you, for they know none of this would even be possible without you.

I remained silent for a moment while I digested what he had said. I looked around the longhouse in amazement of its creation and manifestation. It was a quiet and peaceful atmosphere inside, which usually I enjoyed, but this time I desired a celebration. I looked, once again, at Thorenel and Emalickel. They were already looking at me with relaxed expressions. I smiled at them excitedly and nodded showing my approval for the party. Instead of taking the initiative, as he usually did, Emalickel leaned forward and whispered to me.

Emalickel: Then just say the word and watch the festivities begin.

Thorenel nodded encouragingly at me and leaned in to whisper words of encouragement.

Thorenel: Everything will begin at the very drop of your words. You must exercise your title, Princess. Ever since you first received your crown, your reign has been in the shadows of Emalickel and me. You must start creating your own light unto yourself. There is no better place to start than here, where your villagers honor and respect you unconditionally.

Me: What do I say?

Emalickel: Whatever you want to say. The word is yours, own it.

I looked forward and took a deep breath while I tried to gather the words to say. I wanted my words to sound proper and carry an authoritative tone, like that of a true, respected princess. After a moment I let go of my fear. The silence was more awkward than any words I would manage to speak. So, I simply said the first words that came to my mind, with a confident smile and a loud volume.

116. Artist: Brunuhville
Song: Dance with Dragons

Me: We are ready to enjoy the festivities!

The attendant excitedly rushed back to stand in front of us. She curtseyed again.

Attendant: As you wish, Princess.

She turned around and faced the rest of the longhouse.

Attendant: You heard your Princess! Let the festivities begin!

Lively medieval-Celtic music began to play. A group of six dancers, three male and three females, came to the foot of the throne stairs. They performed a dance which resembled a Renaissance-style routine. They wore matching colors per dance-partner pair. One pair wore purple, another wore red, and the third wore green. Their attire was made of velvet and gold. The ladies wore full-length dresses while the men wore doublets. They danced with grace and flow.

Thorenel leaned in, giving me a reassuring smile and a wink. He made a sound with his mouth, imitating the sound of a fire being ignited in flames.

Thorenel: Whoof! And so, begins her fire with sparks.

The front doors of the longhouse were opened by the guards. Villagers rushed in and filled the room. They came in cheerful and excited. Some dispersed to tables for food and drink, while others danced with a drink in hand. They all conversed among each other merrily.

Thorenel stood up and walked to me. He bowed forward, extending his hand. I knew he was inviting me to dance with him, like a gentleman. I hesitated and looked at Emalickel, and nodded in approval; but that wasn't what I had been seeking from him. I didn't know how to dance in the Renaissance-style. Standing up from my seat, I took Thorenel's hand. Thorenel pulled me into him, and positioned our arms into a formation. Then he whispered quietly in my ear as he spun us around in a circle.

Thorenel: Relax. I will lead.

He did just that. He guided my body with every step, while moving us along the floor in front of the thrones with flow and ease. I started catching on to the movement patterns. As we danced, I couldn't help but wonder where Thorenel had learned to dance.

Me: How did you learn to dance like this? Are you sure you haven't lived in the mortal plane?

Thorenel laughed at my comment. He continued moving us along to the music as he answered through his laughter.

Thorenel: Not that I can recall, but I have spent a decent amount of time observing it! Do you think I have been completely sheltered, my dear?

The music ended. Thorenel held my hand and bowed to be again. Then, he escorted me back to the throne chairs. More music began to play and new dancers took the floor. Emalickel was still relaxed in his seat.

117. Artist: Dyathon
Song: Hope

Emalickel: I must say, brother, I am impressed with your move! And Princess, you were stunning! I couldn't help but watch. And, from the looks of it, neither could anyone else in the room.

All the villagers' eyes were looking in our direction. I hadn't noticed them staring. The last I had seen was them all piling-in and conversing among one another. I was surprised to see them watching us. Thorenel reared back in his chair and pretended to be overly arrogant.

Thorenel: Get used to it. My moves tend to draw a crowd.

I chuckled. Thorenel had a playful sense of humor. Emalickel was used to this, for he always just smiled, shook his head, and rolled his eyes at Thorenel's remarks. An attendant brought by a tray of refreshments and offered it to us. We all took a chalice of mead and some fresh-baked bread. It was fun sitting up there with the revered brothers of Lapoi. I felt important and privileged. Emalickel and Thorenel felt my eyes on them, for they both returned the look and held up their chalices to acknowledge me. We all took a sip together. Emalickel leaned in to speak to me.

Emalickel: You are worthy of us. Do not ever doubt or question that again.

I expressed a confused look at him, pretending I didn't know what he was talking about.

Me: What do you mean?

Emalickel shifted himself to face me more squarely and leaned in closer. He spoke more directly into my ear; thus, he spoke quieter.

Emalickel: Do not pretend I cannot detect your thoughts. They are as loud and clear to me as if you were speaking them with your own voice.

Without taking his eyes off me, he smiled gently as he returned to his original position in his chair. I was rendered speechless, and he knew it. There was no argument to present to him nor denial worth fronting. He knew my thoughts, and that was the end of it. All I could do was acknowledge what he had said by nodding to him.

Emalickel: Do not ever doubt your worth, Hadriel, not ever again. I give you my word, you are more valuable to Thorenel and me than the crown or the royal title or anything else for that matter. Don't you ever forget this—not any of what I have said to you this night.

He maintained his focus on me, waiting for my confirmation of understanding. Blushing, and still rendered speechless, I nodded my head again with a shy smile.

Emalickel: And although I am pleased you are flattered by my words, I want you to know that inflicting feelings of flattery upon you was not the motivation behind all I have disclosed to you. I want you to know I genuinely mean every word I have spoken.

He moved his hand to lift my chin with his finger. He pierced his eyes into mine.

Emalickel: You. Are. Worthy.

118. Artist: Brunuhville

Song: Northwind

The next song had come to an end and the floor calmed down of commotion. An attendant stepped to the foot of the stairs and bowed to us before speaking.

Attendant: Excuse me, Princedoms and Princess, but at this time we would like to propose to you the newest perspective inhabitants of the village.

The attendant bowed and stepped to the side. An armored guard stepped out from one of the side-doors located at the front of the longhouse. Two males and one female followed behind. Their faces were completely covered by a silver helmet. They walked, behind the guard, up the first set of stairs, then across the floor of the long table. Finally, they stopped at the foot of the throne stairs. All three of them went down to their knees. The attendant stepped back into our line of sight to speak once again.

Attendant: Our Principality, they are ready for questioning at your will.

I saw Emalickel and Thorenel nod their heads to acknowledge the attendant's words. The attendant moved to the side again. Emalickel looked over at me.

Emalickel: Would you like to ask the perspective inhabitants any questions?

I answered Emalickel quietly, undetectable by anyone other than Thorenel and him.

Me: I wouldn't really know what to ask.

Thorenel leaned over to me and whispered.

Thorenel: You must continue igniting those sparks of power. Soon you shall have a full-blazing fire.

Emalickel: Ask them the kinds of questions you would ask if you were allowing someone into your home.

I thought for a moment.

Me: How about if you and Thorenel question the first two, and I will follow your lead with questioning the third one?

The brothers both nodded their heads and settled comfortably back into their chairs.

Emalickel: So be it.

Emalickel cleared his throat as he readjusted himself to a more upright position.

Emalickel: Candidate number 1, in the dress, please state your name.

Candidate #1: I am Florrazziel, unified to guardian celestials of Lapoi, Gorandriel and Hassaniel.

Emalickel: And tell me, why do you seek citizenship in Rasaevulus?

Candidate #1: My partners are guardians and are consumed in their duties regarding the mortal plane. I wish to be a part of a unique experience such as has been created here.

Emalickel: I see. Do you have anything to offer to the village of Rasaevulus? In other words, what shall you do in your citizenship here?

Candidate #1: I offer my ability to create fine jewelry. I may be able to offer the finest craftmanship in my work.

Emalickel: You wish to open a shop?

Candidate #1: God willing. Otherwise, I will be just as happy playing a part in the culture itself. My greatest desire is to immerse myself in the experience.

Emalickel: Once accepted, your commitment to this village shall become a priority, and you must be prepared to carry your weight among the others.

Candidate #1: I understand, my Prince.

Emalickel: And you shall be prepared to forfeit your celestial abilities unless called upon in a necessary situation. You must be prepared to fully immerse yourself in the mortal-like experience maintained and valued within these village walls. Do you accept these terms?

Candidate #1: May I ask a question?

Emalickel: Proceed.

Candidate #1: Will I be able to leave the village during the times of Gorandriel and Hassaniel's return, for the duration of their return?

Emalickel paused and looked at Thorenel and me for our approval of her request. Still uncertain of how everything worked, I shrugged and nodded. Thorenel gave Emalickel a look of non-surprise, and then smiled and bowed his head in acceptance.

Emalickel: The Principality has agreed to your request. Now, do you accept all of the terms previously spoken?

Candidate #1: I do.

Emalickel: Then rise and remove your helmet. Step forward before the thrones.

The candidate stood up and removed the helmet from her head. Her long, curly brown hair was down and partially pulled back with fine diamond barrettes. The attendant stepped in to take the helmet from her hands. The candidate ascended the stairs toward us, keeping her eyes to the floor.

Emalickel: Florrazziel, on behalf of the Thrones of Principality, I hereby name you the newest inhabitant of Rasaevulus, granting you all rights to property and coin, and permitting you to dwell freely for as long as you adhere to the terms of your citizenship.

Florrazziel smiled with great enthusiasm. She clinched her fists and shook her arms in excitement. Then she proceeded to step before Thorenel. She took one of his hands into hers and placed her other hand on top. Thorenel placed his free hand on top of the stack, and Florrazziel bowed. As she bowed, she placed the stack of hands to her forehead. Then she moved over to Emalickel and proceeded with the same gesture. Finally, she moved down to me. I copied the gestures of Emalickel and Thorenel with her. Upon lifting her head from my hands, Florrazziel made eye contact with me and spoke.

Candidate #1: It is an honor to consider my name a part of your great work, Princess.

With that, she squeezed my hands within hers and smiled. Then she bowed and proceeded down the stairs to the side of the longhouse. I brought my attention back to the other two candidates on the floor, then to Emalickel and Thorenel. Emalickel turned his head to look at Thorenel, at which point Thorenel looked out at the candidates and proceeded to ask questions to the second candidate.

Thorenel: Candidate number two, in the red attire, state your name.

Candidate #2: My name is Namriel, second in charge of quadrant seventy-two of the Lapoian warriors.

Thorenel lifted his eyebrows and pretended to be impressed.

Thorenel: Tell me, why does a warrior desire a place among the village of Rasaevulus?

Candidate #2: Because I too want more than just to be another warrior among the crowd. I want to stand for something more specific and specialized.

Thorenel took a sip from his silver-jeweled chalice.

Thorenel: Mm humph.

He took his time swallowing the mead and placed his chalice back into the holder in the arm of his throne chair. He cleared his throat before continuing.

Thorenel: And might I ask how you see yourself standing for more here?

Candidate #2: By becoming a part of the armed guards and offering my sword to protect the greatness of the village in the honor of our Princess.

This time, Thorenel seemed genuinely impressed at the candidate's well-chosen words. He looked over at Emalickel and me.

Thorenel: Well, you just can't argue with that. I think we are done here.

He looked back in the direction of the candidate.

Thorenel: Rise, Namriel. You may remove your helmet and step before us.

The candidate removed his helmet and handed it to the nearby attendant. Then he walked up the stairs exhibiting strong posture.

Thorenel: On behalf of the Thrones of Principality, and pending your successful training with the armored guards of Rasaevulus, I hereby welcome you as one among the great village of our beloved Princess.

The candidate bowed.

Candidate #2: It is my honor. I am truly grateful for your hospitality, my Princedoms and Princess.

Namriel proceeded with the hand-stacking custom—beginning with Thorenel, then with Emalickel, and finally with me. Afterward, he gave us a final bow and proceeded down the stairs. There was one candidate left. Emalickel and Thorenel's eyes fell on me. I knew they were waiting for me to take my turn and question the final candidate. Nervous, but displaying a front of confidence, I brought my chalice to my lips for a sip. I held it in my hand while I began my questions in a similar fashion to that of Emalickel and Thorenel with the other candidates.

Me: Candidate number three, wearing the blue attire, please tell us your name.

Candidate #3: My name is Cliviticus Gwydion, and I humbly seek a place among your great village, Princess.

Although I recognized his name, I maintained a neutral demeanor.

I noticed movement out of the corner of my eye, in the direction of Thorenel and Emalickel. Despite the commotion, I proceeded with the same questions as asked of the other candidates.

Me: And, Cliviticus, why do you—

Thorenel shifted himself to sit forward, on the edge of his throne chair and abruptly interjected.

Thorenel: Remove your helmet, candidate number three!

119. Artist: Brunuhville
Song: Wolfborn

My interview had been interrupted by Thorenel's loud and sudden outburst. He brought his elbows to rest on his knees, and his hands were clasped together with the fingers tightly interlaced. His body language appeared wrathful, for he appeared like a tiger, ready to pounce in an ambush. Clive reluctantly removed the helmet from his head, making the helmet seem even more solid and heavy. Once his face had been revealed, Clive slowly brought his eyes to our direction. The attendant stepped in briefly to take the helmet.

Thorenel: What exactly are you doing here? And how did you even get here in the first place?

Clive: Seronimel sent me... at my begging request. I seek belonging. I will never be accepted among the celestial guardians or warriors of Lapoi, they will never respect or appreciate me. I wish to find a place in which I can call home; a place in which I can belong.

Thorenel abruptly stood up from his seat.

Thorenel: And just what makes you think THIS is where you belong!?!

Clive answered with his head down.

Clive: This village holds something very special and unique—an experience similar to that of a perfect life on Earth—a simple life with purpose and pride. I desire to belong to such a home; to belong in a place of such peace and comfort.

Thorenel raised his voice and spoke articulately.

Thorenel: Where you BELONG, Cliviticus Gwydion, is back in Haffelnia, left for dead! You are a traitor!

Clive retaliated in his own defense. He pointed at me, seeming to fight tears.

Clive: I died protecting HER, the very Princess of Lapoi!

Thorenel: No! You died ATTEMPTING to protect her! But you failed. Had we not shown up, the outcome would have been much different! WE are the reason our Princess is safe . . . WE are the reason YOU are even alive!

Clive: With all-due respect, you are the reason she was put into danger in the first place. Had you not brought her into your celestial activities, then she would not have been held hostage by Barthaldeo to begin with.

Thorenel bucked himself up.

Thorenel: I dare you to say that again—this time, closer to my face!

Thorenel maintained an intense stare on Clive. Clive remained in his position, but with his head respectfully downward. After a moment, Thorenel walked down the stairs to stand directly in front of Clive. Thorenel towered over him and spoke with his arms crossed at his chest.

Thorenel: You do not deserve to be alive, Cliviticus. At best, you deserve to still be stuck in Haffelnia where your arrogance and rebelliousness landed you in the first place!

Thorenel looked over Clive's head, at the rest of the villagers in the longhouse.

Thorenel: Inhabitants of Rasaevulus, might I inform you this perspective villager once turned his back on the Principality of Lapoi and refused to follow a direct order given by your Prince, Emalickel.

Clive attempted to redeem himself.

Clive: That was long ago. I have since been humbled during my entrapment in Haffelnia.

Thorenel continued, completely ignoring Clive's comment.

Thorenel: This candidate is not even a celestial, and we are still trying to figure out what to do with him. This man not only turned his back on the celestials of Millattus and acted against our direct instruction, but he also embellished his own power and denied the true power of those celestials watching over him—which, might I add, is blasphemous to God!

Emalickel stood up from his throne chair.

Emalickel: Enough of this, Thorenel! That is all irrelevant now.

Thorenel quickly turned around to face Emalickel.

Thorenel: Is it, brother!?! Is it irrelevant that the village be

disclosed of the selfish, outlandish, rebellious, power-hungry nature of a potential inhabitant of their village? He doesn't belong here. He is nothing more than a rodent! He deserves nothing more than—

Emalickel: I said ENOUGH!!!

Emalickel's voice was a thunderous roar as he stood up and interrupted Thorenel. Everyone in the longhouse froze while Emalickel's voice echoed throughout the walls. He stood there, glaring at Thorenel, clenching his jaw. Annoyed, he spoke through his teeth.

Emalickel: The Principality has yet to make a decision—a decision which shall be made collectively among the three of us.

Clive was looking at me, with disappointment and sorrow. I felt bad for him that his questioning-session had turned so ugly. In the short moment of silence following Emalickel's statement, I stood up and spoke with my hands folded at my waist.

Me: May I say something here?

All eyes turned to me. Emalickel turned around to see me and folded his hands down in front of him. Both he and Thorenel bowed their heads at me in approval of my request.

Me: Although I am not aware of what exactly took place in Clive's past with the celestials of Lapoi, I am aware of his present, and everything I have seen from this man has been nothing but the demonstrations of a kind-hearted, genuine, and good gentleman.

I walked down the stairs to stand beside Clive. He smiled in relief, seeming grateful for my words.

Me: He saved my life, and risked his own, many more times than just once. The first time, he helped me escape the wrath of a dragon. Then, he saved me during an attack of wild, savage beasts—monsters like I had never seen before. Afterward, he cleaned and nursed my wounds. He provided shelter, food, and drink to me. He made potions that helped me see Lapoi, bringing me much-needed peace and reassurance. Barthaldeo didn't care about my fate, he was just using me for ransom. He had already told me that if I died, he would just find the next best choice to hold for ransom. Without Clive, I would not have survived, not long enough for ANYONE to save me.

I stepped forward to stand and face Thorenel and Emalickel.

Me: Haffelnia has indeed humbled him and made him a changed man. I have trusted this man with my life on several occasions, and I would trust him with it again. Therefore, I trust him as an inhabitant of the village. Whatever he did in the past, he deserves a second chance, a chance at redemption, a chance to prove himself as the man he has become today—not the man he may have been in the past. Is that not what our King would do? Would Christ turn his back on a man because of his past? Should we not follow the example of our great King?

Everyone remained silent. Not a sound was heard, nor a movement was made. I turned around to glance at Clive and offered him a sympathetic smile. Turning back around, I looked at Thorenel.

Me: That is all I wanted to say.

Then, I walked back up the stairs and returned to my throne chair. Emalickel and Thorenel watched me the entire way. After

I sat down, Thorenel took his eyes down to the floor, where he paused. Finally, he cleared his throat and spoke with a calmer and quieter voice.

Thorenel: I must say, Princess, it seems the sparks within you have started to flame. I am impressed.

120. Artist: Atis Freivalds
Song: Above the Light

He turned to face Clive again, and spoke in a louder tone so the rest of the longhouse occupants could hear.

Thorenel: Cliviticus, although my opinions of you remain unchanged, the words of our Princess have reminded me to release you from my resentment.

Thorenel turned and proceeded up the stairs to stand next to Emalickel. Both of them held themselves as strong and confident. Emalickel's hands were still folded in front of him. Thorenel rested his hands at his waist, by using his thumbs to hang from his belt.

Thorenel: Our Princess has spoken. You should be grateful for her empathies. Her presence among the Principality has added an element of balance to our throne. She seems to support your stand, and seeing how she is among one of the Principality, and how this village is her own, your request will be considered. You shall have your answer by nightfall.

Thorenel nodded his head to Clive, and turned around to return to his throne chair. Emalickel went back to his chair, as well. Clive closed his eyes and smiled, then opened them again as he spoke.

Clive: I am grateful for your hospitality.

Clive bowed, and then turned around to walk toward the front door. I could hear mumbling among the crowd. When he arrived at the front door, Clive nodded at the armored guards, who then opened the door for him. Then he proceeded out of the longhouse entirely. The door closed behind him and he was gone. The mumbling among the crowd continued.

Emalickel scanned the room noticing the awkwardness. He looked at the nearby attendant and placed his elbow of the armrest of his throne chair. He snapped his fingers to get her attention. She immediately noticed. Emalickel twirled his finger in the air, signaling for her to cue the music.

Attendant: And now, may the festivities continue with the entrancing moves of the synchronized step-dancers!

121. Artist: Brunuhville
Song: Medieval Legends

The mood of the crowd shifted to one of excitement. They clapped and made sounds of joyful hollering. The music began playing. It sounded like Celtic-folk music consisting of fiddles, flutes, and bodhran drums. The tempo was fast-paced and upbeat and carried a simple, catchy rhythm. The music played for a moment before the step-dancers began coming out from behind the arches. They came out in a single file line, facing the thrones, and performing the exact same motions with each other.

The team of dancers comprised males and females. The males wore loose black pants with dark-green tunics and white belts. The females wore green, knee-length dresses with black panty hose underneath. Over their dresses, the females wore white aprons. Their hands hung firmly at their sides while their feet did coordinated movements similar to jumping, tapping, and flapping. The movement of their feet accompanied the bodhran drums, making similar sounds as they stomped and clicked their feet with the beat.

An attendant came before us with a tray of hors d'oeuvres. She offered each of us an empty plate to hold items from the tray including sushi, toasted bread topped with cheese, and crackers with a meaty dip. We indulged in the food and kept the attendants busy with keeping our chalices full. We conversed with each other about random things, such as the drunken stupor of some of the villagers in the longhouse. Emalickel and Thorenel cut-up with each other as they usually did. They reminded me of brothers in every way. They carried-on with each other, teasing and making back-and-forth witty remarks. At the end of each word-battle they would laugh and rough each other up, playfully pushing and punching on each other as brothers do.

Hours passed, and the last light of day ceased to shine through the windows. It had been dark outside for some time. The lively music went uninterrupted, and the commotion of the festivities was on-going. Through the evening, we found ourselves engaged in conversations with the villagers. At times, they would approach our thrones to introduce themselves and share their stories with us.

After a while, Thorenel became restless. Seemingly, he had mingled for as long as he could. Finally, he looked at Emalickel and used his head to point in the direction behind our thrones. Emalickel turned to me and leaned in to speak discreetly.

Emalickel: Would you like to get out of here? We could all get more relaxed in the longhouse chambers. I could send for a tray of hors d'oeuvres and mead.

122. Artist: Wardruna
Song: Solringen

Thorenel had already stood up. He was stretching-and readjusting his upper body. He twisted his torso to each side. Then he rolled his shoulders back a few times and stretched his neck to each side. I smiled at Emalickel with satisfaction, for I, too, grew bored of the confinement of my throne chair. I nodded at him and responded.

Me: I would like that very much.

By this time, Thorenel had moved to stand in front of me, but he was looking at Emalickel. Thorenel nodded his head to Emalickel and then offered me one of his arms to escort me. Emalickel stood up from his throne and stepped out to the top of the stairs. Thorenel led me toward the back of the longhouse and around a corner. As Thorenel and I exited down a hall behind the thrones, I heard Emalickel.

Emalickel: Guardian Kentiel, we shall retire for the evening. I leave you in charge of overseeing the village. Ensure the attendants have the longhouse cleaned by morning. Please relay our upmost gratitude to everyone for such a warm, wonderful evening.

Kentiel: Yes sir. I will see that it is all taken care of, Prince Emalickel.

Emalickel: Also, please see to it that our village candidate, Cliviticus Gwydion, is made aware of his acceptance to inhabit Rasaevulus, pending the final approval of the Dominion.

Kentiel: It will be done, my Prince.

After we had turned the corner, Thorenel and I continued halfway down a hallway, until we came to a solid-bronze door on our left. This was the only door along the entire twenty-foot hallway. Fancy beige curtains hung above the doorframe and were tied to the sides, creating an opening in which to walk through. A crowned-lion tapestry hung on the wall at each side of the door. Also, hanging on the wall, next to each of the tapestries, were sconces lit by fire. In front of each tapestry, was an armored guard, standing at attention. The armored guards acknowledged Thorenel and me as we proceeded inside.

An attendant, wearing an elegant red-velvet dress, was finishing with placing two trays on a rectangular table in the back-right corner of the room. She turned to us and bowed before gracefully exiting. The room was square, containing four walls, each measuring about twenty feet. The right-most wall was not actually a wall, but rather two enormous stone archways, each containing a glass double-door opening. Outside the glass doors was a balcony overlooking the foggy, moon-lit fjord.

Thorenel sat down on a rectangular ottoman at the foot of the bed. He began removing his boots. I walked over to the glass archways to have a closer look. The view was captivating. I couldn't help but think about my life on Earth and wonder when I must return to the ordinary world. I reflected on the magnificence of all I had seen and experienced during my times in Lapoi. I thought about how routine and mundane life would be upon my return to the mortal plane, but at the same time, I remembered many happy memories on Earth and how precious and priceless those moments were. I wondered what would come of my mortal attachments, and if I would be able to have them after my mortal death.

The door closed as Emalickel entered the chambers. The music and commotion of the main longhouse room could still be heard, but had become muffled within the enclosed walls. I heard the steps of Emalickel's boots on the wooden floor as he approached me. He placed his hands on my shoulders.

Emalickel: Quite the view, isn't it?

We continued standing there, admiring the scene in silent peace, when I heard Thorenel grunting to himself. He was making sounds of frustration on the bench as he fought to remove his boots.

Thorenel: These boots are more trouble than they are worth!

I turned my head to look at Thorenel. Emalickel remained behind me with his hands still resting comfortingly on my shoulders. He, too, had turned his head in the direction of Thorenel who continued the struggle with removing his boots.

Thorenel: Why is this so difficult? I just don't understand!

Emalickel chuckled to himself and then teased at his brother.

Emalickel: It seems as though you, brother, have not had enough practice in the experiences of mortality.

Thorenel jerked his head up and responded with irritability.

Thorenel: Then by all means, mister expert, do walk me through this procedure of boot-removal.

Emalickel responded in a playful, sarcastic tone.

Emalickel: First off, it would help you immensely if you unbuckled them along the outside of your leg there, genius.

Even though Thorenel's struggle was cute, I understood why he was having such a hard time adhering to the customs of mortal practices exercised in the village. Thorenel found the buckles on his boots and finally managed to remove each of them. He then walked over to the table, near the arched doors overlooking the fjord, and began pouring himself a drink from the tray.

123. Artist: Adrian Von Ziegler
Song: Ohori Village

Meanwhile, Emalickel returned his attention to me.

Emalickel: Tell me, what thoughts consume your mind. You seem... weary.

I refocused my sights to the scenery outside and remembered my previous thoughts.

Me: If you truly are practicing the mortal expectation of this village, then how would you know I was weary?

Emalickel: Because I know you, very well, and your demeanor is not one of complacency.

By this time, Thorenel had poured himself a drink, and took a sip while turning to focus his attention to me. Neither of them said anything, but I could feel their attentiveness.

Me: It's just that . . . I struggle with the feeling of living two separate lives, one completely different from the other.

Thorenel turned to set his drink down on the table. He picked up another chalice and began pouring another drink. I walked to stand even closer to the arched-doorways. Thorenel picked up both chalices and walked over to me. He handed the second chalice to me. I thanked him and gratefully took it in my hand before continuing.

Me: I am attached to the memories of my life on Earth, yet I am deeply drawn to this life here in Lapoi. I can't choose the

favor of one over the other. I want them both, and I fear the loss of one over the other. Neither of them is expendable to me.

Emalickel gently squeezed his hands on my shoulders and leaned into my ear as he spoke.

Emalickel: And what makes you think you must choose one over the other?

I shook my head.

Me: Because I cannot see it being any other way.

This time, Emalickel whispered in my ear.

Emalickel: You do not have to choose.

I didn't understand.

Me: What do you mean I don't have to choose?

Emalickel removed his hands from my shoulders and stepped forward, from behind me. He looked out at the fjord and took a deep breath before answering.

Emalickel: To be more specific, when the time comes, and everything is complete, both planes of existence will blend beautifully into one.

Me: How? How will I be able to have the things I love from Earth, right here among the things I love in Lapoi?

Emalickel dropped his head, as if in defeat. Thorenel stepped-up, to interject and provide an answer.

Thorenel: You ask questions in which you are not ready to comprehend the answers. All we can offer you, in this

moment, is reassurance that everything you love, you shall have.

The answer was unfulfilling, non-specific, and vague. I wished the two of them would try harder to be more specific, even if they didn't think I would be able to comprehend what they may say. Emalickel looked up and peered at me analytically.

Emalickel: Are you truly seeking security about your future valuables, or are you rather seeking to determine which place, Lapoi or Earth, holds more truth to the reality of its existence?

I was silent as I tried to process his question. After a moment, Emalickel further clarified.

Emalickel: You see, Hadriel . . . Adrienne, you cling tightly to the things in which you love and to the things in which bring you comfort. The more real they seem, the more invested you are in them, and the more dependent you become on their continued existence. You fret about which place is more real in order to make a decision on which one in which to invest yourself; but what you fail to understand is that they are both equally real.

Me: Even if I were able to accept them both as being equally real, how can I experience one without lacking the other?

Emalickel: Again, that will be taken care of in due time.

Looking from the tops of my eyes, I tilted my head at Emalickel in annoyance of his vagueness. He slouched his posture and looked over at Thorenel. Returning his eyes to me again, Emalickel placed one of his hands on my shoulder.

Emalickel: I could show you a vision, but that would require me to use my celestial powers. Besides, you would not be able

to understand what you saw—you do not yet have the capacity to interpret it.

Thorenel began walking toward the door at the front of the room. He placed his chalice on the arm of a nearby chair. He cleared his throat, and began removing his royal cloak while adding to the conversation.

Thorenel: If you ask me, I am not convinced either of these matters is what truly bothers you. You already know and believe, with all your heart, there will be a satisfactory resolution when all is complete of Heaven and Earth.

He hung his cloak on one of three bronze hooks positioned on the wall near the door. I kept my eyes on him, looking at him intriguingly. He began carefully adjusted the cloak so that it hung neatly, without any folds or wrinkles.

Thorenel: And even though you do not know exactly how it will be when that time comes, you feel at peace with it. Your confidence and trust in the Word of God grant you that comfort.

He turned around and walked back in my direction, passing by his chalice on the arm of the chair. He stopped behind me and began removing my royal cloak as he continued.

Thorenel: It sounds to me like you are troubled, not by which place is more real, nor how your separate lives in Lapoi and Earth will someday blend, but rather how you can accept being a part of both worlds without casting one or the other aside as being of less significance to you.

He finished removing my cloak and walked over to hang it on the middle hook. As he did this, he further elaborated.

Thorenel: You feel torn between two worlds, and you feel

compelled to choose one as being exalted over the other. The reality is they are both equal. Neither one of them becomes abandoned when you experience the other. Your consciousness is the source of all your experiences. It is vast, and it can exist anywhere you direct it.

He finished straightening out my cloak. Emalickel had walked over to the table in the corner to pour himself a drink. Afterward, he returned his attention to Thorenel, who had brought himself to stand in front of me.

Thorenel: When you direct your consciousness to Lapoi, you can still recall your experiences of the Earth. When you direct your consciousness to the Earth, you can still recall your experiences of Lapoi. When recalling an experience, there is no physical tangibility to it—there is only an image which plays-out in the form of collected thoughts, like a memory, within your consciousness. Does that make it any less real? And does that mean all other memories are casted aside as being less important?

I remained silent in anticipation of his point. He began slowly pacing in front of me with his hands behind his back. He looked at the floor as he continued his lecture.

Thorenel: When you recall your Earthly experiences, while consciously focused on Lapoi, do you doubt their authenticity? Why then, do you doubt the authenticity of your Lapoian experiences while consciously focused on the Earth?

Although he still had not addressed my true dilemma, he did provide me with much-needed clarity regarding my tendency to doubt the reality of Lapoi. I processed what he had said and concluded that the only reality we truly have is the ever-changing present moment. Everything else exists only in thoughtform. All past experiences and all wonders of the future come from the conscious mind as nothing more than a collection of images in the form of thoughts.

Me: I understand your point. My doubts have been inconsistent. Why do I doubt the reality of Lapoi, but not the reality of Earth? The experiences of both places are recalled using thoughtform, so why do I continue to doubt the truth of Lapoi's existence while my experiences of Earth remain undoubted?

Thorenel continued his pacing.

Thorenel: Exactly. And I think there are three answers. First of all, you have more experiences on the Earth. Secondly, the illusion of time allows you to arrange your experiences of Earth in a chronological order, making it seem more vivid and defined. And lastly, your experiences on Earth are so deeply immersive that you become consumed by its demands; intricately focusing your attention to it and therefore involving your persistent action within it.

I was speechless. Even in the past, when Thorenel's celestial abilities were activated, I had never heard him speak such profound wisdom. He was right, and I needed to hear such a lecture. It provided me justification and reasoning for why I needed to put my doubts to rest.

Me: I'm impressed by your wisdom. You're really good with your words, Thorenel.

Although I was smiling at him, I became troubled. The core of my most deeply-rooted conflict between Lapoi and Earth had finally revealed itself to me. Just as a cork being held under the water rapidly rises to the surface upon being released, my inner-most dispute did the same. Thorenel had stopped pacing.

He turned his head to look at me from the side. He was analytical.

Thorenel: Why then . . . why are you still so weary?

This caught me by surprise. Knowing he wasn't endowed with his celestial ability to hear my thoughts, I didn't expect for him to pick-up on my remaining troubles. There was no use in trying to deny his intuition of my feelings. I took a deep breath, trying to formulate my best, most clear, presentation of the root of my troubles.

Me: On the Earth, I often become distracted by thoughts of Lapoi, and I feel guilty because it consumes my focus and attention from the things of importance to me on Earth. In Lapoi, I have recently started feeling that same distraction by thoughts of Earth, and I feel guilty because it takes my attention away from the things of importance to me here.

Emalickel put down his chalice and stepped in beside Thorenel. Giving me his full attention, he crossed his arms at his chest and lowered his eyebrows in concentration.

Emalickel: Please, we must get to the very core of this. Do not use any filters nor dance around in attempt to find the right words. Open up completely and bare the nakedness of your troubles before us.

Me: When I am on Earth, my feelings for the two of you seems immoral and wrong; and when I am here, thinking about my life on Earth, it takes away from my connection to both of you. I always feel torn, clouded, withdrawn, and confused. I fear I will never be able to live fully, in either place, without distraction or guilt stemming from the other.

Although it had been difficult to share this so bluntly with them,

I also felt a sense of relief. Thorenel stepped closer to me and leaned down to bring his eyes level with mine. I felt tears begin to pool in the lower lids of my eyes. Thorenel cupped my face in his hands and spoke reassuringly.

Thorenel: You have done nothing wrong, in either world, in which to feel guilty or ashamed.

Emalickel moved himself to support me from behind, placing his hands on my back. A tear managed to escape from behind the shield of my lower eyelid. It trickled down my face as I interjected.

Me: But you said both experiences were equally real, which means I am indeed living separate lives. That makes me feel guilty because—

Maintaining his hold of my face, Thorenel interrupted.

Thorenel: Do not let it fill you with guilt. All of which we have said is true, but perhaps you need clarification. On the Earth, you live in a mortal flesh, and that flesh has not ever left its sacred and rightful place on the Earth. In Lapoi, you live in your spirit-form. Your spiritual experiences here have not compromised the morality of your flesh. They are separate—in a different place and time, if you will. Feeling guilty about your experiences in Lapoi, would be like feeling guilty for past lives on Earth. Although they are connected, they are not overlapping; they are not co-existing.

Me: But I am deeply invested in things of both Lapoi and Earth, in a singular overlapping time and place—right now, in this life. I feel guilty for thinking about one place while being present in the other.

Emalickel entered the conversation.

Emalickel: You are prematurely blending your life on Earth with your life in Lapoi. The human-state of mind cannot comprehend a morally acceptable way of doing this. Perhaps we should have waited in seeking you until the completion of your awakening.

I heard Emalickel sigh, and I felt him release his hands from my back. He seemed distressed and exasperated.

Emalickel: You have shared your experiences from Lapoi with the people of the Earth, thus inviting them to influence you with their inhibited perceptions and inaccurate beliefs and hasty conclusions regarding a place and time in which they know nothing about! Thanks to Haelael, they too have become corrupted and choose to be judgmental hypocrites. They are closed-minded, ignorant, self-glorifying, know-it-alls, and I remember why I withdrew myself from their futile affairs a long while ago!

Thorenel released his hold on my face and hesitantly looked up at Emalickel.

Thorenel: They are not all that way, brother.

By this time, Emalickel had begun rapidly pacing behind me. I could tell he was appalled at the happenings on the Earth. He yanked his cloak from his back and flung it up on one of the wall-hooks by the door. With fast, heavy steps, he walked to the bench at the foot of the bed and sat down to begin removing his boots.

Emalickel: Well then, I am speaking of the ones who have induced this brainwashing effect upon our Princess—making her feel immoral and impure! She has done nothing wrong and their uninvited, misinformed, manipulative opinions have jeopardized her perception of us and of herself! Now she

feels torn and guilty, and for no reason whatsoever, except that it doesn't follow the human-standard of what is considered morally acceptable of a place and time that doesn't even apply to them! And it all stems from their insecure, selfish, self-gratifying senselessness!

He had loosened the laces of his black tunic and rolled up the sleeves. Even though he was disgruntled, I couldn't help but admire the intense passion behind his defense for me. I rarely had seen him in such an uncontrolled emotional state. It was usual for him, but at the same time, it flattered me that he was lashing-out like that on my behalf.

The display of him removing articles of clothing, through his anger, made it hard not to stare at him with lustful thoughts. He stood up and worked to unbuckle his belt and loosen his pants at the waist. Then he sat back down with heavy force. He rested his elbows on his knees and dropped his face into his hands for a moment of silence. None of us said a word. I turned around to square myself with Emalickel. With his head in his hands, he finally mumbled to himself.

Emalickel: How did I fail at foreseeing this? I should not have disrupted your mortal life and gotten you involved in any of this. I was being impatient, and I rushed to interact with you too soon before your awakening. I never should have gone to meet you in the astral plane at the lake that night, long ago.

With his fists clenched at his sides, Thorenel abruptly stomped his way toward Emalickel.

Thorenel: Watch your words, Emalickel.

Taken aback by Emalickel's comment, I went up to him and kneeled on a large, white, fur rug at the foot of the bench. I placed my hands on each of Emalickel's arms.

Me: Do not ever think or say anything like that again, Emalickel.

Remaining silent, he looked up at me from his hands. I continued.

Me: That statement, the sheer thought of such a thing being true, hurts me and brings me more pain than any of my collective troubles combined!

The tears I had been fighting, all began to escape at once. Emalickel removed his hands from concealing his face. He rested his hands in his lap and brought his head up to face mine. Looking at me with sorrow, he swiped the tears from my cheeks with his fingers. His eyes toggled between mine.

Emalickel: Then I shall never think of it again.

We maintained eye-contact as Emalickel aided me to stand with him. Thorenel consoled me by placing his hands supportively on my shoulders.

Thorenel: Nothing which transpires will ever be held against you. Not here, nor on the Earth. We will forever be your pillars of support, confidently flying your tapestry through each and every battle. A battle is not always easy, but it is always temporary. This is merely one of those battles, and it too, is temporary. The outcome shall always fall in the favor of our King, in whom we place our trust in all of our decisions. This battle will have no different outcome than all the rest. We shall all overcome and will find ourselves blending flawlessly when comes—the new Heaven and the new Earth.

Emalickel looked at Thorenel and smiled. Then, he returned his eyes to me.

Emalickel: He speaks the truth. It all shall be so.

124. Artist: Whitesand
Song: Luna

Our eyes toggled again, and I felt myself leaning into the comfort of Emalickel's embrace. Our lips approached each other until they finally met. Emalickel grabbed my face, pulling it into him more closely. Thorenel began to pull me closer to him from behind. I turned around and allowed it. Then, Emalickel stepped to stand beside Thorenel. I turned to him for another passionate embrace, removing his shirt in the process. Thorenel teased the side of my neck with his lips, as Emalickel concentrated on dancing his tongue with mine. All the while, both brothers began working gently at loosening and removing my dress from my shoulders.

We moved collectively to the large, wooden bed behind us, framed by four tall posts at each corner. White, cashmere-soft sheets were covered by a luxurious fur blanket. As I scooted myself backward onto the bed, I removed the shirt from Thorenel's back while indulging in the taste of his lips. We continued to freely express our love without any shields of clothing or any burdens of shame. I had forgotten how smooth and inviting both of the brothers' bodies were. Their skin glowed a soft, bronzed-hue in the ambient candlelight.

That night was the first time I was able to enjoy the physical company of both brothers. I felt so very privileged to experience this with them, knowing there were countless females, both in Lapoi and on Earth, who would give anything to share an intimate night with the powerful and handsome Royal-Princedoms of a celestial planet. I, on the other hand, had given nothing, yet I happened to receive personal invitations from both brothers during my first visit to Lapoi. And still, there I was with them, once again receiving an open-invitation to savor their magnificence.

What made all of this even more astounding was the fact in which they had disclosed to me, prior to ever becoming intimate with them—I remembered the words Thorenel spoke during my first visit to Lapoi, *"Celestials who unify with a mortal female will have such a deep, unconditional love for her that she becomes their only partner for eternity. They quite literally become a part of each other forever."*

I felt safe and comfortable in the protection of their presence. I knew I could do anything with them without reaping any judgement or haste on their part. If I wanted to, I could decide to perform grotesque acts with them, and they would humbly oblige, respecting my desire without judgement. Alternatively, I could decide never to be intimate with them ever again, and they would still humbly oblige and respect my desire without haste. There was no expectation of me from them; there was also no right or wrong when it came to the three of us being (or not being) intimate. This fact even further drove my desire for them. Just the sight of them filled me will unconditional love and passion.

As if relishing in the grandeur of Emalickel and Thorenel wasn't enough satisfaction in itself, my body also found physical satisfaction as the brothers took turns in their roles among me. They rotated every so often, changing out their dominant positions of duty. Although they were very traditional in their approaches to providing physical pleasure, they were both of expert-level in achieving success with it. No physical pleasures on Earth compared to that which was administered upon me by them.

I enjoyed my slightly vulnerable position of being outnumbered by the two of them, as well as being overpowered by their strength and their capabilities. It stimulated me to know there was an entire village right outside the walls of our room, who all knew better than to interrupt us, for they feared the power and wrath of the Princedom brothers.

125. Artist: Luke Richards
Song: Look to the Stars

After each of us had received satisfaction, we all laid on our backs. I was positioned protectively between Emalickel on my right and Thorenel on my left. I thought for a moment, how utterly pleasing it was that we were all three alone and together, having shared the secrets of our intimacy. Our bodies warmed each other, skin-to-skin, without barriers, under the soft fur blankets. In the privacy of that room, we would not be disturbed through the entire night. Thorenel looked over at me and grinned, as he maintained his relaxed position with his arm under his head.

Thorenel: There is no other emotional or physical sensation, in all of creation, that is as utterly satisfying as sharing that with you.

Emalickel managed to mumble his agreeance through his satisfactory exhaustion.

Emalickel: I must second that.

Thorenel: What do think, Princess?

Although I agreed completely, there was one thing missing.

Me: There is nothing like it. Although I do know one thing that would make it even better.

Fully alerted, both brothers turned their heads to me in attention, anxiously waiting for me to continue.

Emalickel: And what might that be, beloved?

Me: If you both stayed right here, through the night, and I could wake up to glory of you both, still here in this bed with me come morning.

Both Emalickel and Thorenel smiled and turned their heads back toward the ceiling while they answered in relief of the simplicity of my spoken desire.

Emalickel: Of course. We shall remain in this bed with you throughout the entirety of the night, until you awaken come tomorrow morning.

Thorenel: You have our word. We will sleep beside you this night, and when you awaken, you shall still see us, right here, at each side.

There was nothing more I needed in that moment. Completely content with everything, I closed my eyes and drifted into sleep almost immediately.

10

CONCLUSION

126. Artist: Olexandr Ignatov
Song: Emotions

The next morning arrived. I found myself still in the private chambers of the longhouse. I was lying on my back and noticed the candle-lit chandelier hanging from the vaulted ceiling. As promised, Thorenel and Emalickel still lay next to me. They both appeared to be asleep. Thorenel was to my right, on his stomach, with the fur bedding pulled just above his hips, exposing his smooth, bare back. His head was facing my direction and rested on his forearm. Emalickel was to my left, on his back, with one of his arms behind his head. The fur covering of the bed was pulled just above his waist. The exposed skin of his bare chest was glowing of soft-bronze in the golden light of morning. His chest rose and fell as he breathed slow, deep breaths. I moved my head, back and forth, to look at each of them, trying to make minimal noise. I did not want to risk waking them, for I wished to absorb the magnificent image of them without interruption. I became deeply entranced by the perfection of them.

Emalickel opened one of his eyes and exhibited a relaxed smile. I became embarrassed, knowing I had just been caught staring lustfully at him.

Emalickel: Do not be embarrassed. Only the company of your eyes could be so utterly flattering.

I heard Thorenel yawn.

Thorenel: Yes, the pleasure is all ours to be of such a distraction to your sights.

I turned my head again, back to Thorenel. He had just awoken, blinking with squinty-eyes. He lifted his head from his arm and smiled at me.

Thorenel: Good morning, bright eyes.

I returned the smile.

Me: You're both here. You kept your word.

Thorenel raised his head and repositioned himself to prop up on his forearm.

Thorenel: As we always will.

127. Artist: Gaelic Storm
Song: Sight of Land

He rubbed his face and groaned.

Thorenel: Why does my stomach feel like it is caving in on itself?

He moved to the edge of the bed, hanging his feet to the floor. He rubbed his face in his hands once more, and cleared his throat.

Thorenel: Shall we ready ourselves to return to the palace? This sensation in my stomach is most uncomfortable, and I wish be to rid of it.

I chuckled at him. I still found his inexperience in mortality rather cute. Emalickel responded.

Emalickel: Toughen-up, brother. You are only feeling the pains of hunger. The palace has prepared a full-course meal for our return.

Emalickel turned himself to lean on his right arm to better face me. Then he continued.

Emalickel: We have a full day ahead of us. After we eat, we shall commence at the spa-pool on the Grand Balcony, where we may refresh ourselves before preparing for the re-crowning ceremony.

I slowly rose to a sitting position on the bed. Thorenel was on the bench at the foot of the bed, once again struggling to dress himself. He stood up and walked over to retrieve his cloak from its hook on the wall. His shirt was on backwards. He looked down at his boots and asked with all seriousness.

Thorenel: Do I have on YOUR boots, Emalickel? They feel awkward.

He had put them on the wrong feet. The outer buckles were positioned inward. Emalickel had put on his pants and stood up to fasten them. He took one look at Thorenel and burst out laughing.

Emalickel: Oh, brother! Tsk, tsk, tsk. Being mortal just does not suit you, does it?

Perplexed, Thorenel looked down at himself and raised his arms out to the sides in a fashion of misunderstanding. He looked back up at Emalickel and shook his head obliviously.

Thorenel: What?

Emalickel stroked his chin with his fingers, pretending to think deeply. Then he walked over to Thorenel and stopped directly in front of him. He looked down at Thorenel's boots, and then up at his shirt.

Emalickel: Well, for starters, your tunic is facing the wrong way. The laces should lay against your chest, not against your back. As for your boots, they each belong on a specific foot, and let's just say you have not gotten that exactly right either.

Thorenel scoffed and removed his shirt in frustration. Then, he returned to the bench and sat down to resume the struggle with his boots.

Meanwhile, I rose out of bed to retrieve my dress. It was draped across the back of a bedside chair. Emalickel had slid his arms into the sleeves of his black tunic. He raised his arms up and placed his head through the neck-hole, then tugged the shirt to fixate it comfortably on his torso. By this time, I had slipped into my dress.

Thorenel had just finished switching his boots to the correct feet. Before buckling them all the way down, he stood up to test their comfort. In the process of sitting back down, a bursting sound of flatulence ruptured from his rear. He sprang back up to a standing position, clinching his glutes together. He shielded his hands over the area from where the sound had originated and looked at Emalickel and me, horrified and concerned. He hollered in a panic.

Thorenel: What in the hell was that!?! Did you hear that!?!

Emalickel nor I could restrain from laughing hysterically. Thorenel remained clueless and stared at us annoyingly.

Thorenel: Although I am glad the two of you have found the humor in this, I still fail to see it that way. I am quite concerned! It felt like something just literally escaped from the seat of my trousers!

The more Thorenel talked about it, the more hysterical Emalickel and I became. Thorenel's obliviousness, while making all those remarks, sent us out of control, barely able to breathe through the all laughter. I had fallen to my knees on the floor with tears of laughter leaking from my eyes. Emalickel further provoked the humor.

Emalickel: You have every right to be concerned, brother! I would be, too, had a noise like that escaped my trousers!

Emalickel hunched over, propping his arm on the back of a nearby chair for stability. Still completely lost, Thorenel rolled his eyes at Emalickel, while Emalickel laughed himself senseless. Thorenel went back to the bench where he had been sitting. Taking a closer look, he ran his hand along the cushion. Having found nothing out of the ordinary on the cushion, he was about to give up. Just as Thorenel was about to sit back down and resume fixing his boots, Emalickel regained enough control to serve himself another helping of laughter at his brother's expense. In a matter-of-fact tone, Emalickel spoke.

Emalickel: Have you been able to confirm nothing did, in fact, escape from your rump? Perhaps it would be a good idea for you to check the seat of your trousers, brother!

128. Artist: Gaelic Storm
Song: The Farmer's Frolic

Taking Emalickel completely serious, Thorenel frantically unbuttoned his pants and dropped them to his ankles. With a determined look on his face, he bent himself over to investigate the inside seams. By this time, I was laughing so hard, I had rolled myself into a ball on the floor.

After a few minutes, Emalickel and I managed to compose ourselves. Thorenel had finally gotten himself together, and Emalickel explained the process of flatulence to him. Apparently, celestials seldom encounter this biproduct of digestion. After fulfilling Thorenel in a brief lesson of human anatomy and physiology, we were all finally ready. We each stood near the hooks on the wall, and fastened our cloaks to our shoulders. I made sure to pull the hood of my cloak over my head, to conceal the messy hair I had acquired in the night.

Then, we proceeded out to the main room of the longhouse. Besides a few attendants, the room was quiet and empty. The long table had been cleared of everything except candles and a few floral arrangements. Everything was neatly in place. The wooden floors had been swept and mopped, free from any dust or debris. The entire floor was lustrous, as if it had been polished. The room carried a fresh-cut wood scent, like that of a new house, with a hint of lemon. We stopped next to the throne chairs, as an attendant, wearing a yellow and white noble-style dress, stepped out from the side of the room.

Attendant: It is an excellent morning, my Principality. May we offer you coffee, perhaps with some breakfast?

Thorenel looked down and placed a hand on his stomach. He smiled and began to speak.

Thorenel: That sounds splendid! Prepare—

Emalickel: It is a very kind gesture, but we must be on our way to the palace now.

The attendant bowed her head and returned to the side of the room. Thorenel, still coddling his stomach, looked at Emalickel with resentment. Kentiel approached us and respectfully bowed his head.

Kentiel: All is order here, my Principality. I will see to it the armored guards are ready to escort you. They will ensure your journey from the village goes uninterrupted.

Emalickel: You are doing fine work here, Guardian Kentiel. We value for your noble services. You shall remain in charge during our absence, sending notice of any concerns directly to the palace.

Kentiel bowed his head.

Kentiel: You have my word, Prince.

Although the village was aware that Emalickel wasn't technically the current prince, as that title still belonged to Dennoliel, it showed Kentiel's greatest upmost respect for Emalickel by addressing him in this manner.

129. Artist: Garry Ferrier
Song: Atonement

Kentiel turned around and headed toward the front door of the longhouse. Thorenel removed his hand from his stomach and extended it in the direction of the front door.

Thorenel: After you, my beauty.

I took a moment to take-in one last view of the fantastic longhouse of Rasaevulus—the elaborate craftmanship, the tapestries, the high ceilings, and the warm atmosphere. Then, I proceeded down the throne stairs. Emalickel and Thorenel were directly behind me. As I passed the long table, I ran my hand along the glossy, polished wood. I looked at the grandness of the columned-archways along the sides of the room, and even noticed a balcony running atop both sides. There was still much to be explored of the longhouse, but I knew the brothers had pending business in which to tend back at the palace.

We walked down the stairs near the entryway. The interior armored guards opened the door for us. When I stepped outside, there were already six armored guards, standing in a horizontal line, facing away from the longhouse, with their hands behind their backs. Our three white horses were also waiting. They stood, facing away from the longhouse, in front of the line of armored guards. Arwynn was positioned at the very front. Trojan was behind her, slightly to the right, and Thunder was to the left of Trojan. The armored guards had left a gap between themselves, in the middle, to allow space for us to access our horses. Kentiel was waiting, directly to the side of the exterior front-door. He extended his white-gloved hand to aid me down the stairs. I picked up the hem of my dress, with one hand and held his hand with the other, until I had reached the bottom of the exterior stairs. I released Kentiel's hand and took a few steps forward to wait for Emalickel and Thorenel. They both trailed down the stairs after me, acknowledging Kentiel as they brought themselves to stand with me.

130. Artist: Audiomachine
Song: Remember Not to Forget

Emalickel guided me to Arwynn and assisted me in mounting her. Then, he stroked the side of her neck and patted her shoulder before turning around to approach his own horse, Trojan. Arwynn pawed at the ground a few times with her front leg. I heard Thorenel call from behind me.

Thorenel: She is happy to see you, Hadriel!

I turned my head to the left, as far as I could, and looked at Thorenel through the corner of my eye. He had already mounted Thunder and was adjusting himself on the saddle more comfortably. Emalickel grunted as he hoisted himself upon Trojan's back. He, too, shifted his posture to a more comfortable position. The armored guards moved into their positions on-foot. Two of them were in the front, two were at each side, and one was in the back. Kentiel called from the base of the longhouse's exterior stairs.

Kentiel: They are ready, upon your word, Prince Emalickel.

Emalickel: No, Kentiel, they are ready upon the word of Princess Hadriel.

Emalickel knew I did not like being in charge, but I understood why he kept pushing it upon me. He was preparing me, and establishing my authority, for the future of my, more permanent, residency in Lapoi. I exhaled my breath in frustration and turned my head right to glare back at Emalickel. He was looking at Thorenel, smiling connivingly with him. Noticing my eyes on him, Emalickel returned his sights forward and winked with an upward nod at me. I shook my head in defeat as I returned it forward. I muttered to myself, but loud enough for those around me to hear.

Me: It is too early for this, Emalickel . . . unfortunately, it is also too early for a glass of mead.

Having heard my utterance, the two armored guards in front me drew their eyes to each other, and then back at me, smiling in amusement. Their amusement put me at ease, knowing they had picked-up on the hidden-humor of my smart-remark to Emalickel. I took a deep breath, in and out, and gathered my words to prevent any stuttering. Straightening my posture to a more upright position, I allowed the words to roll from my tongue.

Me: Well then, let us begin.

The guards began walking. I gently tapped the reins on Arwynn's neck. I heard Thorenel click his tongue and Emalickel whistle. We progressed collectively down to the village, traveling the cobblestone roadway. Most of the villagers were awake, but instead of being gathered along the sides of the pathway, they tended to their everyday businesses, apparently unaware of our departure. As we passed through, several of them noticed us and scurried to send us their humbled farewells.

When we had arrived at the front gate, the large arched doors opened. The armored guards who had guided us, dispersed to the sides. I continued leading under the giant, stone gateway to the other side. Emalickel and Thorenel brought their horses to walk beside me as we continued forward, into the dewy green meadow. As the horses walked, I turned to looked back, in admiration, at the village of Rasaevulus—a place I would forever remember.

131. Artist: Mattia Cupelli
Song: In Quel Sorriso (In That Smile)

We walked our horses a bit further into the meadow before we came to a stop. Uncertain why we had stopped, I looked over at Emalickel to my right.

Emalickel: We shall take a short-cut to the palace, but first, let me make us more presentable.

I noticed the wind began to pick-up. It swirled around us for a few seconds before subsiding. When all was calm again, I looked down and saw that I was wearing the flowy black dress with the golden rope wrapped elegantly above my waist. I still had my cloak draped behind over my shoulders, but it no longer covered my hair. Instead, my hair had been fixed neatly into a simple donut-shaped bun worn high and tight like a princess.

A forcefield surrounded us all and gradually faded into a bright light. For several seconds, I was unable to see anything except white light. A warm wind drifted around us, carrying the sweet scent of vanilla, followed by another aroma of wintergreen. Then, the light began to fade again until it disappeared completely. We were still on our horses, but had arrived in the front courtyard of the majestic Palace of Lapoi. The palace appeared to radiate in a beam of light piercing from the sky between the cover of clouds.

Emalickel and Thorenel made shuffling sounds as they dismounted their horses. Thorenel walked around, in front of Arwynn, to my right side. He offered his hand to help me dismount. The three of us proceeded toward the front doors of the palace. Two guards, standing at the doors, bowed their heads to us and opened the doors.

The palace Throne Hall was empty, with the exception of a few guards. The two white lions, at the top of the throne stairs, sat up in attention upon our entry. Thorenel held up his hand and called to them.

Thorenel: At ease boys.

The lions groaned, almost as if they were disappointed at the lack of a potential action, and they both lazily returned to their prone positions. Emalickel moved to walk in front, while Thorenel and I followed behind him. We continued straight, along the black runner of the main aisle of the Throne Hall. As we approached the throne stairs, Dennoliel was making his way inside from the Grand Balcony. He smiled and held his arms out in welcome, as he descended the throne stairs to meet us at the bottom.

Dennoliel: There you are! I was beginning to wonder what happened to you. Neither of you could be reached last night.

Emalickel: Was there a problem?

Dennoliel: No, there were no problems. I assumed you were just enjoying exclusive time with our Princess.

Dennoliel gazed at me from head to toe. Thorenel stepped to stand in front of me, shielding me from Dennoliel's sight.

Thorenel: And of that, you are correct, Dennoliel.

Dennoliel: I still wear the crown, can you not respectfully address me as Prince, brother Thorenel?

Thorenel chuckled to himself, almost cockily, and shook his head.

Thorenel: Do not let it go to your head. The Princedom power of the crown pumps through the veins within Emalickel and me—whether we physically bare it upon our heads or not.

Dennoliel maintained his eyes on Thorenel. Emalickel stepped in.

Emalickel: Shall we make our way to the spa-pool? There is much to discuss before the ceremony.

Dennoliel answered, without removing eye-contact with Thorenel.

Dennoliel: Certainly. Romenciel is already there.

Emalickel turned to me and extended his hand to his left, toward the Dining Hall.

Emalickel: I will escort you to the Dining Hall, Princess. It is midday here in Dillectus. An appropriate meal is waiting.

When we entered the Dining Hall, the table had already been set on the table under the massive window in the back. Serving celestials were attending to the table, ensuring it was presentable. I walked with Emalickel to the table. He pulled out my chair and allowed for me to settle into it.

Me: Are you going to the spa-pool?

I looked at the table, noticing two places had been set for eating.

Emalickel: Yes, and after you eat, you shall join us there.

Me: Why are there two place-settings?

Just then, there was movement at the doorway of the Dining Hall. I was pleased to see it was Clive. He was making his way to the table. Emalickel looked in his direction and smiled.

Emalickel: Clive! I am happy you could join the Princess!

Emalickel bent down to me while Clive continued making his way to the table.

Emalickel: I figured you would enjoy the company.

It was very thoughtful. Emalickel smiled genuinely at me. He nodded to Clive before turning to leave the Dining Hall. Before he left, Emalickel stopped in the doorway.

Emalickel: I shall see you shortly, Princess.

132. Artist: Mattia Cupelli
Song: Meraviglia (Wonder)

Clive sat down at the other place-setting. He removed the napkin from under the eating utensils, and fixated it in his lap. He folded his hands on the table in a mannerly fashion.

Clive: It is an honor to be here with you, Princess.

I had just finished placing my napkin in my lap. I took my eating utensils in each hand and dropped my posture to look at Clive in a playfully annoyed manner.

Me: There's no need to be formal, Clive. You can call me Adrienne.

He used his fork to pick up a variety of foods from the serving trays on the table. Then he stuffed a big bite of food in his mouth and began chewing. While chewing, he smiled and responded.

Clive: No, I quite like it. Princess suits you!

I was glad he did not harness resentment regarding the matter of his status in the village. I took a bite of food and chewed it up.

Me: I am sorry about yesterday evening in the village. Thorenel just needs some time. You have been good to me. I will make sure he considers your kind heart.

Clive: I understand his reservations. He does not trust me; a problem I have brought upon myself in my past. Then again, I have no regrets. If I had remained obedient to them, I would have lived-out my life on Earth in a place and time of a much worse torment. The path I chose may not have been an easy

one, but at least it has led me into who I have become—a humble man of respect and understanding.

I nodded my head in agreeance and offered words of reassurance.

Me: Smooth seas do not make a skillful sailor. Sometimes it's the journey that best teaches you about your destination.

We continued with our meal until we had finished gorging ourselves on delightful food. We sat back in our chairs to relax and enjoy our warm, satisfied bellies. A serving celestial came by to serve coffee. We savored a cup together, before I needed to make my way to the spa-pool.

Me: So what are you going to do now, Clive Gwydion? Where will you stay while you await a decision regarding your residency in the village?

Clive: Seronimel has taken me under his wing. He has a good, empathetic soul. He seems to be one of the few celestials who understands me and who understands why I made the decisions of my past. It doesn't hurt that he also is of the Princedom brothers. His position of authority keeps any resentful celestials from retaliating against me.

I took another sip of coffee.

Me: I still don't know much about him, but he does seem to be different and less judgmental than the other brothers.

Clive: He says he understands what it is like to be outcasted and shunned. He was the reason the search for me persisted for as long as it did. He had a group of guardians searching relentlessly, around the clock, without giving up. He sees a lot of himself in me, and for that I am grateful.

He finished his coffee and placed the empty cup on the table.

Clive: Seronimel was the one who informed me about Rasaevulus. He knew it would be fitting for me—a place where I would be accepted among others, giving me time to show them the man I have become.

I, too, had finished my coffee. I placed my cup on the table and scooted my chair out to stand.

Me: It is my greatest hope for you to become a part of that village. I assure you, my friend, I will do everything in my power to see to it that you find a place to dwell among them.

Clive stood up and nodded his head to me.

Clive: You are more than a friend to me, Princess. I consider you family. You are the closest thing I have ever had to such —like a sister, who I will always trust and hold dear to my heart.

Smiling, I moved to the side of my chair and stepped into Clive for a hug.

Me: As it is with you; the feeling is mutual.

We patted each other on the back, parting from the hug, and proceeded toward the Dining Hall doors. While we were walking in that direction, I playfully punched him in the shoulder and teased at him.

Me: And don't call me Princess, you big goon!

Clive slung his arm around my neck and pulled my head in, trapping it for a noogie.

Clive: Whatever you say... prissy-face.

When he let me loose, Clive tucked his hands into the pockets of his black, leather jacket. I forcibly knocked into him with my shoulder.

Me: Where'd you get the jacket... cool guy?

Given his 6-foot 3-inch stature, I had barely managed to even move him. Despite his hands being tucked into his jacket, Clive only stumbled slightly to the side. He looked down at his shoulder and pretended to dust it off. Then he looked down at me, as if I were only a nuisance. He bumped back into me with his shoulder.

Clive: In Rasaevulus... midget.

Although he had only bumped me, his size had created enough momentum to cause me to lose my footing. He caught me before I fell. Laughing, I admitted defeat.

Me: Victory is yours... this time.

133. Artist: Mattia Cupelli
Song: Ink

We had exited the Dining Hall and turned left, down the hallway toward the Throne Hall. We arrived to the side of the throne stairs. I could hear male voices coming from the direction of the Grand Balcony.

Me: Well, I suppose I will be heading that way.

Clive: I am headed to the Western Courtyard. Seronimel asked me to meet him there for a game of chess.

Clive placed a hand on my shoulder and smiled.

Clive: It was a pleasure sharing time in your company.

I nodded in agreement.

Me: Perhaps we will do it again very soon.

Clive nodded and removed his hand from my shoulder. He turned and walked toward the front of the palace. The closest door to the Western Courtyard was located in the front hallway, across from the entrance of the Chapel. I noticed a female, wearing a light-blue robe, rushing to approach me from that direction. Recognizing her attire, I knew she was an assistant from the Spa Quarters upstairs. She called to me, waving in effort to get my attention, as she continued rushing down the side of the Throne Hall.

Assistant: Princess! Princess Hadriel!

I waited for her to arrive. She took a moment to catch her breath, then tried to speak again.

Assistant: I waited for you to finish your meal, but wanted to catch you before you went out to the balcony. We have yet to make you presentable this morning.

Humbled by her kindness, I smiled in appreciation.

Me: I remember you from the other day. You helped me get dressed. What is your name?

She seemed flattered I had asked.

Assistant: My name is Eupheshiel, main-assistant of the Spa Quarters of the palace.

Me: It is nice to see you again, Eupheshiel, and to know your name.

She curtsied to me, then looked at my hair.

Eupheshiel: I do hope you will allow for me to, at least, fix your hair before you make your way to the balcony.

Considering how Clive had given me a noogie earlier, I chuckled and agreed. Eupheshiel turned me around, to see the back of my hair. She took it down and ran her hands through it two times.

Eupheshiel: There! All done!

I turned around to face her again, surprised she was already finished.

Me: You're already done?

She held out her hand, and a mirror manifested in it. She held the mirror up to me and spoke with confidence and pride.

Eupheshiel: See for yourself, Princess!

My top-bun had been transformed into silky, bouncy curls.

Me: Wow! Thank you, Eupheshiel. I am glad you were able to catch me before I went out there looking like an untamed parrot!

Eupheshiel chuckled, trying to modestly shield her grin behind her hand. Then, she curtsied to me once more.

Eupheshiel: It is my honor and duty.

She smiled at me, then returned toward the front of the palace. I picked up the hem of my dress and ascended the throne stairs. The brothers were still conversing with one another. I walked behind the thrones toward the three large archways which separated the Throne Hall from the Grand Balcony. The sheer, white curtains hanging from each archway, swayed with the gentle breeze coming from outside. I stepped through the curtains onto the balcony. In the spa-pool I saw Romenciel, Dennoliel, Emalickel, and Thorenel. They noticed me, as well.

Emalickel: There she is, brothers, shining like the most beautiful star in all the heavens.

Thorenel: Please, grace us with your presence, Princess. Join us.

I made my way to the nearest edge of the spa-pool. There were stairs to enter on all sides. The four brothers sat on a bench that had been made into the inner edge of the spa-pool. Steam rose from the surface of the warm, semi-translucent water. A layer of white, nickel-sized beads, similar to pearls, floated on top of the water. The beads appeared to sizzle and carried an aroma like that of sweet peaches and white jasmine. It was a very inviting pool, and I considered getting in, but then I looked down at my attire.

Me: I would join you, but what should I wear? I can't get this gown wet.

Thorenel: You shall wear nothing at all.

I rolled my eyes at him, with a half-amused smile. I casually shook my head, as if shame of his provocative humor. Thorenel kept a relaxed, straight-face. The other brothers also seemed unfazed by his comment. Even Emalickel acted casual. Slightly perplexed, I narrowed my eyebrows, but maintained a playful half-smile.

Me: I know you're not serious. What do I need to wear?

This time Emalickel answered.

Emalickel: You needn't wear anything at all.

He didn't flinch a muscle or even blink an eye. He only remained there, smiling genuinely at me. I burst out loud, laughing in disbelief.

Me: You ARE completely serious!

Emalickel stood up, emerging his chest from the water, and brought himself closer to the stairs. He held out his hand, encouraging me to come in. I looked at Romenciel and Dennoliel, who were sitting across from the stairs. Then, I took a few steps forward and bent down, closer to Emalickel. I lowered my voice and spoke discreetly, trying not to move my lips.

Me: But . . . I would be completely naked.

Emalickel responded quietly back to me.

Emalickel: Do not feel shame in the purity of your most natural state.

Me: But . . . what about Romenciel and Dennoliel?

Emalickel: They, too, are in their natural states. All of us are. This is the way, the custom, and the tradition of the great spa-pool.

My intention was to bring Emalickel's awareness to the fact that I would become naked in front of Romenciel and Dennoliel, but instead I had inadvertently been informed of their nudity. I closed my eyes and shook my head vigorously, fighting the completely nude visual of them from forming in my mind, despite the temptation to glory in it.

Me: No, what I meant was . . . they're both right there.

Realizing my true concern, Emalickel offered reassurance. He spoke loud enough for them to be able to hear this time.

Emalickel: You needn't mind their presence. Your body is a sacred temple. I cannot promise you my brothers will refrain from admiring the aesthetic display of your body, but I can assure you . . .

He turned his head to look at them, before continuing.

Emalickel: . . . they shall not lust for you.

134. Artist: James Paget
Song: Look to the Skies

Thorenel turned his eyes to Romenciel and Dennoliel. They both shifted uncomfortably and exchanged an awkward look. Romenciel cleared his throat and brought his arms out of the water to rest them along the outer edge of the pool. Dennoliel observed him and followed suit. They both glanced up at me, before neutrally focusing their eyes on the waters of the pool. Emalickel turned back around to face me. Once again, he held out his hand, inviting me into the pool. Paranoid of someone seeing me, I looked all around.

Emalickel: Princess, do you trust me? You are safe, and all is well.

I couldn't help but keep my eyes from looking around, as I began loosening the straps at the back of my dress. Once the lacing had been completely undone, I slid each sleeve from my shoulder and pulled each arm out. I stood there for a moment, clutching the dress, keeping it from falling to the floor. My modesty prevented me from being able to let it drop. Emalickel encouraged me, by orally walking me through the process.

Emalickel: If you trust me, then you will smile and hold your head high. Look out at those majestic mountains in the distance. Let your arms rest at their sides. Release the hold of your dress. Then walk calmly, to the stairs here, and take my hand.

My thoughts had been clouded by a slew of other thoughts,

Emalickel's directions helped me tremendously. He knew exactly what I had needed. I took a deep breath and gulped. Then, giving up all resistance, I lifted my chin and presented a relaxed smile as I looked out at the wondrous mountain range in the distance. I let go of the dress, by lowering my arms to my sides, and allowed the dress to drop completely at my feet. I stepped over it and slowly proceeded to walk toward Emalickel. He kept his hand extended to me the entire way. I kept my eyes on the comfort of him. When I had arrived to the edge of the pool, I stopped to step out of my elegant, diamond-accented, shoes. As I did this, I looked over at Thorenel. He was smiling proudly at me, looking me directly in the eyes.

Before I reached to take Emalickel's hand, I managed to look out at Romenciel and Dennoliel. At the time, they still had their eyes focused downward at the water, but they must have sensed me looking at them; for they both looked up at me. Dennoliel's eyes immediately widened. Romenciel's mouth dropped open. They both appeared as a deer would in headlights. Both of their chests were exposed above the water—Dennoliel's was smooth and bare, while Romenciel's had a vague shadow of fine, short hairs. Their chests were rising and falling, rapidly and deeply. Dennoliel licked his lips and pressed them together, forcing his eyes to look down at the water again. Romenciel pushed his head to look upward while he regained control of his breathing. Clearly, they both felt slightly uncomfortable.

Once I had fully entered the water, I noticed how smooth it felt! It was almost like being submerged in liquid satin. It was warm, but not hot. I walked into the water until it rose to just below my shoulders.

I sat down to left of the stairs. There was no room for anyone to sit on my right, for the stairs of the pool were there. Emalickel had moved to the other side of me. Meanwhile, Thorenel swam over to sit on the other side of Emalickel. Romenciel and Dennoliel were directly across from us. Making myself comfortable on the bench, I looked out at Romenciel and Dennoliel again. They still seemed to be working on recomposing themselves.

Emalickel was right, neither of them had ogled me, nor offended me or made me feel uncomfortable. They did look at me, and they both seemed quite flustered; however, neither of them had done anything wrong by looking. As for them becoming flustered, I felt they had demonstrated immense self-control. Not only did they restrict their eyes from overindulging, but they refrained from shooting me any looks or from making any comments alluding to a sexual desire. I realized I didn't mind them seeing me. In fact, it made me more comfortable with them and provided me a great deal of trust in them. Even if they had felt desire, I appreciated their respectful and noble behavior in the presence of my vulnerable, uncomfortable, exposure. It revealed a lot to me about each of their characters.

Once we were all resettled in the spa-pool, Romenciel tried his best to get things back on-track. He looked at Emalickel attempting to redirect his attention back to a conversation in which they had been engaged, prior to my arrival.

Romenciel: Shall we get back to the topic you were discussing, Emalickel?

Collecting his thoughts, Emalickel took a moment to revisit this topic in his mind. Every so often, I noticed either Romenciel's or Dennoliel's eyes would fall on me. They both maintained a collected demeanor, making it hard to read them. I wondered what they were thinking and wished I had the ability to hear their thoughts. Finally, Emalickel spoke to resume their previous topic of conversation prior to my arrival.

135. Artist: Brunuhville
Song: Path to Queensgarden

Emalickel: Our King has chosen to begin a Great Awakening among man-kind. Those who are drunk on materialism and selfishness have suppressed their ability to feel the effects of this awakening. They will be left behind. Those who are simple and open will remember their places of origin in the Garden of Eden. They shall feel the effects of this awakening as the spirit within them raises frequency.

Dennoliel: I was aware of the coming of this time, but when exactly will it begin to transpire?

Thorenel: It is currently being put into place.

Romenciel: We Princedom have already received permission to practice a few unusual customs during this time of change. For one, I have been granted access to the mortal plane. I have recently been visiting there in my astral form, scouting among the mortals to find those who may become a part of an elite force of leaders and warriors. They will be needed during the coming time of change.

Dennoliel: What do we need to be doing with the guardians?

Emalickel: Just as Romenciel has been empowering the chosen elite-mortals with the energies of the warriors, you will need to provide the elite-mortals with the energies of the guardians. Both of you shall also prepare all the celestials under your authority, for there will certainly be an increased

demand for their presence as this process continues to unfold.

The brothers all sat there, nodding their heads together. I could tell they were internally processing everything. After a moment, Dennoliel brought his brothers' attention to the lingering issue regarding Xabiel.

Dennoliel: In other matters, I find it of significance to point out that Xabiel slept in Versallus last night. I am finding it harder and harder to trust him. What are we to do with him?

Thorenel: You speak as though he deserves to be outcasted, but we cannot just toss him aside—he is our brother.

Dennoliel: You must let go of your brotherly attachment to him before we can make a justified decision.

Emalickel: What Thorenel meant was that Xabiel is of the Princedom line. Although we have the authority to strip him of a ranked-position, it would be an overreaction to cast him aside like a piece of trash.

Dennoliel: He has become a pestilence, and there is nothing we can entrust in him anymore.

Romenciel: Mind you, Crown-Prince Dennoliel, his hands obediently helped me release the Nephilim—a task of which he was utterly terrified. I would count that as an act of entrusting in him.

Emalickel: You enjoy working with him, Romenciel?

Romenciel: He has always been my partner in helping me oversee the warriors. Although he carries an abundance of arrogance, he has never let me down, nor done me wrong.

Dennoliel: That's not to say he never will, especially given his

recent demonstrations of adolescent behavior. You've had your hands tied with him on numerous occasions, Emalickel. I am surprised you are so forgiving of his behavior.

Emalickel: He has already been stripped of his ranking among the warriors, ruining his credibility. The celestials of Lapoi will no longer listen to any of his commands. What more do you want?

Dennoliel: He should be exiled to infantry!

Emalickel stood up in the water, exposing himself to halfway down his thigh. Without care of that, Emalickel roared in Xabiel's defense.

Emalickel: He does not! I understand he can be an egotistical nuisance, but he isn't a downright evil celestial!

Dennoliel abruptly rose to a stand, also exposing himself in the process.

Dennoliel: He swiped the Crown of Lapoi from me, Emalickel! He wore it upon his head and threatened to keep it there! He craves control and power—as time progresses, so will his appetite.

Thorenel: Might I ask how he managed to swipe the crown from you?

Dennoliel dropped his head and looked around at his brothers, shamefully, from the tops of his eyes.

Dennoliel: He picked it up without my knowing.

136. Artist: J. T. Peterson
Song: Crystal

Romenciel: How would he do that without your knowledge? Seems difficult since it transmits its own vibrational energy.

Everyone remained quiet, waiting for Dennoliel's explanation. Finally, Emalickel broke the prolonged silence.

Emalickel: So where did you misplace it, Dennoliel?

Dennoliel: It doesn't matter how, when and where the crown was stolen from me! What matters is the fact that Xabiel behaved unacceptably, and I predict his behavior will not improve in the future! I have seen it from him, time and time again; and it only continues to worsen!

Dennoliel brought himself to stand at the foot of the pool-stairs and paused.

Dennoliel: Which is why I shall send him into exile for infantry to redeem and humble himself.

Thorenel looked over at Emalickel. Emalickel tilted his head toward Thorenel, looking at him through the corner of his eye. Emalickel smiled, for he had already predicted going down this path of a power-struggle with Dennoliel. Emalickel looked down at the water and shook his head in preparation for a fallout with Dennoliel. Emalickel rose to his feet. Crossing his arms at his chest, he walked to stand on the opposite side of Dennoliel at the foot of the pool-stairs.

Emalickel: And just how do you plan on enforcing that? You are aware that, although many of the celestials often disagree with Xabiel's actions, they will not find your decision to put him away as justifiable. You will lose much respect to have abused your power like that. Thus, you will have stooped to the very level of Xabiel, and you will be deemed a hypocrite, brother.

Dennoliel: I am not worried about my popularity among the beings of our realm! My primary concern resides in the best interest of Millattus. Xabiel has shown recklessness in his approach. He continues to threaten the safety of Millattus by defying orders. So, whether or not you choose to see this as a concern of priority, I choose to see it as such!

137. Artist: 2WE1
Song: Expectations

Emalickel locked his eyes on Dennoliel and began leaning in toward him, intentionally invading his personal space. Dennoliel subtly began taking steps backward, up the pool-stairs, as Emalickel continued pushing himself forward. The two of them, nearly touching foreheads, continued this routine until they were both out of the pool. They gazed at each other with such intensity, as a pit-viper before it strikes. Sensing the possibility of a physical altercation, Thorenel jumped-up, from where he sat in the spa-pool, and positioned himself to stand ready at the foot of the pool-stairs. Emalickel spoke through his teeth at Dennoliel.

Emalickel: Those are strong words, Dennoliel. Your title as Crown-Prince has made you rather full of yourself. You are ambitious, young-brother, I will give you that; but understand that no matter what you enforce upon Xabiel while bearing the crown, I will always have the final say. Your title is temporary, but mine is eternal.

Dennoliel yelled and shoved Emalickel back using a wave of white energy from the palms of his hands. Although the force caused Emalickel to stumble backward, it did not knock him far nor did it cause him to fall.

Dennoliel: Yet, I am the present beholder of this crown! My orders are to be followed, and I shall command Xabiel into isolation!

Emalickel rushed toward Dennoliel, lifting him up by the neck with one hand. He scowled at Dennoliel, clenching his jaw.

Emalickel: Then I shall seize that crown from your big, square head!

Dennoliel forcibly flung himself down, and waved his arms in a large circle, resulting in his body becoming fully endowed in his golden, Princedom-Guardian armor. He bucked himself at Emalickel, trying to make himself appear larger. Emalickel scanned Dennoliel—head to toe—exhibiting a sly smile while speaking to him through an arrogant laugh.

Emalickel: And exactly what do you think that fancy armor is going to do?

Emalickel raised his arms to the sky, and a golden beam of light radiated down on him. The golden beam of light burst into an explosion of white-light, revealing Emalickel in the Royal-Princedom battle-armor. It was carbon-black with dark-red and golden accents. It was much larger and more elaborate than the Princedom-Guardian armor on Dennoliel. In each of Emalickel's hands, he clenched an Ulfberht sword. He immediately brought them both to point directly under Dennoliel's neck.

Almost immediately reacting with Emalickel, Thorenel had brought himself to the top of the pool-stairs and had also conjured onto himself a full-set of the Royal-Princedom battle-armor. Romenciel called out, remaining in his seat, trying to remain calm.

Romenciel: Don't do it, Thorenel. Let them hash this out.

Thorenel remained back, but he stood in an offensive position, ready to fight. Dennoliel became stiff with fear. Moving nothing but his eyes, Dennoliel noticed Thorenel had also conjured the royal armor onto himself. Knowing he would not stand a chance against both Royal-Princedom brothers, Dennoliel spoke slowly and in a calm manner, taking care not to make any sudden moves.

138. Artist: Audiomachine
Song: Hallowed Dawn

Dennoliel: He doesn't deserve any more chances, Emalickel. We have given him more than enough warnings but have yet to see any improvement in his behavior. Exiling him to infantry will suit him and perhaps shall even better him.

Emalickel kept his stance, with his swords still pressed firmly to Dennoliel's neck. Emalickel breathed in effort to regain control of his anger.

Emalickel: Do you even hear yourself!?! You are acting no better than him. He has done nothing severely wrong. Where is your soul, brother? Despite how easy it would be for me to thrust these swords, upward into your neck and outward through your thick skull, you are my brother, and I would not be able to bring myself to do it!

He slowly brought the swords down and sheathed them at each of his hips. He did this in a well-practiced, two-step manner, all the while maintaining his fierce glare, fixated only inches from Dennoliel's face. Dennoliel exhaled in relief, but tried to keep his strong demeanor. Emalickel closed the conversation.

Emalickel: Regardless of what you decide to do with our brother while you wear MY crown upon your head, I can

assure you, he will be freed upon my word—and that is the end of this, Dennoliel!

The balcony fell silent again as the two brothers starred at each other and steadied their breathing. Thorenel sheathed his swords. Footsteps approached the balcony from inside the palace. An attendant in red, velvet robes stepped out. He stopped just outside the archways and made an announcement.

Attendant: Excuse me for interrupting. Xabiel is here and has requested to see Emalickel.

139. Artist: Whitesand
Song: Her

Emalickel, Dennoliel, and Thorenel all three began walking to go inside.

Dennoliel: Being the present Crown-Prince, I shall join this meeting.

Thorenel: I am with you, Emalickel . . .

Thorenel glared at Dennoliel, who walked beside him, and added to his words with animosity.

Thorenel: . . . in case anything *unexpected* shall transpire.

Emalickel stopped briefly and turned back to face Romenciel and me.

Emalickel: Excuse us. We will return shortly.

Emalickel turned back around and resumed walking into the palace. I looked at Romenciel. He was still sitting across from me, with his arms spread-out along the back of the spa-pool. He had been watching his brothers, but then brought his eyes to me. He cracked a smile and nodded his head at me. It was evident, by his ability to remain relaxed and composed during the whole ordeal with his brothers, that he had seen his fair-share of battles. He even had a sense of humor about it. He lifted his hands to shrug while making a playful remark.

Romenciel: It has been another typical family reunion here on the Grand Balcony of Lapoi.

I cracked a smile at him, amused by his humor. There was still much to know about Romenciel. I had never really gotten to know him on a more personal level. Although being in the nude with him in a pool wasn't the setting I had in mind, I took advantage of the limited time I could find in his company. I followed up to his previous comment.

Me: I can honestly say, I did not see all of that coming.

Romenciel scoffed to himself and shook his head. He pressed his lips together and smacked them in a manner of casual, non-surprise.

Romenciel: And yet, it is just another Tuesday in the grassy savannah for the all-male lion pride.

He gazed to his left, out at the wheat-field in the east. He squinted his eyes and nibbled on his lower lip, as if in deep thought.

Me: You haven't said much in all of this. What is your perspective?

Taking in a deep breath and exhaling it vocally, Romenciel gave a big stretch. He briefly scratched the top of his head. It was adorned with dark-brown, wavy locks of hair, extending down, well beyond his shoulders. The front portion of his hair was always pulled-back, out of his face, secured in a messy bun behind his head.

Romenciel: I always find that Emalickel and I favor each other, especially when it comes to our opinions and the way in which we think things should be operated.

Me: So, you think Dennoliel is over-reacting about Xabiel?

Romenciel: I believe in justice and punishment, but I also believe in understanding and redemption. There must always be a balance.

Xabiel is our brother, and he always will be. I shall never support matters regarding the demise of those close to me.

Me: Are there any brothers you don't get along with?

Romenciel burst out laughing, shielding his mouth with his hand.

Romenciel: There is not a brother of mine whom I dislike, but each of them carry certain traits of which I am not fond.

I smiled with excitement to learn something new.

Me: What traits? Tell me!

Romenciel shot me a confused, yet amused, expression.

Romenciel: Why are we discussing this!?! Shall you go next!?!

I had gotten his point. Embarrassed that I had been invasive, I dropped my head and apologized.

Me: I'm sorry. I didn't mean to overstep; it's just that you are so mysterious. Our paths rarely cross, you and me, and when they do cross, there's no time to talk. We don't ever get a chance to become better acquainted.

140. Artist: Whitesand
Song: Beyond Horizon

He removed his arms from the back of the pool and cleared his throat. He repositioned himself, scooting to edge of the bench, and leaned himself forward, closer to my direction.

Romenciel: Perhaps you are right, Princess Hadriel. Ask me something you would like to know about me, and then I will ask you something I want to know about you. How about that?

I was so very pleased he understood my desire to know him, and that he had realized it to be of equal importance to him. I smiled with excitement again.

Me: I would like that very much!

I gathered my thoughts to think of a really good question that would provide a lot of information for an answer. I gave Romenciel a sly smile.

Me: Ok, how about this? Tell me your story, from beginning to end.

Romenciel ran his hands down his face, pretending like he was weary, but I caught a trace of a smile. He folded his fists together, below his chin, to make a place for it to rest. He looked up and teased at me.

Romenciel: Well, this is just not fair. You are unmanageable. We should have made up more rules before we began.

Knowing my request was way too much to ask, I scaled it back a bit.

Me: Alright, let's compromise. How about you just tell me the

beginning of your story—like your roots and some early memories?

Romenciel: That is something I can manage.

He proceeded to let his hair down. Some of it fell to the front and rested on his chest. Some of it also fell down the sides of his lightly bearded-face. The waves in his hair appeared glossy, as if they contained gel, but really, it was because the individual strands of his hair were thick and shiny. He began talking as he redid the hairstyle.

Romenciel: As you know, in a time before much had begun, all Princedom brothers were created from one energy which became divided into three parts. Emalickel and Thorenel comprised the first part, Xabiel and I comprised the second, and Dennoliel and Seronimel comprised the third.

By this time, Romenciel had finished pulling the front of his hair back into a new, less-messy bun. He briskly moved himself to sit beside me, to point out a moving picture in which he must have created in the water. There were three glowing orbs of light—one was blue, one was red, and one was yellow.

Romenciel: Each of these energy-sources became divided into halves, and so began the dawn of six Princedom brothers who would oversee one of nine realms in creation.

The image played-out, following perfectly to his words, as if I had been watching a documentary on television.

Romenciel: None of us remember anything leading up to that point. Our earliest memories are images of discovering new lands while we explored Lapoi and established our leadership system.

I was so intrigued; I couldn't help but to interject a question.

141. Artist: Trevor Jones
Song: Promontory

Me: Do you have any specific memories from that time?

Thinking, he shook his head.

Romenciel: Nothing of great significance comes to mind. After the number of warriors rapidly grew, from one-hundred to one-million, I mostly found myself training them and leading them into battles for various reasons. Given that my past has revolved around training and battle, I have almost become unfazed by it.

Me: Is that why you were so relaxed earlier, when Emalickel and Dennoliel were hostile?

He stood up and walked to the other side of the pool, with his hips still submerged under the water. His back was turned to me as he looked out at the Valley of Dillectus and reflected aloud.

Romenciel: When someone has been conditioned in such a way as me; having experienced and seen things from my perspective, it is a rare occasion that I exhibit concern for minor encounters. I know my brothers very well, especially Emalickel. I know he would not act with poor-judgement. He has always demonstrated a remarkable level of self-control, even in times of intense rage. What we just witnessed was nothing more than Emalickel demonstrating his dominance over Dennoliel. It will always be Emalickel who truly holds the right, the wisdom, and the power to provide for the best interest of Millattus. This realm, and everything within it, depends on his responsibility. He would never put any of it in jeopardy.

He turned back around to face me before continuing.

Romenciel: Emalickel and Thorenel view this realm as their child, in that they must provide everything needed for it to grow, evolve, and flourish. They must lead it and make decisions that would secure the divine fate of it. Xabiel and I were created fully equipped to ensure Millattus is protected, guarded, and defended from anything which may compromise its fate. Dennoliel and Seronimel were created fully equipped to ensure the beings within Millattus are guided and directed in a manner that fulfills the realm's fate. Emalickel knows the loss of any Princedom brother would leave this entire realm vulnerable and would render it severely weakened.

Romenciel shook his head and smiled with confidence.

Romenciel: This is something I know, in which the other Princedom brothers do not. Emalickel is aware that I know, but he is also aware I shall never share this among the other brothers; for it would showcase Emalickel's dependence on them, which would give them leverage in undermining his authority.

Then, Romenciel's expression turned serious.

Romenciel: Something else I know, in which Emalickel is NOT aware, is that he holds the power, strength, and wisdom to single-handedly ensure Millattus has all of which it needs.

The fact that he disclosed this information to me—information in which no other celestial was aware—showed Romenciel's trust in me. It made me feel that I could also trust him. I felt like he saw something in me, something unique and neutral, something in which compelled him to disclose what he had just shared. He nodded his head and stared at me. Taking a moment to process all of this, I stared back at him. I wanted to know what he was thinking.

Me: Tell me, if no one knows this, why did you choose to share it with me?

He laughed nervously and began to pace around the pool as he joked.

Romenciel: Now hold on just a moment! The rules were that we each get to ask the other SOMETHING, not TEN things!

Romenciel looked up in the direction behind me. I turned around to see what caught his eye. Emalickel was standing there. He had returned to the balcony. He shook his head, in distress, and let out a deep sigh.

Emalickel: Why must I always clean up the messes of our younger brothers?

142. Artist: Audiomachine
Song: The Messenger

He was looking at Romenciel. Romenciel proceeded to the stairs of the spa-pool and began ascending them. As he continued up the stairs, I managed to fixate my eyes out at the Valley of Dillectus, despite my curiosity of Romenciel's stature.

Romenciel: 'Tis one of the smaller sacrifices a Prince shall make for his kingdom, brother

Emalickel: Even when I am not technically the Prince?

Romenciel: You are always the Prince, Emalickel. You know this.

I turned around to approach the spa-pool stairs. By this time,

Romenciel had already clothed himself in the Princedom-Warrior attire. He was adjusting his cloak to drape it smoothly over the back of his shoulders. Noticing I was emerging from the pool, Emalickel walked over and offered me his hand. Upon taking his hand, I become endowed with the cover of my long, black dress again.

Romenciel had already headed back inside the palace. Emalickel began escorting me in that same direction. We stepped down the stairs and stopped next to the thrones. The Throne Hall was empty, except for the two white lions and a few warriors standing guard in their designated areas. I saw Eupheshiel, my assistant, standing at the bottom of the next set of stairs, below the thrones. She was looking up at me, as if waiting. Emalickel turned to face me, taking both of my hands into each of his.

Emalickel: The crowning ceremony will begin shortly. Eupheshiel shall take you to the Spa Quarters to prepare you.

Although I knew my time in Lapoi would come to an end following the ceremony, I felt ready for my departure this time; for the brothers had much business to handle, and they would be deeply occupied with that during the time to come. I smiled gently at Emalickel and nodded willingly. He escorted me down the stairs where we stopped next to Eupheshiel. He bent down to place his face level with mine.

Emalickel: I am anxious to lay my eyes on the beauty of you again, in this very spot, quite soon.

He leaned in to kiss my cheek before releasing my hands and sending me to Eupheshiel. She and I turned to walk down the long, black, aisle rug. As we walked, I turned around to see Emalickel again. He stood proudly and watched as Eupheshiel and me made our way toward the main archway at the front of the palace. 2

143. Artist: Thomas Bergersen
Song: New Life

The walls in the Throne Hall echoed the sound of Eupheshiel's heels while we continued under the archway. We turned right and walked down the hall until we came to the stairs at the end. These stairs led us to the second level of the palace, where the Spa Quarters was on our right.

Upon entering the Spa Quarters, there were several female assistant celestials waiting inside to make me presentable. They dressed me in an ivory ballroom gown, similar to the one I had worn for the homecoming ceremony in Lapoi. It contained long-sleeves, but was of an off-the-shoulder style. The sleeves were made of a light, sheer, chiffon material, which also overlaid the entirety of the dress.

The top portion of the dress was fitted to my torso and blended elegantly into a full, flowing, bell-shaped bottom, which grazed the floor with a diameter of about six-feet. The neckline and bottom were trimmed with a sash made of short, soft, pure-white fur. The portion around my torso contained an abundance of cream-colored, flowery fluffs which varied in size from half-a-centimeter to half-an-inch.

On the bell of the dress, these same fluffs were present, but they were more widely dispersed, except for around the lower trimming where they were more abundant. Throughout the bell of the dress, there was a series of golden-glittery embroidery designs which were sewn in random vertical arrangements along the length of the bell. Down the back of the dress, the bell luxuriously trained the floor, eight-feet beyond the bottom.

The assistants tended to my hair. They created a smooth circular-bun on the lower right side of my head, resting just behind my right ear. The bun itself measured about five-inches in diameter and was accented with diamond jewels. The only other jewelry I wore were a pair of small, dangly, diamond earrings containing the Lapoian Triquetra symbol, and I also wore a matching diamond necklace. I stepped into the elegant heels with thin, diamond straps, as the assistants performed a final touch-up to my face.

144. Artist: Really Slow Motion
Song: Miracles

They escorted me to the door which led to the hallway of the second floor of the palace. Before opening it, another assistant came before me to place the sparkling, diamond-filled, Lapoian Princess crown upon my head. Then the door opened. A warrior stood there, ready to escort me to the Throne Hall. He had been standing guard, just outside the door, and was looking down the hallway as I stepped out of the Spa Quarters. Eupheshiel made him aware I was ready.

Eupheshiel: Our Princess is ready for escort.

The warrior turned his head and looked as if stunned. He scanned his eyes from my crown to my gown, and then blinked several times and shook his head.

Warrior: Please forgive me for looking, Princess, but you are absolutely radiant. It is a privilege to be your escort.

I gave him a reserved, but genuine smile, and stepped out from the doorway. He offered his arm, and we began walking toward the stairs to the left. Eupheshiel and a few other assistants followed behind us. I picked up the hem of my dress as we proceeded down the curved staircase and made our way down the front hall of the main level of the palace.

Halfway down the hall, the doors to the Throne Hall were still closed. When we arrived, two warriors were stationed in front of the main archway doors. With their golden rods in hand, they stomped the rods on the ground three times. The echoing sound of the rods brought the rumbling of voices within the Throne Hall to a complete silence. Then, the massive doors of the Throne Hall opened, revealing the bright glow of light within the Throne Hall. It was packed full of brilliant celestials dressed in armor and in robes. A beautiful, majestic tune of music played. The escorting warrior brought me to stand, under the main archway, at the entrance of the Throne Hall. Eupheshiel and the other assistants tended to the train of my dress, ensuring it was spread-out to lay perfectly behind me. Then all of them stepped aside and nodded for me to continue down the aisle toward the thrones.

145. Artist: Whitesand
Song: Adventure Begins

I stepped carefully along the perfectly pressed, black, aisle runner-rug, lined in gold along its outer edges. Only the ambient music that played within the Throne Hall could be heard, except for the echo of the massive main doors as they closed quietly behind me. Steadily, I walked down the one-hundred-yard central aisle, toward the opposite end. Standing at the end, at the base of the throne stairs, was Thorenel. His posture was tall and confident with his hands folded down in front of him. Although he was far away, I could tell his face held a satisfied smile. He wore the formal Royal-Princedom suit, complete with his crimson-red cloak, lined on the inside with white fur.

Romenciel was stationed to the left of the throne stairs with Seronimel beside him. Romenciel stood wearing his casual, dark-red tunic with black pants, under his black Princedom-Warrior cloak. Seronimel, despite his placement alongside the warrior-leader, Romenciel, still wore his formal Princedom-Guardian attire of a white top with black pants and his white cloak lined, on the inside, with gold satin.

Dennoliel was atop the throne stairs, seated comfortably on the leftmost throne chair. He was wearing the white Princedom-Guardian cloak with golden inner-lining. Even though he had become the Crown-Prince, this didn't mean he dawned the Royal-Princedom cloak—as that would only be worn by Emalickel and Thorenel.

The light of Auruclerum was beaming-in through the white, chiffon curtains draped in front of the three massive archways of the Grand Balcony behind the thrones. The light illuminated the entire throne area like a stage. I continued taking myself down the aisle. Celestials filled the entire Throne Hall, on both the main level and on the balconies of the upper level. Their eyes all fell onto me. I smiled gently and kept my eyes forward, on Thorenel, until I had finally reached him at the end of the aisle. I was not quite sure where to go or what to do from there, so I stopped in front of him. He nodded his head regally at me. Then he gave me brief instructions using his thoughts.

Thorenel: ***Stand next to me and face the main doors. Wait for Emalickel.***

Just then, the music slightly faded. The room remained perfectly quiet. Nobody even seemed to move. After a moment of building-anticipation, the giant main doors of the Throne Hall opened, once again, and the music regained its power. Around the corner of the main archway doors, emerged Emalickel. He stepped onto the black aisle runner, wearing his formal Royal-Princedom attire. He began walking toward the thrones. Every celestial in the Throne Hall bowed respectfully as he passed them and progressed down the aisle. They looked-up to Emalickel, for he was their source of comfort and security.

After a few moments, he had reached Thorenel and me at the base of the throne stairs. He stopped at the foot of the stairs and looked upward, at Dennoliel, who rose to a stand in front of the throne chairs. By extending his arm outward, Dennoliel motioned for Emalickel to join him at the top of the stairs. Before he proceeded up the stairs, Emalickel held out his hand, offering for me to take hold of it. I looked at Emalickel and trustingly placed my hand into his.

We ascended the throne stairs together until we stood at the top with Dennoliel. Emalickel squeezed my hand before moving to step closer to Dennoliel. I looked down at Thorenel, who still stood at the base of the throne stairs. He beamed at me and winked, which was his way of providing reassurance.

146. Artist: Future World Music
Song: Anthem of the New World

Dennoliel reached up to remove the crown from his own head and presented it to the crowd while he spoke the ceremonial words.

Dennoliel: The Crown of Lapoi represents supremacy among

the entire realm of Millattus. May he who bears this crown, adorn it with great honor in their title as the Prince of Lapoi. May all who come into the presence of the Prince, embellish him with great respect, obedience, and admiration.

Still holding the crown high, Dennoliel turned to face Emalickel.

Dennoliel: Today, our kingdom welcomes the return of its Royal-Princedom, the sovereign leader of all Millattus—Prince Emalickel!

The celestials roared in celebration. Emalickel gazed out at them and smiled humbly. Then, he turned back toward Dennoliel and looked down to kneel on one knee. The celestials became quiet again.

Dennoliel regally placed the sparkling gold and diamond crown upon Emalickel's head, where it seemed to rightfully belong. Adorning the Crown of Lapoi, Emalickel slowly rose to a proud, standing position. As Emalickel rose, Dennoliel kneeled. Emalickel placed his hand on Dennoliel's right shoulder, signaling acknowledgement. Dennoliel rose and bowed his head to Emalickel, then turned to descend the throne stairs.

The celestials cheered in celebration of their Royal-Princedom. Emalickel held his hand out to me and showed me to my throne chair. I sat down at the edge, trying to exhibit good posture. Smiling proudly, Emalickel sat back and relaxed in his throne chair while he watched the joyful crowd.

147. Artist: Fearless Motivation
Song: Work on Yourself

When the Throne Hall had become semi-quiet again, Emalickel

sat forward and began speaking. Soft empowering music faintly began to play as he spoke.

Emalickel: There are many matters concerning Millattus which need to be addressed. Although it is imperative that we come to a place of resolution regarding these matters, it is also imperative that we find ourselves grateful for the blessings bestowed upon us. We shall give the glory to God for all of these things. We shall continue to sing our praises to Him for His mercy and for His grace. There is more to come; and with that, there is more to be overcome.

Emalickel stood up from his throne chair. He raised his voice, speaking slowly and articulately, so that it echoed clearly all through the palace.

Emalickel: We shall rise-up and honor the name of our King! As His sons and daughters, we have been chosen to live in the name of His righteousness, for He has given us a place among eternity! We shall stand behind Him, until the day comes that we shall stand before Him. We shall let our knees bow at the perfection of His Majesty and His Omnipotence!

As he spoke the final words of this statement, Emalickel removed the crown from his head and dropped to one knee, placing the crown on the floor in front of him. The faint music had increased to a volume of motivation. The celestials were moved by Emalickel's words, as if the very Spirit of God had entered the Throne Hall. They all collectively took to their knees, and knelt with their faces to the floor. I, too, felt this spirit and brought myself down to my knees with my eyes to the floor.

The wind picked-up through the archways of the Grand Balcony. The chiffon curtains blew with intensity, as a sweet floral-scent filled the Throne Hall. The scent was familiar, perhaps like that of gardenias, and brought with it a feeling of comfort and security.

The Throne Hall became immensely illuminated in a golden light, which glowed all throughout, reflecting from every piece of gold within. It was as if the brightness and contrast of the room had been increased to a maximum. Everything appeared washed-out as all colors turned to white—everything became white. The armor of the celestials reflected as mirrors. The white marble floors appeared like water.

The palace walls seemed to tremor a thunderous quake while everyone within it maintained their kneeling positions. Not an eye looked up. Not a body flinched. Everyone remained frozen, in their inferior positions, stunned by the power of the presence which swarmed through the room. Goosebumps raised themselves upon my neck and scattered all down my arms. My heart trembled with fear and also with excitement. Several tears of respectful humility fell from my face.

The room continued to vibrate with a radiant power. It swarmed through the atmosphere, pouring rain of love and security on each and every soul present in that room. With my head still bowed low, I heard the two white lions begin to shuffle their feet. I peeked up and saw that they were standing on all four legs, something I had never seen them do before. They both raised their heads upward, toward the ceiling, and let out a series of booming roars which shook the floors beneath our hands and knees. Their roars seemed lively, rather than intimidating, as if they were speaking greetings of welcome to the unique presence among the room.

There was not a thought in my mind which questioned the source of the presence. It seemed to speak without words. It flowed through me, like a whirlwind of piercing light, activating a feeling of which I cannot describe in any word, other than heavenly.

After a few moments, there was a stillness—a quietness which overcame us all. We remained low, but slowly raised our heads to look upon one another. I would forever remember the magnificence of that experience; seeing tens of thousands of revered monumental celestials, kneeling with dignity before the spiritual presence of the one King, whom they called by many names, but who remained as the one King above all of creation. He had been there, gracing us with His undeniably timeless presence, reassuring us of His infinite sovereignty and never-ending existence.

Emalickel brought himself to his feet. The celestials followed-suit. Silence remained among us until Emalickel finally brought himself to speak.

Emalickel: Let that be an indication of our prevalence in all matters which may concern us. We shall tend to these matters, but in a time to come. I assure you all, as your Prince, we will overcome any and all trials that may be set before us.

He turned to me and extended his hand. I knew what was next to take place. My time in Lapoi was quickly approaching its ending, but I felt at ease; for I had seen and experienced more than I once had known, taking part in many things which were profoundly moving to my soul. I was anxious to share it with the mortal world and record it in a text where it would remain forever written. I took Emalickel's hand and prepared myself to say to goodbye.

Emalickel: For now, we shall bid farewell to our Princess, who continues to play her part among the spiritually evolving mortals of Terra, where she shall persist in her quest to share

the vision of destiny, leading all who see it to find their rightful places among eternity.

148. Artist: Fearless Motivation
Song: Proof

After he said this, the front doors of the palace began to open, letting in the brightness from outside. Standing in the opening of the arched doorways, was a beautiful pure-white horse. It was Arwynn. She was led by a celestial-guard wearing the standard white-robed attire, to stand under the main archway of the Thorne Hall. Then, the guard stopped with Arwynn as they came onto the black aisle-runner. After taking a moment to pause with purpose, the guard began walking Arwynn down the aisle, toward the thrones where I stood.

Although the two white lions, at the top of the throne stairs, had resumed to sitting upright at attention, they did not seem phased by her presence; for their eyes squinted and blinked in a rather relaxed manner. As Arwynn slowly marched down the aisle, her hair seemed to glow of pure white in the resonate lighting of the palace. The celestials watched as she steadily paced herself along the central rug, whipping her white tail behind her along the way.

When they had reached the foot of the throne stairs, the guard let go of Arwynn's reins and walked off to the side. Arwynn remained in place, still whipping her tail. On her back, she wore the black, velour blanket, trimmed in gold, with the golden triquetra symbols on each side. Thorenel stepped closer to her and took the reins loosely in one of his hands. She pawed the floor with one of her feet, as if anxious to take me upon her back. Emalickel stepped forward and descended the throne stairs to the half-way point. He held his hand out to me again, to assist me down the stairs. I took his hand and began stepping down the stairway. Emalickel smiled and spoke to me directly, yet loud enough for all to hear.

Emalickel: I assure you, this will not be your last ride upon her, Princess.

Thorenel still held onto the reins while Emalickel hoisted me up to sit in the elegant saddle upon Arwynn's back. Thorenel guided her around to face the front of the palace and Emalickel moved up to stand to the right of Thorenel. Eupheshiel stepped out from her place in the crowd and hurried toward me. She adjusted my dress so that the train was secured from dragging. She also repositioned my cloak to drape smoothly over Arwynn's back and hips. Before returning to her place in the crowd, Eupheshiel peered up at me and offered words with a kind smile.

Eupheshiel: Always an honor to serve you, Princess Hadriel—in the past, present, and upon your future return.

She bowed her head and went back into the crowd. Emalickel and Thorenel were watching from their positions in front of Arwynn. They kept their eyes on me, as if awaiting my acknowledgement for them to escort me. I showed them a wide-smile and nodded my head once at them.

149. Artist: Really Slow Motion
Song: Beneath the Starry Skies

They both turned forward and guided Arwynn along the aisle, with me upon her back. I noticed the other four Princedom brothers had positioned themselves to follow behind us. We slowly made our way toward the front doors of the palace. The celestials among the palace folded their hands down in front of them and respectfully bowed their heads as we passed them by. We continued forward until we exited under the grand archway of the Throne Hall.

The massive front doors of the palace began to open. As we emerged outside and into the main courtyard, the coral-hued light of Auruclerum pierced our eyes. The courtyard was empty, with the exception of a few celestial-warriors who stood guard in designated places. We stepped-out to follow along the paved pathway which led to the main exterior gates of the walls surrounding the palace. A slight gust of wind blew, and I saw the grass of the courtyard ripple like soft green waves.

When we had arrived at the outer gates, they opened very slowly. We exited toward the gently rolling grasslands in front of the exterior palace walls. The grasslands extended for about a half-mile in front of us, until they blended into the rocky cliffs sloping into a beach. To the left of us, the grasslands flourished for about two-miles until coming to a hillside of wheat. To the right of us, the grasslands rolled into the woodlands about one-mile away. When we had emerged from the gates completely, Emalickel and Thorenel turned back to look at me. They both grinned with excitement in their eyes.

There were an uncountable number of celestials present on the land, both warriors and guards. There were also hundreds of Nephilim. They all filled the entire block of land between the palace and the beach, and for miles to the east and west.

The light of Auruclerum suddenly became brighter, as if it were peeking between the clouds, casting a golden-hue onto everything outside. Tiny, white, fluffy feathers began falling from the sky—millions of them came pouring down. They seemed to glow as they gracefully swayed back and forth, dropping endlessly all around.

The palace gates closed behind us, making a deep rumbling sound. At that very instant, as if it were a signal, every being in the land dropped their heads down and lowered themselves into a kneeling position. Nephilim dropped to one knee, warriors kneeled behind their swords, and guards bowed forward. An abundance of feathers continued falling from the sky at a steady pace. My perception of time slowed. All sounds around me became quiet and muffled. Everything seemed to move in slow-motion as I absorbed that scene of a magical fantasy happening right before my very eyes.

150. Artist: Really Slow Motion
Song: Becoming

Still holding onto the back of Arwynn's neck, I looked up to see the source of the feathers. They were coming from the puffy white clouds which filled the entirety of the sky above. The feathers fell slowly, like snow. They trickled down all around the grassland, covering it in a blanket of white.

Time was still moving very slowly when I heard the muffled yell of Emalickel and Thorenel as they signaled for Arwynn to begin trotting. Still holding the reins, they faced forward and led her pace. The celestials and Nephilim rose to stand upright again. They clapped and cheered—smiling and yelling joyfully at us. All across the grassland, I saw golden sparkles of light reflecting from the armor of the divine beings who surrounded us. In front of us, the water of the ocean twinkled like all the stars of the heavens. Feathers continued to fall from the clouds of the blush-colored sky.

Once again, Emalickel and Thorenel turned their heads around to see me while they continued guiding Arwynn's trot. They both exhibited wide, playful smiles that revealed their pearly-white teeth. A few feathers had sporadically landed in their hair and on the crimson cloaks that folded behind their shoulders. They squinted their eyes in delightful laughter. Time still appeared to pass in slow-motion while I gazed in awe at the two Princedom brothers who preside over the entire realm of Millattus, and with whom I was privileged to share a never-ending intimate love.

The feathers fell until they completely blanketed the grass. The white of the ground reflected onto the brothers' faces, illuminating them and accentuating their aqua-blue eyes. Arrows of love shot into the pit of my stomach. They stirred within me, making it hard to breath correctly. They gave me a hard-to-resist yearning to be encompassed within a tight embrace from them, never to be let go.

They both looked forward again. Gradually, I resumed hearing sounds more clearly and perceiving time at a normal pace. We were nearly at the rocky cliffs overlooking the beach. I noticed the stone pathway which allowed for easy passageway to the white sandy shores.

In front of this pathway, however, I noticed something else. It was something which had not been there in any of my other visits to Lapoi. It was a large, black and purple oval, which hovered and swirled one foot above the ground. The oval was about six feet tall and three feet wide. Then, I recognized what it was—it was a portal, just like the ones I had seen in the past. This would be the place I would depart from Lapoi and return to Earth.

151. Artist: Really Slow Motion
Song: End of an Era

Emalickel and Thorenel slowed Arwynn to a walking pace as we approached the portal. I looked around me. Romenciel, Seronimel, Dennoliel, and Xabiel were still trailing behind Arwynn. All the other celestials and Nephilim were standing calmly. They stared at me through the falling feathers. Emalickel and Thorenel let go of Arwynn's reins and stepped to either side of her. They both looked up at me. Emalickel spoke to me first.

Emalickel: Are you ready?

I grabbed the reins from the back of Arwynn's neck. I slowly turned my head to look behind me as I replied to him.

Me: No . . . not yet.

I rested the reins on the left side of Arwynn's neck, signaling for her to turn to the right. I had her turn around until I was facing the opposite direction, looking directly toward the palace. I scanned the entire scene, from left to right, taking my time to engrain a mental picture of everything. I wanted to be sure I would be able to recall everything, precisely and in great detail, after I had returned to the mortal plane. I wanted to remember the moment perfectly.

My eyes took-in everything. The ground was covered in a sheet of white feathers. The sky was pick with traces of lavender and reminded me of a glorious Earth sun-rise. The celestials and Nephilim were packed across the feather-covered land. They stood with professionalism, still reflecting the glistening golden light of Auruclerum from their various attires. The Nephilim wore all-black cloaks which created beautiful contrast with the white of the ground. Most astounding, however, was the palace. It was a giant, radiant, stone fortress. It was illuminated by a beam of light that glowed down directly from Auruclerum.

Thorenel moved to the right side of Arwynn. He held out his

hand. I took it as a signal that it was time to start the process of returning home. Taking his hand, I slid from the side of Arwynn and down on the ground. Thorenel had moved his hands to support my hips as I dismounted.

Thorenel stepped to the side and looked over at his four brothers who stood in a horizontal line in front of Arwynn. All of their eyes were fixated on me. I walked to stand before Romenciel. He was at the far right of the line.

152. Artist: Whitesand
Song: Melodic Dreams

Romenciel exhibited a slight smile, but his face was otherwise serious. He placed his hands on my shoulders and lowered his head to better square his eyes with mine.

Romenciel: Be strong. Keep your focus on God, knowing that the deceit of darkness aims to disconnect you from His peace. Certainly, you don the full Armor of God, as surely as my celestial eyes can physically see it. Remember this, Princess, always.

I nodded my head and absorbed his words. He saw a physical armor on me, an armor in which I could not see—a divine armor which I had always thought was figurative in the Biblical book of Ephesians. This excited me and empowered me. My smile grew wider. In gratitude, I clasped Romenciel's arms as they still rested on my shoulders.

Me: Thank you, Romenciel. Your words provide me with much-needed reassurance, and strength, and empowerment.

He stood upright and pulled me into him for a strong and genuine hug. After several seconds, he released his hold on me and nodded in approval. Then, I moved down, to the left, to stand in front of Seronimel. I stopped and grabbed one of his hands with mine. I squeezed it within my hands, as if giving it a hug. Seronimel smiled and clasped his other hand onto the pile.

Seronimel: May your journey be safe, Princess. Keep your guard up, but should it come down, rest assured, we guardians are there, and we WILL protect you.

I lowered my eyes to the ground and smiled humbly.

Me: I appreciate that, truly. I'm fond of you, and I'm glad I've come to know you better.

We made eye-contact once more and gave each other's hand a final squeeze before I moved down the line to stand in front of Dennoliel.

Dennoliel took my hands into each of his. He exhibited a grand smile.

Dennoliel: Princess! It has been a great pleasure spending this time with you. Your company has been a joy. I speak on behalf of all the celestials when I say it has been wonderful having your presence here and to be a part of your safe return to Millattus.

Flattered, I smiled at him and nodded in approval. He bowed and released my hands as I moved down to Xabiel. Although Xabiel had been difficult during most of my visit this time, Xabiel managed to crack a genuine smile before he spoke.

Xabiel: Well, Princess… please hold no grudges against me for my less than noble behavior recently. I hope you know none of them were intended against you.

I understood what Xabiel was trying to say. He had not done

anything to act directly hasty toward me, and I was surprised by his statement in swallowing his pride. I placed my hand on his shoulder and squeezed it reassuringly.

Me: I don't hold any grudges against you, Xabiel. Your intentions are well-meaning, and I know that.

I paused for a moment before teasing him to make light of the conversation.

Me: You just make sure to behave yourself while I'm gone. I can't keep your brothers from killing you while I'm mortal!

Xabiel chuckled and bowed his head to me, in gratefulness.

153. Artist: Mattia Cupelli
Song: Two Souls

I turned around to walk back toward Thorenel, who remained standing beside Arwynn. When I arrived to him, I looked up at his face while holding back tears. I knew the end of my time in Lapoi was only moments away. Thorenel stood there and rested his hands on my hips, while he stared down at me with a gentle smile. My stomach sank in dread as I locked eyes with him. He pulled me into him, with great passion, and clutched my head to his chest. He squeezed me ever so tightly, sending chills down my back. Then, he leaned down to press a kiss to my forehead. After a moment, he moved his hands to hold my face, maneuvering it to look up at him. Maintaining his gaze in my eyes, he leaned down and slowly tilted his head to the side. Leaning in further, he closed his eyes and allowed his lips to meet with mine. Almost immediately, I reached up with both my hands, and pulled his face more firmly into mine. We held ourselves there, resistant to part ways. I felt a tear escape the corner of my eye as a lump of sorrow swelled within my throat. Trying to be strong, Thorenel completed the kiss. Even though we had parted from the kiss, we both continued to embrace each other's face. Thorenel bent down to level his eyes with mine. With our faces only a few inches apart, we toggled our eyes several times —long enough to absorb the image of the soul behind them. Finally, Thorenel closed his eyes and pressed his forehead against mine.

When Thorenel and I separated, Emalickel moved to stand beside us. He stood patiently with his hands folded down in front of him. I could see that he was smiling, but there was a glimmer of sorrow within his eyes as they sparkled at me. I stepped away from Thorenel and collapsed in the warmth and security of Emalickel's arms. I felt his chest rise and fall, as he took a deep breath and exhaled. He held my face and brought me to look at him. Our eyes froze on each other. We became very serious as our eyes danced. His eyes always seemed to pierce into me, as if he saw deep inside of me, into an aspect within me of which even I was unaware. He hunched his shoulders forward, and I felt him squeeze my face with more passion. Then, he brought himself closer to touch his forehead firmly against mine. He held it there for a moment before whispering words of strong, passionate reassurance.

Emalickel: Call for me and know, in that very moment, I am right there with you.

He brought his lips to press them against my forehead, where he retained them solidly. I closed my eyes, fighting the tears which began accumulating beneath them. He pulled me into him, clutching me closely, with all his strength. His hand stroked the back of my head and further pulled me in, while we remained close together. I felt him shake as he held me, as if resisting to let go.

Thorenel stepped closer to Emalickel and placed his hand on his shoulder for encouragement. Emalickel loosened his grip of me and stepped back with his hands on my waist. He looked down at me, offering a comforting smile before nodding his head for me to proceed with my journey. Then, he brought both his hands to remove the crown from my head. It glittered as he slowly brought it to rest at his waist.

Emalickel: Your crown will always await you securely, right here, until your next return—Princess of Lapoi.

Emalickel straightened himself to an upright stance. He held his head high with a stiff upper lip. Thorenel, still with his hand on Emalickel's shoulder, nodded his head and managed to cock a reassuring smile at one corner of his mouth.

After pausing for one final gaze at the two of them, I gulped the lump of sorrow down my throat and slowly turned around toward the portal. I stroked my hand down the side of Arwynn as I took a few steps toward the swirling oval. Before stepping inside, I paused, and turned around for one last look at the Kingdom of Lapoi, a piece of my soul, a timeless image that would forever remain in my heart through the rest of my days on Earth. My Princedom brothers were illuminated far brighter than anything else in sight.

Thorenel: We await your return, beloved. You will see us again, and eventually, forevermore. Rest assured—you have my word.

A tear dropped from the inner corner of my eye. My stomach sank with dread of the coming moment of my departure. Emalickel encouraged me.

Emalickel: You must be strong, Hadriel. You are adorned with the full Armor of God. Have trust, and always remember to let

faith prevail. Now go—live your purpose, be righteous, share your gifts. Great things await ahead.

My head dropped to the ground as I slowly turned around to face the portal. The image of everything had been secured within my mind. I carried the image with me as I stepped into the spinning purple-black vortex. Sparing myself the pain of looking back, I focused on replaying the words of Thorenel and Emalickel echoing in my mind. Their words recycled again and again, until all in view became completely dark.

154. Artist: Fearless Motivation
Song: Work on Yourself

My body felt as if it were being pulled out of a deep-sleep. I felt tired and groggy. I could hear the soft humming of a bedroom ceiling fan. My eyes began to open. The room was dimly lit by the light of early-morning. I was in my own bed, back in my peaceful country home on Earth. My black and white tuxedo-cat was curled-up by my feet, sound asleep. As I laid there for a minute, my mind began recalling details from Lapoi. I slowly sat up in the bed and rested my head in my hands as I processed everything, trying to digest all that had happened.

Lifting the covers from my legs, I brought myself to the edge of the bed. The sun was slowly rising outside. The light coming through the window was becoming brighter. Although the events of the past night were soaring through my mind, I still followed my usual morning routine. I went to the bathroom counter and grabbed my hairbrush from the cabinet.

I glanced at myself in the large, rectangular mirror secured to the wall over the counter. As I began brushing through my hair, something immediately captured my eye. I froze with the brush still in my hair. Slowly leaning in toward the mirror, my eyes narrowed in deep concentration. I continued closer to the mirror to further analyze what I was seeing.

Then, my jaw dropped open. My eyes widened in disbelief. I removed the brush from my hair, ever so cautiously, and gently placed it on the countertop. I reached my hands up to retrieve something from the upper left-side of my head. Pinching it between my fingers, I slid the item down through the long strands of my brown hair. Once it was free, I raised it up for a better look in the light. My postulation had been deemed correct. There, between my thumb and forefinger, I held a single, small, white feather. Its soft individual barbs were blowing gracefully with the movement of air within the room.

The feather was about the size of a dime. It contained no shaft and no hard rachis, but rather appeared to be completely composed of light, fluffy after-feather—exactly like the ones that had fallen from the sky in Lapoi!

My heart raced in excitement! I wasn't even sure what to do or think! My hands began shaking as every nerve in my body reacted to my adrenaline. I began pacing around the bathroom and talking to myself in whispers of excited denial.

Me: What!?! No way! Really!?! How is this possible!?!

I tried to be reasonable and figure out a logical explanation. I thought of every possible way that feather could have found its way into my hair. There was no answer. There was absolutely nothing made of feathers in the entire house—no pillows, no blankets, no clothing—nothing of any kind.

Besides, what would be the chances of finding such a feather in my hair on the very same night as I visited Lapoi where white feathers, of the same size and texture, had fallen in my final moments there? Not to mention, I had lived in that house for ten years and never seen, found, nor came across any white feather before. My mind continued spiraling in search of other ideas from where it came.

Then, I recalled the times the brothers had told me to resist doubt. Their voices echoed in my head. *Doubt is the enemy. Never doubt. Always trust, and let faith prevail.* There I was, remembering the brothers' words, with a physical artifact of reassurance in my hand, with no possible logical explanation as to how it had appeared, and yet I was still doubting.

My pacing led me out of the bathroom and into the living room, where I continued to pace in astonishment while looking at the feather in my fingers. I paced, back and forth, in front of the couch several times, wondering what to do and what to think. I tried to remain calm and collect my thoughts.

Then, I stopped in front of the end-table. My eyes moved to the floor. Resting on the side of the couch, was my black laptop with the red logo in the center; the same laptop in which I had recorded my previous visits to Lapoi. It captured my attention and beckoned to me. My eyesight almost seemed to zoom into it, as it were begging me to open it and begin recording the experience.

Giving in, I reached down to pick it up. I sat on the couch and carefully placed the fine feather on the end-table next to me. The laptop rested in my lap as I opened it up. The all-black keyboard lit-up with red keys. I used them to type my password, then I opened a brand-new document—a blank canvas which would soon hold every detail my mind could recall of that most-recent experience in the celestial plane. I hit the enter button several times to take the curser half-way down the blank page. I typed the word “Emalickel.” Then, I hit the enter button once more and typed “Release of the Nephilim.”

I turned my head to the end-table on my right and looked at the little soft feather once more. I became absorbed by the magical sight of the white, glowing artifact from Lapoi. Perhaps it had been sent back with me as both a gift and as a sign—a gift of the brothers’ reassurance and a sign of their reality. My eyes absorbed great detail of the beauty of that feather as it gently fluttered with the air of the room. Then, I looked forward and upward. I displayed a smile of great gratitude and spoke aloud.

Me: Thank you.

I nodded my head and reiterated.

Me: For everything.

The feather remained on the end-table next to me, as I began typing the words to describe my experience. The feather sat there, in the purest form of beauty, as a humble reminder that nothing is ever a coincidence.

THE END

VERSES

"You intended to harm me, but God intended it for good to accomplish what is now being done, the saving of many lives." Genesis 50:20

"The LORD will fight for you, and you shall hold your peace." Exodus 14:14

"Behold, I am sending an angel ahead of you to guard you along the way and to bring you to the place I have prepared. Pay attention to him and listen to what he says . . ." Exodus 20:20-21

"One thing I ask from the Lord, this only do I seek: that I may dwell in the house of the Lord all the days of my life, to gaze on the beauty of the Lord and to seek Him in his temple." Psalm 27:4

"Blessed is the nation whose God is the Lord, the people he chose for his inheritance." Psalm 33:12

"Take delight in the Lord, and He will give you the desires of your heart." Psalm 37:4

"He will cover you with his feathers, and under his wings you will find refuge; his faithfulness will be your shield and rampart." Psalm 91:4

"You women who are so complacent, rise up and listen to me; you daughters who feel secure, hear what I have to say!" Isaiah 32:9

"They are the ones who will dwell on the heights, whose refuge will be the mountain fortress. Their bread will be supplied, and water will not fail them. Your eyes will see the king in his beauty and view a land that stretches afar." Isaiah 33:16-17

"A hand touched me and set me trembling on my hands and knees. He said, [. . .] "Do not be afraid. Since the first day that you set your mind to gain understanding and to humble yourself before your God, your words were heard, and I have come in response to them." Daniel 10:10-12

"I consider that our present sufferings are not worth comparing with the glory that will be revealed in us." Romans 8:18

"For in this hope we were saved. But hope that is seen is no hope at all. Who hopes for what they already have? But if we hope for what we do not yet have, we wait for it patiently." Romans 8:24-25

"Do not conform to the pattern of this world, but be transformed by the renewing of your mind. Then you will be able to test and approve what God's will is—his good, pleasing and perfect will." Romans 12:2

"For you were once darkness, but now you are light in the Lord. Live as children of light [. . .] everything exposed by the light becomes visible—and everything that is illuminated becomes a light. This is why it is said: "Wake up, sleeper, rise from the dead, and Christ will shine on you." Ephesians 5:8

"For our struggle is not against flesh and blood, but against the rulers, against the authorities, against the powers of this dark world and against the spiritual forces of evil in the heavenly realms. Therefore put on the full armor of God, so that when the day of evil comes, you may be able to stand your ground, and after you have done everything, to stand." Ephesians 6:12-13

"Do not forget to show hospitality to strangers, for by so doing some people have shown hospitality to angels without knowing it." Hebrews 13:2

"If any of you lacks wisdom, you should ask God, who gives generously to all without finding fault, and it will be given to you. **6** *But when you ask, you must believe and not doubt, because the one who doubts is like a wave of the sea, blown and tossed by the wind." James 1:5-6*

"I have much more to say to you, more than you can now bear." John 16:12

"many false prophets have gone out into the world. This is how you can recognize the Spirit of God: Every spirit that acknowledges that Jesus Christ has come in the flesh is from God, but every spirit that does not acknowledge Jesus is not from God. This is the spirit of the antichrist, which you have heard is coming and even now is already in the world. You, dear children, are from God and have overcome them, because the One who is in you is greater than the one who is in the world." 1 John 4:1-4

"I looked, and there before me was a white cloud, and seated on the cloud was one like a son of man with a crown of gold on his head and a sharp sickle in his hand." Revelation 14:14

"After this I looked, and there before me was a door standing open in heaven. And the voice I had first heard speaking to me like a trumpet said, "Come up here, and I will show you what must take place after this." At once I was in the Spirit, and there before me was a throne in heaven with someone sitting on it. And the one who sat there had the appearance of jasper and ruby. A rainbow that shone like an emerald encircled the throne." Revelation 4:1-3

"At that time Michael, the great prince who protects your people, will arise [. . .] at that time your people—everyone whose name is found written in the book—will be delivered. Multitudes who sleep in the dust of the earth will awake: some to everlasting life, others to shame and everlasting contempt. Those who are wise will shine like the brightness of the heavens, and those who lead many to righteousness, like the stars for ever and ever." Daniel 12:1-3

APPENDIX A

PRONUNCIATION KEY

Key:

- a - **a**pple, **a**lligator
- ā - **a**pe, **a**corn
- ä - f**a**ther, **ah**
- ch – **ch**ase, **ch**ip, **ch**astise
- ə - **a**bout, circ**u**s, gall**o**p
- ē - **e**at, b**ee**
- e - **e**lephant, **e**gg
- i - **i**gloo, **i**ndigo, **i**guana
- î - **i**ce, **eye**s
- ō - **o**ats, t**oe**, b**oa**t
- û - he**ar**d, **ur**ge, t**er**m
- ōō - b**oo**t
- th - **th**is, **th**at, **th**e
- ô - **or**e, f**or**, h**oa**rse
- ö - **ou**ght, c**au**ght, p**o**t

Names/ Characters:

- Barthaldeo (bär · **thöl** · dē · ō) –antagonist celestial from Haffelnia
- Clive Gwydion (clîv) (**gwi** · dē · un) –mystic from the cave on Thermaplia
- Civiticus (klə · **vit** · i · kəs) –the full first name of Clive Gwydion
- Emalickel (ē · **mal** · i · kel) – the primary Royal-Prince of Lapoi
- Thorenel (**thôr** · e · nel) –the secondary Royal-Prince of Lapoi
- Romenciel (rō · **min** · sē · el) —brother of Emalickel who oversees the Warriors of Lapoi
- Xabiel (eks · **ā** · bē · ul) –brother of Emalickel who accompanies Romenciel with the Warriors of Lapoi
- Dennoliel (de · **nä** · lē · el) –brother of Emalickel who oversees the Guardians of Lapoi
- Seronimel (se · **rä** · ne · mel) –brother of Emalickel. Second to Dennoliel
- Hadriel (**hā** · drē · el) –Lapoian name given to Adrienne of Earth
- Zamadriel (zə · **mä** · drē · el) –the feminine aspect united with Romenciel and Xabiel
- Haelael (**hā** · lel) –the deceiver who manipulates mortals into disobedience to God.
- Gahndriel (**gön** · drē · el) –dark skinned celestial who questions Thorenel
- Drakahdra (drə · **kä** · drə) –the Nephilim who found Adrienne on Thermaplia
- Rahnukah (rö · **nōō** · kə) –one of the Nephilim residing in Versallus

- Uthesiel (yōō · **thē** · sē · el) –a celestial serving in the Palace of Lapoi
- Florrazziel (flôr · **rä** · zē · el) –candidate #1 in the village of Rasaevulus and the feminine aspect united with Gorandriel and Hassaniel
- Gorandriel (gôr · **ön** · drē · el) –guardian of Lapoi who is unified with Florrazziel
- Hassaniel (ha · **sön** · ē · el) –guardian of Lapoi who is unified with Florrazziel
- Namriel (**nam** · rē · el) –candidate #2 in the village of Rasavulus
- Kentiel (**kin** · te · el) –celestial guardian in charge of the village of Rasaevulus during the absence of the Principality.
- Eupheshiel (yōō · **fē** · shē · el) –a feminine assistant celestial in the Spa Quarters of the Palace of Lapoi.

Places/ Locations/ and other things:

- Millattus (mi · **la** · tus) –one of the nine realms of the Universe (divine status) whose celestial planet is called Lapoi. Millattus is the realm of mankind.
- Lapoi (lə · **pöi**) –the celestial planet of Millattus where Emalickel presides
- Auruclerum (ə · **rōō** · clē · rəm) –the giant star of Lapoi (like the Sun)
- Jesserion (je · **sir** · ē · än) –one of the nine realms of the Universe (divine status) filled with the feminine celestial aspects of Millattus. This is the origin place of all female mortals.
- Ithilliah (i · **thil** · ē · ə) –the celestial planet of Jesserion

- Haffelnia (ha · **fel** · nē · ə)—one of the nine realms of the Universe (dark status)
- Umgliesia (ōōm · **glā** · shē · ə)—the celestial planet of Haffelnia where Barthaldeo presides
- Thermaplia (thûr · **mä** · plē · ə) –one of three mortal planets in Haffelnia
- Gaddorium (gu · **dôr** · rē · um) –one of the nine realms of the Universe (dark status)
- Yahrinstahd (**yä** · rin · städ) –one of the nine realms of the Universe (dark status)
- Odalveim (**ō** · dəl · vîm) –one of the nine realms of the Universe (unknown status)
- Norohmba (nôr · **äm** · bä) –one of the nine realms of the Universe (unknown status)
- Chasstillia (cha · **stil** · ē · ə) –one of the nine realms of the Universe (unknown status)
- Salheim (**sal** · hîm) –one of the nine realms of the Universe (unknown status)
- Versallus (vû · **sä** · lus) –land on Lapoi inhabited by the freed Nephilim
- Rasaevulus (rö · **sā** · vōō · lus) –Princess Hadriel's mortal-like village created in Lapoi
- Triquetra (trî · **kwe** · trə)—trinity symbol adopted by the Lapoian Princedom brothers
- Ulfberht (**ulf** · bût)—Viking-like sword wielded by the Princedom brothers

Language Articulation:

- Uhn ah tufah nich (ōōn · ö · tōō · fö · nēk) – Nephilim chant literally translated as "*We are afraid not*"

APPENDIX B

MUSIC PLAYLIST CREDITS

1. Artist: Whitesand
Song: Eternity
Album: (Single Release)
Available: YouTube @ Whitesand, soundcloud.com/marty-naslau, patreon.com/Whitesand

2. Artist: Whitesand
Song: Story of the Wind
Album: (Single Release)
Available: YouTube @ Whitesand,
Soundcloud/martynaslau, patreon.com/Whitesand

3. Artist: Efisio Cross
Song: If You Fall I Will Carry You
Album: (Single Release)
Available: Amazon Music, iTunes/ Apple Music

4. Artist: Danheim
Song: Gungnir
Album: Herja

Available: Amazon Music, iTunes/ Apple Music

5. Artist: Clint Mansell
Song: Lux Aeterna (LOTR Version 6:30)
Album: Requiem for a Tower
Available: YouTube, Amazon Music

6. Artist: Really Slow Motion
Song: Hero
Album: Elevation
Available: Amazon Music, Bandcamp, Google Play

7. Artist: Audiomachine
Song: Tangled Earth
Album: Decimus
Available: Amazon Music, iTunes/ Apple Music, YouTube @ Audiomachine, www.audiomachine.com

8. Artist: Mark Petrie
Song: Celestial
Album: Soundtrack for a Blockbuster
Available: Amazon Music, iTunes/ Apple Music

9. Artist: Paradox Interactive
Song: Drums of Odin
Album: War of the Vikings
Available: Amazon Music, iTunes/ Apple Music

10. Artist: John Dreamer
Song: Becoming A Legend
Album: (Single Release)
Available: Amazon Music, iTunes/ Apple Music

11. Artist: Audiomachine
Song: Existence
Album: Millennium/Existence
Available: (Pandora Extended version on YouTube @ Pandora Music), Amazon Music, iTunes/ Apple Music, www.audiomachine.com

12. Artist: Fearless Motivation Instrumentals
Song: Revival
Album: Sounds of Power
Available: Amazon Music, Google Play, iTunes/ Apple Music, www.fearlessmotivation.com

13. Artist: Charles Bunczk
Song: The Inner Light
Album: (Single Release)
Available: YouTube @ Epic Music World, soundcloud.com/epicmusicworld, patreon.com/EpicMusicWorld

14. Artist: Thunderstep Music
Song: They Are Coming for Us
Album: Dystopia
Available: Bandcamp, iTunes/ Apple Music, YouTube @ Thunderstep Music, soundcloud.com/armando-de-moura

15. Artist: Wardruna
Song: MannaR Liv
Album: Runaljod Ragnarok
Available: Amazon Music, iTunes/ Apple Music

16. Artist: Olexandr Ignatov
Song: Rising from the Ashes

Album: Forgotten Reality
Available: Amazon Music, Audiojungle, Bandcamp, Google Play, iTunes/ Apple Music, Soundcloud, www.olexandrignatov.com

17. Artist: Antti Martikainen
Song: Otherworld
Album: Set Sail for the Golden Age
Available: Amazon Music, Bandcamp, Google Play, iTunes/ Apple Music

18. Artist: Hi-Finesse
Song: Another World
Album: Stratus
Available: Amazon Music, iTunes/ Apple Music

19. Artist: Audiomachine
Song: Black Cauldron
Album: Chronicles
Available: Amazon Music, Google Play, iTunes/ Apple Music, YouTube @ Audiomachine, www.audiomachine.com

20. Artist: Paradox Interactive
Song: Drums of Odin
Album: War of the Vikings OST
Available: Amazon Music, iTunes/ Apple Music

21. Artist: Paradox Interactive
Song: Terror from the Sea
Album: War of the Vikings OST
Available: Amazon Music, iTunes/ Apple Music

22. Artist: Songs to Your Eyes (Tybercore)
Song: Termination

Album: Heroes of Chaos
Available: Amazon Music, iTunes

23. Artist: Whitesand
Song: Eternity
Album: (Single Release)
Available: YouTube @ Whitesand, soundcloud.com/marty-naslau, patreon.com/Whitesand

24. Artist: Mikolai Strinski, Marcin Przbylowicz, Percival
Song: The Nightingale
Album: The Witcher 3 – Wild Hunt OST
Available: iTunes/ Apple Music

25. Artist: Mikolai Strinski, Marcin Przbylowicz, Percival
Song: Cloak and Dagger
Album: The Witcher 3 – Wild Hunt OST
Available: iTunes/ Apple Music

26. Artist: Olexandr Ignatov
Song: Rising from the Ashes
Album: Forgotten Reality
Available: Amazon Music, Audiojungle, Bandcamp, Google Play, iTunes/ Apple Music, Soundcloud, www.olexandrignatov.com

27. Artist: Antti Martikainen
Song: At Journey's End
Album: Eternal Saga
Available: Amazon Music, Bandcamp, Google Play, iTunes/ Apple Music

28. Artist: Mark Petrie
Song: Ultrasonic

Album: Genesis
Available: Amazon Music, iTunes/ Apple Music

29. Artist: Two Steps from Hell
Song: Evergreen
Album: Vanquish
Available: Amazon Music, iTunes/ Apple Music, YouTube @Two Steps From Hell www.twostepsfromhell.com

30. Artist: Audiomachine
Song: Enoch
Album: Magnus
Available: Amazon Music, Google Play, iTunes/ Apple Music, YouTube @ Audiomachine, www.audiomachine.com

31. Artist: The Secession (Greg Dombrowski)
Song: Unbreakable
Album: Reflections
Available: Amazon Music, Bandcamp, iTunes/ Apple Music

32. Artist: PostHaste Music (Mark Petrie)
Song: Renewed Spirit
Album: Volume 8 - Drama
Available: Amazon Music

33. Artist: Twelve Titans Music (David Edwards)
Song: Bound by Purpose
Album: Ascend the Starless Sky
Available: Amazon Music, iTunes/ Apple Music

34. Artist: Audiomachine
Song: Earth Shaker (Drums)
Album: Drumscores

Available: YouTube @ Audiomachine, www.audiomachine.com

35. Artist: Fearless Motivation Instrumentals
Song: Revival
Album: Sounds of Power
Available: Amazon Music, Google Play, iTunes/ Apple Music, www.fearlessmotivation.com

36. Artist: Really Slow Motion
Song: Shine Like the Sun
Album: Illume
Available: YouTube @ Really Slow Motion; other RSM tunes at Amazon Music, Bandcamp, Google Play, iTunes/ Apple Music

37. Artist: Peter Gundry
Song: The Last of Her Kind
Album: The Elixir of Life
Available: Amazon Music, Google Play, iTunes/ Apple Music, www.petergundrymusic.com

38. Artist: Audiomachine
Song: Hallowed Dawn
Album: Awakenings
Available: Amazon Music, Bandcamp, Google Play, iTunes/ Apple Music, YouTube @ Audiomachine, www.audiomachine.com

39. Artist: Danheim
Song: Tyrfing
Album: Munarvagr
Available: Amazon Music, Bandcamp, Google Play, iTunes/ Apple Music

40. Artist: Rok Nardin
Song: Destroyer of Worlds
Album: (Single Release)
Available: YouTube @ Rok Nardin, soundcloud.com/rok-nardin, facebook.com/roknardin.composer

41. Artist: Audiomachine
Song: Lord of the Drums
Album: Trailer Acts: Act 1-7
Available: YouTube @ Audiomachine, www.audiomachine.com

42. Artist: 2WEI
Song: Expectations
Album: Escape Velocity
Available: Amazon Music, Google Play, iTunes/ Apple Music, YouTube @ 2WEI

43. Artist: Peter Gundry
Song: A Nostalgic Dream
Album: (Single Release)
Available: Amazon Music, Google Play, iTunes, www.peter-gundrymusic.com

44. Artist: Adrian Von Ziegler
Song: Walking with the Ancestors
Album: Fable
Available: Amazon Music, Bandcamp, Google Play, iTunes/ Apple Music

45. Artist: PostHaste Music (Mark Petrie)
Song: Renewed Spirit
Album: Volume 8 – Drama/PHM Presents: Best of Mark Petrie
Available: Amazon Music, Google Play, iTunes/ Apple Music

46. Artist: Antti Martikainen
Song: The King of the Highlands
Album: The Last Chronicle
Available: Amazon Music, Bandcamp, Google Play, iTunes/ Apple Music

47. Artist: Really Slow Motion
Song: Legendary
Album: Sigma
Available: YouTube @ Really Slow Motion; other RSM tunes at Amazon Music, Bandcamp, Google Play, iTunes/ Apple Music

48. Artist: Two Steps from Hell
Song: Amaria
Album: Battlecry
Available: Amazon Music, Google Play, iTunes/ Apple Music, YouTube @Two Steps from Hell, www.twostepsfromhell.com

49. Artist: Steve Jablonsky
Song: My Name is Lincoln
Album: The Island OST
Available: Amazon Music, Google Play, iTunes/ Apple Music

50. Artist: Antti Martikainen
Song: At Journey's End
Album: Internal Saga
Available: Amazon Music, Bandcamp, Google Play, iTunes/ Apple Music

51. Artist: Antti Martikainen
Song: The Land of Eternal Winter
Album: Creation of the World
Available: Amazon Music, Bandcamp, Google Play, iTunes

52. Artist: R. Armando Morabito (feat. Julie Elven and Tina Guo)
Song: Sea of Atlas
Album: Days of Tomorrow
Available: Amazon Music, Bandcamp, Google Play, iTunes/ Apple Music

53. Artist: Antti Martikainen
Song: Eternal Saga
Album: Eternal Saga
Available: Amazon Music, Bandcamp, Google Play, iTunes/ Apple Music

54. Artist: James Paget
Song: The Hero Within
Album: Rubicon
Available: Amazon Music, Bandcamp, Google Play, iTunes/ Apple Music

55. Artist: Adrian Von Ziegler
Song: Maiden's Lullaby
Album: The Complete Discography
Available: Bandcamp, patreon.com/AdrianvonZiegler

56. Artist: Fearless Motivation Instrumentals
Song: Redemption
Album: Sounds of Power 7
Available: Amazon Music, Google Play, iTunes/ Apple Music, www.fearlessmotivation.com

57. Artist: Fearless Motivation Instrumentals
Song: Day of Purpose
Album: Sounds of Power 7

Available: Amazon Music, Google Play, iTunes/ Apple Music, www.fearlessmotivation.com

58. Artist: Audiomachine
Song: Through the Darkness
Album: Ascendance
Available: Amazon Music, Google Play, iTunes/ Apple Music, YouTube @ Audiomachine, www.audiomachine.com

59. Artist: Audiomachine
Song: Slash Bash
Album: Drumscores 2
Available: YouTube @ Audiomachine, www.audiomachine.com

60. Artist: Blue Lion Music
Song: Everything Ends Here
Album: (Single Release)
Available: YouTube @ Blue Lion Music

61. Artist: Dean Valentine
Song: A Fire Shall Be Woken
Album: Viking OST
Available: Amazon Music, iTunes/ Apple Music, soundcloud.-com/dean_valentine

62. Artist: J. T. Peterson
Song: Honor and Gold
Album: Petrichor
Available: Amazon Music, Google Play, iTunes/ Apple Music

63. Artist: Rok Nardin
Song: Hell Rising
Album: (Single Release)

Available: YouTube @ Rok Nardin, soundcloud.com/rok-nardin, facebook.com/roknardin.composer

64. Artist: Audiomachine
Song: Taste of Blood
Album: Leviathan
Available: YouTube @ Audiomachine, www.audiomachine.com

65. Artist: Audiomachine
Song: Bloody Brigade
Album: Drumscores 2
Available: YouTube @ Audiomachine, www.audiomachine.com

66. Artist: Antti Martikainen
Song: The God of Thunder
Album: Eternal Saga
Available: Amazon Music, Bandcamp,
Google Play, iTunes/ Apple Music

67. Artist: Audiomachine
Song: Famine
Album: Drumscores 2
Available: YouTube @ Audiomachine, www.audiomachine.com

68. Artist: Really Slow Motion
Song: Legendary
Album: Sigma
Available: YouTube @ Really Slow Motion; other RSM tunes at Amazon Music, Bandcamp, Google Play, iTunes/ Apple Music

69. Artist: Philipp Beesen
Song: Shadow Warrior
Album: Memories - EP

Available: Amazon Music, iTunes/ Apple Music, soundcloud.-com/philipp-beesen

70. Artist: Tom Player
Song: Desolation
Album: Resonance Theory
Available: Amazon Music, Google Play, iTunes/ Apple Music

71. Artist: Hans Zimmer
Song: Time
Album: Inception OST
Available: Amazon Music, Google Play, iTunes/ Apple Music

72. Artist: Soundcritters
Song: Stardust
Album: Starbound
Available: Amazon Music, Bandcamp, iTunes/ Apple Music

73. Artist: Fearless Motivation Instrumentals
Song: Revival
Album: Sounds of Power
Available: Amazon Music, Google Play, iTunes/ Apple Music, www.fearlessmotivation.com

74. Artist: Really Slow Motion
Song: Gates of Pearl
Album: Battle Angel
Available: Amazon Music, Bandcamp, Google Play, iTunes/ Apple Music, YouTube @ Really Slow Motion

75. Artist: Ivan Torrent
Song: Afterlife
Album: Immortalys

Available: Amazon Music, Bandcamp, Google Play, iTunes/ Apple Music

76. Artist: Judah Earl
Song: Creation
Album: (Single Release)
Available: soundcloud.com/judah-earl, www.judahearl.com

77. Artist: Antti Martikainen
Song: Throne of the North
Album: Throne of the North
Available: Amazon Music, Bandcamp, Google Play, iTunes/ Apple Music

78. Artist: Marcin Przybylowicz
Song: On the Champs-Désolés
Album: The Witcher 3: Wild Hunt OST
Available: Amazon, Google Play, iTunes/ Apple Music

79. Artist: Zack Hemsey
Song: Don't Get in My Way (Instrumental)
Album: Ronin (Instrumentals)
Available: Amazon Music, iTunes/ Apple Music

80. Artist: Wardruna
Song: Völuspá
Album: Skald
Available: Amazon Music, Bandcamp, Google Play, iTunes/ Apple Music

81. Artist: Marcus Warner
Song: Among the Giants
Album: 39 Seconds

Available: Amazon Music, Bandcamp, iTunes/ Apple Music

82. Artist: Dominik A. Hecker
Song: Hear It, See It, and Feel It
Album: (Single Release)
Available: YouTube @ Dominik A. Hecker, www.dominikhecker.bandcamp.com, soundcloud.com/dominikheckermusic,

83. Artist: Antti Martikainen
Song: Spirit Creek
Album: Eternal Saga
Available: Amazon Music, Bandcamp, Google Play, iTunes/ Apple Music

84. Artist: Peder B. Helland
Song: Earth in the Sky
Album: (Single Release)
Available: Amazon Music, Bandcamp, iTunes/ Apple Music

85. Artist: Adrian Von Ziegler
Song: Song of Brotherhood
Album: Starchaser
Available: Amazon Music, Bandcamp, Google Play, iTunes/ Apple Music, patreon.com/AdrianvonZiegler

86. Artist: Thomas Bergersen
Song: Illusions
Album: Illusions
Available: Amazon Music, Google Play, iTunes/ Apple Music

87. Artist: Wardruna
Song: MannaR Liv
Album: Runaljod Ragnarok

Available: Amazon Music, iTunes/ Apple Music

88. Artist: Antti Martikainen
Song: Northland
Album: Eternal Saga
Available: Amazon Music, Bandcamp, Google Play, iTunes/ Apple Music

89. Artist: Fearless Motivation Instrumentals
Song: Day of Domination
Album: Sounds of Power 7
Available: Amazon Music, Google Play, iTunes/ Apple Music, www.fearlessmotivation.com

90. Artist: Audiomachine
Song: Homecoming
Album: Tree of Life
Available: Amazon Music, Google Play, iTunes/ Apple Music, YouTube @ Audiomachine, www.audiomachine.com

91. Artist: Whitesand
Song: Eternity
Album: (Single Release)
Available: YouTube @ Whitesand, soundcloud.com/martynaslau, patreon.com/Whitesand

92. Artist: Audiomachine
Song: Morningrise
Album: Worlds of Wonder
Available: Amazon Music, Google Play, iTunes/ Apple Music, YouTube @ Audiomachine, www.audiomachine.com

93. Artist: Olexandr Ignatov

Song: Our Fates are Bound Together
Album: (Single Release)
Available: Amazon Music, Audiojungle, Bandcamp, Google Play, iTunes/ Apple Music, Soundcloud, www.olexandrignatov.com

94. Artist: Inward Oceans
Song: Rolling Through
Album: Weather the Storm
Available: Amazon Music, Google Play, iTunes/ Apple Music

95. Artist: Really Slow Motion
Song: Suns and Stars
Album: Elevation
Available: Amazon Music, Bandcamp, iTunes/ Apple Music; other RSM tunes at Google Play, YouTube @ Really Slow Motion

96. Artist: Antti Martikainen
Song: Northland
Album: Eternal Saga
Available: Amazon Music, Bandcamp, Google Play, iTunes/ Apple Music

97. Artist: Trobar De Morte
Song: The Bear's Dance
Album: The Silver Wheel
Available: Amazon Music, Bandcamp, Google Play, iTunes/ Apple Music

98.
Artist: Antti Martikainen
Song: Sons of Avalon
Album: Eternal Saga

Available: Amazon Music, Bandcamp, Google Play, iTunes/ Apple Music

99. Artist: Really Slow Motion
Song: Purple Skies
Album: Iron Poetry
Available: Amazon Music, Bandcamp, Google Play, iTunes/ Apple Music

100. Artist: Fractured Light Music
Song: Salvation
Album: Immortal
Available: Amazon Music, Bandcamp, iTunes/ Apple Music

101. Artist: Wodkah
Song: The Last Butterfly
Album:
Available: Amazon Music, Bandcamp, iTunes/ Apple Music, Soundcloud

102. Artist: Brunuhville
Song: Forevermore
Album: Age of Wonders
Available: Amazon Music, Google Play, iTunes/ Apple Music

103. Artist: Brunuhville
Song: Timeless
Album: Timeless
Available: Amazon Music, Bandcamp, Google Play, iTunes/ Apple Music, YouTube @ Brunuhville

104. Artist: Fearless Motivation Instrumentals
Song: Proof

Album: Sounds of Power 8
Available: Amazon Music, Google Play, iTunes/ Apple Music, www.fearlessmotivation.com

105. Artist: Two Steps From Hell
Song: Piece of Mind
Album: Dreams and Imaginations
Available: Amazon Music, Google Play, iTunes/ Apple Music, YouTube @Two Steps From Hell, www.twostepsfromhell.com

106. Artist: Marcus Warner
Song: Africa
Album: Liberation
Available: Amazon Music, Bandcamp, Google Play, iTunes/ Apple Music

107. Artist: Howard Baer
Song: Highland Dance
Album: Celtic Mystique
Available: Amazon Music, Google Play, iTunes/ Apple Music

108. Artist: Audiomachine
Song: Between Heaven and Earth
Album: Magnus
Available: Amazon Music, Google Play, iTunes/ Apple Music, YouTube @ Audiomachine, www.audiomachine.com

109. Artist: Andrea Pascali
Song: Hope Send
Album: (Single Release)
Available: reverbnation.com/andreapasandr, soundcloud.-com/andrea-pascali

110. Artist: Steve Jablonsky
Song: Tessa
Album: Transformers: Age of Extinction
Available: Amazon Music, Google Play, iTunes/ Apple Music

111. Artist: Brunuhville
Song: Spirit of the Wild
Album: Age of Wonders
Available: Amazon Music, Bandcamp, Google Play, iTunes/ Apple Music, YouTube @ Brunuhville

112. Artist: Whitesand
Song: Legend of the King
Album: (Single Release)
Available: YouTube @ Whitesand, soundcloud.com/martynaslau, patreon.com/Whitesand

113. Artist: Antti Martikainen
Song: A Forgotten Kingdom
Album: Throne of the North
Available: Amazon Music, Bandcamp, Google Play, iTunes/ Apple Music

114. Artist: Brunuhville
Song: Wolfborn
Album: Age of Wonders
Available: Amazon Music, Bandcamp, Google Play, iTunes/ Apple Music, YouTube @ Brunuhville

115. Artist: Alan Lennon
Song: Strive
Album: (Single Release)
Available: soundcloud.com/user-458982226

116. Artist: Brunuhville
Song: Dance with Dragons
Album: Fantasy Journey: Celtic Collection/ Aura
Available: Amazon Music, Bandcamp, Google Play, iTunes/ Apple Music, YouTube @ Brunuhville

117. Artist: DYATHON
Song: Hope
Album: Decadance
Available: Amazon Music, Bandcamp, Google Play, iTunes/ Apple Music

118. Artist: Brunuhville
Song: Northwind
Album: Northwind
Available: Amazon Music, Bandcamp, Google Play, iTunes/ Apple Music, YouTube @ Brunuhville

119. Artist: Brunuhville
Song: Wolfborn
Album: Age of Wonders
Available: Amazon Music, Bandcamp, Google Play, iTunes/ Apple Music, YouTube @ Brunuhville

120. Artist: Atis Freivalds
Song: Above the Light
Album: (Single Release)
Available: Amazon Music, Bandcamp, Google Play, iTunes/ Apple Music

121. Artist: Brunuhville
Song: Medieval Legends
Album: Fantasy Journey: Celtic Collection

Available: Amazon Music, Bandcamp, Google Play, iTunes/ Apple Music, YouTube @ Brunuhville

122. Artist: Wardruna
Song: Solringen
Album: Runaljod – Yggdrasil
Available: Amazon Music, Bandcamp, Google Play, iTunes/ Apple Music

123. Artist: Adrian Von Ziegler
Song: Ohori Village
Album: The Complete Discography
Available: Bandcamp, patreon.com/AdrianvonZiegler

124. Artist: Whitesand
Song: Luna
Album: (Single Release)
Available: YouTube @ Whitesand, soundcloud.com/martynaslau, patreon.com/Whitesand

125. Artist: Luke Richards
Song: Look to the Stars
Album: Maximum Impact Aurora
Available: lukerichards.com, audionetwork.com

126. Artist: Olexandr Ignatov
Song: Emotions
Album: Piano Scenes
Available: Amazon Music, Audiojungle, Bandcamp, Google Play, iTunes/ Apple Music, Soundcloud, www.olexandrignatov.com

127. Artist: Gaelic Storm
Song: Sight of Land

Album: Gaelic Storm
Available: Amazon Music, iTunes/ Apple Music, www.gaelic-storm.com

128. Artist: Gaelic Storm
Song: The Farmer's Frolic
Album: Gaelic Storm
Available: Amazon Music, iTunes, www.gaelicstorm.com

129. Artist: Garry Ferrier
Song: Atonement
Album: (Single Release)
Available: www.mapletapemusic.com

130. Artist: Audiomachine
Song: Remember Not to Forget
Album: Life
Available: Amazon Music, Google Play, iTunes/ Apple Music, YouTube @ Audiomachine, www.audiomachine.com

131. Artist: Mattia Cupelli
Song: In That Smile
Album: Fly
Available: Amazon Music, Bandcamp, Google Play, iTunes/ Apple Music, YouTube @ Mattia Cupelli

132. Artist: Mattia Cupelli
Song: Wonder
Album: Fly
Available: Amazon Music, Bandcamp, Google Play, iTunes/ Apple Music, YouTube @ Mattia Cupelli

133. Artist: Mattia Cupelli

Song: Ink
Album: Broken Hearts
Available: Amazon Music, Bandcamp, Google Play, iTunes/ Apple Music, YouTube @ Mattia Cupelli

134. Artist: James Paget
Song: Look to the Skies
Album: Believe
Available: Amazon Music, Bandcamp, Google Play, iTunes/ Apple Music

135. Artist: Brunuhville
Song: Path to Queensgarden
Album: Timeless
Available: Amazon Music, Bandcamp, Google Play, iTunes/ Apple Music, YouTube @ Brunuhville

136. Artist: J. T. Peterson
Song: Crystal
Album: Petrichor
Available: Amazon Music, Google Play, iTunes/Apple Music

137. Artist: 2WEI
Song: Expectations
Album: Escape Velocity
Available: Amazon Music, Google Play, iTunes/ Apple Music, YouTube @ 2WEI

138. Artist: Audiomachine
Song: Hallowed Dawn
Album: Awakenings
Available: Amazon Music, Bandcamp, Google Play, iTunes/ Apple Music, YouTube @ Audiomachine, www.audioma-

chine.com

139. Artist: Whitesand
Song: Her
Album: (Single Release)
Available: YouTube @ Whitesand,
soundcloud.com/martynaslau, patreon.com/Whitesand

140. Artist: Whitesand
Song: Beyond Horizon
Album: (Single Release)
Available: YouTube @ Whitesand,
soundcloud.com/martynaslau, patreon.com/Whitesand

141. Artist: Trevor Jones
Song: Promentory
Album: The Last of the Mohicans OST
Available: Amazon Music, Google Play, iTunes/ Apple Music

142. Artist: Audiomachine
Song: The Messenger
Album: Chronicles
Available: Amazon Music, Google Play, iTunes/ Apple Music,
www.audiomachine.com

143. Artist: Thomas Bergersen
Song: New Life
Album: Sun
Available: Amazon Music, Bandcamp, iTunes/ Apple Music

144. Artist: Really Slow Motion
Song: Miracles
Album: Premium Series: Prophecy

Available: YouTube @ Really Slow Motion; other RSM tunes at Amazon Music, Bandcamp, iTunes

145. Artist: Whitesand
Song: Adventure Begins
Album: (Single Release)
Available: YouTube @ Whitesand, soundcloud.com/martynaslau, patreon.com/Whitesand

146. Artist: Future World Music
Song: Anthem of the New World
Album: A Hero Will Rise
Available: Amazon Music, iTunes/ Apple Music

147. Artist: Fearless Motivation Instrumentals
Song: Work on Yourself
Album: Sounds of Power 8
Available: Amazon Music, Google Play, iTunes/ Apple Music, www.fearlessmotivation.com

148. Artist: Fearless Motivation Instrumentals
Song: Proof
Album: Sounds of Power 8
Available: Amazon Music, Google Play, iTunes/ Apple Music, www.fearlessmotivation.com

149. Artist: Really Slow Motion
Song: Beneath the Starry Skies
Album: Supremacy
Available: YouTube @ Really Slow Motion; other RSM tunes at Amazon Music, Bandcamp, Google Play, iTunes/ Apple Music

150. Artist: Really Slow Motion

Song: Becoming
Album: Miraculum
Available: Amazon Music, Bandcamp, Google Play, iTunes/ Apple Music

151.
Artist: Really Slow Motion
Song: End of an Era
Album: Miraculum
Available: Amazon Music, Bandcamp, Google Play, iTunes/ Apple Music

152. Artist: Whitesand
Song: Melodic Dreams
Album: (Single Release)
Available: YouTube @ Whitesand, soundcloud.com/martynaslau, patreon.com/Whitesand

153. Artist: Mattia Cupelli
Song: Two Souls
Album: Waves
Available: Amazon Music, Bandcamp, Google Play, iTunes/ Apple Music, YouTube @ Mattia Cupelli

154. Artist: Fearless Motivation Instrumentals
Song: Work on Yourself
Album: Sounds of Power 8
Available: Amazon Music, Google Play, iTunes/ Apple Music, www.fearlessmotivation.com

APPENDIX C

Visual Aids

The following pages are rough-sketches, drawn by the author, to help the reader obtain a clearer vision of certain parts of the Palace of Lapoi.

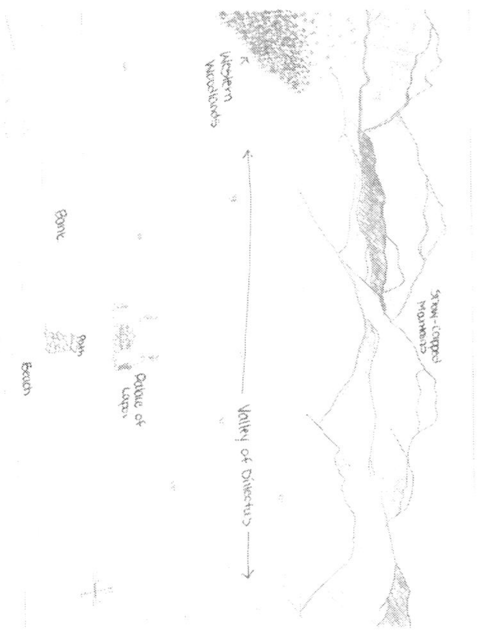

Aerial view of the Palace of Lapoi and its surrounding land

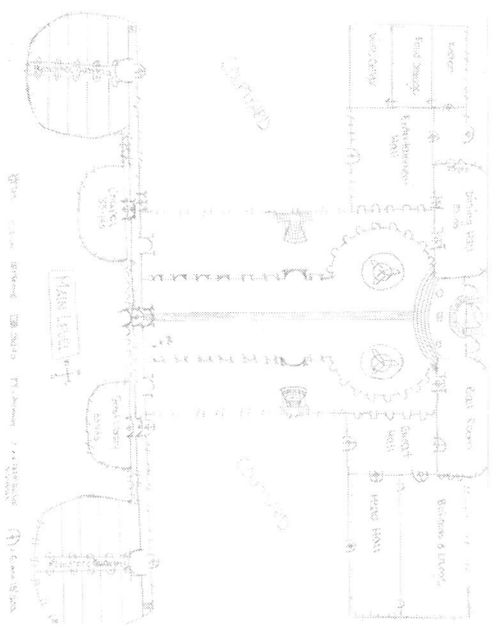

Blueprint sketch of the main level of the Palace of Lapoi

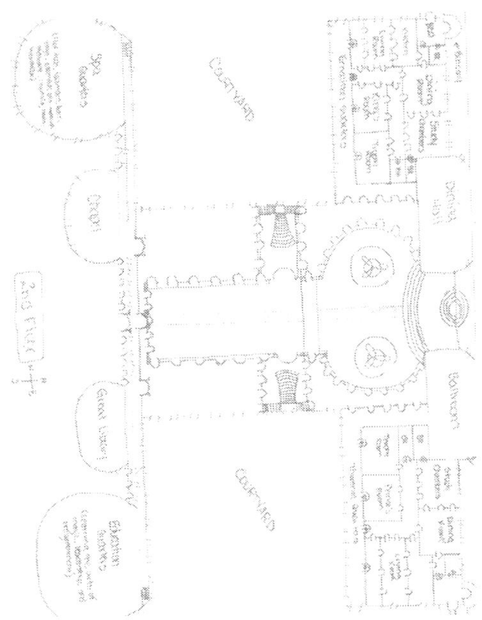

Blueprint sketch of the second level of the Palace of Lapoi

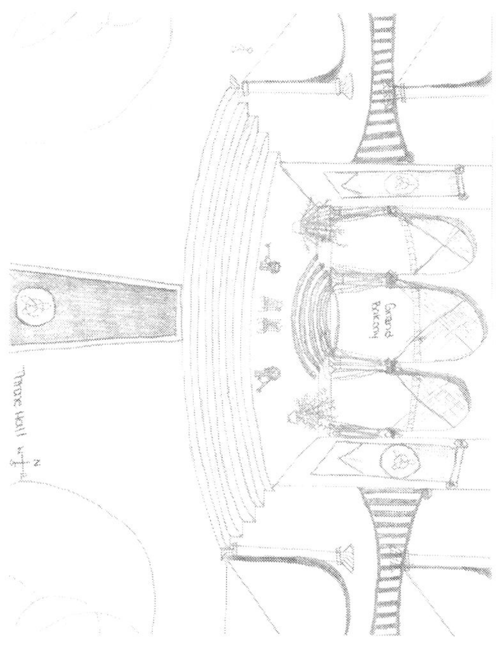

Throne Hall - facing the throne chairs from the view of the central aisle

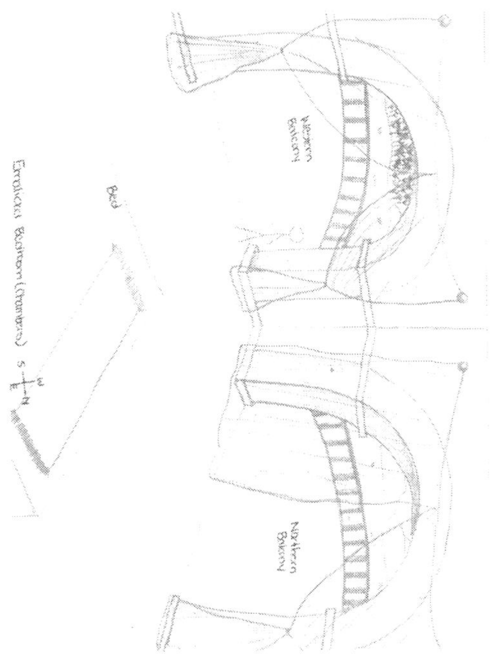

Emalickel's Bedroom Chamber in the palace

The emblem in Lapoi that represents Hadriel, Princess of Lapoi

ABOUT THE AUTHOR

A. M. TRUE became an author unintentionally. Her first novel, *Emalickel: The Celestials are Real*, was written over a period of five years after a very vivid dream she experienced. During that time, she had been avidly recording her dreams for memory recall. The first novel was one such recording. Initially, she kept this dream private, known only by those closest to her. In 2018, she decided to make it public.

Born in 1984 in the United States, True enjoys living a quiet, simple life in the rural country. She has a profound love and respect for life, nature, and animals. A deep thinker and dreamer, she enjoys moments of quiet and serenity. Aside from a few select shows, she does not watch television, but prefers expanding her mind in topics of science, history, and spirituality. During the school year, she works as an elementary teacher. In her free time she enjoys archery, home improvement, landscaping, playing Elder Scrolls V: Skyrim on Playstation 4, and listening to music. She also has played the cello, piano, and guitar. Her favorite types of music include Celtic/traditional Irish, cinematic scores, classic rock, and the music of the 1960's.

A. M. True still regularly recalls and records her dreams. Who knows what she will share next?

facebook.com/authoramtrue

instagram.com/authoramtrue

amazon.com/author/amtrue

74191778R00269

Made in the USA
Columbia, SC
10 September 2019